STRONG
HOLD

SARAH CASTILLE

sourcebooks
casablanca

Library of Congress Cataloging-in-Publication Data

Names: Castille, Sarah, author.
Title: Strong hold / Sarah Castille.
Description: Naperville, Illinois : Sourcebooks Casablanca, [2018] | Series: Redemption ; 5
Identifiers: LCCN 2018010277 (softcover : acid-free paper)
Subjects: LCSH: Mixed martial arts--Fiction. | GSAFD: Erotic fiction. | Love stories.
Classification: LCC PR9199.4.C38596 S77 2018 | DDC 813/.6--dc23 LC record available at https://lccn.loc.gov/2018010277

Published by Sourcebooks Casablanca, an imprint of Sourcebooks, Inc.
P.O. Box 4410, Naperville, Illinois 60567-4410
(630) 961-3900
Fax: (630) 961-2168
sourcebooks.com

Printed and bound in the United States of America.
VP 10 9 8 7 6 5 4 3 2 1

Shayla

"COME BACK."

My whisper fades into the night as I stare out from the balcony of the Lucky Dollar Motel. Maybe if I look hard enough, wish desperately enough, it won't be true. Maybe Zack was joking when he said he was moving to Seattle. Maybe this pain in my chest isn't the agony of my heart breaking, but something else.

I hold up my hand when I see headlights in the distance, coming down the highway. That's Zack. I know it. He probably just went for a drive to clear his head. We'd waited ten years for tonight, and although it was beautiful, it was also intense.

It's your first time, baby. We'll take it slow.

My heart sinks when the car drives past and the bright red lights disappear into the night, swallowed up by the thick fir trees that crowd the sides of the road.

I take a deep breath and then another, trying to crush the steadily rising panic in my chest, telling myself it's all going to be okay. Any minute now, the door will open and Zack will be there, looking at me with those beautiful warm, brown eyes, his sable hair mussed from our lovemaking, his jaw rough with stubble, his sensual mouth curved in a smile. Oh, the wonderful things Zack could do with his mouth.

And the horrible words he could say.

I'm moving to Seattle.

"He's coming back," I say firmly, although there is no one around to hear me. You don't invite spectators to your very first time. It's just you and the boy you have loved since you were eight years old. It's the beating of hearts and the merging of souls. It's the start of what is supposed to be forever, not the end of an era.

It's my big chance. I'm finally going to be someone. I'm going to make something of life. I'll show the whole damn town they were wrong about me.

"No." I say it because a sob is forming in my chest, and I don't want to cry. But the pain is an unstoppable force, ripping through my throat in a bid to be free. Turning my back on the empty road, I tear the covers off the bed, fling the stained sheets across the room. An empty condom wrapper falls to the floor.

I will not cry.

This is all just a misunderstanding. Maybe I'm still asleep, and when I wake up, Zack will be beside me, his strong arms holding me tight. He will tell me that he wants to be with me.

That we're going to go to San Diego like we planned, and he's going to become a carpenter and train at night in an MMA gym. And I will dance with the San Diego Ballet Company, and every month, we'll come back to Washington to see his sisters and my mom and brother in Glenwood.

I'll live my dream, and you can live yours.

Except this was my dream—Zack and me together forever. Who knew I would wake up alone in a cheap, dingy motel room wearing a rumpled dress and the dragonfly necklace Zack gave me when I turned sixteen, his scent still on my skin.

I squeeze my eyes shut and hold my breath, but nothing can stop the sob that erupts from my throat. I yank a drawer from the dresser beside me, spilling the contents on the floor. School books. Dance bag. Acceptance letters from ballet companies in San Diego, Miami, Denver, and New York.

San Diego wasn't my first choice for an apprenticeship. The ballet company is small and not well known. But Zack wanted to go to California. He wanted to be an MMA star, and that was where all the good coaches and training centers were based. It was also a good place to find work as a carpenter, and if we were going to live together, we needed money to pay the bills.

So I didn't tell him about New York. I kept the letter hidden from everyone except my mom. Of course, she couldn't understand why I planned to go to San Diego instead of New York. In the world of ballet, New York is everything. The best choreographers. The best dancers. The best directors. I didn't want the best. I wanted Zack. But Zack didn't want me.

I know we're supposed to go to San Diego, but what could I say when one of the top MMA coaches in the country drove all the way to our town to offer to coach me if I could start right away? It's what I always dreamed about. He's picking me up in an hour, but I'll call you and we'll work something out.

I was happy for him. But what about me? What about our plans for the future? How could he make that kind of decision for both of us without even giving me a call? When he accepted the offer, he had to know it was too late for me to apply for an apprenticeship in Seattle, and taking a year off dancing would be the end of my career. But did he really think I would still move to a city I never wanted to live in, away from the people I care about, and dance with a company that offers no real future? Alone?

I know San Diego is far away, but it will only be a few years…

Years.

I wade through the pile of covers and grab a pillow. With a howl, I fling it across the room. I throw another pillow and another, but the pain inside me doesn't go away. If my big brother, Matt, were here, he'd say he told me so. He'd never liked Zack. He said nothing good had ever come out of the Shady Pine Trailer Park, and especially not a kid whose parents had snorted their lives away.

I didn't care where Zack lived or how much money he had. I didn't care what he did for a living or how broken his family was. I loved him, and nothing else mattered.

Loved. Past tense. An unconscious slip. Because my stupid heart still feels *love* present tense. But what will I feel tomorrow when he doesn't come back? Or next week? Or even next year? How will I feel after the years he expects me to wait for him? After he so callously threw away all our plans for the future? I can't imagine *love* future tense with anyone other than Zack. I wasn't made to love anyone else. But I've learned a truth tonight. Love isn't worth the pain.

Shayla

"WINNER BY A KNOCKOUT...BLADE SAW!"

Grinning wide, Jimmy "Blade Saw" Sanchez holds up his arms in a victory salute after I announce his arrival at Redemption, Oakland's premier mixed martial arts gym. Everyone cheers, although they were all at the fight on Saturday night for his big win—and my humiliating defeat. I lost big-time to lightweight newcomer, Camilla Rizzo, putting me one step further from my dream of winning the amateur title belt and eventually going pro.

I didn't join Redemption to become a professional MMA fighter. I came here four years ago to learn how to fight, with no aspirations beyond being able to walk alone at night without suffering panic attacks. Who knew a graceful ballerina had a hidden talent for martial arts and a violent side that came out in the ring?

"The recruiters are going to be swarming this place any minute now," Jack "Sadist" Caldwell says as I turn and drumroll my gloved hands on the speed bag. "I can smell them coming."

"You didn't smell them coming when they recruited you."

Six feet four inches tall, 250 pounds of rock-solid muscle, eyes as blue as the Redemption mats, thick, blond hair buzzed down to a number two, Sadist is by far the largest fighter in Redemption. Until two years ago, he'd dominated the amateur super heavyweight rankings, but a health scare changed everything. He went on the Paleo diet and dropped so much weight, he had to start fighting as a heavyweight, where he dominated the field. It wasn't long before he was snapped up by one of the world's biggest promotions, changed his fight name from Rampage to Sadist, and now he's Redemption's second biggest star—Max "Torment" Huntington, the owner of Redemption is, of course, number one.

"It's hard to see yourself as others see you." He stills my speed bag, and his expression turns serious. "You fought a good fight last night."

"I got punched in the face twice by a rank amateur with only one fight under her belt, and now I look like a raccoon with this black-and-blue mask." I knock his hand away. "And then she caught me in a submission that I'd learned how to escape my second week at Redemption. It wasn't a good fight. It was pathetic." I smash my fist into the speed bag half a dozen times before pausing for breath. "And it's not the first time. I've been sliding down the ranks all year. I don't know what's wrong."

"Have you talked to Torment?"

I lift an eyebrow. No one voluntarily seeks out Torment unless they have a death wish. Although he has been helping me train, he is a formidable man, a virtual MMA god who runs Redemption with an iron fist. Torment used to be a champion underground fighter and turned down many offers to go pro. Even today, the recruiters are still after him, but with a multimillion-dollar business to run as his alter ego Max Huntington, and a new baby girl at home, he has neither the time nor the interest in being a star.

Sadist laughs. "Wrong question."

"Definitely the wrong question. And if you see him, try to keep him distracted and away from me. I'll be in the practice ring with Sandy. We're running through the striking techniques I'll be teaching my junior girls' MMA class tomorrow night."

"The kids are gonna love your new look," he says as he turns away. "Maybe I'll talk to the guys about giving you a new ring name. Instead of Shayla Tanner, a.k.a. Shilla the Killa, you can be a.k.a. Ricky the Raccoon."

"Ha ha. Very funny." I started teaching at Redemption after Torment roped me into helping out with the kids' MMA classes when one of the instructors got sick. The girls in the class were more interested in the fact that they had a female teacher than learning the moves, and they peppered me with questions. I'd never thought of myself as a model or mentor for anyone, but they made me realize I could give something back to the sport that had helped me reinvent myself after my ex-husband, Damian Peters, destroyed the only life I had ever known. I wanted to empower them so they could become fighters, too.

I cross the mats toward the practice ring, taking in the enormity of what is now one of the top MMA training gyms in California. The vast 25,000-square-foot warehouse in Oakland's Foster Hoover Historic District is more of a home to me than my apartment in Rockridge. Spotlights shine bright on the electric-blue mats and glint off the equipment. Fighters of all shapes and sizes grunt and groan over in the free weights area. Cardio machines whirr and spin to the steady thud of running shoes on the track that circumnavigates the gym. Tag "Fuzzy" O'Donnell, a cop by day and my co-coach with Torment, barks abuse at a group of newbies in his Fight or Flee class. Over on the grapple mats, the first aid attendant, Makayla, sometimes known as Doc, otherwise known as Torment's better half, tends to a woman who has managed to get her head stuck between the legs of a full-size submission dummy.

"Oh my God!" Sandy's hand flies to her mouth as I climb through the ropes, an almost comical move, given she's wearing fight gloves twice as thick as mine. "Sadist told me what happened last night. Are you okay?" She runs her glove through her long, platinum-blond ponytail and heaves a deep breath, her generous breasts straining against her too-small, too-tight pink sports top. Sandy loves her breasts, as do most of the male fighters at Redemption. I don't think I've ever seen her show less than three inches of cleavage, but then if I had breasts like hers, I would show them off, too. Unfortunately, years of intense ballet training meant I developed late, and when I did, I didn't have much to show for the effort.

"Does it really look that bad?"

She grimaces and shrugs. "You look kind of Zorro-esque. Maybe if you use a little concealer—a lot of concealer—you won't scare the kids. And actually, it kind of goes with the grunge thing you've got going on outside the gym. If you wear those patterned, ripped leggings, clunky shoes, and that black leather dress you had on the other week under your flannel shirt, people will just think it's part of your style. Does it hurt?"

"Only when I blink."

Sandy gives me a sympathetic smile. A lot of people at Redemption don't like Sandy, a wealthy socialite who was once engaged to Torment, chased after him when he was with Makayla, and twice broke poor Blade Saw's heart. But we've always gotten along. She has her flaws—when there are unattached men around, she forgets she has friends—but when it's just us or we're out with the Redemption gals, she's all sorts of fun. She also has a big heart, and although she doesn't talk about it, she does a lot of charity work for underprivileged kids.

"Why didn't you stay home and put some ice on it? Hide out for a few days?" She stretches on the mat, checking out the guys in the gym as she warms up. She just went through a bad breakup and has decided to follow my lead and give up relationships in favor of casual hookups.

"The last time I tried to hide after losing a fight, Torment found me." I don't have to mock a shudder; the fear is real. "He came to my apartment and almost broke down my door. He's a big fan of getting right back in the ring after you lose a fight. He threatened to cut off my membership and break my legs if I didn't get down to the gym."

Sandy laughs as she jumps to her feet. We practice together a few times a week. She's a recreational fighter, whereas I have been trying to work my way to the top of the amateur circuit for years.

"You could have stayed home," she says. "A recruiter from MEFC showed up first thing this morning, and he's been in Torment's office ever since. We've been taking bets on who's caught their interest. Imagine. Another Redemption fighter in the pros!" Without any warning, Sandy lunges from the side, clearly hoping to take advantage of my distraction. But we've played this game before, and I've been ready for her since she dropped into her ready stance.

"I think it will be Blade Saw. He just won that big fight." Mega Extreme Fight Championship, or MEFC for short, is one of the world's top MMA promotions and features the top-ranked fighters of the sport. They are always looking for new talent, and Blade Saw's recent wins have been turning heads. Spinning, I feint right, but my kick goes wide. Sandy dives in with a straight left that glances off my shoulder. I move in fast with a right hook, dropping Sandy to her knees.

"My money is on Renegade." She gestures to the cage where Renegade is tossing a newbie around for fun. "He's only a few fights away from a title belt."

My stomach tightens as it always does when I see Renegade. He's a great guy with a good sense of humor and one of the most laid-back fighters at Redemption. But he looks so much like Damian, I always have to take a moment to assure myself that the man with the blond hair and blue eyes, the lean, toned body, and the chiseled jaw is not the man I loved and married and shared a bed with for four long years. I wanted so desperately for Damian to fill the black hole in my life that had consumed me since Zack left, I didn't see what lay beneath his caring and compassion—a deep-rooted insecurity that eventually drove him to the edge.

Sandy's gaze flicks to someone behind me, and she jumps to her feet. "Torment just came in." And then her eyes widen. "He's got the MEFC recruiter with him. Oh my Lord. Look who it is."

Taking advantage of her lack of focus, I lunge forward and wrap my arm around her neck in a choke hold. Out of the corner of my eye, I spot Torment walking toward us with the recruiter by his side. Sandy manages to spit out his name before my brain registers what I am seeing.

"Zack Grayson."

My breath catches, and the world freezes around me. *Zack?* My gaze locks on the man talking to Torment, and memories of the past breach the walls that have kept me safe for the last seven years. The day he found me at the bottom of Devil's Hill. The touch that woke our souls. The strange friendship between a thirteen-year-old boy and an eight-year-old girl that no one understood. The easy conversations. Our first kiss when I turned sixteen. Cuddles under the stars. Sexual exploration. And then the night we came together and broke apart.

He'd wanted to make something of himself, and he had. Three-time winner of the MEFC middleweight title belt, Zack is an MMA legend. He is a master of five different martial arts and once won a title fight despite having a broken arm. He is his ring name personified, a "Slayer" in every sense of the word. Fiercely aggressive in the cage, he was feared and admired when he was fighting, revered and respected since he retired. But I know what kind of man he really is. A slayer of the heart.

My grip loosens. Sandy spins out of the hold and clips me a good one in the chin.

I stumble back and lose my balance. My head thunks against a metal pole, and I go down hard. Taste blood. See stars. Or are they hearts? For a long moment, I don't move. Lights twinkle above me. Fade to black. I am lost in a sea of pain.

"Wake up."

I open my eyes and blink away the blur. People are murmuring around me. Sandy is talking to someone named God and apologizing over and over. A male voice calls for Makayla, and I hear the pounding of feet. Drawing in a deep breath, I inhale the scents of stale sweat and disinfectant. The smell of home.

"Shayla?" Sadist's usually gruff rumble of a voice is surprisingly soft and gentle. "Talk to me."

Of course Sadist is the first one in the ring. And he must be worried. No one calls me Shayla at Redemption. Torment has decreed that we must use ring names only in the gym, and the team gave me the worst ring name ever. Shilla the Killa I was named, and Shilla the Killa I will be unless I can break out of the middle of the amateur pack and earn the right to a better name.

"I thought I'd take a little rest," I mumble. "I'm still tired from Saturday's fight."

"Good idea." Makayla says, joining Sadist on the mat beside

me, her hazel eyes dark with concern. "I'll just check you over. Doctor Death is in the first aid room dealing with a sprain."

"Thank goodness." Doctor Death, a heart surgeon, amateur fighter, and Redemption's official ring doctor is too gorgeous for his own good, and the last thing I want is to succumb to the touch of his beautiful surgeon's hands.

Sadist unlaces my gloves while Makayla does her thing, poking and prodding and patting me all over. Sandy kneels beside me. "I am so, so sorry. I didn't mean to hit you like that. Well, I did, but I thought you'd move your face out of the way."

"I was…distracted." Although I've tried to avoid local and live stream events where Zack has fought, it has been impossible over the years to avoid seeing pictures of him online and in magazines where he has endorsed everything from gloves to protein shakes. But nothing could have prepared me for the in-person, breathtaking visual feast he has become in the seven years since we were together.

With that long, dark, rock-star hair; the lean, powerful body; hard planes of muscles concealed beneath a tight MEFC T-shirt; and three days' worth of groomed stubble on a firm, cleft chin, he has the kind of tear-off-the-clothes, jump-into-bed, fuck-me-till-I-die good looks that make women do stupid things. Like celebrating their eighteenth birthday by having sex for the first time with him at the Lucky Dollar Motel.

Why did age have to make him even more breathtaking than I remember? Why, why, why did he have to come to Redemption of all the gyms in all the states in the country?

Why did he walk away and leave me?

"He is yummy, isn't he?" Sandy whispers, glancing up. "I'm going to invite him out with the team tonight, maybe take him back to my place. I know he's got a reputation as the sport's biggest man whore, but how often do you get a chance to sleep with an MMA legend?"

Just once. And then he'll walk away. His well-earned reputation started with me.

Desperate to get away in case Zack recognizes me, I push myself to sit.

"Don't get up yet," Makayla says, frowning. "Just give it a minute. You hit your head pretty hard."

"I'm fine."

"You don't look fine," she says when I stand, my gloves hanging loose on my hands. "You're very pale."

"It's the black eyes. They make my skin look paler."

"I'd really like to take you to the first aid office for a proper check." Makayla helps me climb out of the ring. "Sandy said you blacked out for a few seconds. I want to make sure you don't have a concussion."

"Really. I'm good." I take a step forward, and the mat swirls below me.

"Whoa. Easy there." Strong hands steady me, pull me into a broad, hard chest.

Disoriented, I fall into brown eyes flecked with gold. Warm, like the hands around my waist. Steady, like the touch on my skin bared between my shorts and sports top. Unyielding. Betraying. Painfully familiar.

Pain.

I fight my body's response, the tug deep in my soul, reminding myself why I'm here. Zack left. Damian picked up the pieces. And then I was destroyed all over again.

"Let me go, Zack."

3

Zack

"Shayla?"

For the longest moment, Zack's brain couldn't process the sight in front of him.

Seven years, ten months, and twenty-seven days. That was how long it had been since he'd seen her. That was how long it had been since he'd lived a life without regret.

He felt a dangerous heating of his blood as he stared at the woman in his arms. Her slim, lean, graceful dancer's body was now powerful and strong, but the classic beauty of her oval face shone through the mask of bruises. Her eyes were still the dark blue of the violets he'd picked for her when she turned thirteen, and her beautiful long hair was shorter and tied into a ponytail that swung behind her.

His gaze dropped to her ripped shirt and torn, black leggings. No wonder he hadn't recognized her right away. She was supposed to be fangirling Nureyev, not Nirvana.

"What are you doing here?" His hands tightened around her

waist as he tried to control his emotions. He hadn't ripped his heart out of his chest and walked away so Shayla could wind up bruised and beaten in an MMA gym in the worst part of Oakland.

And married. He had almost forgotten that only a year after they'd split up, she had married another man.

"I train here."

She tried to pull away, but Zack firmed his grip. He'd let her go once, and he'd regretted it every single day of his life. He wanted answers, and he wanted them now.

"Why aren't you dancing?" he demanded. He'd followed her ballet career until he'd won his first amateur title belt and MEFC had come calling with an invitation to the pros. With his belt in one hand, a contract in the other, and his worth now splashed on screens and magazines across the globe, he'd gone to New York to find her, only to discover she was with someone else.

Shayla bristled. "Because I'm not."

"That's not an answer." He instantly regretted his abrupt tone. Although he'd thought nothing could hurt more than discovering he had been so quickly and easily replaced, the death of Tadashi "the Mountain" Okami not long after had utterly destroyed him, leaving him emotionally scarred and quick to anger.

"That's all you're going to get." She twisted away and he released her, caught in a maelstrom of emotion. It was almost too much to take in. Shayla. Redemption. Her drastic career change. And the hostility he had never expected to face. He had given her everything. Sacrificed everything. He had left her to make himself worthy. He had set her free so she could fly.

"Shay…" He breathed in a lungful of her scent, his stomach doing a strange twist at the familiar fragrance of wildflowers.

"Leave me alone."

"I just want to talk."

Pain flickered across her beautiful face. "You're seven years too late."

"Give me a chance to explain."

"I don't care, Zack. It's all in the past. I've moved on and so have you."

"You don't mean that."

"Don't tell me what I mean." Her eyes glittered, brittle and hard. "You don't know me. Not anymore."

He felt her words like a knife in the chest. He had known Shay better than he had known himself. He knew what moved her and what made her smile. He knew it was harder for her to give up candy than it was to dance until her feet bled. He knew she was strong, brave, compassionate, and fearless. He knew she loved him so much, she would never leave him, even if it meant giving up her dreams.

"Shay…" He trailed off, suddenly aware of all the eyes on them, the slight sway of bodies as people leaned in to hear. If he could just get her alone… "Let's take this somewhere private." He grasped her hand, intending to lead her away.

"Don't touch me." She slapped him, the sound of her hand striking his cheek echoing through the gym.

"What the hell was that?" He didn't feel physical pain from

her blow—he'd suffered much worse in the ring—but her very public show of anger stung both his pride and his hope that after so many years, he might be forgiven.

She looked back over her shoulder as she walked toward the door. "That's the 'fuck off' I never got to say."

Shayla

"WHAT'S GOING ON?"

Torment fixes me with his deep, dark gaze. After a terrible night in which Damian haunted my dreams and Zack tormented my waking moments, I am ill prepared for a meeting with Torment. When he called me to his office this morning, I had to fight the urge to run and hide. I broke the rule against fighting outside the practice ring when I slapped Zack yesterday, and I can only pray Torment will let me go in one piece.

"I'm sorry." I figure Torment will appreciate the straightforward approach. And it's not like I can lie. Redemption is worse than high school for gossip, and given the number of people who were at the gym last night, guaranteed everyone knows I slapped Zack Grayson.

What the hell was I thinking?

"Unsatisfactory," Torment says. "Try again."

"Well…" I twist my hands in my lap, supremely uncomfortable with having to discuss my personal life with Torment.

Although I respect him as a fighter and a coach, we've never really had a personal conversation. Torment isn't really a chatty kind of guy. How Makayla gets along with him, I'll never know.

"Zack and I have a history. We grew up together. Dated. It ended badly. I guess I still have unresolved feelings." I'm not embarrassed about slapping Zack. It was the goodbye I never got to say.

"I'm not interested in your relationship issues." Torment cuts me off with an irritated wave of his hand. "I'm talking about the fight on Saturday night."

Burn, cheeks, burn. Can this entire situation get even more humiliating? Of course he doesn't care about relationship issues. He's running a gym, and training fighters. All he cares about is making good fighters better. "Right. The fight. Well, I don't know what happened. I started strong—"

Torment cuts me off again. I'm not sure why he even needs me here, since he's not really interested in my answers to any of his questions. "I was there. I saw the fight. Your opponent is known as a grappler. She works best rolling on the mat because she lacks the stamina of a striker. That was obvious when she dropped her hands and exposed her chin over and over again. You needed to use defensive wrestling and striking to get a knockout." He leans forward and scowls. "Just like we planned."

I slump down in my seat like I'm in middle school and being told off by the principal. Except this time, Zack isn't going to be waiting outside, threatening to beat anyone who makes me cry. "I thought it would be too risky."

My heart pounds wildly as Torment drums his fingers on his desk. I knew this talk was coming. This is the fourth fight in a row I've lost over the last few months, and Torment doesn't like losers.

"I never had any doubts you were ready to step up to the next level," he says. "You have the skills, the fitness, and the strength. You decimated the entire lower tier of amateurs. But last year when we moved you up to fight a different class of fighters, you started holding back. Is it a matter of confidence? Do you not think you're as good as them? Or are you afraid of more experienced opponents?"

"I'm not afraid." I hum a few bars of Masterplan's "I'm Not Afraid," trailing off when Torment's scowl deepens. So much for lightening the mood. The power metal song is a little slick for my taste anyway. After I left New York, I purged all my playlists of classical music and dance pop, replacing them with the angst-filled, angry, frustrated lyrics, dirty guitar sounds, and heavy drumming of lighter grunge bands like Stone Temple Pilots, Pearl Jam, and Queens of the Stone Age. Only they understood my pain.

"I've talked to Fuzzy," Torment says after my brief musical interlude. "We think it might be better if you pulled out of competition until we can find out what's holding you back."

"I'll lose my shot at the amateur title belt and my chance to go pro. It will be another year before I can try again." I want this more than I want anything else. I want to prove to myself that no one can destroy me. That no matter how far I fall, I can get up again.

Determined to empower myself after my career and marriage imploded in New York, I moved to San Francisco and trained as a security guard. Now, as a senior security consultant for Symbian Cloud Computing, I have a gun, Taser, and nightstick, and I know how to use them. But success as a fighter has eluded me. I am good, but not good enough. I want to be a pro. Not because of the fame and fortune, but because I need to know in my heart that if anyone ever tries to hurt me the way Damian did, I will be able to defend myself. My biggest fear is to be a victim all over again.

"You would need to win your next three fights to get into the finals," Torment says. "And right now, that doesn't even look like a possibility."

Torment doesn't pull his punches in the ring or out.

My hands clench into fists in my lap. I've been through far worse. The two most important men in my life left me—my dad when he died in a car accident just after my seventh birthday and Zack when he walked out on me—and the third, Damian, betrayed me, morphing from caring friend and gentle lover to violent, alcoholic, abusive spouse. I lost my marriage, my friends, and my career because of him, and I almost lost my life.

In the big scheme of things, taking a step back from the competitive circuit is not a big deal, and yet I feel sick inside. For four years, I've trained and sweated through pain and blood and bruises for a chance to show the world that I'm a survivor, that I could come back stronger than ever, that I'm worthy of being the role model the young girls in my classes think I am.

Maybe I was wrong.

For the first time since I sat down, concern flickers across Torment's face. "I know what you're capable of. I've seen you grow as a fighter, and I know you can grow more. We'll put our heads together and come up with a plan."

"Okay. Thanks." I feign enthusiasm, but I'm dying inside. Fuzzy, Torment, and my personal trainer, Stan Roberts, have already put in hours of their personal time to help me get to where I am. I can't possibly ask for more. Stan only charges me half his normal rate, and Fuzzy pretends he hasn't raised his coaching fee during the time I've been at Redemption. I offered to pay Torment once and almost lost an arm.

After I leave Torment's office, I head into the gym and take a quick look around for any sign of Zack. Still reeling from the huge setback, I can't bear the thought of seeing him right now. Zack made it to the pros faster than any other amateur on the circuit, winning his title belt only a year after he moved to Seattle. Unlike me, he brought no baggage into the ring when he decided to become a fighter. He didn't have a body shattered by a fall down two flights of stairs, a heart destroyed by betrayal, or a mind twisted by fear. He had no one and nothing to hold him back.

And yet, for all the hurt in my heart, my body still responded to his touch. It was always that way with Zack. We had a connection from the moment we met. All the more reason to stay away.

For the rest of the afternoon, I manage to avoid Zack as he scouts out potential recruits, flirts outrageously with his female fans, signs autographs, and talks with the pro fighters while ambitious amateurs swoon in his wake. Although he retired four years ago, everyone fully expects him to make a big comeback. So, of course, they all want to be his new BFF.

"Hey, Zack, can I get you a protein shake?"

"Can you sign my gloves?"

"Will you pose for a picture?"

"It must get lonely traveling all the time, sleeping alone in your hotel…" Sandy, of course, doesn't waste any time. She knows what she wants, and for her, Zack is triple A–grade fresh meat.

I tell myself I don't care. Zack is nothing to me. Like I told Torment, we had a history, but now we've moved on. So why does my stomach clench when I hear the deep rumble of his voice? Why am I hyperaware of his presence when I'm trying to ignore him?

By the time my training day is over, I am more than happy to escape to Silicon Valley for my late shift as a security guard at Symbian Cloud Computing.

After running from the nightmare that was my life in New York, Redemption was one part of taking back my life; training as a security guard was the other. It was as close to my secret childhood dream of becoming a police officer like my dad as I could get while still recovering from my injuries. Although there is no possibility of promotion, I can use my fight and self-defense skills, work the hours around my training schedule, pay all my gym and training bills, and I get along so well with my coworkers Joe and Cheryl, I haven't looked around for anything else.

Long rays of evening sun filter through causeways lined with trees as I pull my Volvo into the parking lot. The company compound consists of four two-story, T-shaped buildings that appear to have been haphazardly dropped in the middle of an industrial estate along with a smattering of trees and a circular flower garden. Our main security desk is in the central reception building.

"Hey, Joe." I take a seat behind the plexi-glass bulletproof barrier Symbian erected two years ago after spies from a rival software firm broke into the building and tried to steal company secrets.

Joe Robinsky, age fifty-seven, widowed, no kids, no hair, one heart bypass under his tightly cinched belt, gives me a nod. "We've just got building three tonight. Management put extra security on the other buildings, because everyone's staying late to meet some deadline." He bites into what appears to be a mayo, butter, and processed meat sub on pure white bread.

"I thought you told me the doctor ordered you to cut out white carbs and bad fats." I pull out my plastic containers and show him my fight diet evening meal—steamed chicken and veg, and whole grain rice with a chocolate protein shake for dessert. "I'm happy to share."

"Can't eat that shit," Joe says. "I need real food."

"I don't want to lose you." I hand him one of my containers. "I was worried sick when you had your heart attack. What would Cheryl and I do without you?" Joe, Cheryl, and I have worked the evening shift together for almost two years. We make such a good team, Joe turned down an offer to take on the slightly higher paying late-night shift to keep us together.

Joe waves the container away. "Don't worry about me. It'll take more than a sandwich to put me out of commission, and if it does, I'll see my Lizzie that much sooner."

My heart squeezes in my chest. Joe's wife died three years ago, and he still misses her something fierce.

I strap on my utility belt and angle my cap to avoid the bump on my head. My uniform consists of a silver polo shirt bearing a Symbian Security badge, shapeless navy pants, a security belt complete with gun, Taser, nightstick, walkie-talkie, and cuffs, and an extremely unflattering blue cap. "Don't say things like that. I like working with you. You know the last time you were in the hospital, they paired me up with Sol DeMarco. He spent half his shift hiding in the basement watching sports on his tablet and the other half telling people he could take me in the ring with one hand tied behind his back."

"Not a chance," Joe says.

"Definitely not with these pythons." I mock a body-builder pose, flexing my biceps.

Joe chuckles and then calls out as I leave the building, "Remind me never to get on your bad side."

My tension eases as I walk the perimeter of the building, enjoying the cool stillness of the night. Maybe I can take some extra shifts while Zack is around. Usually, recruiters only stick around for a couple of days, wining and dining potential new fighters or scouting for talent. I'll just have to rejig my training sessions so I'm there when he's not around, and then he'll be gone and out of my life for good.

I cross over to the parking lot, and something rustles the

bushes in front of me. Heart thumping, I turn on my flashlight and push the branches aside.

"Jesus Christ. Get that thing outta my face." The throaty rasp of Cheryl Walker's voice cuts through the night air. A botched thyroidectomy a few years ago damaged one of the nerves leading to her voice box, leaving her with what she describes as a "chain-smoking, phone sex hooker voice" but what Joe says is downright sexy.

"I thought you were a raccoon." I lower the flashlight and round the bush to the parking lot, where Cheryl is picking something off the ground.

"You know many five-foot-three-inch raccoons with big boobs and a little extra junk in the trunk?" She pats her ample bottom and grins. Her curly, dark hair is even more wild than usual, and her green eyes are wide and framed in long lashes. I've never known anyone like Cheryl. She says what she thinks, and she lets it all hang out. Compared to her, I'm positively repressed.

"Not personally. What are you doing in the bush?"

"Dropped my keys." She leans closer and frowns at my face. "Talk about raccoons. What happened to you?"

"Bad fight on the weekend."

Cheryl snorts. "Welcome to my life. I had a bad fight with the damn ex, so he decided not to pick up Amber even though Tuesdays are supposed to be his daughter and daddy nights. I had to drop her off with my sister again."

"Report him to family services."

"Tried it." Cheryl sighs. "He straightened up for about two weeks, and then he turned deadbeat again. I knew that about him when I married him, but the sex was so damn good. You know what I mean?"

"Sure," I say, although I don't. As the ballet company's artistic director, my ex, Damian, was creative at work, not so much in bed. It wasn't until I'd moved away that I realized he had married me not because he truly loved me but because I helped his career and fed his ego. He liked that I was twelve years younger than him, awed by his power and reputation, and willing to do his bidding. He showed me off to his friends, boasted about our relationship, and used me as an adornment when he wished to impress. As I became more successful, I opened doors for him, giving him an edge over the new generation of choreographers who were snapping at his heels. In return, he gave me stability and security, helped me build a career, and made me feel wanted again.

After I left Damian, I didn't date for over a year, and when I did, it was just casual hookups with men who were friends of friends or part of my social circle. For the most part, they were uniformly dull, mild mannered, and totally unthreatening, which translated into lackluster performance in the bedroom.

"I'm on patrol with you tonight," Cheryl says. "I'll let Joe know I'm here and we can finish patrolling the parking lot together."

She is gone no more than five minutes when my walkie-talkie crackles into the silence. "Got a guy in the front lobby who's looking for you," Cheryl says. "You want me to bring him out with me?"

"I'm not expecting anyone. Who is it?"

"He says his name is Grayson. Zack Grayson."

5

Shayla

"ARE YOU KIDDING?" MY BREATH CATCHES IN MY THROAT. "ZACK Grayson is at reception?"

"He just showed me some ID," Cheryl whispers in a pathetic attempt to keep her voice down. "Zachary Richard Grayson from Seattle, Washington. Age: thirty. Hair: dark, long, and curling deliciously at the ends where it brushes his shoulders—broad ones, I should add. Height: six feet, two inches. Weight: two hundred pounds of pure muscle. Eyes: melted chocolate with golden sparkles. He's wearing a Led Zeppelin T-shirt, leather jacket, jeans low on his hips. And the package..." She exhales loudly. "Do you know him? Please tell me he's not taken."

"Yes, I know him. And I have no idea if he's taken, although going by his reputation, I would guess not. But I don't want to see him. Tell him we aren't allowed visitors at work."

Cheryl makes a choked sound over the walkie-talkie. "He's not the kind of guy a single woman turns away."

"Please, Cheryl."

A moment passes, and the walkie-talkie crackles again. "Apparently, 'no' wasn't the answer he wanted to hear. You want me to cuff him and call the cops, or maybe just take him home with me?"

I tip my head back and groan. Cheryl may be tough, but maturity and years of experience as an MMA fighter have filled out Zack's muscles, added character in the form of a few scars and imperfections to his still breathtakingly handsome face, and given him the force of presence to put fear into even the toughest of security guards. He is Slayer, and I don't want Cheryl to get slayed.

"Send him out front. I'll meet you at building three." I straighten my uniform and walk toward the front of the building. Zack is the last person I want to see, but damned if I'm going to run away.

Fifty yards from the door, Zack emerges from the darkness. Raw power rolls off him with each stride of his long legs. My gaze drops down, taking in the faint ripple of his abs and the flex of hard muscle beneath his jeans. If I thought he looked hot in the gym, he looks even hotter in the semidarkness, where the shadows only add to his dark sensuality.

He halts a short distance away, and his gaze travels from my face to my shoes and up again. When his chin dips for what appears to be another leisurely perusal of my body, I give an exasperated sigh.

"Have you never seen a woman in a uniform before?"

Zack doesn't miss a beat, nor does he appear to be embarrassed. "I've never seen you in a uniform before. I like it."

For a moment, I lose the power of speech. With its shapeless, straight cut and heavy-duty polyester twill-weave material, the Symbian uniform is not made to show off a woman's assets. "Very funny. I see you haven't lost your sense of humor."

"You're lucky I have a sense of humor. The last person who got a strike past my guard…"

He trails off and my heart squeezes in my chest because we both know he wasn't thinking when he spoke. The last person who hit him in the ring wound up dead, although it wasn't Zack's fault.

"I'm sorry." I'm not sure if I mean I'm sorry for what happened with Okami or what happened at Redemption, but his face softens just enough that I know he understands.

"What are you doing here?" I fold my arms across my chest, bracing myself against the memory of the night I looked up an online video of his fight with Okami after seeing Zack's name in an article about an event in which a fighter died. Even if the cameras hadn't shown the devastation on his face, I knew in my heart he was in pain. "How did you know where to find me?"

Zack stares at me, his lips tipping up at the corners. Of course he won't say. One thing about Zack, he may have come from the wrong side of the tracks, but he was never the kind of guy who would rat someone out. He was loyal to people even if they didn't deserve his loyalty, respectful even if they hadn't earned his respect.

Not that I really need him to tell me who gave my location away. "You talked to Sadist."

He gives a noncommittal shrug. "You don't want to mess with a head injury. I wanted to make sure you were okay."

"I'm okay."

Zack steps closer, so close that I can feel the heat of his body through my thick polyester uniform, inhale the heady scent of his intoxicating cologne. "Then why are you wearing your hat to the side?"

My hand flies up, and I push the cap straight. "I was going for a jaunty look."

"Jaunty?" Zack raises an amused eyebrow. "Never heard of a jaunty security guard."

"And I never heard of a top MMA recruiter driving out to an industrial estate on a Friday night for no reason."

"You're hurt. I could see the bump on your head before you left the gym. How's that for a reason?" He gently removes my cap, and his fingers run lightly over my head, sending a delicious shiver of memory down my spine.

"This is where you bumped your head the first time I met you." Zack slides his fingers through my hair, strokes my head so gently, it's hard to believe he is one of the best MMA fighters in our local gym or that he has a reputation for getting into fights every weekend at the bars in town.

"That was the best fall of my life." I nuzzle his neck beneath the pale light of the moon. Behind him, the "Sweet Sixteen" banner my friends made for my birthday swings between two pine trees in the back-yard, casting a faint shadow on the lawn. "I'm sixteen now, Zack."

He groans, wraps his arms around me. I can feel his erection, hard against my stomach. "Yes, you are."

"That's the legal age of consent in Washington State," I whisper.

"Shay…"

"Please, Zack." I grind my hips against him, desperate to be close, to feel his skin against mine. "Can we go to your place? I want you to be my first. My only. I want you to be mine."

"I've been yours since the day we met." He leans down to kiss my cheek, and I turn so our lips meet. Almost instantly, his arms tighten around me, and he invades my mouth like he needs to claim me. I've never kissed any boys except Zack, but I know nothing will ever compare. I feel his kisses deep inside me, filling my heart until I think it might burst with happiness.

"You know what I mean." I press my palm over his erection, run my fingers along the hard outline of his shaft. He rocks his hips against my hand, and a thrill of excitement shoots through me. Zack has never let me touch him there before. Maybe tonight...

"God, I want you." His hand hovers over mine, as if he's torn between letting me continue and pushing me away.

Heart pounding, I reach for his belt, my fingers sliding over the smooth leather, brushing the hard ridges of his stomach beneath his T-shirt. I'm willing to take the risk of someone finding us if it means I can have what I want. Right here. Right now.

"No." With a shudder, he covers my hand and draws it away. "We're going to wait until you're eighteen. It's the right thing to do. I don't want people to say I took advantage of you, and I don't want you to have any regrets. Because once we do this, you'll be mine. Mine forever."

"Do you promise?" I lean my forehead against his broad chest. "Do you promise that you'll never let me go?"

Zack reaches into his pocket and pulls out a silver chain. "This is my promise. Happy sixteenth birthday."

I hold the chain up, and a dragonfly pendant sparkles in the moon-light, tiny blue crystals embedded in its delicate wings.

"It's beautiful. It looks like the dragonflies we saw down by the lake." I turn so he can fasten it around my neck. "I'll wear it always."

"And I'll love you always." He whispers so quietly, his voice is almost lost in the breeze. "No matter what happens, that will never change."

"Shay?" Zack's voice pulls me out of the warm memory and into a sea of pain. He never kept his promise. The night I turned eighteen, everything changed.

My hand flies to my neck where the dragonfly lies hidden beneath my uniform. After I left Damian, I started wearing it again, a silly hope that one day, I'd find the kind of love and joy I had with Zack.

"I have to get going. I'm on patrol." I take my cap from his hand and settle it on my head. "Thanks for stopping by. I'm fine." I take one step back and then another, but I can't force myself to turn away. For years, I heard his voice around every corner; I thought I saw him in every crowd. Even after I married Damian, I never stopped thinking about Zack. And now here he is, but there is a huge chasm between us that I'm not prepared to cross.

"Is someone picking you up after work?"

"No. I drove myself."

He takes a step closer, his body perilously close to breaching my personal space. "It's not every day a guy bumps into a girl he hasn't seen for seven years. I'm jamming in Sunnyvale tonight. Come by after work and we can catch up."

Ah. I'm just "a girl he hasn't seen for seven years." Not "the girl I loved since I was thirteen years old" or "the girl who wanted me to be her first" or even "the girl I bitterly regret fucking and abandoning in a cheap motel."

"No, thanks. I have an early start tomorrow morning." I hesitate when he doesn't move. "You're still playing electric bass?"

Zack listened to a lot of Led Zeppelin when we were together and steadfastly maintained that John Paul Jones was the best bassist of all time. I loved watching him play. Sometimes I would fall asleep at his trailer, watching his fingers gently strumming over the strings, his long hair falling forward to cover his face, his deep voice sliding in and out of my dreams.

"It's the only way I know how to relax." Zack tucks a wayward strand of hair behind my ear, his fingers trailing lightly over my skin, his low, husky voice caressing my senses.

Desire, deep and dark, awakens within me, and my body practically melts, the way it always melted when he touched me. My first sexual feelings were for Zack. He held my hand one day when I was thirteen, and instead of the warmth of friendship, I felt something else. Something dangerous and exciting that only got more intense as our relationship deepened.

Something I shouldn't be feeling now.

"Well, have fun. I guess I'll see you at Redemption, unless you're heading out tomorrow."

"I'll be around." His words are casual, but even after seven years, I can sense his disappointment, and it still twists me up inside. I used to feel the same way when I disappointed my father. Unlike my mother, who demanded so much because she wanted to live her lost career as a ballerina through me, my father loved me without judgment or expectation, and because he never asked anything of me, I always felt bad when I let him down.

"Good night, Zack." I walk away, but before I turn the corner, I can't help but look over my shoulder. Our gazes lock, and I am swept up in a rush of emotion so fierce, it tears my breath away.

But then I remember another time emotion threatened to overwhelm me and how it felt to have my heart ripped out of my chest. I remember how I came to be at Redemption and why I need to move forward. Not back.

6

Zack

Z ACK WATCHED S HAYLA FROM ACROSS THE GYM, WONDERING IF
she realized just how many male fantasy buttons she pushed.
Or did she know how many dudes were surreptitiously
watching her teach striking techniques to a group of avid
tween girls, several of whom looked like they shopped at the
same grunge gym wear store as her? He couldn't get over
her 180-degree change of style since he'd last seen her in
Glenwood, but he liked the badass clothes that teased a man
with glimpses of her beautiful body while at the same time
warning him away.

He knew he shouldn't have gone to see her at work last
night. Her slap at the gym had made it abundantly clear that
she hadn't forgiven him for walking away. But what was he
supposed to do when he saw her icing her head after every session? Or walking out with a visible bump? Nobody at the gym
seemed particularly concerned, but then they probably didn't
understand the danger of a head injury the way he did. If she'd

been his, he would have been in the car and breaking every speed limit to get to Redemption to look after her.

But she wasn't his. She was Damian's wife. Tall, blond Damian with the square jaw and lean, dancer's body. One year after Zack had left her in that cheap motel, he'd made the mistake of going to New York to find her, only to discover that her brother, Matt, hadn't lied to him the night Zack had finally worked up the courage to call.

She belonged to another man.

Even today, he couldn't believe she had so quickly replaced him. Had Damian offered her all the things Zack couldn't give her? Money, stability, a nice house in a cozy suburb, and a normal, middle-class family. Did he buy her expensive presents, take her to fancy restaurants, and buy her pretty clothes? Was he worthy where Zack was not?

Why hadn't she waited for him? Just one year. Zack could have given her everything she wanted and the one thing he knew no man could give her like he could. Love. With every ounce of his soul.

"I've got all the stats you asked for this morning," Torment said, coming up beside him. "You want them emailed or in hard copy?"

"Email is fine." He glanced over at the man beside him, assessing his size and strength against his own. Even in professional circles, Torment was a legend from his underground fight days. He had only ever lost one fight, and that was when his competitor hit him over the head with an illegal set of brass knuckles and almost took his life. Every fighter dreamed of the chance to face Torment in the ring, but rumor had it only his closest friends at Redemption were given that opportunity.

"She's a solid fighter." Torment folded his arms, leaned against the wall beside Zack, nodding in the direction of Zack's gaze, which was, as it had been since he walked in the door, fixed on Shayla. "Probably the best female fighter at Redemption. She's got a good grounding in both striking and grappling techniques. You'll see from her stats that she's lost her last four fights, but we're coming up with a plan to get her over the hump. I'm confident she can make it happen. But frankly, I'm surprised MEFC is interested in her right now."

MEFC wasn't interested, but as one of their top recruiters, Zack was expected to scout for new talent as well as entice top amateurs into the MEFC fold. He had already sent in his report letting his bosses know their original target, Blade Saw, wasn't ready for the pros and not worth the early investment. Usually, he would head out of town after the report was done or the targeted fighter signed, but now that he'd found Shayla again, he needed a reason to stick around. With female fighters in high demand, assessing her potential was a good excuse.

Torment obviously wanted to know why Zack would be interested in a fighter who had just lost her last four fights, but Zack didn't rise to the bait. "How long has she been with the club?"

"Four years," Torment said. "She started out taking karate and judo classes and moved on to jiu-jitsu. When I saw her potential, I encouraged her to work on striking and start fighting. She was phenomenal right out of the gate. Very focused and intense."

Zack forced himself to look at Torment although it meant tearing his eyes away from the woman he had thought he'd never see again. "Any idea what happened in those last fights?"

"I'm sure you know that sometimes strength and technique aren't enough. If there's something going on in a fighter's personal life or inside her head, it comes out in the ring."

Personal life? Zack's chest tightened at the thought of Shayla with her husband. Jealousy had been a huge problem for him when he and Shayla were together, fueled in no small part by his insecurity about his trailer park roots and his dysfunctional family.

"That was the case for me," Torment offered. "I worked through a lot of issues in the ring over the years."

"We all do." Zack's mother, an abuser of any substance that would help her forget her own traumatic past, had overdosed when Zack was twelve years old, and he had always felt some measure of responsibility for her death. If he'd been smarter, tried harder to be good, spent more time looking after his sisters, done more to keep his abusive father away... His mother had needed him, and he'd let her down, just as he'd let down his sisters, Viv and Lily, who had needed Zack to protect them from their alcoholic father until he drank himself to death. Every time he wasn't there to intervene was another black mark on his soul. Even after he had been granted guardianship of his sisters and they were no longer at risk, the need to help and protect them was there, as if it were hardwired into his brain.

During those tumultuous teenage years, he had wanted to protect Shayla, too. She was the one person he would not fail. But his determination to keep her safe had landed him in detention again and again for picking fights with guys who even looked at her the wrong way. If not for a school counselor who had suggested he take up MMA at a local gym to relieve his anger and frustration, he had no doubt he would eventually have landed in jail.

"If something is going on with her, she's keeping it close to her chest," Torment said. "She doesn't share much about her past or her personal life. Even Sadist hasn't been able to get much out of her over the years, and he can get just about anyone to talk."

Zack's gaze flicked back to Shayla. She was cooling her class down on the mats while talking to a tall Ken-doll-type dude with a square jaw, blond crew cut, and too much tan. He seemed overly familiar with her, putting his hand on her arm, then her shoulder, patting her on the back, and leaning in close. Too close to be a friend.

"Who's that?" He braced himself for the answer he didn't want to hear.

"Her personal trainer, Stan Roberts." Torment shot Zack a sideways look. "He's one of the best. He took her on because he believes in her."

Zack took an instant dislike to Stan, who didn't seem to be able to keep his hands off Shayla. It didn't make any sense. He and Shayla weren't together anymore. And it wasn't like he had lacked for female company over the years. Before the

Okami fight, he'd had everything—fame, fortune, and countless women fighting for his attention, few of whom he'd ever seen more than a handful of times and none of whom had filled the emptiness inside him.

"You think she has what it takes to go pro?" he asked.

"You're the recruiter," Torment said. "You tell me."

Recruiter. Not fighter. Even after three years in the business, he still found it hard to be on the outside looking in. Recruiting was as close as he could get to the sport without stepping into the ring, but after the Okami fight, he knew he could never cross the ropes again. No one understood his decision. His boss, Kip Matthews, head of MEFC recruitment, pressured him constantly to return, as did his fans and fellow fighters. But there was only one person who had ever truly seen him, one woman who would have understood his pain.

"I didn't think you'd come." Zack smiled as the little girl made her way along the path at the top of Devil's Hill where he'd been waiting for the better part of the hour. He didn't know what he was doing here, especially after taking a beating yesterday afternoon from her brother. Matt hadn't believed that his eight-year-old sister had taken his bike for a joyride and had pinned the blame on Zack instead.

She sat beside him, her knees still bandaged after her fall yesterday, long hair falling over her shoulder. She was a cute kid. And she smiled a lot. No one in Zack's trailer park ever smiled.

"You said you'd be here."

"I guess I did." He'd offered to teach her to ride down the hill before his encounter with Matt, and a promise was a promise.

"And I thought you might need some bandages after what Matt did to you. I had some in my dance bag. I get hurt a lot in ballet."

She didn't look like a ballerina. Sure, she was skinny enough and pretty, but the ballerinas he'd seen on TV were tall, graceful, and willowy with poufy skirts, and their arms looked like they were blowing in the breeze.

"I'm okay." The cuts and bruises Matt had given him were nothing compared to the beatings he got when his dad came home drunk from the bar.

"No, you're not." She peeled the paper off one of the bandages and carefully placed it over the cut on his forehead. Zack didn't like to be touched, and it had been years since he'd let anyone tend his cuts and bruises, but when her fingers brushed over his skin, his body stilled, a calm settling over him like nothing he'd ever felt before.

Before Zack even realized he had moved, he was halfway across the gym toward her, thinking how that day on the hill wasn't the first time she had wanted to help him but the only time he'd let her. Over the years, he'd pushed her away when she had tried to look after him, whether it was bruises from fights or slipping grades because he had to work to support his two younger sisters. In his mind, it was his job to look after the important women in his life. Not the other way around.

"Shay."

She looked up, startled. "Zack. I thought you were gone."

He'd thrown her off. Well, that was something. At least he had some effect on her.

"I still have work to do at Redemption." Although chasing

after Shayla to find out what had happened in the years since he left her wasn't technically work, he had enough leeway with his job that he could spin things to suit his personal agenda.

"This is Stan, my personal trainer." She nodded at the blond dude beside her.

"Slayer." Stan grabbed Zack's hand and pumped it up and down. "It's an honor. I followed all your fights. That night you fought Paul Renardo in Denver... I was there. Greatest fight ever. Can I get a picture?" Stan pulled out his phone, and Zack posed with him for the obligatory selfie before Shayla sent Stan to tend to her class.

She waited until he was out of earshot before turning on Zack. "What are you doing here?"

"Recruiting."

Her lips pressed into a thin line. "I mean here on this mat, talking to me. Obviously, I'm not in the running, and if you're looking for friendship, any chance of that was obliterated when you walked out the door seven years ago."

Zack winced. He had always regretted how he'd handled the situation, but after bumping into Matt outside the local drugstore where he'd gone to buy condoms for their first night together, it had seemed like the right thing—the only thing—to do.

"You're destroying her life, you fucking selfish bastard." Matt shoved him against his car. *"She was accepted to apprentice in New York, and she's going to turn it down tomorrow to go to San Diego with you. I always knew you'd drag her down, you worthless piece of shit."*

"What the hell?" Zack shoved Matt back, something he would never

have dared to do before he started training at the local MMA gym, but a few years had made all the difference.

"The ballet company in New York is everything," Matt spat out. "It's the best in the country. Dancing with them could launch her international career. It's what she's been working toward since she was three years old, and you're taking it away from her. There is nothing for her in San Diego. They have a small, unknown ballet company that offers her no real prospect for advancement. She'll be nothing. All that work. All the hours, the pain, the tears, the damn money we spent, the sacrifices we made. All. For. Nothing."

Matt punctuated each of the last three words with a shove, but for the first time since Zack had started MMA, he didn't fight back. Shock stayed his hand. Why hadn't she told him? But even as he asked himself the question, he knew. She was afraid he'd make her go to New York. And that was exactly what he was going to do.

"I knew about the New York offer," he said. "Matt told me. I did what I had to do to get you to go."

She stared at him aghast. "So you lied? About Seattle and the coach…"

He shook his head. "I never lied to you. I did have a visit from a top coach in Seattle that day. He did make me an offer, and he was heading back to Seattle that morning, but I could have gone the next week, and at that time, Seattle wasn't where I thought I needed to be to make it in MMA. But Matt said you planned to turn down your offer the next day. I couldn't take the risk. I needed you to hate me enough that you would want to be as far from me as possible. In New York."

Her hands balled into fists, and her voice thinned. "That wasn't your call. And doing it that night? You certainly gave me a first time to remember. If you think I'm going to thank you, it's not going to happen. It was the wrong choice for me, and not just because I didn't get to make it."

He bristled under her anger, but before he could respond, Stan returned with Shayla's class in tow. "This is Slayer," he said to the group of girls who looked to be no older than twelve. "He's one of MMA's biggest stars." He rattled off all Zack's accolades, and the girls' eyes widened. "If you ask nicely, I'm sure he'll show you a few moves."

Shayla shook her head. "I'm sure Slayer is busy, and we have—"

"Pleasepleasepleasepleaseplease." The chorus of young voices rose above the noise in the gym.

"How can you say no to that?" Stan flashed his snow-white smile, and Zack had to fight the urge to relieve him of a few of his teeth.

Shayla shook her head. "We're actually done for the day—"

"Pleasepleasepleaseplease." The little girls pleaded until she gave a grudging nod. She'd always had a soft spot for kids.

"We were going to learn how to escape a choke from the guard today, but we ran out of time," she said to Zack with a shrug. "Maybe you could show them how's it done."

Zack grabbed the opportunity and bit back a smile. "I'll need a partner, and you just volunteered. On your back."

Her eyes narrowed, and he was damn sure he heard the softest growl. Lips pressed tight together, she lay on the mat in front of him, knees bent but together.

Zack raised an admonishing eyebrow and gently pushed her legs apart. He'd always enjoyed winding her up. "Open for me."

Her cheeks heated, and she bit her bottom lip, the way she'd done at fourteen when she had wanted to kiss him but was too shy to ask. By sixteen, she wasn't shy at all, and his resolve had been tested every time they were together. Much like now. Damn, she was sexy. His blood rushed to his groin, and he shifted his weight, regretting that he hadn't worn a cup.

"Like that's ever going to happen again," she muttered under her breath. "You made it pretty clear how you felt about me when you left me alone in that run-down hotel."

"If it helps, this isn't easy for me either," he said quietly. "You made it pretty clear how you felt about me when you hauled ass out of town only two days later." He grabbed her shirt, rolling them before his body overrode his mind and gave way to the heat between them. With one hand, he pulled her down until she was lying on top of him, her cheek against his chest, her hips pressed tight against his, an exquisitely painful pleasure that threatened his self-control.

"You can't have it both ways," she murmured softly, her breath warm against his skin, despite the T-shirt between them. "You can't be upset because I left town after you walked away. I was going to go to San Diego for you, Zack. To support you while you tried to build your career as a fighter. To help you. I could have deferred New York. But you never gave me a chance. You never wanted my help. You lived your life like a martyr, making selfless choices without letting people save you in return."

Her heart pounded a rapid beat against his chest, her body soft and warm. She still fit perfectly against him, as if they were made for each other, as if they had always been one person, not two. In that moment, the years that separated them seemed only minutes, the pain of loss only the smallest nick and not the brutal slice of a dagger that had torn a gaping wound in his chest.

She wiggled against him, seeking an escape, and he bit back a groan. Damn her. Damn her bitter truths and her sweet body and the betraying longing of a wounded heart.

"If you were mine, I wouldn't let you do this with another man." He grabbed the back of her shirt and pulled his elbow around her head, holding her in place for the submission. "I called Matt once a few years back. He told me you were married. How does your husband stand it?"

"We aren't together anymore."

Zack's chest constricted as he tried to process her words, and he made the critical mistake of loosening his grip.

"You should always try to escape at the earliest possible moment," Shayla said to her rapt audience, bridging up quickly to slip her head free. Twisting into half guard, she scissored her legs around him, taking advantage of his distraction. Only instinct and muscle memory saved him from being submitted by an amateur, honed after years of drills and dozens of fights. He rolled and mounted her, straddling her hips in a dominant position. A blush crept up her neck, her lips parting, but when he looked in her eyes for arousal, all he saw was pain.

"Am I hurting you?"

Even as the question dropped from his lips, she wrapped

her right arm around the back of his neck, grabbed her left bicep with her right hand, and pulled him down so their cheeks pressed together. When he felt her left hand slide under his neck, ready to crush his throat, he flipped her, easily escaping the submission. He could have let her have the win in front of her class, but there was a small part of him that couldn't stop fighting, even though he'd hung up his gloves.

Did it really make a difference? She hadn't even made an effort to come after him or contact him after their night together. Walking away had been the hardest, most gut-wrenching decision of his life, but he had always believed he had done right by her. He had given her the only gift he had to give—he had let her go. And she had gone. Two days later, she'd been on a plane to New York, and one year later, she was with another man.

"Class dismissed." Shayla looked away, smiled at her class. "I'll see you all next week."

"You did well," Zack said, looking down at her as the girls walked away. "But you left yourself vulnerable at the end."

"Story of my life."

He leaned forward, palms to the mat on either side of her shoulders. "I want to hear all about your life, Shay. Everything."

"From the night you used me and threw me away?"

Bitterness laced her tone, and he knew finding his way through those walls was going to be an uphill battle, especially when he had walls of his own.

In those last moments before he'd slipped out of their bed and out of her life, he'd held her against him, breathed in her scent, felt her heart beat slow and steady in her chest, and wished he were a different man with a different past and the hope of a future where he could be everything she needed him to be. Now silence stood between them. Secrets he could never share.

"I never wanted to hurt you. Leaving you was the hardest thing I've ever done, and I've regretted that decision ever since, but I had nothing to offer you. You had a chance to go to New York and make something of your life. I didn't want to take that from you."

"So you took my choice from me instead?" She pushed herself back to her knees. "You destroyed me. I loved you. You were my world. My breath. The other half of my soul. And once you were gone, I was lost. I'd never felt pain like that, and I have no intention of ever opening myself to it again. It leaves you vulnerable. And when you're vulnerable, the worst things can happen."

"I don't want to fight with you," he said. "Not after I've found you again."

"Dammit." She scrambled to her feet. "You didn't *find* me. I wasn't *lost*. If you really wanted to see me, it wouldn't have been hard to track me down. You could have read about me in the news, called Matt, or even watched my performances online like I watched your fight with Okami..."

She trailed off when he stood, angry with himself for still feeling the pain of that wound and perversely disappointed that she hadn't been there to heal him when he had needed her most.

"Zack." She reached out, her tone softening. "I'm sorry. I shouldn't have..."

"It's fine."

"No, it's not." She touched his hand, covered it with her own. "If it was, you'd still be fighting."

He pulled his hand away, loving and hating that she still knew him so well.

"I almost called Viv and Lily to get your number—"

"You wouldn't have reached them," he said abruptly. "They moved to Seattle shortly after you left."

"How are they doing?" She gave a wistful smile that made his heart hurt, because if he closed his eyes, he could almost imagine they were back in Glenwood having a conversation about everyday things.

"They're doing fine."

"I still miss them," she said.

They missed her, too. Viv especially, because she and Shayla had been closer in age with only three years between them. Lily was a year older and Zack one year older than her. Viv was also the most outgoing of the three siblings and the peacemaker of the family. A creative soul who flitted from one project to the next, Viv had shared a love of music with Shayla as well as a willingness to take risks that Lily could never understand. And yet it was Lily, with her springy dark curls and dry sense of humor, who could make Shayla laugh. Lily who had been their rock when Viv was first diagnosed with leukemia.

He hesitated, wondering if he should tell Shayla about Viv's illness. But if she did ever reach out to them, it would be better that she knew. "Lily works as an accountant. Viv runs a jewelry business from home. They moved to Seattle because Viv had leukemia and it was easier to get treatment in the city, but she's in remission now."

They had suspected something was seriously wrong in the weeks before he'd left Shayla, and he'd already started preparing for the worst. One of the reasons he'd decided to train in Seattle was so he could be there if Viv needed him. It wasn't a burden he had wanted Shayla to bear.

Her hand flew to her heart. "Oh my God. Poor Viv. It must have been so hard for you and Lily."

And just like that, she was in his arms, compassion her undoing.

It was clearly meant as a friendly hug, but Zack couldn't stop himself from holding her tight. She fit so perfectly against him, felt so right in his arms, he almost couldn't believe they'd been apart for seven years.

He rested his cheek against her head, closed his eyes, and pretended it was real.

7

Shayla

AFTER A SLEEPLESS NIGHT TRYING NOT TO THINK ABOUT ZACK AND the feel of his arms around me, I drag myself through training the next day and almost get myself knocked out by a newbie with a powerful right hook. By the time I arrive at the Protein Palace later that night, I have a pounding headache, and I'm looking forward to being distracted by the antics of the Redemption team.

Once a '50s-style burger joint, the Protein Palace is now run by a couple of retired MMA fighters who serve up protein in every way, shape, and form. With its shiny, red vinyl stools and booths, glistening chrome, and sparkly tiles, the restaurant has retained its '50s charm but smells of wheatgrass and whey instead of ice cream and grease.

Sadist waves at me from a table in the corner. The team meets at the Protein Palace on Thursday nights for protein shakes, and then we move on to the clubs and bars. After my devastating fight on the weekend and the shock of seeing Zack again, the alcoholic part of the evening can't come soon enough.

"She's rocking the Protein Palace today," Sadist says, eyeing my clothes. Unlike the Redemption crew, who wear T-shirts and either shorts or jeans, I'm ready to party in a Nirvana T-shirt over a tulle skirt, thick-soled shoes, and my favorite black fedora.

"Someone has to give the Redemption team a bit of class." I take a seat beside Jimmy "Blade Saw" Sanchez, Redemption's very own James Dean but with Latino style, and give a wave to the rest of the guys crowded around the table.

"So, what's the deal with Slayer?" Darkly handsome Blade Saw is two-fisting protein shakes tonight and alternates between straws as he talks. "He's still kicking around. I thought the recruiters came in with a contract all ready to sign, and *bam*, someone's lucky day."

"Our girl here got the *bam* all right." Sadist grins. "Zack asked Torment for all her fight stats."

"He did?" I stare at Sadist, aghast. "MEFC doesn't recruit fighters on a losing streak."

"Maybe he's trying to 'recruit' you in the other sense of the word." Blade Saw snickers, setting off a chain reaction of juvenile sexual innuendo from the other fighters at the table. It's like I'm in high school all over again.

"Give it up. She only has eyes for me." Donald "Doctor Death" Drake, fresh from chasing waitresses around the café, pulls up a seat at the table and puts his arm around my shoulders. The blond-haired, blue-eyed, chisel-jawed heart surgeon is a part-time ring doctor at Redemption and sometime fighter. Just like me, Doctor Death dreams of one day going pro. Unlike me, he spends the rest of his time feeding his sex addiction.

Unfortunately, he always seems to go for women who are wanted by other men, and suffers the inevitable consequences.

"Who?" I pretend to search the restaurant, and Doctor Death gives an irritated huff.

"Just because I'm beautiful is no reason to turn me down." He preens, smiling at himself in the mirror on the wall.

I open my mouth to make a snappy retort when pain stabs through my skull—the third time today. Just a flicker and then it's gone, leaving a dull ache behind.

"You okay?" Doctor Death's doctor radar must have kicked in, because his smile is quickly replaced by a worried frown. "Makayla told me what happened. Sometimes concussions don't present right away."

"I'm fine. Really. I have a hard head. And it's not like I lost consciousness or anything. It's just a headache. I'm probably dehydrated." At least that's what I keep telling myself. A few missing seconds doesn't count.

"I have to swing by the hospital tonight," he persists. "I'm happy to take you so you can get checked out."

"Would I make it there with all my clothes on?"

"My reputation precedes me." He puffs out his chest and chuckles. "Women have been known to tear off their clothes in my presence, and if you feel the need, I won't stop you. But in my medical opinion, it would be better to wait until after you've had your head checked. Subdural hematomas really put a damper on vigorous sexual activity. We can have more fun if you're conscious."

A disturbance near the door draws our attention. Zack is

here. How irritating. This was supposed to be my night to get drunk and forget he ever walked back into my life. But chances are he'll never make it to our table. Already, the crowd is three deep around him with no end in sight, and there are fangirls clinging to him like flies.

Zack's star power keeps him occupied and away from our table for the next hour. He signs napkins, arms, cheeks, and even the curve of one woman's ass. Before long, he is steered to the wall bearing the Protein Palace logo to pose for pictures with his fans. I don't want to watch him, but I do. I've never loved anyone the way I loved Zack. I opened myself fully to him. I gave him everything, and he filled me so completely, I never wanted more. Every time I see him, the memories come flooding back. Ten years of happiness destroyed by one night of pain.

"He's been checking you out," Doctor Death says, a scowl marring the perfection of his handsome face as he stares at Zack, posing with two eager fangirls.

Zack looks devastatingly gorgeous tonight in his tight, black skull-print T-shirt, stretched deliciously over his muscular chest, and a pair of well-worn jeans, snug in all the right places. From the way the fangirls have latched on to his biceps, I'm not the only one to notice.

"I heard a rumor you had a history together," Doctor Death continues.

"We grew up in the same town. That's about it."

Zack catches me watching him, and in that second when our gazes connect, I remember every reason why I loved him. The way the gold flecks sparkled in his dark eyes when he was happy, the way he watched over me, his easy laughter, the feel of his body against mine, his lips on my lips, his breath on my skin, his hands—God, the things he could do with his hands—the steady beat of his heart as we lay together making dreams for a future we would never have.

After Zack finishes posing for pictures, Fred "Bulldog" Jenner, a heavyweight fighter from a rival gym and one of Sadist's fiercest competitors, challenges Zack to an arm wrestle. Such is how fighters entertain themselves when they're training. No fights in case of injury, no excessive drinking because of calories. But when fighters are pumped, as they usually are at this time of day, they need an outlet, and the Protein Palace has a special table set aside for the occasion.

Zack graciously accepts the challenge. Although he and Bulldog are evenly matched in height—two or three inches over six feet—Bulldog is actively training and must outweigh Zack by at least fifty pounds of solid muscle. Still, Zack clearly hasn't let himself go as many retired fighters do. There isn't an inch of fat on his toned body. And God, those biceps…

Not wanting to be left out, I join the crowd around their table. Although this is just for fun, there is more at stake than just a friendly arm wrestle. Zack was a big, big name in the sport, and Bulldog is shooting for the pros. A win over Zack sends a message that Bulldog is the man to beat. Out with the old and in with the new.

My heart thuds in my chest when Bulldog clasps Zack's hand. Although it makes no sense, I want Zack to win. He started from nothing and worked hard to get to where he is, and no one knows that better than I do. Despite what happened between us, I am a secret Slayer fangirl, too.

Biceps flex. Hands grip. A hum of excitement winds its way through the crowd. Bulldog grunts, and his arm shakes. Sweat beads on his forehead. He shifts in his seat, and his chair scrapes over the tile floor. The air thickens with the primal scent of testosterone. I'm surprised I don't suddenly grow a beard.

Someone turns up the music, and the Black Keys' "Everlasting Light" plays through the speakers. Zack's lips turn up at the corners. He lifts his gaze and smiles at me.

Because this was our song. We both loved this band with its steady beats, old-time sound and meaningful lyrics. "Everlasting Light" was the song Zack strummed on his bass while I practiced at the studio late into the night. It was the song he asked the band to play when he danced with me at my grad. It was the song he sang softly to me after we made love. I believed the lyrics as if they were his words. I believed he wanted to be everything to me. They were the last words I heard him say. They are the last words I want to hear now.

A sigh escapes my lips, and although there is no possible way he could have heard me over the music or the chant of the crowd, his face tightens, and the gold in his eyes fades to black.

Wham. Bulldog's hand goes down. Sandy lifts Zack's arm in a victory salute. The crowd cheers, and people surge forward to congratulate the victor.

"Who's next?" someone shouts.

The crowd hoots and hollers, and names get bandied about. The noise makes my headache worse, and I turn back to the

Redemption corner, looking for Doctor Death. Maybe I will take that ride.

A chair scrapes over the floor. And then a table. People shift to the side as if to give way.

My pulse kicks up a notch, and I know, even without being able to see through the crowd, that he's coming for me. I want to run. I want to hide. But pride and my stupid thudding heart hold me in place.

"How about it, Shay?" Zack saunters up to me, all smiles after his win, like we weren't just fighting yesterday in the gym before I found myself in his arms. "You want to take me on? I remember you actually won one of our arm wrestling competitions."

"I cheated." A lump rises in my throat at the memory of leaning across a table and kissing Zack on the lips to distract him so I could win.

"I remember." He clasps my hand and pulls me close. Heat radiates from him, sinks into my bones. I breathe him in, and I am engulfed in the scent of home—pine trees and flowers and wild heart of the Rocky Mountains.

"Zack…" I tear my gaze away and glance over at the crowd. "You should get back. I think your fangirls are worried."

His voice drops, sexy and low. "They should be."

"Don't let me keep you," I say, pretending not to have heard him. "As soon as I find Doctor Death, I'm heading out."

His cheeky smile fades. "You and Doctor Death?"

"He's giving me a lift."

Disappointment flickers across his face, but he rallies quickly. "I can take you where you need to go. I think he's a little busy right now." He tips his head to the restroom hallway where Doctor Death is giving one of the waitresses the benefit of his surgeon's hands.

"I guess I'm driving myself."

"I'll walk you out." He doesn't wait for my response. Instead, he presses a warm hand against my lower back, and we walk out the door as my Redemption teammates nudge each other and whisper like a bunch of teenagers.

"My car is over there." I point to the Volvo at the far end of the parking lot. "I used to have a Jeep, but I left it in New York."

"With your husband?"

I glance over at him, but he's staring straight ahead as he guides me through the parking lot. The marriage thing seems to bother him a lot, although I don't know why. Every time I saw him in the news or online, he had a different woman on his arm. Sometimes two.

"Yes." As far as I know, Damian is still in New York. He was charged and convicted for the assault, but he managed to plea-bargain his way out of jail. He got a slap on the wrist, and I lost my career and almost my life. A travesty of justice, but that's how the system works when you're a famous artistic director with connections in the highest places.

"Good."

I fight back a smile. "I see someone still has a jealousy prob-lem. How can you be jealous of a man you don't know?"

"Because he had you." He stops beside my car and pulls me close, brushing his thumb over the sensitive skin on the inside of my wrist, sending my pulse skittering out of control. I don't want to feel anything for him, but I do. I should pull away, but I can't. I need to make him understand how he made me feel, but I don't have the words.

How can you explain the feeling of your soul pouring out of your body, a pain so fierce, you can barely breathe, a heart shattered beyond repair, the pieces scattered over an ocean of sorrow, lost so deep, they can't be found? How do you share unstoppable tears, thick with memories, draining you of everything but the barest flicker of life?

Yes, it was young love, first love, teenage love. But that is the most intense love. The love you remember for the rest of your life, because you know nothing of the world except this one perfect person with whom you connect on a level neither of you understands. Zack was my everlasting light, my sun and stars until he fell from the sky and turned my world to ice.

I feel that sharp stab in my head again, lift my hand to my temple to try and ward off the pain. Zack wavers in front of me, his eyes growing dark with concern.

"What's wrong?" He releases my wrist, takes another step toward me until he is so close, I can feel the delicious heat of his body.

"Headache. A bad one. I made an appointment with my family doctor for the end of the week, but it's been getting worse. Doctor Death was going to take me to the hospital to get it checked out. He said subdural—"

Whoosh. I am off my feet, cradled in Zack's arms, and it feels like I never left. He smells of the meadows where we lay on lazy summer days, the cinnamon whiskey he sneaked out of the bar and kissed into my mouth, and the pine from the tree he climbed every night so he could lie with me until I fell asleep. He smells of comfort and safety. He smells of home and love and longing and everything I have ached for since we parted.

"What are you doing?"

"I'm taking you to the hospital."

"I'm okay to drive. Put me down." My words don't sound convincing, even to me. And I am torn between forcing him to release me and enjoying the feeling of being cared for after so many years alone.

Zack stops beside a blue pearl Acura NSX. It's a beautiful car. Sleek. Powerful. Very him. But… "Seriously? Blue? It's kind of sedate for you."

"It's a rental." He pulls out his key fob and unlocks the door, still holding me easily against his chest. "I have a red one at home."

"Of course you do." Zack always drove red vehicles and maintained only a lesser man would drive anything else.

He chuckles. "I guess some things don't change."

But a lot of things do. I am not the same person I was seven years ago. Trust is a luxury I can no longer afford. I no longer believe in fate or hope or everlasting love, and I don't take chances.

I study the sleek, black leather-and-chrome interior as he bends and gently places me on the seat, like I'm a breakable treasure. I've never ridden in a vehicle that cost over two hundred thousand dollars. Living paycheck to paycheck, I can't even imagine having that much money to spend on a car.

"What do you think?" Zack's words are almost inaudible over the roar of the motor as he peels out of the parking lot. If we drive at this speed to the hospital, I might make it back to Redemption to pick up my car before the Protein Palaces closes.

"It'll do." I grin and run my hand over the sleek dash. When Zack used to pick me up in his dad's rusted-out Ford half-ton truck, we loved to talk about the cars we would buy if we won the lottery. He was always partial to the Venom, because it resembled the head of a snake. I wanted the fastest car, which meant my dream car changed every time a manufacturer figured out a way to improve performance.

"You're a hard woman to please."

I shrug, enjoying the game despite myself. "It can't go over 190, so really, what's the point?"

"Still a speed demon, I see." He accelerates, only to have to slam on the brakes when we hit a light. "Do you need to drive that fast for your work as a security guard?" He revs up with a squeal of tires when the light turns to green. "Seems kind of dangerous."

"I'm dangerous."

He laughs out loud, that familiar deep rumble vibrating through my body. "Good thing I wasn't around when you applied for the job. I might have tried to talk you out of it."

"Nobody could have talked me out of it." I stare out the window, watching the blur of the city. "I wanted to be able to defend myself. I wanted to be strong and capable. If life hadn't turned out the way it did, I would have become a policeman like my dad. Nobody ever intimidated or pushed him around."

"You were strong," he says quietly.

"Not strong enough." I struggle to hold back the memories of the night Damian attacked me, how easily he knocked me to the ground, how it took less than half an hour to destroy everything it had taken me a lifetime to build.

"Where were you?"

I startle when I hear Damian's voice coming from the darkness. With a sigh, I flip on the switch to see him sitting in a chair facing the door, a bottle of vodka in his hand.

"I told you before I left the studio, and in the many texts I answered over the last few hours. I went for a drink with Stefan and Violet." I place my handbag on the hall table and pull out my phone. We have been playing out this scene more and more often as my career has taken off. Although Damian gave me my start in the company, he's become jealous of my success, and our marriage has started to suffer. Caring has become controlling. Protective has become possessive. And once the rumors started that he might be replaced with a younger artistic director, he has become increasingly insecure about our age difference. Now, I can't meet a friend for a drink without Damian showing up or calling a dozen times to find out where I am or who I'm with. He is obsessed with the idea that I will leave him for a younger man, and his baseless accusations have led to fights that can be heard on the street.

"You're lying. You went to see him."

"Who?"

"Your lost love." He sneers. "The fighter who broke your young heart and left you ripe for the picking. I checked the search history on your computer. You've been visiting MMA sites and reading about him."

My heart skips a beat. His paranoia is getting out of control if he's checking my computer. Violet and Stefan were right. I need to leave him before it's too late. But where will I go? What will I do? Although his influence in the company is slowly fading, Damian is still a powerful person in the ballet world. One word from him and no company on the East Coast will hire me.

"Don't be ridiculous. I saw an online article in my news feed about a fight in Newark where one of the fighters died. I recognized his name, so I decided to check it out."

He lets out a breath. "He's dead?"

"No. The other guy died, but Zack was absolved of blame, because his opponent went into the fight knowing he had a life-threatening condition and against doctor's orders." *After seeing the video, I'd read every article I could find to see what happened to Zack.*

"Zack." He takes a drink straight from the bottle of vodka he brought home after his last visit to Russia. "You never loved me the way you loved him. If we ended it today, you wouldn't sob for me alone in a dark room. You wouldn't pine until you were skin and bone. You wouldn't break. You'd probably trample me on your rush out the door."

"It was just an article, Damian." *Now I'm getting irritated. I'm tired of this. Tired of defending myself. Tired of his suspicions. Tired of his baseless accusations.* "You're reading too much into it."

"Am I? Where were you *really* tonight?" *His handsome face curdles.* "Did you go to console him because he took another man's life? Did you make him feel better by spreading your legs?"

"You're disgusting." *My stomach clenches even though I've done nothing wrong, because I thought about it. After I saw the video of the fight, I could feel Zack's pain. I could see his devastation. Even though he'd been cleared of wrongdoing, he would never forgive himself. It would destroy him. Despite everything that had happened between us, I wanted to be there for him, if only for the memories of all the good things he had done for me. And didn't that just say everything about the state of my marriage.*

"You're drunk."

"Of course I'm drunk," he shouts. "That's what you do when you get fired. You drink. But you aren't supposed to drink alone. Your wife is supposed to be at home waiting for you on the worst day of your life. Not out fucking another man."

My heart sinks. We both knew this was coming. Ticket sales were down. Donations were drying up. The board of directors had decided to move in a new direction by hiring two young choreographers, ostensibly to help Damian modernize the company, but we all knew what was coming. Damian, with his traditional background and classical training, struggled to keep up, and I guess today they put him out of his misery.

"I'm sorry they let you go. I truly am. But don't take your anger out on me. I've never cheated on you. I was with Stefan and Violet since I left the studio. You can ask them about it tomorrow."

"Give me your phone." He holds out his hand. "I'll ask them now, and then you can answer for your lies."

My heart pounds wildly, but I walk over to him. I don't need to be afraid. We've danced this dance before. He's angry and he's hurting, but Damian is not a violent man.

Damian takes the phone from my hand, but instead of calling my friends, he throws it across the room.

"What are you doing?"

"You never loved me," he snarls, and I realize drink isn't the only

thing clouding his mind. "It was always him. Even though he broke
you and I put you back together, you still want him."

I take a step back, and he grabs my hand so tight, my fingers
squeeze together.

"Say it."

"Let me go. You're hurting me."

"Say it," he shouts.

"What else are you on?" I struggle in his grasp. "You're acting
crazy. I don't want him. I married you. I've been faithful to you. I've
supported you. What more do you want from me?"

"Love." He squeezes my hand so tight, I scream. "You were supposed to love me until death do us part."

"Stop, Damian. Let me go." I slap and punch at his face until
he releases me, and then I back up to the door. "I'm done with this.
I'm done with your drinking and your jealousy and your inability to
believe that I have been faithful to you. I'm sorry they let you go, but
maybe now you'll stop obsessing over what they are going to do. You're
a great choreographer, a great artistic director, and I'm sure you'll find
a company that appreciates your talent, but I can't do this anymore."

"Shayla." His face falls, and his voice softens. "Baby, I'm sorry. It
was a terrible shock. Please. Don't go."

"You hurt me. I think you broke something in my hand."

He crosses the room and picks up my phone. "At least take your
phone so you can call me and let me know you're safe. You shouldn't
walk around alone at night without it."

"Okay. Thanks." Off guard now that he is back to his old self, I
reach for the phone, but before my fingers can close around it, he grabs
my wrist and twists my arm behind my back.

"Cunt." He twists my arm more, forcing me to my knees, and the pain almost blinds me. "You're running to him, aren't you? You just can't get out the door fast enough."

"No." I gasp as he twists my arm again. "I'm going to stay with Violet. She has an extra room."

"So you planned it. You were already planning to leave me." He gives my arm a further wrench, and I hear a crack. Bile rises in my throat, followed by a nauseating wave of pain. A scream pierces the night, and I realize it's mine.

"You don't leave me." He releases my arm, and I crumple on the floor. "You're mine. I made you what you are. You don't get to walk away."

I roll to my side, cradling my arm. I just want to lie here and process the pain, but my mind is screaming danger, and I need to get away. Too late, I realize the cost of my hesitation. The blow comes out of nowhere, a thud of his foot against my ribs that takes my breath away.

"Stop. Please."

But he doesn't stop. He follows me as I scramble away, backing me against the door. With fists and feet, he strikes me everywhere, and I only have one arm to fend off his blows. I scream and wonder why no one comes to save me. Desperate for a weapon, I roll and grasp the umbrella stand. It falls, and Damian stops beating me to laugh.

"Was he really worth it?" He walks up beside me and carefully rights the umbrella stand, then without warning, he stomps on my outstretched hand. I can hear bones break, but I don't feel any pain, because I passed that threshold long ago.

"There is no him. He left me and never came back."

"Liar." He picks up his baseball bat from between the spilled *umbrellas. His eyes narrow as he taps it against his palm. I know what's coming next, but I don't have the strength to run.*

"Shayla?" The worry in Zack's voice pulls me out of the memory before it gets to the worst part. I haven't thought about that night for years. Being around Zack is bringing back a past that I'm just not prepared to deal with again.

"Are you okay?"

"Just…thinking how different things would be today if I could do the things I can do now way back when." No way would I have let Damian beat me. One blow and it would have been him bouncing down the stairs that night instead of me.

"Fighting?" He pulls up at yet another light and drums his thumb on the steering wheel. For some reason, that small, familiar gesture makes my heart squeeze in my chest.

"Yeah."

"You didn't need to fight when we lived in Glenwood," Zack says, misunderstanding. "You had me."

"And then I didn't." I should never have let Zack protect me. I should have learned how to protect myself.

"And then you found someone to replace me."

I've never known Zack to obsess about something the way he is obsessing about Damian, and I can't decide if it's jealousy or something more. "I never replaced you. No one could replace you. I moved on, and from what I saw in the press, you did, too. You'd probably forgotten about me when you walked into Redemption."

Screech. Zack yanks the steering wheel to the side and pulls the car up along the curb. His chest heaves, and tension radiates from every pore. "Did you forget about me?"

You still love him.

"No."

"Why would you think I could ever forget about you?" His hands curl around the steering wheel so tight, his knuckles turn white.

"Because I never saw you again. You never came to New York to find me."

Zack shifts the car into gear and pulls out into the road. I don't need to see his face to know he's as angry and frustrated as I am; I can read it in the set of his jaw, the tension in his shoulders, and the fact that we're driving at least forty miles an hour over the speed limit. We drive in silence until we reach the hospital, and then he turns to me and says, "I did."

8

Shayla

WE DON'T GET ANOTHER CHANCE TO TALK AFTER WE REACH THE
hospital, but Zack doesn't leave my side. After I check in, we
wait most of the night in the crowded waiting room, making
small talk, mostly about MMA. Zack is still very much a part of
the world, and although he doesn't fight, he still stays up-to-date
on all the new developments and trains every day.

Finally, I see the doctor. After running a few tests, he diag-
noses a mild concussion.

"Ease up on the training for the next four days," he says,
handing me a prescription for painkillers. "Very light exercise
only. And since you're in a high-risk occupation, book that time
off work. I didn't see anything serious on the CT scan, but come
back if it gets worse."

Zack preens as we leave the hospital in the soft early-morning
light, chest puffed out, a swagger to his stride. I can't bear to
look at him for the smug smile on his face. Finally, I can't take
anymore. When we reach his vehicle, I turn and glare.

"Say it. I know you're desperate. So spit it out."

He lifts a mock quizzical eyebrow as he opens the door. "Say what?"

"Don't even pretend you don't want to say it, or you'll force me to go against medical advice. I'll run around the parking lot, jump up and down, and grapple with the next person who walks out the door."

His smile fades. "You wouldn't dare."

He's right. I won't take the risk. But once upon a time, I would have.

"Just say it and put me out of my misery."

"Told you so," he says, unable to hide his smirk. "I knew it was a concussion when I held you at Redemption."

"Did that feel good?"

"Yes, it did." He holds my door open while I climb into his vehicle and leans over to clip my seat belt. His shoulder brushes against my breasts, and we both freeze.

Zack's gaze holds mine. He tips his head so our foreheads touch. His eyes close for the briefest moment, and he draws in a shuddering breath. It is the first time he has shown anything but a calm determination to ensure I get proper medical care, and I realize this has taken a toll on him, too.

"Thank you." Unable to stop myself, I cup his jaw in my hand. His face is bristly with a five-o'clock shadow, but it is the same beautiful face that has haunted my dreams.

"Pleasure." He draws my hand to his lips and kisses my palm.

My heart flutters in my chest. Zack was a master kisser. We used to take a blanket to the field near his trailer, and he would kiss my fingers one by one, working his way up my arms so slowly, I would feel drugged with pleasure and anticipation by the time he reached my lips. Then he would roll on top of me, blanketing me with his warmth as he plundered my mouth while I ground against the only thing he wouldn't give me.

I hear the sound of footsteps, voices heading toward us. Zack moves back, leaving me bereft.

"Where to?" he asks after he climbs into the car beside me.

"222 Foster Street in the Lower Haight. You can just drop me off. I'll be at the gym later today, so I'll probably see you there. I'm going to watch the tapes of my old fights to see what I've been doing wrong."

"You're not going to the gym." He starts the engine, and the quiet parking lot is suddenly filled with sound. "I'm taking you home to rest. That's what the doctor said." His voice drops to a low rumble. "Do I need to come inside and tie you to the bed to make sure it happens?"

All my blood rushes down to where blood shouldn't rush when you're sitting in a car beside a sexy hunk of male perfection who has just spent all night beside you in the hospital.

"Um...no. That's okay." I shift uneasily in my seat, wondering why someone invented panties and how much cooler things would be down below without them. "And actually, he didn't say I had to rest. He just said ease up on the training."

"He meant rest." Zack peels out of the parking lot like we've just robbed a bank, tires screeching around the corner. Then he blasts down the road.

"I'm curious." I gasp when he narrowly misses a woman with

a baby stroller. "I was going to ask this question on the way to the hospital, but I was busy holding on for dear life. Why did you settle for the Acura if you wanted to drive like you're in the Indy 500?"

"They were out of Indy cars."

"Hate it when that happens." I rub my hand over my forehead as we weave through traffic at the speed of light.

"You okay?" He drops one hand to my thigh, his warmth seeping through my jeans.

"Yeah. Mostly tired." We drive in silence for a few blocks and narrowly miss cars, pedestrians, motorcycles, and almost run a red light. I can tell from the way he nibbles on his bottom lip that something is bothering him, simmering under the surface. He's distracted, and I am almost about to tell him to put both hands on the steering wheel when he squeezes my thigh.

"Does it hurt?"

"Not much since I took the painkillers the doctor gave me."

He pats my thigh. "I meant your leg. I saw the scars."

My body tenses even though I should have known the question was coming. Although I asked him to step outside when the triage nurse asked me about past injuries, he would have seen the scars at the gym and again when I was walking around in my hospital gown.

"Sometimes," I say honestly. "I still have the pins in it. I've been afraid to go through the surgery to get them out. The specialist said they could stay in, so I just live with it."

He shifts in his seat, and his hand tightens on my thigh. "What happened?"

"I fell down a flight of stairs," I say, giving him the half-truth that I've repeated so many times, I almost believe it. "I broke my leg and a couple of other bones, too."

"Is that why you don't dance anymore?"

"Yes."

He draws in a ragged breath. "I can't imagine how hard it must have been to give up your dream."

Hard doesn't even begin to describe waking up in the hospital alone and being told that the life you have known since you were three years old is over, that you will never dance again or feel the music lift you and carry you across the stage. All the blood, sweat, and tears I shed were for nothing because I trusted another man, and I was betrayed again.

"It led me out here, so I guess it turned out okay in the end. I love fighting and training at Redemption, and I enjoy my job. I have a new dream now. I'm going to be a professional fighter, like you were."

He reaches for my hand, threads his fingers through mine. "I should have been there for you."

If Zack had been there, Damian wouldn't have found me crying in the changing room after rehearsal one night. He wouldn't have held me and soothed me and said all the kind words I needed to hear. He wouldn't have insisted on taking me out for coffee, making me laugh, showing me the beauty of New York. I wouldn't have fallen for him and married him. If Zack had been there, I would still be dancing.

"Did he look after you?" he says into the silence.

"Who?"

"Your husband."

"Mom and Matt were there. Mom stayed in the hospital with me, because I had casts on my arms—"

"Jesus Christ." Zack yanks the steering wheel to the side, and moments later, we are parked behind a gas station. At this early hour, there is no one at the pump, and the cashier is inside watching TV.

"What the hell kind of fall was it?" He scrubs his hands through his hair. "How high were the stairs? Were they concrete?"

"I don't want to talk about it."

"Shay." His voice cracks, breaks. "Please. Tell me. I need to know."

With a sigh, I unclip my seat belt and turn toward him. If this is what it takes to get me home, I'll give him the details I gave Torment when I first joined the gym. "I broke my right arm, some bones in my left hand…"

You won't be calling him now, will you?

"And a few ribs…"

Did you think I wouldn't find out? Kick. *You're still in love with him.* Kick. *All those fucking years and you couldn't let him go.* Kick.

"My left shin…"

I've been practicing my swing.

"I had a few bruises, a concussion, broken nose, black eyes…"

I made you what you are, and I can take it away. No one wants a broken, ugly ballerina. If I can't be part of this world, neither can you.

"And, of course, my leg…"

You want to go, bitch? I'll let you go. I'll let you go to fucking hell. Forever.

I lean back in my seat. "Can we go home now?"

Silence. And then, "Your husband. Where was he?"

Your husband has been arrested. He is in jail and faces multiple charges in connection with the assault. If he makes bail, you may wish to get a restraining order…

"Away."

Zack shouts a string of expletives and pounds on the dash. This isn't just about me, I realize. It's about him. He protected me from the first day we met, and it's killing him that he wasn't there to protect me when I needed him the most.

"Stop it," I shout over the noise. "Enough. It's over. It doesn't matter."

"Why the fuck did you marry him?" He runs a hand through his hair. "Why didn't you wait for me? It was one year. You acted like what we had was nothing, like what we had never mattered."

Now it's my turn to get angry. "Of course it mattered. You were everything to me. But what did you expect me to do? We had made a plan for the future, and you just threw it away without even talking to me. Did you think I'd go to San Diego and sit around alone, waiting for you to achieve your dreams and forget about mine?"

"I left because I loved you," Zack says. "I found out about New York and I knew it was the only way to make you go. I thought you'd forgive me when you realized it was the right choice, and we'd pick up where we left off. But that clearly wasn't the case, because you didn't just jump into another man's bed right away; you got married. We never had a chance."

How can he be so clueless? I feel like my sweet Dr. Jekyll

who took me to the hospital has suddenly turned into the evil Mr. Hyde. Pushing open my door, I step out of the car. "I can't even believe this conversation. I'm calling a cab."

"Don't run away from me." Zack exits the vehicle and grabs my hand. "I want to know. What was it about him that made it so easy for you to move on? Was it that he had money? Or a college degree? Or was it his family? I'm pretty damn sure he wasn't a high school dropout who grew up in a trailer park with a drug addict for a mother and an abusive alcoholic for a dad."

"Don't." My hand flies to my throat where my dragonfly necklace is tucked under my shirt. "I missed you so much, I couldn't breathe. Everything reminded me of you. Every dance. Every song. I saw you on every corner. I kept hearing your voice on the street. My heart shattered the day you left me, and it has never been the same. I just wanted the pain to end."

"It never ended for me."

Zack cups my face between his hands and kisses me. His lips are soft and sweet and painfully familiar. My heart beats wildly in my chest, and I melt against him. I don't want to kiss him, but I do. I move my mouth against his, explore the painfully familiar seam of his lips with my tongue. He tastes of coffee, bitter and sweet, and I am lost in a sea of emotion so deep, I don't know if I'll find my way home. His hands wrap around me, pulling me in, and the risk of getting swallowed in his embrace wakes me up. I step back, tear myself away, my chest heaving.

"You can't do that." A wave of anger surges through me, disappointment that I have been so weak when I have spent years learning how to be strong. I force myself to remember how I felt the night he left me, the hollowness that consumed me in the weeks and months that followed, and the vulnerability that left me open to a relationship that almost killed me. "I can't do that. We can't go back, Zack. Things can't be the way they were."

His face smooths to an unreadable mask. "It won't happen again."

"No. It won't."

He draws in a ragged breath and holds open my door. "I'll take you home."

I get in the car only because I don't want to stand in a parking lot at six in the morning trying to find a cab. Zack settles in his seat, and a few minutes later, we are back on the road. But something has changed. I am aware of him now in a way I wasn't before. I can feel the tension in his body as if it were my own. I can taste him on my lips. His warmth lingers on my skin.

"You hate me, don't you?" he asks, the tension in his voice belying his calm demeanor.

"I could never hate you. You're still a part of me. But you hurt me so badly, I don't think I'll ever get over it."

"You recovered from your accident." He drops his hand to my thigh, tentatively this time, but I don't push him away. After what happened between us, I need this connection even though it might be the last time we're together. He left me once. No doubt he'll leave me again.

"That's different. I had Redemption."

He pulls up in front of my apartment, his face thoughtful. "Maybe I need Redemption, too."

9

Zack

ZACK HEAVED HIMSELF OFF THE MAT, BLOOD DRIPPING FROM HIS *forehead, his left arm dangling uselessly at his side. Gritting his teeth against the pain, he pulled himself to stand. His fingers gripped the cold metal wire of the fight cage, and his chest constricted with each rasping breath.*

No pain. No blood. No guts. No glory.

Except for the first time in his MMA fight career, glory was slipping out of reach.

Across the cage, his opponent, Tadashi "the Mountain" Okami, licked his lips, his gaze flicking to the championship belt on a table in full view of the cameras. The thunderous crowd in the arena, only a small fraction of the millions who were live-streaming the big event, bayed for blood.

Zack's blood.

After watching Zack win the MEFC middleweight title belt three years in a row, the fans wanted something new. And Okami had promised to provide. After a brutal knockout loss, the aging five-time MEFC light heavyweight champion had shed some serious weight to go after Zack's middleweight belt. And right now, four minutes into the fight, he was up on points and looking as fresh as a goddamned new recruit.

Okami's dark eyes flicked to Zack's broken arm, and a smirk played over his tanned, broad face. If either of them called out Zack's injury, the ref would end the bout, giving Okami a technical knockout victory. But Okami wasn't the kind of fighter who would be satisfied with a technical win. He wanted a fight to the finish, and he would keep going until the end. It was up to Zack. Fight or fall?

A choice that was no choice. Zack Grayson had never walked away from a fight. Not even when he was six years old and facing an opponent three times his size. He shut out the raucous cacophony of the bloodthirsty crowd and drew in a lungful of thick, humid air, scented with sweat and fear, stale beer and cigarettes.

Okami grinned.

Zack cracked Okami with a right hand down the pipe. And another to the body. He dove in deep with a single leg but couldn't get a takedown. Okami feinted right, then lunged for Zack's broken arm.

Pain fuzzed Zack's brain, and his legs trembled as Okami landed blow after blow on his head and broken arm. His vision became hazy, his mind shifting between past and present.

Memories assailed him. Another life. Another beating. Screams. Blood.

His vision sheeted red, and he launched himself across the fight cage with the last of his strength, throwing knees and elbows as his body moved on autopilot, doing what it was trained to do. Protecting his left side, he drove a surprised Okami into the fence, dropped level for a single to take Okami down. Quick to his feet, Okami landed a grazing head kick, knocking Zack to the side. Zack poleaxed his opponent with a short, chopping right hand to the chin. Okami's head bounced backward, and his legs folded under him from the knee. He cursed, and Zack followed him down for the final punch.

Winner by knockout…Zack "Slayer" Grayson!

Even through the haze of bloodlust, the fog of memory, and the thrill of victory, Zack knew something wasn't right. He knelt beside Okami, put his hand on his opponent's chest, waited for a breath.

He prayed, although he wasn't a praying man.

And then he shattered.

—∿∿—

Zack awoke drenched in sweat from his nightmare. His phone buzzed beside him on the night table. He reached for it, trying to clear his head. On the road for most of the year, he had become used to having to orient himself in strange hotel rooms every time he awoke, but when the nightmares came, he needed a few extra seconds to pull himself out of the darkness.

Pushing himself to sit, he grabbed his phone, surveying the rich woods and jewel tones of the penthouse suite. Although he was now a recruiter and not an MMA star, MEFC still treated him well. No doubt because they expected him to make a comeback and they didn't want him jumping ship for another promotion.

"Where the hell are you?" Kip Wilson, VP of MEFC and Zack's boss, never wasted time on pleasantries.

"San Francisco."

"You're supposed to be in Rio."

Zack swung his legs over the side of the bed and shook off the last remnants of the fight that still haunted his dreams.

"Yeah, I know."

"Well, what the fuck happened?"

Shayla had happened. And although it was clear she still hated him, he couldn't stay away.

It made no sense. He'd been hurt, too. First, when he'd found out from Matt that she'd been hiding her New York acceptance from him. And then again, after they'd finally made love and he'd suddenly been hit with the enormity of what she had entrusted to him. She was his. Body and soul. But was he really ready for that responsibility? Was he worthy? What if he turned into his father?

The two hurts had armored his heart, making it easier to justify cutting her loose. But they were nothing compared to the gut-wrenching moment, just over a year later, when Matt told him she was married. And even that had paled in comparison to the pain he had suffered when he went to New York and saw her with her new husband from across the street. He knew that he shouldn't try to find her, but part of him couldn't believe she had moved on so quickly, that the promises they had made to each other were a lie.

After their kiss last night, he was more confused than ever. He had felt their connection, the electric current between them that was as strong now as it had been when they were together. Despite the fact that she had chosen another man, that bond was why he had never been able to move on. Last night, she had made it clear, she had no interest in getting back together with him, and he couldn't blame her. But what the hell was he supposed to do when his heart wasn't going to let him walk away?

"Something personal came up. I needed some time to sort it out."

"I need you in Rio now," Kip barked. "There's a hot new fighter storming up the amateur circuit, and the vultures are circling. I know of three other promotions who have recruiters down there already. Our stable is getting smaller, and market share is dropping. The higher-ups are worried, Zack. We've just lost our two biggest stars to injuries and another twenty to the competition. And on the women's circuit, we're down to only thirty female fighters worldwide."

Zack knew the drill. They were always losing fighters, always desperate to find the next big star. He'd go to Rio, recruit the fighter, and then Kip would send him to another country, and then another… It didn't end. But then he'd never wanted it to end. Recruiting gave him the financial security he needed to care for his sisters, and the constant travel kept him too exhausted to think about the man who had lost his life in the cage.

Although he had been cleared of any negligence or wrong-doing after the MMA governing body discovered Okami had entered the ring against doctor's orders and fully aware of a potentially fatal subdural hemorrhage, Zack couldn't bring him-self to fight again. He had been pushed past his limits in the cage that night—of pain, of endurance, of restraint—and he'd lost con-trol. Although no one blamed him, he couldn't help but wonder if he would have noticed that something was wrong if he hadn't let loose the beast inside him, his father's only legacy to his son.

"Zack? Are you listening? Rio. I need you on the next plane. This kid is gold. He's going to be the next you."

He hoped not. After years of beatings from his father, school fights, bar brawls, and ambushes by Matt and his friends, he'd developed the kind of street-fighting skills that gave him an edge in MMA. He'd trained hard in Seattle, motivated at first by the need to prove his worth, and then for the amateur sponsorships that paid the medical bills after Viv had been diagnosed with leukemia. After a winning streak that wouldn't quit, he was recruited by MEFC. And then everything changed.

Just as it was changing now. He'd found Shayla, and nothing in his life would ever be the same. Leaving her was his biggest regret. Despite his pain, he couldn't make the same mistake again. Even if they couldn't resolve the issues between them, he wouldn't be able to live with himself if he didn't at least try to rekindle the friendship they had lost.

Rio was a problem. He had to go where Kip told him to go, and he couldn't afford to lose the job. Viv had been going through some tests, and if it turned out her leukemia had returned, he would need the medical insurance he had arranged for her through MEFC to cover the cost. His stomach clenched at the thought of Viv having to go through chemo all over again. She had been devastated to lose her long, buttery-blond hair, because it was her only link to our mom, who she could barely remember. Ever practical, Lily had dragged her to a store that sold wigs, but Viv had opted to wear colorful scarves and headbands that she dyed herself in yet another artistic venture that she gave up before it was really off the ground.

"You got a girl there? I feel like you're only half listening."

Zack drummed his fingers on the night table. He needed to

give Kip something or be faced with yet another impossible choice.

"What if I could get you a female fighter?" he asked, thinking quickly. Shayla was on the cusp of success. He'd reviewed her stats with Torment and watched videos of her fights, but it was only last night when they'd talked that he began to suspect what was holding her back.

Fear.

She was afraid to take a risk. She'd lost touch with the girl she used to be, and once she'd found herself in the ring with a higher class of fighters, fear held her back. He didn't know what had happened to change her, but if she could find herself again, tap into that little girl he'd met on Devil's Hill, she could be one of the best professional fighters in her weight class. To do that, she needed to shake things up. New coach. New trainer. New plan.

"A woman?" Kip's voice rose with interest. Female fighters were few and far between, and the good ones were in high demand. A female fighter would be gold for a promotion like MEFC. "Is she the one you were considering at Redemption?"

"Yeah."

"What's her name?"

"Shayla Tanner."

"Never heard of her."

"You will. And in three months, she'll be wearing the MEFC brand."

"Three months?" Kip sighed. "She's not ready now?"

"No," he said honestly. "She's got the skill and the potential to be a star. With the right coach, I think she'd have a shot at the amateur featherweight title, and that's three months away. She's worth the investment." Almost every winner of an amateur title belt was signed to the pros. It was a ninety-nine point nine percent guarantee.

"So you want me to hire a coach? Do you have someone in mind?"

Zack squeezed his hand into a fist. "Me."

Kip laughed. "Is this another Grayson reinvention? First a fighter, then a recruiter, now a coach?"

"I don't think anyone else could do the job."

Silence.

The skin on the back of Zack's neck prickled. Kip was only quiet when he was planning something, and Zack had a feeling it wasn't going to be good.

"Are you sleeping with her?"

"No." At least something good had come from Shayla pushing him away last night.

"I've got a new recruiter I could send to Rio," Kip said, musing. "But he's not you. He doesn't have your experience, your contacts, or your star appeal. If I send him, I'm taking a risk of losing my golden boy—"

"A good female fighter is worth three golden boys," Zack said, interrupting. "You know that."

Kip chuckled. "Not sure if I like having your negotiation skills used against me. But how about this? I'll give you the three months to train her, but it comes out of your vacation. You have four months banked, since you've barely taken any time off since you started. If she finishes in the top two at the title fight, we sign her, and I triple your usual bonus. If she doesn't win…" He paused, and Zack's pulse kicked up a notch. "You go back in the cage."

"No." Kip had been trying to get him back in the game since he'd hired him as a recruiter, and Zack knew his possible comeback was the real reason he'd been given the job.

"C'mon, man." Kip sighed. "It's been four years. Yes, what happened was brutal, but it wasn't your fault, and the likelihood of it ever happening again is almost zero. The fans haven't forgotten you. I have sponsors calling me every day asking about Slayer. The MMA world needs a new hero, and MEFC needs a star fighter who's going to draw the crowds— someone with a story, a history. That's you. Zack Grayson. The comeback kid."

For the briefest of moments, Zack allowed himself to imagine the thrill of stepping into the cage, the burst of adrenaline at the sound of the bell, letting everything fall away except the basic primal instinct to conquer the enemy. He heard the roar of the crowds, smelled the sweat and blood, felt the vinyl under his feet and the hard mesh at his back. Every fight was a reminder of the nights Matt and his friends had ambushed Zack in the back alleys or side roads of Glenwood. Every win was the realization of the dreams he'd had when he had lain bruised and bleeding on the ground.

"It's not going to happen. She's going to win the title belt." He hadn't been there to save her from the fall that destroyed her dream of being a dancer, but he would damn well be there to help her realize her dream of becoming a professional fighter.

It was his path to Redemption.

Now, he just had to convince Shayla it was her path, too.

10

Shayla

"THIS ISN'T SO BAD. I MUST BE IN GOOD SHAPE."

I look over at Cheryl, sweating it out beside me on the treadmill. After Joe's health scare, I convinced both of them to give the gym a try. Joe lasted one night and called it quits, but Cheryl shows up every now and again, ostensibly so I can help her work out, but in reality to ogle the men.

"This is a warm-up." I walk beside her at a doctor-mandated "light exercise" pace.

"Maybe for you," Cheryl huffs. "But any faster and they'd be peeling me off the mat. Plus, how would I be able to appreciate the view if sweat was dripping down my face? I need a clear field of vision."

"Who's replacing me at work tonight?" When the gym closes at nine p.m., Cheryl is heading out for what was supposed to be *our* ten p.m. to five a.m. shift.

"Sol." She sighs. "I'm going to have to spend another shift slapping his hands away from my ass. He's just back from a one-month suspension for sexually harassing the female security team over at building three. I heard he was really angry at Symbian, even though all he got was a slap on the wrist. Apparently, he wants to sue them for five million dollars. He's a nasty piece of work."

"What about your complaint?" I wave to Rampage and Blade Saw as they head toward the door. Ten minutes before closing, the gym is nearly empty. Cheryl and I are the only people on the cardio equipment, and there are a few stragglers over at the free weights.

"It was lumped in with the others. Apparently, my ass wasn't special."

"I wish he'd grab my ass." I increase my speed another notch. My heart's not even beating hard, and after last night's kiss with Zack, I am desperate to burn off some of my tension. "I'm just dying for an excuse. Last time I worked with him, he told me MMA is a man's sport, and if he was in charge, he'd make all the female fighters wrestle naked in a mud pit. One of these days, I'd like to get him alone and show him just how hard I can punch."

"I kinda wish for that, too," Cheryl says. "It would be something to see." She slows her treadmill down to a very slow walk. "You know something else I'd like to see? The hunk of manliness who came to see you at work the other day. You said he was an ex. What's going on with him?"

"Nothing." Just talking about Zack makes me feel overwhelmed by feelings I don't want to have, longings I thought were buried so deep, they would never resurface. How can I move forward when the past keeps dragging me back?

"Yeah? Well, it didn't look like nothing to me." She pats her brow with a white towel, and it comes away with a slight rose tinge. Every week, she tries a new look, and this week, she has dyed her hair hot pink. "After four husbands, I know all about ex relations."

"What's that supposed to mean?"

"That dude was sex on a stick, and he wants you bad. Who drives out to a industrial estate just to check a bump on your head?"

"He hurt me, Cheryl. Badly. He tore out my heart and stomped it on the ground. I never got over it." I force myself to keep to the slow pace, mindful of the doctor's advice. At least I'm feeling a bit warmer. Or is it thinking about Zack that has heated my blood?

"What did he do?"

I tell Cheryl about my past with Zack right through to our night in the cheap hotel and my decision to move to New York. Cheryl knows about my life as a ballerina and that I moved to San Francisco after an accident that ended my career. She also knows that I was married, although not how it ended. "I didn't see or hear from him again until he walked into Redemption," I tell her as our feet thud on our respective treadmills. "He told me he did it for me, so I could live my dreams without him holding me back. But it was my choice, and he took it away from me. I can't forgive him for that."

"Hmm."

"What's that supposed to mean?"

She shrugs. "Sounds to me like his intentions were good but his execution was poor. He was trying to do the right thing."

"Poor doesn't even come close to how I felt that night. And it was the wrong thing. Totally wrong. It took me down a path that ended my career."

"But now you're a fighting machine." She wheezes between words and stabs at the control panel to lower the speed.

"A broken fighting machine. Things aren't going so well. I've hit a plateau."

"Maybe he can help you." She slows to a walk. "He owes you, and if he used to be such a big star—"

"I can't." My feet thud on the treadmill, and I feel the first bead of sweat on my forehead. "Last night he kissed me, and it was just wrong. I can't risk falling for him again. I can't forgive him."

Cheryl's treadmill finally stops, and she bends over, holding her knees as she gasps for breath. "I never knew you had so much anger eating you up inside."

"I never thought of myself as angry." I felt sad and despondent. I grieved his loss. But I never felt real anger until he walked back into my life and made me question the choices I'd made in New York. "At least, I wasn't angry before. But maybe I am a bit now. I'm angry at myself for not fighting for what I wanted. I just accepted that the relationship should end because he wanted it. I moved away, and then I married the first man who was kind and showed an interest in me, because I was young and scared and alone, and I wanted someone to take care of me."

"I got married too young," Cheryl says. "I was only seventeen the first time. I thought I was in love, but I didn't know what love was."

"I thought I knew what love was, and then I realized I was

wrong." I grab my water bottle from the holder and take a long, cool drink. "It doesn't matter anyway. I was pretty hard on him last night. I'm sure he's given up and jumped on a plane by now."

"I think he'll be back." She stands and grabs her towel, patting her face down.

"How do you know?"

She grins and lifts her chin in the direction of the door. "Because he's heading this way."

I look up and almost fall off the treadmill. Zack is stalking toward me, and he doesn't look happy.

"You were supposed to rest," he growls, stopping in front of my machine. "This does not look restful."

"You remember Cheryl from Symbian." I gesture at a grinning Cheryl to deflect his anger.

Zack gives her a curt nod and then scowls at me. "Get down. Now. I'm taking you home."

"The doctor said light exercise. I'm barely moving. And I think you're confusing me with someone who has to do your bidding."

"Actually, you're doing four times the speed I was doing," an unhelpful Cheryl says. "And you're sweating. Profusely. Isn't that dangerous after you bump your head?"

"Don't you have to be at work in an hour?" I shoot her what I hope is a death stare, but it just makes her laugh.

"I do." She sighs. "As much as I would like to stay and watch the fireworks, I'd better get going. But I will expect a full briefing when you're back at work."

Zack waits until Cheryl is out of earshot before he starts in on me again. "A few days wouldn't have killed you."

"Yes, it would have. I'm already on a downhill slide. I can't let my fitness level slip." I increase the speed on the treadmill just to show him he has no hold over me. "If you're done chastising me for nothing, I have a run to finish."

"I need to talk to you." He folds his arms over his chest. His biceps bulge from beneath the sleeves of his MEFC T-shirt, and I try not to drool.

"Maybe tomorrow. I can fit you in after my marathon and before I climb Mount Everest."

"Now." He reaches over and hits the emergency stop on the treadmill.

"Hey. What are you doing?" I glare at him as the machine slows to a stop. "I was just warming up."

"You'll mess up your system if you do cardio in the evening. You won't be able to sleep. If you don't sleep, your muscles don't repair themselves. If your muscles don't get repaired, you risk injury. Injury means you're out of the game. Maybe for good."

"This was Stan's idea." I push the start button. "He's a professional. He knows more about these things than you."

Wham. Zack stops the treadmill again. "No one knows more about these things than me. That's what I want to talk to you about."

"Yo! Shilla!" Blade Saw shouts from the doorway. "Sadist and I are going for a drink. You two are the only ones left in the gym. Lock up when you're done." He tosses the keys to me, but Zack intercepts and snatches them out of the air.

"Give me the keys."

"We need to talk." He nods to Sadist and Blade Saw as they head out the door. "But not here."

"Why not here? We're alone."

"I want to show you something." He holds out his hand, and although I know I shouldn't take it, I do. Warm and firm, his hand envelops mine, holding it tight as he helps me off the treadmill.

Zack leads me through the gym to Torment's office. Lights flicker on as we walk, thanks to Redemption's new energy-saving light system. We stop in front of the glass door leading to Torment's office, and I peer inside. Torment isn't sitting in his leather chair behind his huge cherrywood desk, glaring at people through the glass wall of the office we are forbidden to enter on pain of death.

"If you were looking for Torment, he doesn't appear to be here," I point out unnecessarily.

Apparently, that isn't a concern for Zack. He tries keys until the lock on Torment's door clicks open, and then he steps into Torment's office. The nifty motion-activated lights go on.

I hold my breath and wait for the apocalypse.

It doesn't come.

"You may not be aware, but this is Torment's office." Safely positioned in the hallway, I point to the nameplate on the door. "No one goes into his office when he's here, much less when he's away. He's killed men for less."

"I've never been one for following the rules." Zack leans on Torment's desk and toys with Torment's pens.

"I feel a bit faint." I take a step back. "I think I might go outside and get some air."

"You are looking kinda pale." Zack gestures to the leather chair in front of Torment's desk. "Have a seat."

I shake my head and lean against the doorframe instead. "What's this all about?"

"What do you see?" He lifts his chin toward the wall where Torment has mounted pictures of all the fighters in the gym who have won title belts or gone pro. I know them all, because I've been at Redemption since it was just a warehouse with a makeshift ring and two guys with a dream.

"Success. Winners. Professional fighters." I shrug. "I'm not sure what you're asking."

"Men," Zack says. "They are all men. How many female Redemption fighters have won title belts or gone pro in the time you've been here?"

"None. But it's not Torment's fault. There just aren't that many women interested in fighting at that level."

"But you are," he counters.

My pulse kicks up a notch. "I was. But you've seen my stats. Things have been going downhill in a big way."

"I can get you on that wall," he says. "I can help you achieve your dream."

Puzzled, I frown. "What are you saying?"

"I can train you, Shay. I can be your coach."

My mouth keeps moving as my brain struggles to process what he just said. "I have a coach. Two coaches. Torment and Fuzzy. And Stan is my trainer. I've been with them since the beginning. Starting all over again…with you…it's too big a risk."

"What you want is on the other side of your fear," Zack says. "They got you to where you are, but they can't get you where you want to go. You are fighting at a new level now. This is where fighters make it or break it. With all due respect to Torment and Fuzzy, they don't know anything about fighting professionally. That's why you've plateaued."

I snort a laugh. "Are you serious? Torment doesn't know anything about fighting? He is probably the greatest fighter in the country. He is still the official holder of the underground title belt. *Underground*, Zack." I emphasize the word. "No rules. No laws. No protection. No mercy. The only time he was ever knocked down was when Misery hit him over the head with a pair of brass knuckles and tried to kill him, and that didn't count as a defeat."

"It's not the same." He bristles, and I realize his ego is bruised. He may not fight anymore, but he is still a fighter, still a four-time world middleweight champ.

My hands find my hips, but my feet remain on the safe side of the door. "Did you know that fighters come to Redemption from all over the country hoping for a chance to fight Torment? It became so ridiculous that he put rules in place. Only a fighter who has won fights against Redemption's top fighters is allowed to challenge Torment. But no one has made it that far in years."

"At my peak, I could have defeated Torment," Zack huffs. "I could still beat him. It's all smokescreen and mirrors. He's hiding behind his fighters. Maybe he was good once, but now he's afraid if he steps in the ring, everyone will discover he's just an ordinary man."

Incredulous, I cross the threshold and close the distance between us. "You think he's afraid?"

"I think you're afraid." He strokes a rough finger along my jaw. "But you don't have to be. Let me take you down that hill one more time."

Emotion bubbles in my chest. I wasn't afraid of Devil's Hill. Even after I fell off Matt's bike. I welcomed Zack's help for the skills he could teach me, but I never felt fear like I do now. The thought of starting all over again, and with Zack, sends a chill down my spine.

"You have a job," I protest.

"I haven't taken a vacation in four years. I have more time owed to me than I know what to do with." His hand slides beneath my ponytail, and he strokes his thumb over my nape. "Anything else?"

I scramble for all the reasons this is not a good idea. "I can't pay you. I'm already financially stretched, and that's with Stan and Fuzzy discounting their fees and Torment coaching me for free."

Zack gives a disgusted snort. "I would never take money from you. It's covered."

Without any other reason for turning him down, I take the easy way out. "It wouldn't work. We have too many unresolved issues between us. A past. I haven't forgiven you, Zack. Seeing you every day…training with you…it would be too hard."

He leans in close, rests his forehead against mine. "Since when did you, Shayla Tanner, ever turn away from something because it was too hard?"

Since you left. Since I didn't have you to lean on or to catch me when I fell.

"I'm not the same person anymore."

"Then be that person, because the girl I left behind didn't let anything stand in her way. Not even me."

I pull away, torn between what he's offering and the emotional price I will have to pay. "I can't train with you. It's too much. Too confusing. I don't know how I feel about you anymore. I don't want to start something that isn't going anywhere. I don't want to lead you on."

He doesn't even flinch at what, to me, seem harsh words. "Then we'll keep it strictly professional."

"Professional?"

Zack nods. "It will be no different than your relationship with Torment and Fuzzy."

Keeping it professional will protect my heart. It will give me a shot at achieving my dream. It will mean having Zack back in my life but without the risk of getting involved. I hesitate for a heartbeat, and then I nod. "Okay."

His eyes warm, the gold flecks sparkling in the dim light. "You are still the bravest person I know."

"Not like you. I saw some of your opponents. It took courage just to walk into those—"

He cuts me off with a kiss.

Oh my God. He's kissing me. His lips are soft. Sure. Familiar.

So delicious. So utterly sensual, I cannot pull away. His fingers thread through my hair, holding me still as he kisses me with an intensity that takes my breath away.

Stop.

My head is spinning, and I'm breathing fast as I reach for him, hands gripping his shoulders as I try to hold on. I am aching everywhere, every nerve firing at once in a rush of sensation that sweeps me away.

I am on fire.

"What happened to keeping it professional?" I gasp when he lets me up for air.

"Tomorrow, professional. Tonight, I need you."

His words warm me from the inside out. He slides one arm around my waist, flexes until every inch of my body is pressed tight against him. This close, he molds to my body like he was made to be there. Like we are one person, not two.

Something cracks inside me. Longing breaks free, wraps around Zack, and refuses to let go. I missed him. I missed him so much, it hurts inside. Being with him is like coming home. It feels so right.

"Zack…"

"I got you."

His chest rises and falls with mine. His heart pounds inside my body. I can feel his rock-hard erection against my hips.

Stop.

But it's me who is kissing now. My mouth fitting to his. My moans echoing around us. My tongue searching, touching, tasting. Deeply. Desperately. He shudders, and his tongue caresses mine, velvety soft. So decadent. Erotic. So very, very wrong for me. And yet, I never imagined I could feel like this again, never thought I could be awakened by a kiss.

His fingers stroke gently over the curve of my ear, along my jaw, caress my cheek even as his other hand tightens in my hair, as if he's afraid I will run away.

But there is nowhere I want to run, nowhere I want to hide. There is only Zack.

Zack with his hard body pressed against mine.

Zack with his soft lips on my cheek.

Zack sliding his hands under my ass and carrying me to Torment's desk.

With one sweep of his hand, he clears the desk. Then he lays me back on the cold, hard surface. Papers flutter to the floor around me, like the ashes I will become when Torment finds out what I've done.

Oh God.

"Zack…" My heart pounds, not just in anticipation of what we're about to do in Torment's office but of what might happen if Torment were to find out.

"Don't be afraid," he murmurs against my ear. So confident. Commanding. Dangerous. Dominant. Protective. Passionate. Darkly handsome. He's the kind of man I have always avoided since leaving Glenwood and yet secretly desired. The kind of man I hid from in Damian's arms, only to discover I'd run in the wrong direction.

"I'm not afraid. I'm terrified." My breath is coming fast and hard, and I am wet for him, hot and aching. And I hate myself for it. I am opening myself up to heartache and pain. One night with Zack won't be enough.

"But you're still here." He slants his head and cuts me off with a fierce kiss, bruising my lips, his fingers digging so hard into my skin, my eyes tear. Blood pounds in my temples, my hunger for him raw and wild. I slide my arms around his neck and drag him down for more.

"You've got a beautiful body," he says as he runs his hands down my curves. "I want to lick my way over every one of your muscles. I want to taste you all over again."

He leans over and nuzzles my neck, the rough stubble of his beard scraping over my sensitive skin, and then he cups my breast in his hand and kneads it gently through my clothes. I am on fire, sweat beading and running down my back. I know better than this.

Play with fire and you will get burned.

He rolls my nipple, taut beneath my clothes, between his thumb and forefinger until I arch up on the table, hungry for more.

"There's my girl," he mutters half to himself. "Wanting what I can give her."

Who is this man and where did he learn to talk like that? His sensual words rip down my barriers almost as quickly as his naughty hands. He cups my other breast, squeezing and stroking until I feel swollen and sore and desperate for his hands on my bare skin.

"Torment's desk…" I don't know if I'm warning or wanting, but I stop thinking when Zack presses my legs apart and leans over me. And then he is everywhere, his hands hot under my shirt, his tongue in my mouth, his body pressed up against me, his erection firm against my stomach. I can't think, can't fight. I want him like I've never wanted a man before, and I'll do almost anything to have him.

A door slams in the distance, and I stiffen on the cold wood surface. Zack's head whips around just as the hall lights come on. Heart pounding, I scoot off the desk and drop to the floor to gather up Torment's papers.

"Leave them." He holds out his hand to me.

"Are you crazy?" I stand and dump an armful of papers on the desk. "Blade Saw will tell him he gave me the keys. He'll know I was here."

Zack pulls his ring off his finger. Every MEFC fighter who wins a title belt is given a ring by the MEFC CEO to commemorate the victory. I don't know which of his four title fight rings he is wearing, but when he tosses it on Torment's desk, my hand flies to my mouth.

"Zack." My voice comes out in a strangled whisper. "What are you doing? Your ring…it's precious. He'll know it's yours and he'll come after you."

"I know." He clasps my hand and tugs me toward the door.

"You don't have to protect me," I protest.

"I need to protect you, sweetheart. It's what I was born to do."

11

Shayla

My first day after agreeing to let Zack coach me turns out to be the day after Stan's sometime girlfriend dumped him for an even more ripped, more successful personal trainer from Beverly Hills.

Lucky me gets to avoid the brunt of his anger, because I'm on day two of my light exercise program, but I feel for the rest of the team who have to endure a workout so incredibly brutal, they can barely make it to the water cooler during our halftime break.

"You want some cheese to go with that whine?" Stan shouts as Sandy stumbles across the mats to join me and Sadist in line, hair plastered to her head, clothes drenched in sweat.

"He's a sadist," Sandy mutters under her breath. "I suspected as much, but now I know."

"I'm the sadist." Sadist hands her a towel. "He's stealing all my best lines."

I pat his sweaty shoulder. "You'll always be Rampage to

me." Sadist was the first person I met when I walked into Redemption. In those days, the area was more dangerous than it is now, and he guarded the front door with the ferocity of a rabid dog. Only members were allowed to cross the red line he had painted across the floor, and only his closest friends knew the strength that lay beneath his yellow happy face vest. Now, he's a different man—physically and emotionally. Ever since he hooked up with his girlfriend, Penny, he's become more content, less the Redemption gossip, and more the shoulder to lean on. I've been angling to get him alone all morning so I can talk to him about Zack, but Sandy won't leave us alone.

"Don't send me back," Sandy whispers. "Please. I can't take it. There isn't a muscle left in my body that doesn't hurt. I can't even smile."

Sadist gives her damp head a gentle pat. "You're the one who asked to take Shilla's place this week, but if you really want, I can take him outside. Rough him up a bit."

Sandy sighs. "You outweigh him by about fifty pounds. It wouldn't be a fair fight. And besides, if anyone reported you to the CSAC, you could lose your fight license."

I nod in agreement. The California State Athletic Commission regulates professional and amateur MMA by licensing participants and supervising events. They have strict rules against illegal and underground fights and penalties can be severe.

"How about Slayer?" Sadist suggests. "I've seen him glaring at Stan. He might be up for a little alley fight, and he's not a licensed fighter, so no risk of being sanctioned."

"He hasn't fought in four years," I say.

"He still trains." Sadist's lips quirk in a smile. Although he doesn't gossip as much, he is still the eyes and ears of Redemption. "He asked Torment for a guest pass and he was here at five a.m. when the gym opened. And when I say train, I don't mean keeping fit. He did everything I did—drills, speed work, strength work, jiu-jitsu. He just didn't step into the ring."

Sandy takes her turn filling her water bottle, and I whisper to Sadist, "I think he's getting back into shape because of me. He offered to take some time off his recruiting work and coach me. I texted Torment about it this morning."

"You dog." Sadist gives me what from anyone else would be a friendly punch in the arm and almost knocks me sideways across the floor. "How did you manage that? Are you sleeping with him?"

"No. Of course not." I huff my displeasure. "Why do I have to be sleeping with him? Maybe he sees my potential, and because he's a nice guy, he wants to help me make it to the top."

Sadist laughs. "He's a guy. You're you. And you two have a history."

When I open my mouth to protest, he holds up his hand. "Save your breath. You're gonna tell me you were just friends, but you don't slap a friend who hurts you. That kind of pain only comes from the heart."

"Okay, we used to date," I admit. "But it ended a long time ago."

"Badly, I assume." Sadist puts an arm around my shoulders and leads me away from the water cooler where Sandy is now chatting with Blade Saw. "But now he's back, and he wants to pick up where you two left off."

"Well, that's not going to happen." I lean against the edge of one of the raised practice rings. "What he did…the way it ended…there's no moving on from there."

"Obviously there is, or you wouldn't be talking to him about coaching you," Sadist says.

"It's not personal. It's business."

"Maybe for you, but not for him." He chuckles. "What does he get out of it?"

"A bonus?" I shrug, annoyed at myself for not even wondering about Zack's motives. "I guess if I win the title belt, I'll have to sign with MEFC. They've given him the time off to coach me."

Sadist shakes his head. "You're a free agent. Even if he coaches you to the top, you can sign with any promotion you want, unless he got you to sign something."

"No. He just offered to train me. No strings attached."

"Out of the goodness of his heart." Sadist's lips quiver with a smile. "Or other parts."

"I can't believe you." I punch his arm, and he doesn't even look down, like it was a soft breeze tickling his skin. "Does Penny know you talk like this?"

"It's gym talk. She knows what goes on at the gym. And if you think that's bad, you should hear what comes out of her mouth when something gets her going." His eyes soften. "British swear words are the best. And she knows so many."

Penny and Sadist are one of Redemption's sweet love stories.

He was crushing on her forever, and we could never figure out what was holding him back. But Penny did. Not only did she get her man, she turned him into the Sadist he is today.

"You want my advice?"

"No." I do want his advice, but now I'm afraid that he's going to say something I don't want to hear.

"Well, I'm giving it to you anyway." Sadist grins. "Let it go."

"Let what go?"

"Whatever it is that you're holding onto. Guilt, regret, anger, pain. Let it go and move on."

I look down at my leg. Although I wear knee-length leggings at the gym, the scars from my surgeries are still clearly visible. I've never told anyone about Damian. It was a part of my life I wanted to leave behind. As far as they all know, I fell down some stairs, broke my leg, and couldn't dance anymore. But it is far from the truth of what happened that night.

"Easy for you to say."

"Not easy for me to say." He draws in a breath. "If not for Penny being strong and brave enough to pull me out of the darkness, I would still be stuck in the pain of my past."

I stare at him, incredulous. Sadist is the most easygoing and cheerful person in the gym. "You had a past?"

"We all have a past. It's what you do with it that determines your future. Don't let it limit you, Shay. Don't let it hold you back from going after what your heart really wants."

"I don't know what my heart really wants."

He looks over my shoulder and grins. "I think you do, and he's heading this way."

"Slayer!" Sandy intercepts Zack on his way to me, holding him hostage beside a nearby punching bag. "I thought you were gone. My parents were so disappointed they couldn't meet you. Can you do dinner tonight? They're both still in town."

Zack nods. "Yeah. No problem."

No problem? He kisses me in Torment's office, and now he's meeting Sandy's parents? Is that why he was so quick to agree we needed to keep it professional? I don't want to get involved with him again, but there is no way I can train with Zack if he and Sandy have something going on. I know he's been with other women, but I don't need it rubbed in my face.

"You look fantastic in that gi." Sandy purrs and gets herself struck off my Christmas list forever.

Only then do I notice Zack is wearing a gi, and I almost melt in a puddle on the floor. Zack in his jeans and tight T-shirts is breathtakingly gorgeous. Zack in his fight shorts used to send me into a frenzy of lust. Zack in a black gi, his taut pecs and ripped abs partially visible through the opening, a black belt tied around his waist, is incendiary. No wonder Sandy is drooling.

Zack sidesteps her and joins me and Sadist beside the ring.

"You're a black belt," I say stupidly. Of course he's a black belt. He started training in Brazilian jiu-jitsu as a teenager in Glenwood, and he blew quickly through the belts even then. More than ten years after he started, he would be at the top of his game.

"He's got a black belt in four different martial arts," Sandy says, joining us. "I had to write up his bio for my parents."

Before I can ask why she was writing Zack's bio, I sense

a disturbance in the gym. I glance over Zack's shoulder and see Torment stalking toward us with his henchmen, Ray "the Predator" Black and Jake "Renegade" Donovan in tow.

My heart pounds wildly, and I give Sandy a nudge. "Maybe you and Zack should go grab a protein shake at the snack bar and work on that bio. I'm sure he hasn't told you everything."

"Good idea." She holds a hand out to Zack, but instead of going with Sandy, he steps in front of me, putting his body between me and the oncoming storm.

Torment stops in front of Zack, but his words are directed at me. "Shilla. I got your text. You wanted to talk to me."

Hope flares in my chest, and I step out from behind Zack. Maybe this isn't about his office after all. Maybe, just maybe, he didn't see Zack's ring, or maybe the cleaners picked it up, or maybe he hasn't been in his office this morning.

"Um, yes. Zack has offered to take some time off recruiting to coach me, and I wanted to talk to you and Fuzz—"

"It's a good idea," Torment says. "Shake things up. It might be just what you need."

My tension eases. All okay. "I didn't want you to feel like he was stepping on your toes or that I didn't think you and Fuzz were doing a good—"

Torment cuts me off with a wave. "I want every fighter who walks into Redemption to become the best fighter he or she can be. If this is your path to success, I'm all for it, and I know Fuzz will be, too."

"Okay." My breath leaves me in a rush. "Good. Great. Thank you." I look over at Zack. "Isn't that great?"

If Zack hears me, he doesn't let me know. Instead, his gaze is fixed on the Predator, who is now warming up in the ring, his lean, ropey muscles flexing and bunching as he stretches. The Predator is the state's current underground fight champion. He is also a private investigator who sometimes works for Renegade's attorney girlfriend, Amanda. He and I are good friends. We also had a brief fling, but it didn't last. He was too intense for me, too dominating, and I was glad when he met Sia, a tattoo artist, who can keep him in line. Now that they have a new baby, I don't see him very often, but watching him fight is always a treat.

My skin prickles, and I turn back to Torment. On some unspoken signal, Sadist takes the Predator's place on Torment's right side, and Renegade flanks his left. Almost immediately, tension thickens the air.

"Zack will need a membership if he's going to be here every day training you," Torment says. "He's been coming in and out using the guest pass I gave him when he was representing MEFC." He holds out a purple membership card, and I frown. Why is he telling this to me and not Zack?

As if he knows something is wrong, Zack makes no move to take the card. With a snort, Torment turns and tosses it into the ring where it lands at the Predator's feet.

"What are you doing?" My voice rises in pitch.

"If he wants to coach, he needs a membership. If he wants that membership, he'll have to go and get it."

As if on cue, the Predator slams one foot on top of the card and tips his neck from side to side, making it crack.

Oh. My. God. They want him to fight.

"Seriously, Ray?" I am so pissed off, I am beyond ring names, although I know I'll pay the price for my slip. "What is this? Middle school?"

Torment holds up Zack's ring. "This is giving someone what they asked for."

A challenge. He thinks Zack challenged him by tossing the ring on his desk, but Zack was only protecting me.

"If you're annoyed about your office, blame me. I had the keys. I went in. I made the mess." I take a step toward Torment, and Zack's arm slams into my chest, pushing me back.

"Don't."

"You don't need to protect me." I push his arm away. "I can handle myself. It was my choice, too."

Torment tips his head to the side and frowns. "I'm confused. I'm sure you would never go into my office without my permission—my office, where I keep highly confidential information. That would be grounds for withdrawing your membership at Redemption—the kind of membership Slayer needs if he wants to be your coach."

Sandy grabs my arm, her eyes wide. She's almost as big a gossip as Sadist but with less discretion. "What's going on? Were you in Torment's office? With Slayer?"

I shake her off and glare at Torment. "When did you become such a bully?"

"I was always a bully. You just didn't care."

Maybe I didn't before, but I sure do now. Zack can't fight. After what he went through with Okami, he'll never step into the ring. I have to think quickly. Egos are involved here. Reputation. And pride. "The Predator has an unfair advantage. He knows the ring. He knows the gym. He has his own equipment. If you want a fair fight, Slayer needs time to get used to Redemption."

"Shay…" Zack's jaw tightens. He's not happy with me for interfering, but too damn bad. He's in this predicament because he tried to protect me. Now I'm returning the favor.

"He needs a membership." The Predator toes the card along the mat, and I am a heartbeat away from jumping in the ring and wiping that smirk off his face.

"I have a three-month guest pass at home that I won at the last Christmas party. He can have that."

Torment twists his lips to the side, considering. "Three months. Then he loses the membership or enters the ring." Without further explanation, he turns and walks away. Renegade and Sadist follow after him, like they're guarding his back, except who would dare challenge Torment?

The Predator picks up the membership card and waves it at Zack. "Three months isn't going to change anything. You got the balls or you don't. Why waste time? Get your pansy ass up here, and I'll let you kiss my fucking feet."

"Don't listen to him." I grab Zack's hand and try to drag him away. "He's being an ass. Don't play his game."

"Yeah, Slayer. Listen to your woman," taunts the Predator. "Run away."

Zack's body turns rock solid. I can't move him an inch. His gaze is locked on the Predator, and I know he is seconds away from making the biggest mistake of his life. He might be physically fit, but I know he's mentally not ready to get back in the ring.

"Slayer." Torment shouts over the clatter of weights and the whir of cardio machines. "Three months. You touch him before then, and you'll never step foot in Redemption again."

I send a silent thank you to Torment for defusing the situation and allowing Zack to save face. In that moment, I hate Torment just a bit less.

The Predator blows Zack a kiss and climbs out of the ring, making a big show of tucking the membership card in the pocket of his gym shorts.

"You okay?" I place a gentle hand on Zack's arm, trying to calm him down. His chest is still heaving, his muscles primed and ready to fight.

"Fuck." He shakes my hand off and slams his fist into a nearby punching bag.

"I'm sorry he put you in that position."

Zack slams his fist into the punching bag again, alternating curses with strikes. When he has punched for so long, his gi is wet with sweat, he leans against the bag, panting his breaths.

"What was that about?" I hand him a towel. Torment has set up water and towel stations throughout the gym and has them restocked on an hourly basis.

"I could take him."

I suck in my lips, briefly consider and then quickly discard a lie. Zack is an up-front kind of guy. He would want the truth even if it hurt. "You were a great fighter. When I joined

Redemption, I watched all your past fights. But the Predator fights on the underground circuit. He's never been beaten. He turns into an animal in the ring. At your peak, you might have been able to beat him in a sanctioned competition because he doesn't like rules, but not in an underground ring."

"Not the Predator." He snorts in derision. "Torment."

"Torment?" I bite back a laugh. "No one can beat Torment."

"I can."

My mouth opens to tell him that even at the top of his game, he wouldn't have been able to beat Torment, but I close it again. What's the point in sharing that truth with him? What difference does it make if he believes it? He's never going to have that fight.

"What's with the gi?" I tug on his collar, hoping to distract him. "Are you taking a class tonight?"

"Renegade invited me to teach his jiu-jitsu class with him so I can see what you've been learning," he says in a curt voice. His gaze hasn't left the ring, although the Predator is long gone.

"Maybe I should come," I tease. "Tossing people around and grappling on the mat counts as light exercise, don't you think?"

Zack shrugs, and I have a strong feeling he didn't hear me and an even stronger feeling he's hurting inside.

"Maybe after you're done at jiu-jitsu, we could go grab a protein shake. We don't have to talk about this, but we should talk about what happened last night."

Finally, he tears his gaze away. "Did you change your mind?"

"Not about the coaching, but—"

"I shouldn't have kissed you."

"No." I give a relieved sigh. "I'm glad you understand. If we want to keep this professional, then we have to put our personal feelings aside."

"If that's what you want." His eyes shutter, but not before I see pain flicker across his face.

"Yes, that's what I want."

He closes the distance between us and cups my cheek in his hand. His gaze drops to my lips, and my body heats to one hundred degrees. "Professional."

"Yes," I whisper.

Zack runs his thumb gently over my bottom lip. My head falls back, and my mouth opens for him.

"There she is." He leans down and kisses me so softly, it makes my chest ache.

"What was that?" I ask as he turns away.

Zack looks back over his shoulder, and a slow, sensual smile spreads across his face. "A professional kiss."

12

Shayla

"Your friendly Redemption doctor at your service." Doctor Death smiles when I walk into the first aid room, still rattled from my conversation with Zack. "Where may I put my hands on you?"

My heart sinks the tiniest bit. I was hoping to see Makayla for advice as well as a chat. No one understands Torment like she does, and she's always good for a heart-to-heart. "How about a little professionalism?"

"I'm always professional," he huffs. "Doesn't mean I don't get to enjoy it."

"No hands today." I sit up on his examination bed. "I have a question. Would jiu-jitsu be considered 'light exercise' for someone with a concussion?"

"No."

I mock a frown. "That's not the answer I wanted to hear."

Doctor Death laughs. "I thought you wanted professionalism."

"I want to take the jiu-jitsu class tonight."

"Hmm." He pulls out a little flashlight and shines it in my eye. "Follow the light."

I do as he asks, and then he gently squeezes my head. "Bump gone?"

"Yes."

"Anything show up on the CT scan?"

"No. The emergency room doctor said even the four-day light exercise plan was probably not necessary, but he suggested it out of an abundance of caution, given I was doing MMA."

"Very wise, as all doctors are." He grins. "Headache, blurry vision, sensitivity to light or noise, ringing in the ears, fatigue, trouble concentrating or sleeping, emotional changes like irritability, depression, or anxiety?"

I shift my weight, and the paper under my thighs makes a betraying crinkle. "Um…no to everything except the emotional bit."

Doctor Death smirks. "With respect to the latter, I diagnose a case of an old flame coming back into your life."

"Not you, too." I fold my arms across my chest. "I can't believe how gossip spreads through the gym. Do people not have anything better to do? Slayer and I are just friends."

"And you want to attend the jiu-jitsu class this afternoon for the sake of friendship? Is that right?" He sighs and leans against the counter across from me. "I hope that's the case, otherwise I'll have to delete your number from my special 'Single Ladies' address book."

I slide off the table. "You and me…it's never going to happen."

He sighs again. "I can dream."

"Dream about Sandy. She's your perfect match. I don't know why you two never got together. She's unattached at the moment."

"That's our problem," he says. "We have never been able to coordinate our unattached moments. I'm seeing someone right now. Diane. She works in radiology at the hospital. I think this is the real thing. It's been two weeks and I'm not bored, so I'm going to have Sia tattoo her name on my ass."

I laugh as I reach for the door. "Well then, I plan on coming to your funeral, because the Predator will rip off your arms and legs if he finds out you were alone in a dark room with his wife and nothing on below your waist."

"Sia is a professional," he huffs.

"Maybe she did that kind of stuff before they were married. But now... If he even hears you talking about it..." I shudder. "I can't even imagine what he would do. Ripping off your limbs would probably just be the start. You heard the rumors that he used to be in the CIA before he became an investigator. They know all about torture."

"Maybe I should get it on my arm," Doctor Death muses.

"Maybe give it a bit more time. Two weeks is nothing in the big scheme of things. If it's true love, it will last." My heart squeezes in my chest. Did my love last? Is it still there beneath all the hurt and pain?

Doctor Death snorts. "Good advice from someone as unqualified in the love department as you."

"So what about class?" I say, opening the door.

"If you're just rolling on the mats, I think you should be fine. We worry about high-impact exercise, contact sports, or anything that might give you a second concussion. Also, keep your heart rate down. Anything above seventy percent of your maximum is a risk."

"You're the best." I blow him a kiss, and he pretends to catch it and hold it to his chest.

"I know."

———

Half an hour later, I'm in the jiu-jitsu dojo, talking to Renegade, when Sandy walks in.

"I thought Slayer might need a volunteer to help demonstrate the moves," she says when Renegade lifts a curious eyebrow. Sandy is a striker and has never shown any interest in the submissions, grappling, and floor work we do in jiu-jitsu. She attends classes only rarely and has never progressed past her blue belt.

I force a smile. "How thoughtful."

"You aren't sleeping with Slayer, are you?" she says, drawing me aside. "I would never get in your way."

"No. He's just my new coach. Why does everyone think I'm sleeping with him?"

Confused, Sandy frowns. "You slapped him. You wouldn't have bothered if you didn't care."

"I cared enough to slap him. That's it."

"Well then, it's game on for me."

A slow, predatory smile spreads across her face, and I suddenly regret my feigned nonchalance. If Sandy and Zack hook up, I don't know what I'll do.

Our class today has a disproportionate number of women, given that women account for only twenty percent of the gym members and only two percent of the fighters. With his Greek-god good looks, Renegade alone is enough to fill a class, but add dark, dangerous Zack, and I'm surprised any men made it in the door.

I hide in the back while Renegade explains that over ninety-five percent of street fights finish on the ground, so ground-fighting skills are extremely important for self-defense. Taking an attacker to the ground eliminates around eighty percent of their arsenal. Zack cautions that if there is more than one attacker, however, taking the fight to the ground should be avoided at all costs.

Much to Sandy's disappointment, Renegade and Zack demonstrate moves on each other. Two gorgeous alpha males, lying on top of each other and rolling around the floor trying to force each other into submission, isn't at all disappointing to me. I sit back and enjoy the show.

After the mouth-watering, panty-dampening fight for dominance ends with Zack on top, we pair up. I partner with a newbie named Sue. She is impressed by my purple belt; not so impressed when I put her in a headlock just for fun and to vent some of my Zack-related frustration.

"Let her go." Zack crouches beside us and shows Sue how to free her head from between my legs. Then he sends her across the room to work with another newbie, gesturing for me to remain on my back on the mat. As soon as she is gone, his dark eyes harden. He is barely recognizable as the man who kissed me softly behind the punching bag a short time ago. "What the fuck are you doing here?"

"I don't appreciate the swearing," I huff. "And I'm keeping it light, if you must know. Doctor Death gave me the okay." I push myself to my elbows when his mouth opens again. "Don't even think about asking me to leave. I don't answer to you, Zack. I do what I want."

"I realized that when you got involved in something that wasn't your fight."

Ah. He was annoyed. "I'm sorry, but I'd do it again, because you aren't ready for that fight. And I don't care if you hate me for saying it, because we both know that if you were, no one could have stopped you from climbing into that ring."

Zack stares down at me, lying on my back on the floor. Emotion flickers across his face but disappears so fast, I wonder if my words affected him at all. "Since you're down there, we'll see how you escape a choke from the guard."

"With you?" My heart races as he kneels at my feet, and I take a deep breath and try to keep it below the seventy percent threshold.

"Yes, with me." His dark eyes glitter as he rests a hand on each of my knees and unceremoniously pushes my legs apart. "Spread."

I've done this move countless times in countless classes, but never has my partner set my mind ablaze and my body on fire. Never have I felt that word like a rush of heat in my core.

"Legs around my hips." His voice catches, and I am perversely pleased by the fact that this highly suggestive position that has never seemed suggestive until now is having some effect on him, too.

Acutely aware that we are being watched by the other people in the class, I wrap my legs around his hips. Zack grabs the edge of my gi and rolls, pulling me down with his right hand until I am lying on his body, my cheek against his chest, my hips pressed against what I hope is a cup.

"Breathe," he whispers.

I let out the breath I didn't know I was holding and pray this is over soon.

Zack bumps his hips up until they are tight against mine and grabs the back of my gi with his left hand. Then he pulls his elbow around my head for the choke.

"Escape."

But I don't want to escape. I want to stay here, wrapped in his arms, pressed tight against his body, indulging in years' worth of Zack-on-his-back fantasies in one fell swoop.

"Do you know how?" he murmurs.

Before I can answer, I see pale feet, decorated with perfectly pink nail polish and not a callus in sight.

"Hey, Slayer." Sandy's voice drags me back to the cold, harsh reality of jiu-jitsu class and my conniving and unfortunately single friend. "If you need a partner, I'm free. Renegade had to take Jill to the first aid room. I was a little too rough with her." She laughs. "But I heard you like it rough, don't you?"

And…I'm going to heave.

Before he can answer, I use the distraction to slip my head free. I twist into half guard and scissor my legs around Zack's body. His eyes widen, and suddenly, I have his full, undivided attention.

Zack is stronger and vastly more experienced. He easily evades my every attempt to put him in submission, and our grapple becomes one of chase and evasion.

"Don't let him at your back." Renegade has returned and crouches beside us, calling out helpful tips, because Zack is no longer teaching. He is on the hunt, and I'm the prey.

I quickly turn to protect my back, and Zack rolls and mounts me, straddling my hips, deliciously heavy in just the right place. He looks down at me and gives a satisfied growl as he places his hands on my collarbone, his fingers dangerously close to my neck.

A thrill of desire shoots down my spine, and I bite back a moan.

"Don't just lie there," Renegade barks. "He's giving you a chance."

"Actually, I'm giving him a chance. If he doesn't get off me in three seconds, he's going to suffer like he's never suffered before."

Renegade grins. "Looking forward to it."

I bring both arms inside Zack's guard and slide his arms off my chest. He drops his head, and I wrap my right arm around the back of his neck and grab my left bicep with my right hand. His cheek is against my cheek. His chest is against my chest. His cup is pressed tight against the curve of my sex. With every breath, I inhale his scent of soap and sweat, and every muscle in my body tightens with need.

Somewhere out there, Renegade shouts, "Finish it."

I slide my left hand under his neck, trying to decide whether to use a scissor hand or a fist to crush his throat. And in that moment, Zack moves. Before my brain can process what's happening, he's back in full mount, and I'm flat on my back, hands pinned to the mat above my head.

Oh. My. God. Not again.

"Submit," Zack whispers.

The shiver that explodes through my body almost rips a groan from my throat. I buck my hips, annoyed by the way the thick cotton of my gi dampens the pleasure of his heat against me. I want him in my bed. Naked. I want to tear off his gi and scrape my nails down his back as he pounds inside me, driving me into the bed. The one time we were together, we made love. Now, I want sex. Raw, wild, uninhibited, tear-off-my-clothes-and-throw-me-on-the-bed sex.

Zack's jaw tightens, and his corded throat stiffens when he swallows. "You can't hesitate. Do or die."

"Do." I arch my back and shrimp, trying to throw him off, but he's too heavy, and I'm too tightly pinned.

Zack leans forward. "If we weren't in the middle of class…" he whispers in my ear.

"We're supposed to be keeping this professional."

"If I wasn't being professional, I'd have your clothes off already." Zack releases me and helps me to my feet, all casual as though he didn't just cross a line we'd agreed not to cross. It seems to be one step forward and two steps back.

Almost instantly, he is swarmed by people who want to

know about *that* move and can he try it on them. Confused and annoyed that I can't control this chemistry between us, I head to the locker room for a cold shower. Maybe this was a mistake. Maybe I can't train with someone I once loved more than anything else.

Sandy is talking to Sadist at the front door when I've showered and changed. She follows me out into the parking lot after I wave goodbye to my friends.

"What was that all about?" she asks. "You and Slayer in class?"

"Me messing up a submission." I walk faster, although I know it's not going to make her go away.

"I thought you weren't into him."

"I'm not. We're just working together." I can't even say we're friends, because I don't know if I can just be friends with Zack. I'm beginning to think it has to be all or nothing with him.

"I couldn't work with a guy like him," she says when I stop beside my car. "I mean, look at him. I just want to lick him all over."

So do I.

Is it wrong of me not to want to see Zack with Sandy, even if I can't have him myself? Just the thought of them together makes my stomach twist in a knot. "Actually, Zack and I—"

"Shay. Wait." Zack's shout cuts me off, and I turn to see him walking toward us, closing the distance with easy strides of his long legs. "I've booked the practice ring from eight to ten tonight. Torment gave me the keys to lock up. Since you've got the doctor's okay for grappling, I didn't want to waste time."

Sandy's mouth turns down in a frown. "What about drinks

tonight? I was going to take you out to see my friend's band after we met up with my parents."

"I'll be there for dinner, but I need to be back at eight for Shayla," he says. "I want to get started, because I've got to go to Seattle tomorrow for a few days."

Sandy's lips press tight together, and her gaze flicks from me to Zack and back to me. "Sure. Maybe another night. I guess I'll see you at dinner."

"If you want to spend the evening with her…" I say as Sandy walks away.

"I don't."

"It's okay, Zack." I lean against my safe and solid Volvo. "Really. I don't expect… I mean, I didn't even ask you if you have a girlfriend. Or a wife. Although if you were married, I would have read about it online. Unless it was a secret wedding." I give myself a mental kick. "I'm just trying to say—"

"You're jealous."

Affronted, I stare. "I'm not jealous."

His lips quiver at the corners. "You looked like you were going to deck her when she mentioned going for drinks."

"I was being a good friend." I fold my arms over my chest. "You don't know what she's like. She was engaged to Torment. She broke Blade Saw's heart twice. I was worried for you, in case you had someone. Because that could be awkward." I'm babbling, but I can't stop myself, because I can't get the images of Zack and Sandy together out of my mind.

Zack chuckles. "I'm not with anyone. And I think I can handle myself. But you…" He cups my jaw, his thumb caressing my cheek as his face softens. "What are we going to do about you? Jealous means you still care."

"I am not jealous," I spit out. "I know you've been with other women. Lots of women."

I know, because I read about every single one.

Candy Sunshine confirms romance with MMA fighter, Zack Grayson—"He said I was the one!"

MEFC's "Playboy" Fighters—Who is in Zack Grayson's little black book?

Waitress Jenny Dawson tells all—"I'm going to have Zack Grayson's baby!"

New couple alert! Zack Grayson and porn queen, Kitty Hard. "Slayer slayed me in bed."

Is Zack Grayson dating the president's daughter?

"Rough Stuff." Zack Grayson spotted in exclusive New York BDSM club with A-list actress Noelle Waters. "He likes it rough," staff member reveals. "He likes to make them scream."

"And you'll be with…other women…like Sandy," I continue. "But I can't train with you if you're going to date other women in the gym." I drop my gaze, embarrassed by my admission. "I know it's not fair of me to ask, and it doesn't make sense, but I…just… Don't make me watch."

His face softens, and he leans closer. "That kiss," he whispers, his breath hot against my ear. "In Torment's office. That was nothing?"

"Aside from the fact that we risked both our lives, and you have to pay a heavy price, and I maybe got a little hot from all the activity…nothing."

"And when we touched..." He slides one arm around my waist and pulls me close as if we were alone and not in the Redemption parking lot where, no doubt, we are fueling the overactive gossip mill. "When I held you...nothing?"

My cheeks burn at the memory. "A friendly hug."

"And back there in class..." His hips press up against mine, and his voice drops to a sensual growl. "When I had you underneath me with your hands pinned above your head totally at my mercy...nothing?"

I open my mouth, but nothing is exactly what comes out.

Zack responds with a satisfied grunt. "Something."

"Don't let it go to your head." I grit my teeth and look away. "It was a natural physiological response. I'm genetically programmed to be attracted to handsome, sexy men in peak physical condition. Survival of the species and that sort of thing."

He laughs, and oh God, I missed that deep, rich rumble that rolls right through me. "What about this?" He taps my head. "I've heard the brain can overcome basic instinct and genetic programming. Free will and that sort of thing."

"Yeah, well, it's not working right now. I think it's the gi." Unable to stop myself, I run my hand along the edge of his gi, my fingers trailing over the hard muscles of his chest. "It's...distracting."

His muscles tense under my touch, and a growl vibrates in his chest. "You're distracting."

"We're supposed to be keeping it professional," I remind him, pulling my hand away. I watched his body change from boyhood through his gangly teen years and then fill out when he reached his early twenties. He was ripped back then in a way that made heads turn, but his muscles now are thick and hard, ripened by age and hundreds of fights. When I last saw him, there was still some boy left in the way he held himself, a slight unease with his body. But now, he is all confidence and power. Pure solid man.

Zack grabs my hand and presses it against his bare chest, right over his heart. "You're not making it easy. Your jealousy… knowing you care…feeling that connection… You don't know what that does to me." He is on me before I can part my lips, one hand firm around my neck, his lean, powerful body caging me against the car. His mouth claims mine, stealing my breath away with a kiss that sends a scorching wave of heat through my veins.

"Professional means no kissing," I say when he lets me up for air. Without thinking, I trace the edges of the scar on his forehead, a bitter reminder of Matt's misdirected anger when Zack brought home his mangled bike.

Zack covers my hand with his, trapping it against my cheek. "No kissing," he agrees. "Unless you touch me, and then I can't be held responsible for my actions."

"Fine. No touching." I pull my hand away, pleased that we are setting some ground rules so I don't have to worry about wanting to tear his clothes off in the gym.

His naughty hand skims the side of my face, his thumb stroking over the apple of my cheek as he tips my head back, forcing me to look at him. "I can't train you if I don't touch you, especially when we're rolling on the mats like we just did in class."

"Okay. Professional touching. Nothing else."

He licks his lips like a predator about to feast. "Unless you want something else."

I press my lips together and scowl. "Stop qualifying everything. I know exactly what you're trying to do, and it's not going to work. You can't seduce me, Zachary Grayson. You know exactly what professional means. Now let's shake on it."

He cups my face between his hands and tilts my head back. "Kiss."

"You had your kiss—"

Without warning, his hands drop to my hips, and he yanks me against him. His mouth crushes mine, and his tongue slides between my lips, touching, tasting, claiming. I startle at the urgency of his kiss, the raw heat, the fierce desire. I shouldn't kiss him back, but I can't resist the dark temptation, the firm hand that has found its way to my nape, holding me in place as he coaxes me open for the slow, relentless possession of my mouth.

Blood pounds in my temples, my hunger for him raw and wild. My hand slides up his chest and over his shoulder. I pull him closer, my fingers clutching the soft, silken strands of his hair. My heart pounds in my chest, and the world shatters around me.

I know better than this. When he left me, desolation led me into a darkness far worse than anything I ever imagined. And yet I don't fight it, because I want to feel his hands on my skin, his lips on mine, his arms around me, keeping me safe. I want him to hold me tight, kiss me hard. I want to be the girl who thought she was loved.

"Stop." I pull away. "We're in the parking lot. You don't know the guys at Redemption. They live for this kind of thing. The teasing will never end."

"Fuck them."

He nuzzles my neck, the rough stubble of his beard scraping over my sensitive skin. My body flames, sweat beading and running down my back. Was it always like this with him? Frantic, wild desperation? A fierce hunger for his touch, the closeness of his body? A burning need to be as close as two people can get?

"Zack." I can't think, can't fight. When he touches me, I melt inside. I don't want to feel these feelings, but I can't stop them. I don't want to want him, but I do. Confusion makes my head ache and my heart pound, well beyond the seventy percent maximum.

"This is dangerous," I murmur against his lips.

"I like dangerous."

A door slams in the distance. Footsteps thud in the gravel, getting louder. I push Zack back just as Sadist comes into view. Instead of disappointment that we have to part, all I feel is blessed relief that I have respite from the storm of emotion whipping through my body.

"Shilla. Slayer." Sadist nods a greeting while doing an extremely poor job of trying to hide his smirk.

"Don't get any ideas," I say. "It's nothing."

"Sure." His gaze flicks to Zack, and something passes between them that wipes that smile right off his face.

"What did you say to him in your secret, silent man language?" I ask after Sadist has reached his SUV. "You shut him down pretty quickly."

Zack's face tightens, and he looks away. "Nothing. Just like you said."

13

Shayla

"WELL, LOOK WHO'S HERE. OUR RESIDENT MMA STAR. GUESS we'll be well protected tonight." Sol DeMarco, Symbian's most senior guard greets me with a smirk when I walk into the control room on Friday night.

Six feet tall, his dark hair receding at the temples, and carrying a few extra pounds around his middle, Sol has had an issue with me ever since he found out I was on the MMA amateur circuit. He alternates between mocking me and challenging me to fight when we have to work together, but he never crosses the line the way he does with the other female guards. And that tells me everything I need to know.

"Keep your distance," Joe whispers when I sit down to log in my arrival time. "He lost five grand on the tables in Vegas last week, and Babs left him again."

"Ouch." Sol's girlfriend, Babs, is a woman who likes the finer things in life. When he wins at the tables, she is all sorts of good to him, but when he loses, she walks out the door. He works to feed his gambling habit and keep her happy, but he is always talking about the day he makes the big score.

"Last time, she didn't come home for a month," Joe says.

"Why does he keep taking her back?"

"It's called love. Once you find it, you can't let it go."

My mind turns back to my kiss with Zack before he left for Seattle two days ago. The feelings are still there—the chemistry, the connection. But can you love someone who has cut you so deep you can never heal, who has broken you beyond repair?

"C'mon, honey." Sol holds his arms out by his sides. "Give it your best shot. Gimme a little punch and show me what you give those girlies in the ring. I'll tell you if I feel anything. Or would you be more comfortable in the mud pit behind the fence?"

"Tempting, but I don't think you'd look good in a bikini." I catch Joe's snigger as I stow my bag under the reception desk. "What's he doing here?" I whisper.

"Symbian's put two extra guards on every shift. Apparently, they're launching some revolutionary new cloud technology, and they're worried about competitors trying to steal it. Lucky me gets the pleasure of Sol's company all night. You and Cheryl have been assigned to building two."

"I'm sorry you're going to be stuck with him." Aside from his abrasive nature, Sol is a pain to work with. When he's on patrol, he usually hides in an empty office and watches sports on his phone. His partner is left to pick up the slack, but people rarely report him, because the extra work is better than listening to him complain—his second favorite activity after gambling.

"It is what it is," Joe says.

Cheryl checks in while I'm suiting up, and we walk through the quiet night, checking the grounds on our way to the second of the four buildings that make up the Symbian facility. The air is warm and smells of fresh earth and mowed grass. Symbian's gardeners come twice a week and keep the grounds looking more like a country club than an industrial estate.

"So how's the new boyfriend?" Cheryl checks the lock on one of the side doors of building two, then runs her hand along the edge of the window.

"As you well know"—I turn and glare—"he's not my boyfriend. He's my coach, which, in retrospect, was a mistake, because I couldn't even make it through a jiu-jitsu class with him without wanting to rip off his clothes."

Cheryl nods. "I can see that. If I was in denial about my feelings and pretending he was just a coach, I'd want to rip off his clothes, too."

"Are you done?" I snap.

"No problem with the window." She laughs. "You're wound up pretty tight. What else is going on with your *coach*?"

I am tempted not to tell her, but the whole Zack thing is eating me up inside. I need to talk to someone, and the Predator and Sadist, my usual confidants, now have confidants of their own. "My friend Sandy is after him. When she mentioned they were having dinner with her parents, I wanted to bounce her around the ring. It doesn't make sense. I'm still angry with him. He forced me into the wrong choice. It ended everything—my belief in love, my dance career, my dreams about marriage. So why do I lose all self-control when we're together?"

"You can be angry with him for leaving you but not for the choices you made after that," Cheryl says. "I think in your heart you know that, and the feelings you had for him are probably still there. First love marks you for life. I've been married four times, and yet I'd jump into bed with my first again if I had the chance. He didn't want kids, so we split up, but I didn't love him any less."

I sigh and lean against the building. "So you're saying I'll never get him out of my system?"

Cheryl laughs. "Not if he has anything to do with it. And the way you're going back and forth about him, I gotta wonder if that's really what you want. Would it be that big a risk to forgive him?"

Stones crunch under my feet as we walk along the gravel path beside the building. I used to listen for the same sound when Zack would come to my house in the middle of the night. No matter how quiet he tried to be, I always knew the moment he stepped onto our driveway. "It's not just about him," I say. "It's about all the men I've cared about. I love them, and they betray me. I need them, and they hurt me. I can't feel like that again... like I'm nothing."

"Honey, you're not nothing. You're something special." She gives me a hug, and then she pulls back and grins. "That's why you have me as a friend."

Drained by my outburst, I focus on checking the building perimeter. A smudge of dirt on the window frame halfway along the building has me crouching down in the flower bed, and I spot a footprint in the freshly overturned earth.

"Cheryl!" I motion her over. "Check the door."

She twists the knob and holsters her flashlight. "It's open."

After I hit the emergency button on my radio to let Joe and Sol know we need backup, Cheryl pulls open the door, and we make our way up the stairwell. Emergency lights flicker on the concrete walls. Our feet thud softly on the steps. We emerge on the first floor, and my pulse kicks up a notch when I see light streaming from under a computer lab door midway along the long, white hallway.

Cheryl pulls her pepper spray from her belt. I grab my baton. Although we both carry firearms, the last thing either of us wants is to pull a trigger.

Using hand gestures, I motion for Cheryl to move to the other side. But just as she steps forward, her radio squawks with Sol's voice.

"What's going on, ladies?"

I hear a curse and then a crash. The door slams open, and two men dressed in black burst out of the room. They take a step in our direction, freeze, then take off down the hallway toward the main stairwell. Cheryl runs after them, and I dash into the computer lab to see if they were alone.

All clear. I race back down the hallway and check the other rooms. From outside, I hear the crack of a gun, followed by a scream. Heart pounding, I follow the sound down the stairs and out the door. Joe is on the ground, his face stark white, his Symbian shirt dark with blood. Cheryl is kneeling beside him, trying to stanch the wound.

"Oh God. What happened?"

"They came out the door shooting," Cheryl says. "Joe took one in the chest." Her face tightens, eyes glistening with tears. "He wasn't wearing his vest."

"Where's Sol?"

"He went after them. I'll call 911. You go give him a hand."

Heart pounding, I run around the building and spot the two men near the wire fence. Sol lunges for them, and the taller of the two turns around and belts Sol in the jaw. Sol stumbles back and goes down on one knee.

With a burst of speed, I fly across the gravel. I pass Sol and jump, flinging myself at the nearest intruder. I rip him off the fence and reach for his partner in crime, pulling him down.

"It's a damn girl," the first guy snarls.

"Not like any girl you know." I move quickly with an inside leg kick, winding the first guy and knocking him back against the fence. Then I land a kick on the second and move in with a combo, landing a right hand. My attacker jabs, then winds up and misses his next strike. I kick again and throw a few punches, snapping his head back, and he goes down hard. But my satisfaction is short-lived when I hear the wire twang behind me.

"Sol," I shout. "The other one is getting away. Stop him."

But Sol just stands there, mouth gaping, as I cuff the guy against the fence, while the other runs away.

The police arrive only a few moments later. Cheryl and I stay with Joe until the ambulance takes him away. I call Sadist, my go-to person for exciting news, while Cheryl calls Symbian's head of security to brief him on the break-in. Sadist manages to calm me down while at the same time extracting details about the fight and my first arrest. He then gives a play-by-play summary over the Redemption PA system for the benefit of everyone in the gym. I hear cheers in the background and fighters chanting my name. There is no place like Redemption.

Cheryl, Sol, and I are interviewed by the jaw-droppingly handsome blond-haired and blue-eyed Officer James Morrison and his equally good-looking friend, Detective Bruce Waterton. Cheryl squeezes my hand every time Officer Morrison talks, but if I had to pick one of them, it would be the dark-haired detective whose eyes crinkle at the corners and who has the squarest jaw I've ever seen.

"Shayla was amazing," Cheryl tells Detective Waterton after giving a long, overly enthusiastic description of my fight. "She beat their sorry asses into the ground."

"I weakened them during the chase," Sol mutters when Detective Waterton asks him for his version of the events. "Got in a few punches when we were around the corner. By the time they got to the fence, they could barely walk. That's how the dude was beat by a girl."

Detective Waterton smiles at me and winks to let me know he's not buying Sol's story. My cheeks heat up under his silent praise.

Afterward, Cheryl contacts our supervisor, and he agrees to call in some replacements so we can go to the hospital to check on Joe. He has no relatives in the city, and after his wife died, he stopped going out with his friends. Cheryl and I often take him out for a beer after work when we have an early shift, and I always get him tickets to my fights. On the rare occasion, Cheryl and I will be able to drag him out to see a band, but for the most part, he lives a quiet, lonely life.

Cheryl and I patrol outside the building while we wait for our replacements to arrive and meet up at the parking lot.

"I talked to the paramedic before they took Joe away," she says. "He told me Joe was stable, although he's going to need surgery. He's going to be okay."

"Why didn't he wear his vest?"

She shrugs. "He told me once he's just going through the motions, waiting until he can be with his wife again. Maybe he took a calculated risk because he wanted to be with her. They were childhood sweethearts. Did you know that?"

I swallow past the lump in my throat. "No. I knew they'd been together a long time but not that long."

Cheryl's voice is uncharacteristically soft. "I've never loved anyone so much that I thought I couldn't go on when we split up. I loved all my hubbies, and I was always sad when the relationships ended, but I was never devastated. Maybe that's why I've been married four times. I've been looking for that deep, enduring kind of love. The kind that touches your soul."

I had that. I had it, and I lost it, and I've carried the pain for the last seven years, because our love did endure. I just couldn't see it. Maybe if I had, I wouldn't have married Damian, and Zack and I might have had a second chance. Not that I'm absolving Zack of guilt, but for the first time, I wonder if my actions might have played a part in our separation, too.

Cheryl gives me a nudge, pulling me back to the present. "Maybe I'll get some loving tonight."

"Oh my God. You got Officer Morrison's number, didn't you?"

"He's meeting me at the hospital after his shift. How sweet is that?" She pulls out her phone and shows me his name. "What about you? Detective Waterton was definitely checking you out. Is Zack out of the picture?"

"Zack is—"

The loud screech of tires cuts me off. Moments later, a blue Acura NSX races into the parking lot, jumps the curb, and screeches to a stop only five feet from where we're standing.

"Here."

14

Shayla

WITH A LOUD THUD, THE ACURA DOOR FLIES OPEN. ZACK BURSTS out of the vehicle and stalks across the grass. He is wearing his fight shorts, running shoes, and nothing else.

"Good Lord." Cheryl grabs my wrist, squeezes tight. "I hope you've got some ropes, because you're gonna have to tie me down. That piece of man candy needs some licking, and my tongue is already wet."

I have to admit, half-naked Zack is magnificent, all broad shoulders, taut pecs, and sculpted abs, that faint dusting of hair arrowing down to where my gaze shouldn't go when I'm in uniform and on the job. His muscles ripple as he walks, tat sleeve gleaming under the parking lot lights, hard thighs eating up the distance between us. He is breathtaking. Beautiful.

But for some reason, he doesn't seem happy to see me.

"Where are they?" Zack swivels his head from side to side, checking out the parking lot.

Puzzled, I frown. "Who?"

"The men who attacked you."

"They didn't attack me. They were trying to get away and—"

"One of them is on his way to jail," Cheryl says in a placating tone. "I'm sure by now the police will have apprehended the other one. They aren't a threat anymore. Your girl is safe."

Zack's eyes narrow. "Did anyone check the building? The grounds? Vehicles in the parking lot? Are you sure there aren't any more? Is Symbian putting on extra security?"

"Seriously?" I give an exasperated sigh. "I don't need help to do my job."

"Yes to all your questions." A betraying Cheryl shoots me a grin. "And as soon as our replacements arrive, we're off duty."

Zack grunts his approval, and his gaze returns to me. "You're hurt."

I touch the bandage on my temple and shrug. "Just a few cuts and bruises. I've had worse at the gym. I'm fine."

"You're not fine." He cups my jaw, turning my face so he can inspect my injuries. "Dammit. Why didn't you call me?"

"I was kinda busy chasing a couple of bad guys across the yard and giving them a beat down." I pull my hand away. "This is my job, Zack. I'm perfectly capable of handling a couple of thieves."

"She has a gun," Cheryl adds. "And a Taser. But she didn't need to use them. Not even when they turned on her. You should have seen it. Two massive dudes bearing down on our very own Shayla."

Zack's lips thin, and his face darkens. For a moment, I fear he might lose control.

"Cheryl…" I warn, but Cheryl is on a roll, and nothing is going to stop her.

"It was like David and two humungous Goliaths. They were three times her size and at least twice her weight. I thought for sure they'd rip her to pieces. I had my gun ready in case they knocked her out—or worse."

"Cheryl!"

"Aaargh." Zack roars his frustration and stalks across the parking lot, his chest heaving.

"Too much?" Cheryl asks with mock innocence.

"Way too much. Even after the gross exaggeration of their appearance, I thought he'd hold it together until you said 'worse.'"

She leans against the railing and laughs. "I was checking to see if he's really into you. News flash. He is. Also, he seems to be a very protective sort. Protective can be good or bad, depending on how much bossing around you can take."

"Not much."

Sol comes outside to see what's going on while Zack rages around the parking lot. He is joined by the three security guards Symbian has sent to replace us for the night. Zack takes one look at the uniformed guards and returns to my side, throwing a heavy arm over my shoulders while Cheryl and I get our replacements up to speed on the events of the night.

Although he's the only person in the group without a gun—or proper clothes—he is no less intimidating, and I kind of like having his arm around me, telling me he's there if I need him. Or maybe he's warning Sol and the other guys away. I especially like how he glares at Sol, as if he knows the kind of things Sol is thinking, which I'm sure are even worse than the things that come out of his mouth. However, I don't like it when Zack insists on driving me to the hospital to see Joe.

"Cheryl and I carpool all the time, Zack. Her car is perfectly safe."

"I want you to come with me." Without waiting for my response, Zack stalks to his vehicle.

"You'd better go with him," Cheryl whispers. "He's not going to calm down unless you're with him and he knows you're safe. My second husband, Steve, was just the same. Once those protective instincts are triggered, discussion is a waste of time."

"Seriously?" My head falls back, and I groan. "You make him sound like he's incapable of rational thought. And we're not together, Cheryl. We kissed, and then we agreed it wouldn't happen again. And then it did, but that's it."

"Those must have been damn good kisses, because he's acting like you belong to him. I thought he was going to attack Sol just for looking at you."

"They were good, but they didn't change the way I feel about what happened."

"Then go with him." She gives me a gentle push in Zack's direction. "I promise you won't be sorry. A protective man is a horny man. And he's already got most of his clothes off."

"Joe might be going into surgery. Sex is the last thing on my mind."

"Joe is going to be fine. He probably woke up in the ambulance and asked for a sandwich." Her face tightens, and I know she's just as worried as I am. Cheryl jokes around when she's worried, whereas I bottle everything up inside. "Actually, I'm gonna pick one up for him on my way to the hospital," she continues. "White bread. Lots of meat and lots of mayo. You'd better go with Zack in case I'm delayed searching for my perfect sandwich. I'll see you there." Before I can protest, she's gone.

Zack expresses his pleasure at my decision to ride to the hospital with him by pushing me against the side of his vehicle and crushing my lips in a fierce and very unprofessional kiss that leaves my knees weak and my body trembling. Then he ruins it by trying to kill me as he races through the deserted industrial park at one hundred miles per hour.

"Why do you drive so fast?" I lean back in my seat, take a deep breath.

"I like it."

"Of course you do." I shift in my seat, wincing as the bruises from the fight begin to make themselves known.

Zack frowns. "Where else are you hurt?"

"I took a few body kicks. Nothing serious. I'm wearing a bulletproof vest under my uniform shirt."

With a yank on the wheel, Zack slows to a stop and pulls over at the side of the road.

"Take it off."

His imperious command makes me bristle. "Why?"

"Want to check you out. Now."

"You're so damn bossy. If this is what you're going to be like as a coach, I foresee all sorts of problems, because the new gun-toting, intruder-arresting me doesn't like being told what to do."

His face creases in a menacing scowl. "Is this the game you want to play?"

"Yes." I push open the door and step out into the tall, cool grass, trying to get a handle on the maelstrom of emotion I've been drowning in all evening. First Joe, and now Zack. Fear and loss and longing. It's almost too much to handle.

"Where are you going?"

I lean against the side of the vehicle and look back over my shoulder at his worried face. "I just need to get some air before we go to the hospital. Clear my head so I can be there for Joe when he gets out of surgery."

The door slams. Shoes crunch on gravel. I fight the urge to run as he rounds the vehicle and cages me against the side.

"Stay back." I put up a warning hand between us, and Zack frowns.

"You think I would hurt you?"

"You did hurt me." And yet all I want to do right now is walk into his arms. No matter how bad things were, Zack always made me feel protected and cared for. He could soothe me with just the sound of his voice. When I lay in bed in the circle of his arms, I wanted to stay like that forever.

Zack sighs and leans in to rest his forehead against mine. "What can I do to make things better?"

"Nothing." I turn away, breaking our contact. "Why are you here? I don't need you. I have a gun."

He doesn't laugh at my stupid comment. Instead, he studies me intently. "I can't be anywhere else."

"You make me feel confused, Zack." I don't know if my

adrenaline is crashing after what happened at Symbian or if it has brought all my emotions to a head, but I can barely contain the anger inside me. "Everything was fine until you got here. Now, I'm an emotional mess. It hurts. Seeing you hurts. Touching you hurts. Kissing you causes me pain."

"Why?"

One word and my tension erupts, unleashing all the emotions I've been trying to suppress—sadness, hate, fear, regret, devastation, and despair. "You know my dad left me. He promised he would be there for me always, and then he died. I wanted him to come back so much I ached inside. He understood me in a way my mother and Matt never did. When he was gone, I felt so scared and alone. And then I met you, and I could breathe again." My pain pours out, and although he doesn't touch me, I am safe between the strong arms braced on either side of my trembling body.

"I don't even have words to describe what it was like to lose that again. To lose you." I draw in a ragged breath. "It was like a black hole sucking at my chest, and every day, it took over more of me. New York was overwhelming. I felt alone and afraid, and you weren't there to protect me. I'd never realized how much I relied on you to keep me safe until I was mugged…"

Zack sucks in a sharp breath, but I am already lost in the memory of that terrible night.

"Shayla?"

I recognize Damian's voice in the studio hallway and curl up in the corner of his office, heart still thudding from the slam of the front door. This is my fault. I should have left with the others. I might be from a small town, but I know better than to walk alone in the dark. I can't handle New York. I can't handle being alone and without Zack to protect me.

The door squeaks open, and a sliver of light from the hallway streaks across the room, chasing the shadows away.

"What are you doing here in the dark?" He flicks the switch, and I blink as my eyes adjust to the light, wipe my tears away.

"I was…" A sob rips out of my throat, and he crosses the room to kneel in front of me.

"What happened? Tell me. I came back when you didn't show up at the bar. Gaby said you were right behind them."

"There was a guy. Outside." I draw in a ragged breath. "He was waiting. I was just locking up and he…" I shudder, remembering the press of cold steel against my temple. "He had a gun."

Damian's face tightens in alarm. "Did he hurt you?" He smooths his hands down my arms, and I am at once embarrassed and thrilled that this famous artistic director would have even noticed I was missing, much less try to comfort me.

"No. But I thought…" I can't even voice what I thought when I heard the rough voice behind me, a terror like nothing I had ever known. "He wanted my purse. I threw it as far as I could, and when he went for it, I came back inside and locked the door."

"Thank God you're okay."

He strokes my hair, and I can't breathe for the wave of longing that surges through my body. I need this. A gentle hand. A soothing voice. A kind touch. Someone to look after me who can fill the emptiness in my heart.

"Did you call the police?" he asks.

"No. I was…too afraid to move in case he came looking for me."

"Poor baby." He holds out his arms, and I tremble at the need to be held again.

"I can't." I shake my head. "It wouldn't be right. You're like… my boss."

Damian smiles. He is so beautiful, like some kind of golden Greek god. Some of the dancers think his features are too harsh, but I like his raw masculinity. He is at once sensual and powerful, and I can imagine the days before he was injured when he used to dance for Joffrey, one of the top ballet companies in the country.

"No one is here," he says quietly. "You've just been through a traumatic event, and your boss thinks you need a hug. Are you going to disobey him?"

I lean forward, and he wraps his strong arms around me. His body is slim beneath his crisp, white shirt. He is narrow where Zack was broad. Lean where Zack was muscled. But he is warm and safe, and he smells of Tiger Balm and Deep Heat, makeup, and musty costumes—the scents of my second home.

"Let me take care of you," he murmurs in my ear.

And I do.

"Damian picked up the pieces," I continue, pulling myself out of the past. "He made me feel safe and protected. He put me back together again. And then he broke me, too."

Zack's arms come around me. I lean into him like I leaned into Damian that day. What is wrong with me? I know better than to trust anyone to look after me. That's why I learned to fight and why I have a gun.

"I messed up, sweetheart." He wraps his arms around me, holds me tight. "I was hurt you hadn't told me about New York, and it made me even more certain I was going to hold you back. We suspected Viv was ill, and although Lily had a job, we didn't know how we would pay for her medical expenses. The last thing I wanted was to leave you, but I had nothing. I was nothing. And I knew things were just going to get worse. What kind of life was that going to be for you?"

"A life I chose. I would have wanted to be there for you, to help you and Lily out with Viv."

I adored both Zack's sisters, who were almost total opposites in both looks and personality. Short, curvy Lily with her curly brown hair was fiercely intelligent, highly organized, and would have been intimidating save for her dry wit and quirky sense of humor. Despite their difficult circumstances, she had excelled in school, racking up the scholarships she needed to pay her way through college. By contrast, Viv was tall and slim with waist-length blond hair and an almost ethereal pallor to her skin. Always optimistic and a bit scatterbrained, she had struggled at school, but she had a good heart and was always there to help out a friend in need.

"That's why I walked away," he said. "I knew you would never leave if you found out. I loved you too much for that."

His voice is thick with regret, and I am tired of carrying this anger in my heart. I have been through hell three times and made it back. I am strong now. I can look after myself. I don't need him the way I did before, but I miss having someone to lean on. Someone who cares.

I rest my head against his chest, and he holds me close; he holds me like I haven't been held in forever.

When we reach the hospital, Zack throws on some clothes from a gym bag in his car and I change out of my uniform into the jeans and T-shirt I wore to work. We wait with Cheryl while Joe is in surgery. Zack doesn't talk much, but he is there. Officer Morrison joins us, and Cheryl whispers that it is the strangest and best double date she's ever had.

After a few hours, the doctor gives us the good news. The bullet missed Joe's heart and major arteries, although it caused a lot of damage to his shoulder. We pay him a quick visit in the ICU and promise to come back tomorrow with lots of unhealthy treats. He smiles, but I see something in his eyes I wish I didn't see.

I think about Joe on the drive home. Every morning, he gets up feeling the loss of his wife so deeply that it informs every choice he makes—from the sandwiches he eats against his doctor's orders to the bulletproof vest he refused to wear tonight. Every day, I wake up and make my choices, too. I've chosen anger over forgiveness. I've blamed Zack for setting me on the path that led to the end of my dreams. A different path was open to me, and I chose not to take it.

"We're here." Zack's voice startles me, and I realize that the car must have stopped moving some time ago, because Zack already has the key in his hand.

"Sorry. It's been a long night."

We walk up the sidewalk in the still of the night. Only a few lights shine from the windows of the condos around us. The streets are empty. The air is cool and damp, fragrant with the scent of freshly watered grass.

"Thanks for staying with me and taking me home." I stop in front of my door, look up at his handsome face. Even after a long night, he doesn't look tired. Just thoughtful. Intense.

"Pleasure."

I take a step toward him. And then another. I am so close now, I can feel the heat of his body, smell a trace of his cologne. So familiar. Comforting. Alive.

This is the man who taught me how to live after my father died. He made me feel safe. He filled the emptiness in my chest that I felt so fiercely again tonight when I thought Joe might die.

My hand slides around his neck, and I can't stop myself. I want him. I need him, although I'm not ready to forgive him. Seven years of anger does not just disappear in a couple of days. But I am ready to let him into my life, if only for the comfort of his arms. "Zack." I whisper his name, pull him down until his lips meet mine.

With a groan, he wraps his arms around me and pulls me tight against his body. Our tongues tangle, teeth clash, lips mash together. It is not a pretty kiss or a soft kiss. It is not the gentle kiss of a lover or the chaste kiss of a friend. Raw passion infuses our kiss. Pain and longing, sorrow and even hate.

I pull away, panting. "I need you."

"I'm here, sweetheart."

"I'm not promising anything," I say. "I don't want you to misunderstand."

"I get it, Shay."

"Inside." My chest heaves as I pull away.

We make it into the lobby, and then we are drawn together again like two powerful magnets. We kiss and paw at each other's clothes. Zack cups my ass in his hands and lifts me against him as he strides toward the elevator. I nuzzle his neck, inhale his delicious scent, grind against the bulge in his jeans. The elevator door opens, and Zack steps in and slams me against the wall so hard, my teeth clack together, but God, it feels good, and I am safe with Zack. He may be rough, but I know in my heart he would never harm me.

When the elevator door slides open, he carries me down the hall. Moments later, we are in my apartment. Zack kicks the door closed, pushing me backward as our mouths find each other again.

I nip his bottom lip. Not hard enough to draw blood, but enough to send a message about what I want from this encounter that is so different from any intimacy we have ever shared.

"Jesus." Zack spins me around to face the door, one hand around my waist and one hand at my throat as he pulls me back against his chest. His cock presses against the cleft of my ass, and his fingers rest at the pulse on my neck.

"Is this what you want?" His voice drops husky and low. "I want you so badly, I won't be gentle."

"I almost lost a friend tonight. I don't want gentle. I want to feel. I want to live. I want you to know the fighter side of me because that is what saved me when I lost everything."

Heart pounding, I step back and jab my heel into his instep, then I shove my elbow into his ribs in a move I've used count-less times in the ring. He releases me, and I scoot away, clearing the kitchen counter as I back into the small living room deco-rated in cool gray and teal. Zack's head snaps around, and I run, laughing, fleeing from the predator in my house.

He catches me just as I reach the bedroom. Momentum car-ries us to the bed, and he flips me over, then straddles my hips. The softness is gone from his face. Instead, his jaw is set, his eyes hard and focused as he gives a satisfied growl. He grabs the neck of my shirt and tears it off me like it was made of paper. For a second, I wonder if I can really handle what I've unleashed.

"This is so unfair. You have a weight advantage." I buck my hips, try to throw him forward.

Zack snorts a laugh and shifts his weight, moving into an MMA full mount position with his thighs clamped tight around me. He grabs my wrists and slams them over my head, transferring them both to one hand so he can tease and torture me with the other.

"Submit."

"Go to hell." I arch and wiggle, but the bed is too soft to give me the kind of leverage I need to use my MMA skills to escape.

"This is what I wanted to do to you in Redemption when I had you pinned to the mat in this position." Zack shoves up my bra and cups my breast in his warm palm, kneading it with firm strokes until my nipple is tight and peaked and aching for his touch.

"You have beautiful breasts."

"You wouldn't be touching them if my hands were free." I twist to the side like I did in class, jamming my hip into his groin, but this just seems to inflame him even more. He shifts his weight, forcing me back down, and draws my nipple between his teeth, nipping so hard, I gasp.

With a grunt of pleasure, he turns his attention to my other breast, biting and tugging until I'm writhing on the bed beneath him, so wet, I ache inside.

"Yield."

"No." Our gazes lock in a battle that I know I'm going to lose, because I want him inside me so badly, I'll do anything to have him, including throwing the fight.

Still holding my wrists, he leans back and unbuttons my jeans, shoving them roughly over my hips and down my thighs.

My cheeks heat when he stares and licks his lips like a predator about to feast.

"Beautiful," he murmurs, running a gentle finger over my mons.

"Guess who isn't getting some of that?"

"Every other guy on the planet except me." Zack cups my sex and thrusts two fingers deep inside me. His rough, brutal action takes my breath away, but it feels so good.

"Christ, you're wet." He withdraws his fingers and wipes my moisture along my inner thigh. "You want me bad."

"Don't let it go to your head."

Laughing, he tears open his jeans with one hand and fists his cock. "Too late."

I swallow hard as I watch him stroke. Although we didn't have sex until I was eighteen, we did everything else. But I don't remember his cock being quite so big and thick.

"You always were a bit of a show-off. No wonder you had

sponsors beating down your door." I cringe inwardly at the inelegant reminder of what he lost, but curiously, he grins and reaches into his back pocket for a condom. I try not to think about the fact that he had the condom on hand, how it was within easy reach, or how practiced he is as he rips it open smoothly with his teeth.

"I did enjoy the show aspect of it. Almost as much as the fight." He rolls the condom over his shaft. His body is tense, his thighs rock-hard around me.

I reach out to touch him. I want to know if he feels the same. I want to stroke him until he loses control.

But Zack has his own ideas. He flips me over and grabs my hips, pulling me to my hands and knees. "This isn't how I ever imagined it would be if we got together again."

"Me neither," I mumble with my cheek pressed against the bright red cover that pops a little color into my white and gray room. But this is exactly what I want. Sex, and none of the confusing intimacy that tied us together so long ago.

"Are you okay with this, Shay?"

"Well…" I launch myself forward, making one last mock attempt at getting away, my jeans catching around my knees.

With a low, warning growl, Zack grabs me around the waist and hauls me back. I've never done foreplay like this. Raw, primal, incendiary. I'll be ruined for beta males for life.

"Answer."

"Yes." I look back over my shoulder and grin. "Thanks for asking." When being mauled by a ferocious beast on your bed, always be polite.

Zack tangles one hand in my hair and yanks my head back. His other hand digs into my hip. When he has me immobilized, he pushes me down on the bed, holding me in place with one hand on my lower back. He knows exactly what he wants and how he wants it. After years of looking after myself, it feels good to let someone else be in control.

"Don't move until I tell you to move." He smacks my ass with a firm hand, and I cry out in surprise.

"What the hell?"

"Open those pretty thighs, or I'll do it for you," he demands.

And suddenly I realize I'm not the only one who has changed over the last seven years. The Zack I knew was never rough or demanding in bed. He was always very careful, gentle, as if he was afraid I might break with anything more than a caress. This new Zack has none of those hang-ups. Or maybe he feels different around the new me. All I know is that this isn't the boy who handled me like the most delicate of treasures. Instead, I get Slayer. The beast.

"I'd like to see you try," I challenge, because I know he won't push me too far. The protector in him would never really hurt me.

He smacks me again, harder this time. Pain sheets across my skin, distracting me from my mission of resistance as the burn turns to pleasure.

"Bastard."

"When did my girl get such a dirty mouth?" He smacks my other cheek, the crack of skin on skin echoing in the quiet of my room.

My breaths come in short pants, and I give myself up to sensation, the throb of my pulse between my thighs, the brush of cotton against my nipples, the unbearable ache in my core. I moan softly, and Zack shoves my legs roughly apart with his knee, as far as my jeans will allow.

"Tell me you want me."

"I want you."

"Say my name and tell me you want me." He teases my entrance with the head of his cock, and I let out a moan.

"I want you, Zachary Grayson."

"I want you, too. You can't even imagine how much."

He pushes inside me with one hard thrust, filling me so completely, I almost come right then. With one hand twisted through my hair, he yanks my head back and pistons his hips so hard, the bed squeaks and the headboard bangs against the wall.

Oh God. I've become one of those neighbors.

My arousal climbs fast, and when I'm just about to peak, Zack slides one hand over my hip and drags a rough finger over my clit. Once. Twice. And then he presses just where I need to be pressed.

I come so hard, I lose my breath. Pleasure tears through me, arcing from my clit along every nerve of my body. Zack holds me tight, drawing out my orgasm with hammering thrusts, his breaths quickening, the bed pounding against the wall. Finally, his muscles tighten, and he comes with a guttural groan.

Definitely one of those neighbors. I'll never be able to show my face in the hallway again.

Zack collapses on top of me and threads his fingers through

mine on the softness of the bed, a gentle, tender gesture after the roughest sex I've ever had.

"You okay?" He presses his lips to my nape, and I shudder, feeling curiously empty inside.

"Yes," I lie.

After a few minutes, Zack leaves to dispose of the condom. I feel awkward, uncomfortable, unable to decide what to do. Should I take off my clothes and jump into bed? Or straighten my clothes and wait for him to return? Is he planning to stay, or is he going to leave? What do I want him to do?

Taking the safe road, I fix my clothes, pull on a new T-shirt, and head to the kitchen, where I grab a bottle of water to quench a nonexistent thirst.

Zack joins me a few moments later, dressed as if we didn't just have wild sex only a few moments ago, his brow creased in a frown.

"You sure you're okay?"

"Yeah." I hug myself with one arm and take another sip while Zack prowls around my living room, making me feel curiously embarrassed about my minimalist decor. My apartment is simply furnished but comfy. A gray leather sectional accented with teal cushions surrounds a white block coffee table, and beside it, flush against the dark gray wall, is a tall white lacquer cabinet. A matching white kitchen table sits in the dining area, surrounded by three teal chairs. I've added some softness with a fluffy gray carpet to match the walls, sheer white curtains, and a few potted plants. The kitchen, all white cabinets and black appliances, is tucked behind a counter and open to the rest of the room.

"You don't look okay," he says from the other side of the breakfast bar.

"How do I look?"

"Far away."

I force a laugh, although he's right. I'm wary of getting too close, and I was more than happy to encourage the kind of sex that doesn't involve a lot of cuddling or hugging, soft words or gentle caresses. I wonder if I'll ever be able to allow that kind of intimacy back in my life. I still hurt inside, but being with Zack reminds me of how it felt to feel cared for, to be loved. Although I don't want it, that need is still there. I needed it tonight. I'm so confused.

"People can't look like feelings."

"You can." He rounds the bar into the kitchen and pulls open a drawer. "I could always read you. That hasn't changed. And seeing you dressed and out here with your arms around yourself instead of naked in there, lying beside me, tells me you're not settled. Did I hurt you?"

"No. It was good. It was sex. That's what I wanted."

"Rough sex?" He slams the drawer, and the cutlery inside clatters. "Too rough."

"There were two of us in the bedroom." I offer him the water bottle, but he shakes his head. "If I didn't want it to go where it did, I would have shut you down."

He leans against the counter and crosses his arms. "I don't know what the hell happened. That's not how I wanted things to go, but I can't think when I'm with you. I can't control myself."

"You did control yourself." I squeeze my bottle, making it

crackle. I don't want to have this conversation. It's done, and for some reason, I just want to curl up in bed and cry. "Maybe too much. All the questions…asking if I was okay… To be honest, it was sweet but kind of annoying. If I don't like something, I let my partners know."

Zack bristles. "Your partners?"

"I'm not a nun." I shrug. "I've been with other people since my marriage ended. I know you have, too."

"They didn't mean anything," Zack says quickly, taking a step toward me. "Not like you."

My water bottle becomes a shield. I take a drink I don't want to quench a thirst I don't have. The cool water slides over my tongue and chills me inside as it goes down. "Zack…I'm not looking to start anything up again. It was just…Joe and the chase and the arrest…adrenaline. You know it makes you do crazy things."

He freezes midstep, and I stumble on. "It was good. We got it out of our systems, and now we can move on. Keep it professional like we originally agreed."

He is just standing there, his face an expressionless mask, and for once, I can't tell what he is thinking. Is he relieved? Shocked? Angry? Disappointed?

"You're afraid."

"I'm not afraid." I cross my arms over my chest.

"You are," he says. "You're afraid of risk, whether it's in or out of the ring. It's the one thing about you that has changed. It's what is holding you back from achieving your goals."

"If I were afraid of risk, I wouldn't have become a fighter,"

I snap, irritated that he would presume to lecture me when he knows nothing about my life for the last seven years. "I take a risk every time I step in the ring. You know that better than I do…" I regret the words as soon as they drop from my lips and even more when Zack flinches.

"I'm sorry. That came out wrong. I just meant because you're…were…a fighter…"

"I should go."

He takes a step toward the door, and in that heartbeat of time, I want him to stay. I want things to be the way they used to be, when everything was easy between us. I want to fall asleep in the circle of his arms, listening to the steady beat of his heart. But I don't take the chance. Instead, I let him go. "Thanks for tonight."

"I'll see you tomorrow." He turns back and brushes his lips over my cheek.

Hope flickers, and then he's gone.

15 Zack

"Do it again." Arms folded across his chest, Zack gestured Shayla to her feet. "Try to keep the drill flowing as smoothly as possible until your reactions are natural and instinctual."

She shot him the glare of death as her third training partner of the hour, a scrawny dude Zack had carefully selected for his cowering manner and lack of anything even resembling muscle, scuttled away, only to be replaced by a dude even scrawnier.

"You can't be serious," Shayla bit out. "I'm pretty sure after our training weekend of hell, I'll be able to clear collar ties in my sleep."

"And you'll probably be doing them wrong there, too," Zack snapped. "It's a warm-up and a wrestling drill that even newbies can master. You need to focus. Haven't you been paying attention for the last three days? I set up an underground fight for you on Thursday so you could try out the new techniques, but you aren't even trying to master them."

Finding an underground fight club in a new city wasn't an

easy thing to do, especially for a man who had fought for one of the biggest MMA promotions in the world, making him a "sell-out" to the underground community. Underground fighting was illegal in most states, including California, and the promoters went to great lengths to keep their fights off the California State Athletic Commission's radar. The fight organizers screened and limited attendee lists, texted event announcements only two hours before the fights started, and required everyone to say a code word to get in. Still, underground fights were where many fighters honed their skills, free of rules and regulations, and after a lot of digging, he had discovered that the Predator was Redemption's key contact for the underground circuit.

After only a few grumbled protests, the Predator had made the arrangements for Shayla to fight at Zack's request. They didn't speak about the membership card, but Zack knew the Predator had been watching him train, just as Zack had been watching him. After years on the professional circuit, he had lost touch with the gritty, raw, no-holds-barred fighting of the underground where the Predator had made his name. Although Zack was certain he wouldn't be meeting the Predator in the ring, it made sense to be prepared.

"Are you watching Shayla or the Predator?" Sadist came up beside him, gesturing between Shayla on the mat with her new opponent and the lean, dark-haired Predator bouncing a heavy-weight around the cage, his scarred face a mask of boredom.

"Both."

"If you're looking for weaknesses in the Predator's game, don't waste your time," Sadist said. "He doesn't have any. He also doesn't fight fair. We tried to get him onto the amateur circuit, but he dropped out after a few months because he didn't like the rules. He's all about no-holds-barred street fighting. No limits. No mercy. You know what I'm talking about?"

"Yeah. I do." Matt and his group of thugs had dragged him into more than one alley over the years. Zack had learned street fighting out of necessity, but it was only when he joined the MMA gym that he learned how skill could overcome size or strength in numbers. Every time he stepped into the cage, he remembered those days and how every beating had been a stepping stone to where he was now. Nothing tempted him more than a chance to fight with someone who didn't give a damn about the rules. But he would have to step into the ring to do it. He would have to take the risk that another man would die. "I'm not fighting him."

"He and Shayla are tight," Sadist continued as if Zack hadn't spoken. "I thought there was something going on between them, but then Sia showed up one day, and *boom*. That was it. One day, he's cracking bones and smashing skulls. The next, he's married and has a kid. You find the right girl, and it hits you like that. Maybe you fight it tooth and nail. Maybe it's a long and bumpy road. Maybe you run the other way at first. But when you look back, you realize it was a foregone conclusion the very first time you met."

"You trying to tell me something?"

Sadist shrugged, his gaze on Shayla twisting her opponent into her tenth collar tie of the morning. "Sometimes we're hardest on the people we care about the most."

Was he being too hard on Shayla? Hell, even his coach hadn't asked as much of him when they were just starting out, but he had to be harsh to keep some distance between them or risk hurting her again. He had shocked even himself the other night. His desire—no, *need*—for her had been so intense and all-consuming, he hadn't given a second thought to how rough he'd been in bed. If Zack from then had met Zack from now, he would have punched himself in the damn face.

"Heads up," Sadist warned.

His head jerked up, and he neatly caught the fight gloves Torment tossed down from the practice ring beside them.

"Blade Saw is on his way here, and he needs a partner," Torment said. "I was supposed to be coaching him and Homicide Hank, but Hank's wife just went into labor. It's their sixth kid. Or maybe seventh. No one can keep track. I don't know how he does it. I can't even handle one. Our little girl, Brianna, is more than a handful."

Zack curved his hands around the soft leather gloves. This was exactly what he needed to burn off some steam. Nothing relieved his tension more than a good session in the ring. But after losing it with Shayla in bed, he wasn't prepared to take that risk.

"No, thanks. I'm going for a run after Shayla's done." He tossed the gloves back up.

"Suit yourself." Torment caught them in one hand. "I like to help my fighters succeed. And if you're fighting the Predator, you'll need all the help you can get just to make it out of the ring alive."

Zack bristled. "I don't think it's me you need to worry about."

"So you are going to fight him?" Sadist asked.

Zack gave himself a mental kick for the slip. Staying out of the ring was easy when he was recruiting fighters, but being in the thick of things, part of a world of alpha egos and testosterone, made it damn hard to keep the promise he'd made to himself the night Okami died.

"I didn't say that. Might be that I'm done with Shayla in the three months before the membership expires, and I won't need to stick around."

Torment leaned over the ropes. "You won't solve her problem in three months. It took Fuzz and I four years to help her get where she is today. She came to us broken. She's far from fixed."

Curious, he asked, "How was she broken?"

Torment and Sadist shared a look. "The first year she joined, it was all about rehab," Torment said. "I had her bring in her X-rays so we could come up with a training program to help her get strong again. I never imagined bones could be broken like that from a fall down the stairs. It wasn't just her leg. Her ribs, shoulder, and arm had been broken. And her hand"—he held up his hands in a warding gesture—"was crushed."

Zack felt a prickle of warning sheet over his skin. "Crushed?"

"She let me take the X-rays to a doctor friend of mine, an orthopedic surgeon, because at first, I didn't know how to help her. He said the force necessary to cause many of the breaks couldn't have come from a fall."

The warning prickle turned into a five-alarm fire. What had happened to her in the years after he'd walked away?

"Did you ask her about it?"

Torment worked his hand into his glove. "She told me she was clumsy, and it was a bad fall."

"She's not clumsy."

Torment nodded. "She recovered quickly, probably because she was in such good shape, and she was determined to get better. She's one of the most dedicated fighters in the gym. She's here when I open the door in the morning, and unless she's working, she's usually one of the last people out at night. She went from barely being able to walk to becoming our top female fighter through an incredible force of will"—Torment shook the top rope—"right here in this ring."

Zack ran a finger along the lower rope, feeling the coarse fibers grate over his skin. Once upon a time, he'd been like that. From the day he walked into the Glenwood MMA gym, he wanted to be the best. He wanted to know he would never be powerless before another man, that there would never be another Matt who could beat him to a pulp in the alley. But more than that, he wanted to be worthy. He wanted to show the damn town—no, the world—that he could rise above his upbringing. He wanted to give Shayla something more than a trailer park kid who hadn't even finished high school.

How many times had he climbed into a practice ring without paying attention to the rough feel of the ropes, the tension that allowed them to flex when a fighter fell against them? He curled one hand around the rough fiber, testing the thickness and the strength, while at the back of his mind, he was pulling the ropes apart, climbing into the ring. The mat would be cool and firm under his feet, his opponent wary of facing Slayer in a fight.

"That's why her last four fights are such a mystery," Torment said, climbing through the ropes to join them on the mat. "She moved up to the next level and then slid down. If she loses one more fight, the title belt qualifier will be totally out of reach."

"She's afraid," Zack said, half to himself.

Sadist cocked his head to the side. "Afraid of what?"

"She's afraid to take a risk." He turned to Sadist. "You know what it's like climbing up the amateurs. You're on a roll, winning fight after fight, and then suddenly, you hit a wall. It takes a while to realize that when you get near the top, it's a whole new ball game. Your opponents are a different class of fighter. Suddenly, it's not enough to just know the technique. You need to be something more. You need to anticipate what your opponent is going to do and where he is going to be. You need to have the confidence to take a risk—to go beyond what you've learned and improvise. You need to have the strength to leave yourself vulnerable if you want to win."

"I'd say that's pretty spot-on," Sadist said. "Sounds like your head is still in the game."

Longing ripped through his body. One step and he would be back in the ring, gloves in his hand, a worthy adversary across from him. His fingers tightened around the rope. He could almost hear the buzz of the crowd, the blare of the speakers. He could almost feel the hard mat under his feet, smell the popcorn and hot dogs, the yeasty tang of beer, the sweat of the men who had fought before him. He could see the glare of the lights, the eager faces of the crowd. And then he imagined a scream, like the scream of Okami's wife when she realized her husband was dead.

"Not anymore."

Torment tossed the spare gloves in a box beside the ring. "You need more than your head in the game. You need your heart in it, too."

Zack had never talked about the Okami fight with anyone, never expressed his feelings of guilt or self-loathing. But Torment seemed to understand everything he couldn't say.

"You might want to keep an eye on your fighter," Torment continued, looking over his shoulder. "Looks like she's about to 12-6 Marty and get herself kicked out of the gym."

He looked up and saw Shayla poised over her opponent with her elbow in the air. A 12-6 was a downward elbow strike in which the elbow went from straight up to straight down and was illegal under the Unified Rules of Mixed Martial Arts because of the serious injuries that could result from its use.

"Jesus Christ. What did he do to piss her off?" He raised his voice to a shout. "Shilla. Stand the fuck down."

"She hates that name." Sadist chuckled. "We gave it to her when we saw her potential. We wanted to keep her motivated. Torment came up with a random number of fights she had to win to be able to change it—a number she'd only achieve if she made it to the top of the amateurs—and that became the Redemption rule."

"You're a bastard," Zack said to Torment. "Anyone ever tell you that?"

"I'm a man who gets what he wants." Torment gestured over to the mats, where Shayla was very clearly not standing down and Marty was in need of imminent saving. "I thought you were, too."

16

Shayla

"LET'S GO TELL THE PROMOTER YOU'RE HERE." SADIST PUSHES ME gently through the crowd in the ex-machine shop in Jack London Square, a popular venue on the Bay Area's underground fight club circuit.

Both he and the Predator, a permanent fixture in the underground fight scene, are taking a risk by coming out to support me tonight. Underground fighting is illegal in California and a big risk for any professional fighter or licensed amateur. The CSAC can take away a fighter's license or impose any manner of penalties for even showing up at an underground fight, much less participating. Not that it stops anyone. There is nothing like the raw, gritty, electric atmosphere of an underground fight.

"You shouldn't have come." I look back over my shoulder, half expecting to see a flash of yellow, but after Sadist changed his name, he had to lose the trappings that went with his Rampage persona, and that included his trademark yellow happy face tank top.

"We weren't going to leave you here alone with *him*. He's not part of your team." He shoots a glance at Zack, who is talking to Blade Saw. Of course, once the team heard I was fighting tonight, they came out in force, despite the risks. In addition to Sadist, Blade Saw, and the Predator, my entourage includes Homicide Hank and Doctor Death.

After I register, I warm up in the corner until the whistle blows, signaling the start of the first match. The fights are rotated through various locations, and this venue is rougher than most. Four metal poles with a thick rope strung around them mark the boundaries of the ring. Worn mats have been spread over the concrete floor, and the air smells of wood chips and diesel with a hint of sweat. Huge spotlights set up around the perimeter of the ring provide the only light.

The first few fights result in lots of blood, broken noses, and a few broken bones. Rank amateurs never know when to hold back. Their fights are usually over in less than a minute with one or sometimes both fighters being carried out of the ring to the medic, who has a temporary station near a workbench in the far corner.

"Looks like there is only one other woman here tonight," Zack says, coming up behind me. "She's in your weight class, so you should be evenly matched."

There are no weight classes in the underground. It is a free-for-all where smaller or lighter fighters compete against larger, heavier opponents. The only rules are that men are not allowed to fight women, and the fight ends when someone either passes out or taps out to indicate they give up. Given

Zack's protective nature, I'm surprised he set up the fight, especially with the risk that I might be up against a fighter heavier than me.

"It's hard not to think about the last four fights." I grimace when one of the fighters in the ring staggers backward and whacks his head on the metal post as he falls. My hand flies to my head, and I feel for the nonexistent bump. I've had a few headaches since my fall, but nothing I can't handle.

"You've done some good training over the last week. You'll be fine."

"That's the nicest thing you've said to me all week." Zack has been nothing but professional since our awkward conversation at my apartment, pushing me harder in training than I've ever been pushed before. Although it is what we agreed, I hadn't expected him to be so distant or so cold. And I certainly didn't expect him to be so mean. From his impatience and sarcastic, cutting remarks to his brutal routines, he makes even Torment look chilled out, and that's saying something. I can't joke with him, much less talk to him, and I have felt his emotional absence like a hole in my chest.

Pain flickers across his face so quickly, I wonder if I saw it. "Nice isn't going to win you the title belt."

My name is called, and I check my tape. I'm not wearing fight gloves, but I have taped my hands for the extra power it gives my punches and to compensate for the weakness left over from my horrific accident in New York.

"I know. I just…" I hesitate to say what's on my mind. But I'm in the underground. There are no rules here. It's a place where you can fight any kind of fight, even if it's inside you. It's a place where you can take a risk. "I miss you."

Embarrassed, I turn to leave, but before I can even take a step away, Zack's warm hand covers my nape. He pushes my ponytail aside and presses his lips to my skin. No words, but the gesture tells me so much more.

My pulse kicks up a notch, and warmth floods through my body. "That was better than a shot of adrenaline," I whisper.

"Whatever you need." He kisses my neck again, and then gives me a playful smack. "Now go kick some butt."

I look back over my shoulder and glare. "I hope the irony of giving me a demeaning slap on the ass as you send me off to battle in an underground fight ring isn't lost on you."

Zack chuckles, and between his laughter, the cheers of the team, his confidence in my ability, and the endorphin rush from his secret kiss, I am burning with energy when I step through the ropes.

My opponent, Elsa Blome, is a tall, blond woman with strong features. She is about two inches taller than me with a commensurately long reach, and her low level of body fat makes me want to give up the protein bars and just live on shakes. Someone shouts out "Evil Elsa" seconds after the whistle blows, and she gives me an evil grin.

We touch fists, and everything fades away except the woman in front of me. Adrenaline surges through my body, heightening my senses and throwing Elsa into stark relief. Usually, the adrenaline rush is accompanied by a sliver of tension and a heaping dose of anxiety about how the fight will impact my standing on the circuit. But I feel none of that here. In the grand scheme of things, this fight doesn't matter. I am fighting tonight because I want to fight and not because I have to win.

I track the smallest movement of Elsa's eyes, the flex of her bicep, the slight tremble of her thigh as she presses forward with a kick that I easily evade. Taking advantage of her loss of balance, I smash my fist into her cheek. She recovers quickly, and I am forced into fight stance to fend off her attack with an overhand left, followed by a right. Blood trickles over my brow, and as I wipe it away, I catch sight of Zack now up against the ropes, his face taut and hard.

Too late, I realize my mistake. Even the smallest lack of focus can be an opening, and Elsa takes the opportunity to sweep my injured leg and smash it with her instep as I fall. As if she knows my leg is my weakness, she jumps and smashes her heel down on my shin in a move that would be illegal in a sanctioned fight. Somehow, I manage to knock her off balance as I go down, and we both hit the ground hard.

Pain fuzzes my brain, and I am wrenched out of the ring and flung back into the nightmare that was the evening Damian decided to destroy me.

"I need a drink." Damian tosses the bat aside and crosses the room to his vodka bottle, still sitting on the floor beside his chair.

I suck in one painful breath after another. Even though I just want to lie here and die, a part of me won't give up. Despite the mind-searing pain, I am still driven by the need to escape, and an opportunity has just presented itself. I am beside the door. All I have to do is open it.

Even if I can't get down the two flights of stairs to the street, someone will hear me scream.

Pushing myself to my feet with my good arm, I grit my teeth against the pain and unlock the door. Damian's head whips around as the dead bolt thunks into place.

I freeze. Just for a moment. And then I yank open the door.

The hesitation costs me. Damian manages to cross the room just as I reach the top of the stairs. I open my mouth to scream, but I can't take a deep enough breath before the pain in my ribs cuts off my voice.

"Where do you think you're going?" He grabs my uninjured hand and yanks me toward the door.

"Let me go." My voice is a harsh whisper, my throat bruised from the moment he wrapped his hand around my neck. "I won't tell anyone what you did. I'll leave, and this will be over. You won't have to see me again. I'll even leave the company if you want. Just…please. Let me go."

"Shay!"

Zack's voice yanks me out of the memory. He has one hand on the ropes like he's about to jump into the ring, but I have come a long way since I left Glenwood. I don't need to be protected anymore. The fight only ends if I tap out or pass out. And I'm not ready to do either.

I grit my teeth against the pain and push myself to my feet. My vision blurs, and I shake away the cobwebs. Elsa is up only a half second later, and I move in to strike. It's the kind of risk I don't usually take in a fight. With my brain still fuzzy and my mobility hampered, I'm vulnerable, and my usual tactic would be to fall back and wait for an opportunity to get her on the ground where I have more control. But this is the underground. I've taken one risk tonight. I can take another.

Elsa throws a couple of low kicks, gunning for my sore leg, but I go on the offensive, stuff a takedown, and land a hard knee in her stomach. I go in hard with a right hook and follow through with punch after punch, forcing Elsa to backtrack. She is in all kinds of trouble. I hammer her with punches on the ground and sink in a rear naked choke until she taps out.

The Redemption team cheers, and the ref holds up my hand in a victory salute. Two fighters help Elsa out of the ring. Blade Saw jumps up and down, pumping his fist in the air, but it's Zack's smile that lights me up inside. At least it does, until his gaze focuses on something behind me, and the smile gives way to a shout.

"Bitch. That wasn't a fair fight." Someone grabs my ponytail and yanks me backward. I fly into the ropes, bounce forward, and throw myself to the side, grateful for the skill and training that allows me to stay on my feet to meet my attacker.

But there is no fight. Zack is in the ring, pounding on the dude who grabbed me like he's going for the gold.

The crowd lets out a collective gasp. Zack's fight name reverberates through the shop. Even after four years of retirement, he is magnificent. The fighter in me can't help but appreciate the speed of his takedown, the power of his fists, the ripple of his muscles, and the brutal submission that gives my attacker no option but to surrender before I can even protest that Zack is fighting my fight.

With his bones at risk of breaking, my attacker taps out. Zack releases him right away. He pushes to his feet and glares down at the idiot who I now recognize as one of Elsa's friends. Fighters are a protective alpha bunch. In all probability, Elsa's friend didn't like to see blood streaming down her face, and although there isn't anything he can do in a sanctioned fight, the underground is curiously far more forgiving.

"I think we're done here." I put a hand on Zack's arm, knowing he'll only just have started coming down from the zone. I have only just started coming down from mine.

As if he is oblivious to the fact that we are still in the ring, he slides one hand behind my neck, pulls me close, and kisses me. Deeply. Fiercely. Possessive in his touch. The crowd goes wild, but not as wild as the pounding of my heart.

I pretend not to notice Sadist's smug expression as Zack's arm lands on my shoulders as soon as we are clear of the ring, nor do I respond to Doctor Death's question about how long we've been getting it on. Instead, I let Zack help me limp through the crowd, past the notebooks and body parts being offered up for his signature, the people desperate to know if he's coming out of retirement, and the fangirls wishing they were me.

"I could have taken him," I say when we stop near the entrance where I've stowed my fight bag and clothes.

"I know, but when he grabbed you, it wasn't really a choice."

"Nice to know that much hasn't changed. I felt like I was in high school all over again."

Zack's lips quiver at the corners, and he gestures to a chair near the door. "Have a seat and let me check you over. You took a bad bump to the head. Not good after you just had a concussion."

"It was a very minor concussion and an even more minor bump." I sit on the chair, and Zack kneels in front of me, sifting his hands through my hair.

"You looked dazed for a few moments after you fell."

"Stop worrying." I lean forward and press a kiss to his forehead. "It only lasted a few seconds. I have a hard head."

His forehead creases in consternation. "Maybe we should get you checked out again. Coming so soon after that concussion—"

"Zack." I cup his face in my hands. "I went back to the doctor and got the all clear after my four days off. He knows what I do. He said a few bumps on the head were okay. If I was really worried, I'd tell you. Okay?"

He grunts an affirmation, and I release him.

"Are we good? Can we get out of here now?"

"What about your leg?" He runs his hands down my leg, from my fight shorts to my ankle and back again, practiced and efficient.

"You seem to know what you're doing."

Zack shrugs. "After I retired, I got my high school diploma, a degree in exercise science, and a DPT specializing in sports medicine physiotherapy. I was going crazy sitting around the house reliving the fight over and over again."

"You have a degree?" Emotion wells up in my throat. We had both talked about going to college when we were young, but Zack dropped out of high school to look after his sisters and never had a chance to go back.

He nods, but I see the swell of pride in his chest, the ghost of a smile on his lips.

"That's fantastic. I'm so happy for you. Why aren't you working as a physio?"

He squeezes my calf, his hands warm and strong. "MEFC came to me with the recruiting job just after we found out Viv's leukemia had returned, and I negotiated her medical insurance as a condition of my employment. I didn't mind giving it up. I enjoyed working with athletes, but recruiting keeps me more directly involved in the sport."

"Well, you can keep up your skills with me." I wince when he touches a particularly sore spot.

Zack frowns and runs his fingers over that area of my shin again. "Is that the hardware in your leg?"

"Yeah. It usually doesn't bother me."

"It's working its way out." He takes my hand and runs my finger along my leg where there is a ridge under my skin. "You might want to reconsider getting it removed."

"It's fine. The orthopedic surgeon who did the surgery four years ago said it wasn't necessary. And I don't want to go through another operation with months of downtime." I also don't want to rehash old memories. Better to keep everything locked up inside.

"It's not broken or sprained," he says, standing. "I think you'll have some bad bruises. We'll get some ice on it right away."

I nod at the crowd that has gathered behind Zack as I pull on my track pants. "Maybe not right away. Your fan club is waiting."

"They can wait. My girl needs me." He pulls me to my feet.

"How about I grab an ice pack from the medic while you spread the Slayer love "around?" I suggest. "But no butts or cleavage. Even friendship has limits."

Zack talks with his fans, signs autographs, and poses for pictures while I ice my leg at the medic station. After we're done, I pack up and we head out into the night. During the day, Jack London Square on the Oakland waterfront bustles with activity from the busy farmer's market to the trails for rental bikes. At night, there is a different kind of buzz. Couples walk in the moonlight, and groups of friends head to the open-air movies and restaurants that line the water's edge. The air is soft and warm and fresh with the scent of the ocean.

As we pass the edge of the machine shop, Zack grabs my hand and pulls me into the alley. Next thing I know, I am up against the side of the shop, deep in the shadows, Zack's body plastered against me as he kisses me hard, stealing the breath from my lungs.

"What's that for?" I ask, gasping for breath.

"Proud of you," he says. "That was a great fight. You don't know what it does to me seeing you in the ring like that. I loved watching you dance, but I really love watching you fight."

"You've been holding that in all this time?"

"Wasn't easy."

I give a half-hearted shrug, although I'm happy dancing inside. "I did let her drop me in the first minute."

"It's all about the finish." He feathers kisses across my cheeks, sliding his lips along my forehead and down my nose to devour my mouth again. "And sweetheart. That was one hell of a finish."

A grin splits my face, spreading ear to ear. I am still riding the high of the fight, and I feel ready to take on the world. I want to do something I've never done before. Something crazy and wild like Zack and I used to do. Something I haven't done since we were together.

"I want to celebrate." I wrap my arms around his neck and pull him close. "With you."

His eyes spark with interest. "What did you have in mind?"

"There's an abandoned boathouse down by the pier. The last time we came here to watch the Predator fight, someone broke the lock and we went inside and had a party. Maybe we could…" I trail off when Zack raises an eyebrow.

"I'm beginning to think Redemption is a bad influence— drinking, underground fighting, breaking and entering, gossip, hookups…"

"You're just jealous of our little family."

He laughs. "Maybe I am."

We make our way to the boathouse undetected, and I tug on the broken lock." Are you sure you want to do this? If we're caught…"

"I don't have much to lose as a recruiter, and I can't really do much more wrong than I've already done." He reaches over me and pushes the door all the way open.

There it is. He just can't let it go. Every time I think he's gotten over it, he says something that makes me worry he is never going to forgive himself for what happened with Okami.

"You fought in the ring today and everything turned out okay." I clasp his hand and lead him into the dim, dusty boathouse. "Did you ever imagine that scenario the day you walked into Redemption?"

"Fighting in an underground ring with you beside me?" He shakes his head. "No. Not in my wildest dreams."

"Same for me." I put my arms around his neck and pull him close. "If someone had told me the day you walked into Redemption that my career wasn't over yet, and one month later, I'd be fighting in the underground with you as my coach, I wouldn't have believed them. I almost didn't recognize myself tonight."

"I did." Zack brushes his lips over my forehead. "I saw you in that ring, and I thought, 'there's my Shay.'"

"Zack…" I'm not his anymore, and I'm certainly not the girl he remembers.

"You know what else I thought?" He feathers kisses along my jaw.

"What did you think?" I whisper.

"I missed her."

17

Shayla

"STAY THERE. I'M GOING TO CHECK THINGS OUT." As IF HE regrets sharing his thoughts, Zack turns abruptly and slides the rusty bolt across the door. Then he walks the perimeter of the boathouse, as if staking his territory.

Light filters through torn curtains, casting long shadows on the dusty, plank floor. I recognize the sharp smell of turpentine from the summer Zack took a job with a painting company and the acrid scent of gasoline.

When he's done his walk-around, he leans against a rough wooden pillar, arms folded, spearing me in place with the intensity of his gaze. Behind him, I can see the bay through the boathouse windows and closer, two tarp-covered boats, a long wooden workbench, and an odd collection of tools.

"Everything check out?" I take a step toward him.

He holds up a warning hand. "Stay."

"Why?"

"I want to look at you."

With a laugh, I hold out my arms. "Here I am. I look pretty much the same as when you last saw me two minutes ago."

"Take off your clothes."

Ah. That kind of looking. The kind of looking where scars can't be hidden in the darkness of a bedroom or beneath the shelter of one's clothes. "When I said celebrate, I was thinking of a bottle of champagne."

"When I said take off your clothes," he says, his voice husky and low, "I was thinking of now."

A thrill of fear shoots through my body. Unable to resist the challenge, I take a few steps toward the sheet-covered couch. "Oops. I seem to be walking."

He reacts so quickly, I barely have time to process what is happening. One minute, I'm a few steps from the door, and the next, I'm pressed tight against his chest, his arm around my waist like a steel band.

"You sure you want to play this game?" He spins me and reaches around to unzip my jacket. I shiver as the cool air brushes over my skin. All I have underneath is the sports bra I wore to fight and far too many scars.

"I don't know. This bra is almost impossible to get off."

"You want it off, it's coming off." He slides his hands under the elastic and over my breasts, pushing my bra up as he goes.

"You didn't wait for me to say yes," I whisper.

Zack works the bra over my arms. "You told me last time I was good to go until you said no, and I've never had a problem getting you out of your clothes." He pulls the tight material over my head and drops it on the floor beside my jacket.

"You make me sound like I was stripping down for you every chance I got."

He cups my breasts, squeezing gently. "It was an effort to hold you back."

"What?" I look over my shoulder and glare. "So now you think I'm doing this because I lose control when it comes to you?"

He gives an arrogant shrug. "It happens."

"Women tear off their clothes in your presence and—"

"Yeah."

"I didn't need to know that." Just as I didn't need to know that he dated other girls before I became legal. Although we had a tacit understanding not to discuss that part of his life, it didn't stop me from getting insanely jealous when I heard the rumors. As far as I was concerned, he was mine. He had been mine since I was eight years old, and I couldn't stand the thought of him with someone else the way he couldn't be with me. Just as I can't stand it now, even though our future is uncertain.

"I like that you didn't need to know that." He presses a kiss to my shoulder. "I like that you're jealous."

"I'm not. A whole stadium of ring girls could tear off their clothes in front of you, and I wouldn't care." I tremble as his hands dive beneath my fight shorts, warm fingers stroking my skin. "And just to get your ego back in check, I don't ever remember tearing my clothes off in the frenzy of lust you seem to think I was constantly in around you."

"What about my twenty-second birthday when I won that underground fight in Seattle?" He shoves my clothing over

my hips—panties, fight shorts, and track pants—all in one go.
"When we got back to the hotel, you told me you'd never
seen anything as hot as watching me fight. You tore off your
clothes and pushed me on the bed." He groans and rubs his
hand through his hair. "Hell. I think about that night all the
time. I wanted you so bad. I thought I was gonna fucking die if
I couldn't have you."

I remember that night, how he wouldn't let me touch him,
even though he freely touched me. There wasn't a part of my
body he didn't kiss that night. I had never felt as loved as I did
in that hotel room.

"And what about the night of your prom?" he says softly.
"You were so desperate to show me your sexy lingerie, you
broke into the school library and used a pair of scissors to cut off
your dress when the zipper got stuck."

God, the prom. He remembers everything. I hadn't even
planned to go, because I had no date. When all my school
friends socialized after school in sports or clubs and partied in
the evenings and on weekends, I danced. And when prom dates
were being set up, none of the guys thought to ask me, because
they knew I was with Zack. But for some reason, I felt awkward
asking him to the prom. He was older than everyone else, and
high school had not been a good experience for him. I couldn't
imagine he would want to go back.

Until he showed up at my house on prom night in a rented
tux with a corsage in his hand.

I don't think he expected my memories of the prom to be all
about him. How I thought my heart would stop beating when

I opened the door. How he kept his cool despite Matt putting him down. How his entire face lit up when I came down the stairs in a simple pink chiffon dress that I had worn for my cousin's wedding. And how I spent the entire night in his arms, wishing I could be there forever. Or at least until I could get him alone and convince him to break his damn rule about waiting until I was eighteen to have sex with me.

"Okay." I shrug. "So maybe there were a few times."

"There were more." He kneels behind me and helps me step out of my clothes. "I remember each and every time. Just like I'm gonna remember how you were all over me outside the machine shop, telling me you want to *celebrate*."

"Seriously?" I turn to face him. "I was all over you?"

"Yeah." He grins. "It was hot."

"Just for the record, I was not all over you, Zachary Grayson. And *celebrate* is not a dirty word."

He clasps my hand and presses it against his shaft, hard beneath his fly. "You wanted to put your hand here."

My lips quiver with a smile. "So now you're a mind reader, are you?"

Zack licks his lips. "You wanted to do something naughty."

I pull my hand away and reach for his belt. "Maybe I was thinking naughty as in eating a huge amount of carbs or processed sugar." I undo his belt and tear open his fly. "Naughty doesn't necessarily mean I want to sex it up somewhere people might find us."

His eyes gleam in the dim light. "So if I slid my hand between your legs, I wouldn't find you wet?"

"Hmm. I'm not sure. Let me see." I trail my fingers ever so

slowly down my body, between my breasts, over my stomach and my mound. The pulse in his neck throbs when I slide a finger between my labia, and a sheen of sweat glistens on his brow.

"Check it out." I hold up my finger for him to see.

Zack draws my finger to his lips and then sucks it into his warm mouth. "You taste the same," he murmurs after he releases me. "Sweet."

"Do you taste the same?"

He releases a ragged breath and puts his hands on my shoulders. "Down on your knees, beautiful girl. I'll let you find out."

I drop down in front of him, my knees hitting the rough wood floor with a soft thud. In no time at all, I have his jeans over his hips and my hand wrapped around his thick cock. He is hot and heavy in my hand. *Delicious.*

"I never got to play the other night."

"You won't be playing now." He captures me with his gaze, so dark and intense, I shiver. "Open for me." Zack cups my jaw, rubbing his thumb over my bottom lip as he opens my mouth, giving me yet another taste of his new, dominant self. Or maybe he was always that way and I never got a chance to find out.

My body heats, liquid fire singeing my veins. I lean forward and lick the tip of his cock. Zack groans and sifts his hand through my hair. I swirl my tongue around the silky head, trying to remember what he liked and whether he tasted as salty and sweet as he does now. With my hand tight around the base, I draw my tongue along the underside of his shaft. His fingers tighten in my hair, and when I look up, he is watching, his breath ragged, his gaze fixed on me.

I have tamed the beast.

"Take me," he commands. "All of me. I want to see those sweet lips around my cock."

My cheeks flush as I draw him deep into my mouth. In the years we were intimate, I gave Zack a lot of oral pleasure, although I don't remember him being as big as he is now.

Not that I would tell him…

"Touch yourself," he murmurs as I pull out on an upstroke. "Pinch your nipples."

"Don't hold back your bossy self," I grumble. "Tell me what you really want."

"I want you to stop talking and suck me, sweetheart. I want to feel your hot, sassy mouth wrapped around my cock, licking me until I can't take anymore. And then I want to come inside your hot, wet pussy." He tightens his grip on my hair and tugs me forward.

Arousal throbs between my thighs. I never thought words could have such power.

I draw in a deep breath, inhale the faint scent of soap mixed with the familiar scent of his body, and take him deeper, gliding my tongue along his shaft while I rub my taut nipple between my thumb and forefinger. I can feel every tug in my clit, every pinch as a pulse of heat in my core.

"Fuck. You have a sweet mouth. Take me deeper." He jerks forward, and the head of his cock hits the back of my throat. I gag and pull away. It's been a long time since I let anyone go so deep—since him—and back then, he was different, slower and more gentle. Not the forceful presence he is now.

"Relax." Zack's face becomes thoughtful, and he pushes in again, slowly this time.

When he draws out, I bite down on his crown with the edge of my teeth like he showed me when we first started exploring each other, increasing the pressure until he grunts with pleasure. I relax my throat and then suck, my mouth moving up and down his shaft.

His hand fists my hair, pulling me closer. "You're going to kill me."

Wild with desire, I drop one hand between my legs to stroke my clit as I grasp the base of his cock with the other.

"Christ. You're so fucking sexy. I'm not going to last." He tugs on my shoulders, and I release his cock with a soft pop that makes him hiss in a breath as I stand.

"You did that on purpose to drive me crazy."

"Are you feeling crazy?" Released of all my inhibitions, I do the equivalent of waving a red flag in front of a bull, knowing my bull would never use his horns.

"Over to the bench." He spins me around and lightly smacks my ass. "I want you the way I wanted to take you on Torment's desk. I'm tired of jerking off in the shower to a fantasy that can come true."

"What exactly did you want to do with me on Torment's desk?" I look over my shoulder, teasing. "Curious minds want to know."

A low, warning growl rumbles from his chest. He comes up behind me and curves his hand around my throat, just enough that I can feel the pressure but not enough to cut off my air.

"I'll do whatever the hell I want with you if I know it turns you on."

Nothing has ever aroused me like this. The warning press of his palm on my throat. His commanding presence. His hot, hard body against me. The words that speak to my deepest unspoken needs. A shudder of need ripples through my body, so fierce, I can't hide it.

"I can feel your pulse pound," he murmurs in my ear. He roughly kicks my legs apart and slides a thick finger through my folds. "We never got a chance to explore what really gets you off, and I have a feeling we have more in common than we ever imagined."

"I don't think—"

Oh God. His finger curls to brush against my clit, sending a flush of arousal through my veins.

"What turns you on? Is it this?" He tightens his hand on my throat. "Or is it this?" He pushes his finger inside me, and the sudden burn of pleasure makes me gasp.

He presses his lips to my ear as he holds me immobile, stroking deeper as my insides clench around him. "I think you respond to giving up control."

"No." I grit my teeth and will my body not to respond to the hand on my throat, the huge, heavy body behind me, the relentless thrust and stroke of his finger in my most intimate place.

"Yes, sweetheart."

"I'm not interested in control freaks who want to boss me around." Although Damian wasn't controlling when we first got together, his growing insecurities in our last year together manifested in a need to know where I was and who I was with at all times. Sometimes, he showed up unannounced at bars or restaurants, and I began to suspect he was checking my phone. When I told Matt what was going on, he flew to New York to have a chat with Damian. Things were better for a few months after that, and then Damian was fired.

"I can't." My voice catches, and I shudder. "I can't go through that again."

His entire body goes rigid—and he spins me to face him.

"What do you mean *again*?"

"Nothing. It was a slip of the tongue."

His eyes narrow, and I can feel his anger surge to the surface in a protective wave. "You've always been a terrible liar."

"Maybe I want to do something other than talk about the past when I'm naked in a boathouse and my friends will be coming to look for me soon." I force a laugh, but Zack isn't fooled.

He studies me for a long moment as if he can draw out my secrets with just a look. When no secrets are forthcoming, he brushes his thumb over my lower lip, and then he captures my mouth, igniting a fire inside me. He owns me with that kiss, claims me, sweeps everything from my mind except the feel of his hot hard body against me. His tongue pushes between my lips, ever so slowly, as if he has all the time in the world and our bodies aren't burning for each other, as if his cock isn't pressing insistently against my stomach, and my arousal is not trickling down the inside of my thigh. Our mouths fused together, as he walks me backward to the table on the other side of the boathouse.

Zack tugs off his shirt and spreads it over the table. "Face down. Legs apart. Please."

Laughter bubbles in my chest, beating away the shadows of the past. "You don't have to say please. I like bossy in the bedroom. Just not anywhere else."

"Good to know." He gives a satisfied grunt. "Hold on." He leans over me, spreads my hands wide, and curls my fingers around the rough edge of the table.

With a firm thrust of his thigh, he widens my legs, and then his fingers find my labia to torture and tease.

"Zack…"

Warm hands spread out over my back, stroking gently before sliding down to cup my ass. I tremble in anticipation, but he won't be rushed. He feathers kisses up my spine, over my shoulders, his breath hot on my nape. Beautiful sensations make my body tingle from my head to my toes.

"Please…"

"You don't need to say please." He chuckles, repeating my words. "I've got you, sweetheart. I've just got to grab a condom."

"No. It's okay. I'm on the pill." I want to feel him, bare inside me. Need him to fill me, push away the darkness and the memories, drown me in a sea of pleasure.

"Are you safe?"

"I'm safe. I would never put you at risk."

One hand finds my hip, holds me in place as the smooth head of his cock teases my entrance, gliding through my wetness.

"You're ready for me."

"Very ready."

"Feel me."

He pushes into me, and I feel like I could drown in this moment. I breathe deep, loving the sensation of being filled, stretched, utterly complete. He surrounds me, protects me, makes me feel more than I've felt since we parted ways.

Emotion wells up in my chest, Unexpected. Unwanted. People aren't supposed to cry when they are having sex. But the pleasure is cracking me open, and the sadness is leaking out, dripping down my cheeks in a waterfall of tears.

He pulls back and thrusts in again, slow and steady, like he has all the time in the world, like he is totally in control. I wiggle against him, push back to meet his thrusts. I want him lost like me, overwhelmed by passion, unable to think of anything but the burning need to climax.

"Slow down. I want to enjoy you." He smacks his hand over my ass, shocking me still, but the pain turns into a sensual burn that rips a guttural groan from my throat. "Christ. You tempt a man beyond reason."

One hand thuds onto the table beside me, and the other slides around my hip. And God, oh God, he knows just how to touch me. His slick fingers slide my moisture up and around my clit until I am out of my mind, shaking, aching for release.

"Hold on."

I clutch the edge of the table, and he thrusts faster, harder, stroking deep. His fingers circle closer, feathering every so lightly over my clit. I rest my forehead on his shirt, breathe in his scent as the table squeaks across the floor.

My orgasm cracks through me like a bolt of lightning, making me cry out. My pussy clenches around him in wave after wave of molten heat as he thrusts inside me, drawing out my pleasure. His body goes rigid against me, and his hands grip my hips so hard, I know I'll have bruises tomorrow. I tense in anticipation. Suddenly, he pulls out and groans. Hot liquid splashes over my back. Only when he smooths his essence over my skin do I realize what he has done. Something so primitive and primal, it awakens an almost animalistic want inside me.

Marked.

He marked me.

I push up, look over my shoulder, and almost don't recognize his face, his eyes so fierce and full of male pride.

"You okay?" he asks, leaning down, blanketing me with his warmth.

"I'm not complaining. I thought it was kinda hot."

"You're hot. Sexy. And so damn sweet." He presses soft kisses to my nape, feathers his lips down my spine, making me feel loved all over. I've had sex, but nothing can compare to being with Zack. He knows me, sees me, touches me inside and out...

I give myself a mental shake. I can't go down this road. Thinking of this as anything other than a physical—albeit highly pleasurable—act is to open myself up to a world of pain and heartache.

As if he can sense my emotional withdrawal, Zack pushes himself to stand. "Don't move. I'll find something to clean you up with. There's a sink in the far corner."

"Sure." I watch him cross the floor over my shoulder,

tension etched in every line of his shoulders. "Is everything okay with you?"

Water splashes in the sink. Drawers and cupboards bang as he searches for a cloth. He heard me. This place isn't that big, and I wasn't talking softly.

"Zack?"

Silence.

A few moments later, he returns with a warm cloth that he runs gently over my back, washing away his mark, making me clean. After he returns to the sink, I hunt for my clothes, strewn across the floor.

"What did you mean by *again*?" he asks as he tugs on his jeans. His words almost sound casual, but his tone is anything but.

Damn. I should have known he wouldn't let it go.

"I thought we were done with that conversation," I say, turning away.

"We can't be done with a conversation we haven't even started."

"It's nothing." I pull on my clothes while he leans against the table, watching me in silence. But even his silent disapproval is not enough for me to reveal how deeply I am broken, how I can't trust myself not to make a mistake again. All the men I have cared about have hurt me. Things I thought would make me happy brought me pain.

"Not good enough. You were mine, Shay. Mine. I knew everything about you. And now I'm missing seven years of your life, and you're making me think something bad happened during that time."

"You didn't want those years," I remind him. "So you have

no right to ask me about them. And it doesn't matter what happened then. What matters is what's happening now."

He stares at me so intently, I feel like he can see my soul. "What *is* happening now?"

Now, I am afraid my walls will crack. Now, he's already carrying the burden of Okami's death, and I don't want him saddled with the guilt of my mistakes. Now, I know he will go hunting for Damian if I tell him what happened, and if he finds him, I don't know what he will do.

"I don't know," I answer honestly. "I don't want to get involved, but this…"

"What is this?"

"Sex?" I shrug. "Two people having a good time?"

His face smooths. "Is that all this is to you?"

"Yes." I gesture to the door, dipping my head so he doesn't see the lie on my face. "We'd better get going. The fights will be over, and the team will be looking for us to join them for a drink."

"I won't be able to make it. I'm flying to Seattle first thing tomorrow."

"Oh." I scramble to hide my disappointment, but what did I expect after pushing him away? "What about coaching?"

"You still have Torment and Fuzzy."

I'm not sure if he means he's done with coaching me and I should train with them again or if they are just going to fill in for him over the weekend, but I don't ask because I don't want to be rejected all over again.

Our feet thud softly on the wooden floor as we cross the

boathouse. Zack pulls open the door for me, and I breathe in the scent of the ocean as I step into the cool night air.

We walk back to the machine shop in silence. I should be relieved that I don't have to answer any more questions or tell any more lies, but as the emotional distance fills the space between us, all I feel is an overwhelming fear that I'll lose him all over again.

18

Zack

ZACK TURNED HIS RENTAL SUV ONTO A TREE-LINED STREET IN the heart of Bellevue. He'd bought the house for Viv and Lily after his first year on the professional circuit, letting them choose what would be their first true family home. Lily had fallen in love with the Seattle suburb's trails, woods, and open spaces, perfect for her two rescue dogs. Viv had been drawn by the house's unique architectural design, a cross between a Swiss chalet and a Gothic manor, all tall peaks and angles, with fancy moldings and painted fairy-tale blue.

He tried to visit once or twice every month, coordinating his flights so he could spend weekends with his sisters. When Viv had been ill, the visits were a necessity, but now he came to help out around the house and for the pleasure of their company.

A screech startled him when he walked in the door. Moments later, he was wrapped tight in soft arms, his chest engulfed in a mass of brown curls.

"Lily." He gave his sister a hug. "It's good to be home. How are you doing?"

"Good." She gave him a last squeeze, moving aside quickly as her two golden Labs jumped up to greet him.

Zack kneeled down and ruffled Chloe's fur. Ringo nosed her aside for some attention, and he gave the pup a rub. One day, if he ever settled down, he'd get his own dogs and a big place for them to run, although the way things were going, it wasn't going to be any time soon.

Turning his attention back to Lily, he chatted with her about her accounting firm and new fiancé. Upbeat and energetic, Lily always managed to accomplish more in a day than many people could do in a week. Even when Viv had been ill, she had managed to keep up with her marathon training, run her business, look after the house and dogs, and volunteer at the hospital where Viv was being treated. Of the three siblings, she was the one who had managed to overcome the trauma of the past and succeed both personally and professionally.

"Where's Viv?"

"She's in her studio, finishing up a few designs. I'll go make some lunch while you have a chat." She gave his arm a squeeze. "How long are you staying?"

"I'm just here for the weekend. I took some time off…"

"A vacation?" Lily's eyes widened. "Since when do you ever take vacations?"

Zack shrugged, reluctant to share his reasons with Lily. Although he loved his sister, she had a habit of asking too many questions—uncomfortable questions to which he was pretty damn sure he wouldn't have any answers. "I had some stuff I wanted to do in the Bay Area."

Her lips pressed together, and she lifted an eyebrow, but he made a quick escape before the interrogation could begin and headed to Viv's studio.

"Hey, Viv." He walked into what had once been a spacious dining room but was now Viv's jewelry-making studio, the bright-yellow walls lined with shelves filled with boxes of beads and wires, gemstones, and soldering equipment.

Viv looked up and smiled. Her blond hair had grown out since he'd seen her last and now reached her shoulders. She loved bright colors, and today she wore a brilliant turquoise shirt that made her hair seem even lighter than it was.

"Hey yourself, Big Brother."

He crossed the floor to give her a hug, and she stood to greet him. She had never regained the weight she lost during her first battle with leukemia, and he worried that she wouldn't have the strength for another round of chemo if her illness returned.

"You were just here a few weeks ago. How come we get another visit?"

"I don't spend as much time with you as it is." He took a seat on the stool beside her, careful not to disturb the beads she had placed over the surface of her worktable. "And I took some time off to stick around in San Francisco, so it was a quick flight to come home."

"Well, it's always nice to see you. Hopefully, you'll get to meet Lily's fiancé this time. He's quite the catch."

As always, Viv never poked or pried into his business. Not

that he ever resented Lily's questions, but even as a boy, he'd valued his privacy. Viv had always respected his need to keep his thoughts to himself.

"What's he like?"

"I'm not telling you anything, except to say he's a nice guy and he treats Lily well." Viv grinned. "The days of you trying to scare away our boyfriends, following us to parties, or showing up at Pine Ridge lookout to ruin our make-out sessions are long gone. Save that overprotectiveness for the woman of your dreams."

He winced as her lighthearted comment hit too close to home.

A frown creased her brow. "What's wrong?"

"I found Shayla." It was a relief to say the three words that had so drastically altered his life in such a short time.

Viv's face softened. "In San Francisco?"

"Yeah."

"How is she?"

"Married." Fuck. Of all the things to say. Not *fine*. Or *she's doing MMA*. Or *she quit being a ballerina*. Or *she's more beautiful than when I left*. Just *married*. But that's what had been on his mind since he'd seen her again. Shayla had belonged to another man when she was supposed to be Zack's forever. "She *was* married," he corrected. "She isn't now. It didn't work out."

"Oh, Zack." She covered her hand with his and shared his silence. Viv didn't judge, didn't offer her opinion unless he asked. She understood that sometimes he just needed to talk, and she was always there to listen.

His heart squeezed in his chest at the thought that one day Viv might not be there with her big heart and her gentle smile.

And then he pushed the thought away. She'd just had a few tests. Nothing more.

"I'm coaching her."

"I thought she was a ballet dancer." She settled back on her stool and picked up a strand of wire.

"She was in an accident and broke her leg, so she couldn't dance anymore. She took up MMA. Now she's burning up the amateur circuit. I saw her when I went to her gym to recruit another fighter. I thought I might be able to help her make it to the pros."

"So you managed to fix things between you?" Viv was the only person he'd told about what happened the night he left Shayla. It was the first time she had outwardly disapproved of his actions. If Shayla hadn't moved to New York two days later, he wouldn't have been able to stop her from trying to untangle the mess he had made.

"Not completely."

"Ah. Trouble in paradise."

He scrubbed his hand over his face, returning to the one thing he couldn't get out of his mind. "She was married, Viv."

She plucked a blue glass bead from the tray in front of her. "You knew that. If I remember correctly, you went to New York against Lily's and my advice and saw her with her husband."

"But now she's *not* married, and I see her every day."

With the wire in one hand, she threaded the bead with the other. "Why does it bother you so much? Did you think she wouldn't meet anyone else? I'm not surprised someone else saw the same qualities in her that you did. You made a choice.

You don't get to be disappointed she took the opportunity you gave her. I know you never stopped loving her, because you haven't moved on. But she didn't break your heart the way you did to her."

"You don't pull any punches," he said, his voice thick.

"You wouldn't want me to." She tugged the bead down and selected another. "And it's not like you didn't have a few honeys of your own." When his head jerked up, she laughed. "You think Lily and I don't know about all your women? We follow you online. We know all the gossip about who was seen out with our very secretive big brother."

Zack bristled. "I didn't love any of them. She would have loved this guy she married." It was double betrayal, both of their friendship and the heart.

"There isn't a finite amount of love." Viv strung a final bead on the wire and then closed the clasp holding the ends together. "It's like this circle. Endless."

"I think he hurt her, Viv."

Her smile faded. "Well then, I hope for his sake he's far, far away. You made a name for yourself beating up our boyfriends back in Glenwood before you even started MMA. I can't imagine what you would do now."

Zack toyed with one of the beads on the table. Was that why Shayla hadn't been forthcoming about how her marriage had ended, why she'd tried to shut the conversation down? Was she protecting her ex?

"If he did, it's my fault. I put her in that position. She was mine, and I wasn't there to protect her."

"And maybe she'll be yours again if you don't screw up. She's had a taste of what's out there, and it isn't you. But you aren't responsible for her choices. If you do get back together, at least you'll know she's with you because she wants to be with you and not because she doesn't know her options." She tipped her head to the side, studied him, considering. "Is that why you're coaching her? To get her back?"

"She needed help."

"Does that mean you're going back in the cage, too?"

Zack shook his head. When he'd entered the ring to save Shayla in the underground and the world hadn't ended, he'd briefly considered the idea of fighting again. But this wasn't a simple matter of falling off a horse and getting back up again. He had his father's genes, although his anger was roused not by drink but when someone he cared about was in danger. At least that's what he'd thought until the Okami fight. The dude had been relentless, toying with him until he snapped.

"A man died. I can't forget that."

"Two men died in that cage," she said firmly. "And now I see a flicker of life in the one who has shouldered a blame that wasn't his to bear. You aren't responsible for other people's choices—whether it was Okami stepping into the cage knowing the risk or Shayla getting involved in a bad relationship. You can't save everyone, Zack. And you can't stop life from moving on."

He picked up the bead box, stared at it, set it back down. "She didn't have to get married so fast. It was like everything we had meant nothing."

"I'm sure she thought it did mean nothing after you dumped

her and walked away." She handed him the bracelet she had just finished. "This is for Shayla. So she met someone else. So she jumped quickly into what sounds to me like a rebound relationship. It's totally understandable. She loved her dad and lost him, and then she lost you. It was probably the one thing she feared the most. What's she going to do when she's young and alone in a strange city and some guy comes along and offers her what she needs?"

"What did she need?"

"Safety. Security. Love. All the things a partner is supposed to give you. Or a dad." She pressed her lips together and stared down at her beads. They never talked about their father, and Zack had always assumed she had hated their old man as much as he had. But now, thinking back, he realized their father had never hit Viv. He'd never shouted at her or put her down. In fact, he'd spent more time with her when he was sober than with Zack or Lily, and he had frequently talked about how much Viv looked like her mom.

He missed her.

Zack had spent so long hating their drunk of a father that he had forgotten the man he'd been before their mom had died—a man who had struggled to provide for his family, who had been devastated by his wife's addiction, and who had loved his wife so much, he had turned to the bottle to deal with the pain when she died.

Maybe he didn't have bad genes after all.

Rocked by the revelation, he stood abruptly. "I didn't come to see you for a lecture. I can manage my own life."

Far from being offended, Viv just laughed. "Not very well, as I see it. You help the women in your life, but you don't let them help you. Just like you're doing now." She grabbed his arm just as he moved toward the door, her grip surprisingly strong for her light frame. "If you fix what's broken between you and Shayla, maybe you'll be able to fix what's broken inside you so you can get back to doing what you love."

"I'm not broken," he said, gently removing her hand.

"You don't go through the kind of childhood we went through and come out without a few scars. But they aren't your fault. Mom chose to take the drugs that led to her death. Dad chose to drink and take his anger out on you. Their decisions meant we were alone, and you did your best to look after us, just as you did your best to look after Shayla, and I know part of that was letting her go to make her own choices. You carry too many burdens, Zack. You need to forgive yourself first before you can expect forgiveness from anyone else."

"I never realized you were so bossy." He tucked the bracelet in his pocket.

Viv looked up and grinned. "I learned from the best."

19 Shayla

THE MONDAY NIGHT AFTER MY UNDERGROUND WIN, THE Redemption team heads to the Protein Palace for some healthy post workout treats. We buy protein shakes with extra wheatgrass boosters and big bowls of chicken and steamed vegetables. Blade Saw orders half a bagel on the side and is teased for living dangerously.

"Good atmosphere tonight." Doctor Death indiscreetly eyes up a tall brunette by the juice bar, and I shift my chair to the side so I don't cramp his style.

Sadist cuffs him across the head. "Down, boy. I thought you'd found the one. Weren't you going to get her name tattooed on your ass?"

Doctor Death sighs. "Thank goodness Shilla talked me out of it. She wanted a commitment."

"No." Blade Saw gasps in mock horror.

"Yes. And after only five dates. I couldn't handle it."

Sadist laughs. "So now you're a free man."

"Indeed I am." Doctor Death turns to me and flashes his pearly white smile. "I was thinking candles, soft music, a little Nirvana, and maybe licking wheatgrass off each other as we do a late-night naked workout in the gym."

"Sounds tempting." I don't even try to hide the sarcasm in my voice. "But if Torment caught us licking wheatgrass off each other on his pristine mats, our lives wouldn't be worth living."

"It's not Torment he should be worried about," Sadist says. "It's Slayer. What would he do if he saw Doctor Death doing the nasty with his girl?"

"I'm not his girl."

Blade Saw snorts a laugh. "Beating down some dude in the ring because he pulled your ponytail and then giving you a big fat smooch in front of fifty people says *he* thinks you are."

I guess having sex in an abandoned boathouse might strengthen that claim. But not after I pushed Zack away. He didn't join us for drinks after the underground fights ended, and I haven't heard from him since he went to visit his sisters in Seattle, although I know he came back last night. But I did what I had to do. It was too easy to be with him. Too easy to forget the past and see a future together. I couldn't expose myself to the vulnerability that comes with love.

Doctor Death's shoulders slump. "Scratch fantasy number 342 off my list."

A shadow crosses the table. "Shayla Tanner?"

I look up and smile at the sandy-haired dude who has saved us from Doctor Death's fantasies. In his sharp black suit, white shirt, and navy tie, he is so out of place in the sea of sports gear, muscle shirts, and shorts, he's got to be a recruiter. "Depends who is asking," I say, all cool and collected, although inside, I'm a twisted mess of puzzled excitement. What would a recruiter want with me? Except for the other night, which was an unsanctioned fight, I've lost my last four bouts, and I'm not scheduled to fight again in the near future.

He gives me a crooked smile and hands me his card. "Reg Knight from Radical Power MMA. I saw you fight the other night in the underground. Do you have a minute to talk?"

My mouth opens and closes, but nothing comes out. Radical Power is not a small promotion. They are one of MEFC's biggest competitors and one of the top promotions in the sport. Luckily, Doctor Death comes to the rescue.

"She's just cooling down after another epic fight, but I think we can let her go." Doctor Death gives me a nudge and whispers. "Looks like Slayer has competition in more ways than one."

Reg and I head outside to the small courtyard overlooking the parking lot. Although busy, it's much quieter than inside, and we sit at a table in the corner. I take a breath of cool night air and pretend I'm just talking to a friend and not an ohmyGodprofessionalrecruiter.

"Before we talk, I just wanted to know if you've signed with MEFC," Reg says. "I saw Grayson with you at the underground fight."

"No. He's just coaching me."

"Is that part of some deal you have with them? Are they training you to join their stable?"

I pick at a paint chip on the table. "No. MEFC isn't involved. It's just…Zack and I grew up in the same town. We're…friends."

"Ah. Got it. Good to hear." Reg relaxes in his chair. "I didn't want to step on any toes or waste time if you had already accepted an offer."

Reg says lots of flattering things about me. He says after seeing me in the underground, he thinks I can overcome my four-fight losing streak and still have a chance at making it into the state finals. He talks up Radical Power, telling me how they are the best promotion to work for. Not only do they secure the best fights and the biggest sponsorships, they insure their fighters against injury, and they offer all sorts of benefits MEFC does not. He gets excited, and his blue eyes sparkle as he talks. He's cute, smiley, and very relaxed despite the suit. The waitress flirts with him and brings us complimentary protein shakes. We sip our drinks under the moonlight and talk about life as a Radical Power fighter.

"You would need at least one win for us to make you an offer," Reg says. "And it would have to be against a top ten fighter in your amateur weight class, which would put you in the running for the state finals. We wouldn't expect you to fight in the finals, but it looks better for the promotion if they make an offer to a top ten qualifier. Are you on a card for any upcoming fights?"

"No. My last coach pulled me off the competitive circuit after my last bout."

Reg twists his lips to the side. "Carla Gordon is on the card for the TVP Promotion in three weeks. I know it's short notice, but she's ranked number ten, and if you win against her, you would take her place."

My hands tingle, and I press my lips tight to keep from smiling. "I'll talk to my coach."

"Which one?"

"Get the fuck away from her." As if he knew we were talking about him, Zack strides into the courtyard, a man on a mission with fury in his eyes. He drops a possessive hand to my shoulder as soon as he reaches our table and glares at Reg. "What are you doing here, Knight?"

Reg's smile fades, and the muscles in his jaw twitch. "Grayson. I heard you'd given up the recruiting business."

"You heard wrong."

His abrupt answer doesn't seem to faze Reg, who smiles again and gestures to the chair beside me. "Pull up a seat. We were just talking about the possibility of Shayla joining Radical Power." Reg gives me a warm smile as if he's unaware of the imminent storm. "But now that we've finished the business talk, maybe we could go for a drink."

Thump. Zack spins a chair around and straddles it beside me, draping one heavy arm across my shoulders. "Her coach doesn't want her to go for drinks."

"Actually, the team was planning to hit a local sports bar after we eat," I say to Reg. "I'm sure they would love for you to join us…" My voice trails off when Zack's arm tightens and he yanks me against his side.

"No drinks."

Irritated, I push his arm away. "What's gotten into you?"

"You." Zack twists his hand around my ponytail and yanks my head back for a fierce, possessive kiss that leaves me stunned and breathless.

A crease furrows Reg's brow. "So…are you two together?"

"No," I say quickly. "We're just—"

"Yes." Zack cuts me off, tightening his grip.

"Definitely no. You have issues." I reach behind me and pull my hair free.

Zack snorts. "The only issue I have is why you keep pushing me away."

Mortified by Zack's caveman-like behavior, I give Reg an apologetic smile. "Issues."

"We all have them." He tips his head toward the Protein Palace. "Should we head back? I'm here for a few days and wouldn't mind a chance to check out a local sports bar with the team."

"She's not going drinking with you." Zack leans across the table. "She's mine."

"I'm not yours," I spit out, at once amused and annoyed. It's like he's suddenly become Zack from Glenwood times ten.

"So you are together." Reg frowns. "How does that work recruitment-wise? Like I said, Radical Power might be interested if you get your game on again in your next fight."

"If she signs with anyone, it will be MEFC." Zack gives a satisfied snort and leans back on his chair, tightening his arm around my shoulders.

Reg's gaze flicks to me and back to Zack. "Are you making her an offer, Grayson? Because she told me she hasn't signed with you."

"It doesn't matter." Zack's hand clenches into a fist over my shoulder. "She's not fighting for Radical Power."

"Um. Hello." I pull away and frown, scrambling to make sense of what's going on. "We're talking about hypothetical choices right now. And hypothetically speaking, I would consider all hypothetical options available to me if, hypothetically, an opportunity to sign with a promotion became available."

"Except Radical fucking Power." Zack grunts and pulls me close again as if that's the end of the conversation.

"How about some respect? I don't go around saying M. E. Fucking C." Reg's voice is tight. "Although you deserve it after what happened in Cape Town and Atlanta."

"What happened in Cape Town and Atlanta?" I don't want to know, but I do.

Zack and Reg glare at each other, and I realize their rivalry must go a long way back.

"It's a cutthroat business, love." Reg gives me a warm smile. "You gotta do what it takes to get the best talent, whether it's doing a little wining and dining or coaching and poaching."

Coaching? Is this all a game? Am I misreading Zack the way I misread Damian? "I'm sure you do." I return the smile. No damn way am I going to let him see he rattled me.

"Either way," he continues, "I can't see you signing with MEFC. If you're together, then there's a conflict of interest. If you're not, then maybe Zack's up to his old tricks, and you might want to think about that. He's always got an edge on me when it comes to female fighters. There are some lines I just won't cross, if you know what I mean."

I don't dare glance over at Zack in case I see something in his face I don't want to see. "I can handle myself."

"I'm sure you can." Reg finishes his shake and stands. "I'm not in a position to make an offer right now, but if you can win that Gordon fight—"

"I can," I blurt out. "I will."

Reg smiles. "I guess I'll see you inside then, and if not, I'll be around after your fight."

As soon as he's gone, Zack grabs my hand and half leads, half drags me to the back of the courtyard. "What the hell was that all about? Are you seriously thinking of signing with Radical Power?"

"Are you seriously interfering with my professional career? Your behavior was totally unacceptable. Why shouldn't I sign with them? They're almost as big as MEFC."

"Because they're a shit promotion," he barks. "They aren't going to look after you. They'll throw you into the lion pit, and if you survive, they'll throw you in again and again until you're broken."

I fold my arms and glare. "I don't hear you making an offer."

His lips press tight together, and he swallows hard. "Because you're not good enough. I don't know why he wants you up against Gordon, but guaranteed it's not to help your career. He's a snake, and he's much, much better at playing this game than you."

"He seems like a decent guy, and unlike you, he has faith in my ability." I can feel my face heat with anger. Who is he to tell me what I can or can't do when it comes to my career?

"Christ, Shay." He scrapes his hand through his hair. "You've always been too trusting. Reg Knight is as far from a decent guy as you can get. He's a piece of scum who plans to use you personally and professionally, and I'm not going to let that happen."

"It's my choice. *My choice.*" I thump my chest, looking away so he doesn't see how close his comment about being too trusting hit to home. He needs to understand that it's a decision I have to make, and the price will be mine to pay. "If I want to go out for a drink with him, I will. If I want to fight Gordon, I will. If I want to accept an offer from Radical Power, then I'll accept the offer, and I'll be the best damn fighter they've ever had."

"No, you won't." He thuds his fist on the low stone wall surrounding the courtyard. "I won't let him do to you what I've seen him do to other female fighters."

"I don't need you to protect me." I struggle to keep my voice low so the people in the courtyard don't overhear. "I'm not the teenage girl who knew nothing of the world except what you showed her. I don't even understand what's going on with you. We're professional, and then we're not professional. We're friends, and then we're not friends. You're my coach, and then we have sex, and you run away to Seattle and leave me thinking I'm back to training with Torment and Fuzzy for three whole days."

"I needed some time to get my head around the fact that all you ever wanted from me was physical."

My hands curl into fists so tight, my nails bite into my palms. "That's not fair."

"That's what you told me the other night."

"Right now, I don't want to get involved. Back then, I wanted everything. I was devastated when you left. I felt like a huge piece of me was missing. I was a young girl in a new city I never wanted to live in, with a new ballet company I didn't want to dance for, and I'd never been alone before. I always had you."

"And then you traded me in for him." His voice rises in pitch. "What were you thinking? I left you so you could have a career, so you could go out and live your life, not tie yourself down to some…what? What did he do? What was so compelling about him that you would get married at fucking nineteen years old?"

Bristling, I throw caution to the wind, giving him information I know I should keep to myself. "He was the company's artistic director."

"Jesus Christ." He groans and tips his head back. "He was your boss."

"It doesn't work like that in a ballet company, and you know it."

I hate this. Zack and I never fought when we were together. We disagreed about things like sports teams, how long I spent at the studio, or whether my plans to run/jump/ride/dive were too dangerous—yes, they were, and I always did them with Zack by my side.

"I know the artistic director has a lot of power," Zack says. "I know you don't get the job in a world-famous ballet company without a shitload of experience and a lot of years behind you. And I know you don't sleep with a much younger, innocent corps dancer unless you're a fucking bastard who has no morals and who misuses his power to get what he wants."

Anger surges inside me. Not because he's wrong, but because these were the questions I should have asked myself, the red flags I shouldn't have ignored.

"You didn't want me," I shout, the words I have never been able to say ripping from my throat. "What was I supposed to do? It never got better for me. Every day without you was like dying all over again. Even after a year, the pain didn't fade. I was empty inside, and there was nothing to fill that space, because it was meant for you. Damian was kind to me. He cared. He looked after me, and he helped my career. He wasn't my soul mate, and he never pretended to be, but in the beginning, we both got something out of that relationship that made us happy."

If the words that spill from my heart have any effect on him, he doesn't let me know. Instead, his eyes narrow, and he deepens his tone.

"Do you think I felt any different? Do you think I didn't feel your loss every fucking day? But I didn't give up on you. I didn't throw away a ten-year relationship on the first woman who crossed my path. I still felt you, Shay." He thuds his fist on his chest above his heart. "Right here. And when I knew I could do right by you, when I could give you everything you deserved, I came for you, and you were gone."

If I had just waited, I might still be dancing. But I was looking for someone to fill the hole inside me that my father had left when he died. I'm not looking to fill that hole anymore. I've learned how to take care of myself.

But Zack is back, and I don't know how to fit him into my life.

Zack's face softens. "That wasn't fair of me," he says quietly, mistaking my silence for an admonition. "I can't stand the thought of someone else making you happy. I can't bear the thought that you loved someone other than me." He digs into his pocket and pulls out a bracelet. "Viv sent this. She said there was more than enough love to go around. I think the message was more for me than for you."

I take the beautiful bracelet, a fine silver band with deep blue and violet beads interspersed with silver charms and a single silver heart. "It's lovely," I say, sliding it over my hand. "How is she?"

"She's good." His jaw tenses, and he looks away. "She's having tests, because she's been very tired, but I'm sure it's because she's been overdoing it. Ever since she went into remission, she's determined to squeeze every second out of life."

Suddenly, all the pain and heated words between us don't matter. Zack has always been very respectful of his sisters' privacy. If he's telling me about her tests, then he's more than worried; he's scared.

"She's strong. And she has you." I wrap my arms around him. Our bodies cleave together, our connection snapping back into place with every shared beat of our hearts. This is how it always was with us. Touch brought us together. Touch bridged the gap between us. Touch spoke the words that we could not always say.

"Shayla?" Reg's voice echoes in the courtyard.

"He's coming back," I whisper. "Why is he coming back?"

"Because he's a fucking shark and he smells blood in the water," Zack growls. "He promises to make all your dreams come true, and it's only when the dust settles that you realize you've signed away your soul."

"Is MEFC so different?"

"I'm different." He covers my mouth in a searing kiss. "I won't lie to you. You're not ready. No matter what I had riding on that contract, I wouldn't sign you now, because you would get hurt if you stepped into that ring with fighters who are at the top of their game. But we can get you there. And when we do, you can fight for MEFC." He hesitates. "If you want."

I acknowledge his concession with a smile. "We?"

"You and me, sweetheart. I'm here for you in any way you need me to be."

"There you are." Reg rounds the corner, all casual, like we weren't wrapped around each other in the dark.

Releasing me, Zack greets Reg with an irritated nod. "Thought you had the good sense to give up."

"Thought you'd have the good sense not to resort to the same old tricks," Reg counters. "Especially not after what happened last time."

I shoot Zack a questioning look, but his entire focus is on Reg.

"Were you looking for me?" I step out of the shadows, put my game face on.

"Don't fall for his bullshit." Reg hands me an envelope. "You're an outstanding fighter. And we're not the only promotion who sees your potential. Beat Gordon, and you'll have options, but you'll see that Radical Power has one of the most fighter-friendly contracts in the business. We don't need to resort to dirty tricks to get you to sign. And we don't disrespect our fighters. I thought you might want to take a peek at the contract. Use it as motivation. If you sink Gordon, I've got a few things to sweeten the deal."

"Thanks."

He takes a few steps away, then looks back over his shoulder. "Don't jump into anything for the wrong reasons. Make sure you do what's best for you."

"He seems nice," I say after Reg is out of earshot, solely to wind Zack up. But my head is spinning. My dream is in reach, but Zack thinks I'm not ready for it. Zack who, apparently, has been sleeping with the fighters he's been recruiting. Fighters like me.

"He's not."

I toy with Viv's bracelet. "So you never seduced a female fighter to get her to sign a contract?"

Zack scrubs his face with his hands. "It's a very competitive business. We do what we have to do to make the deal happen. Sometimes women…fighters…enjoy spending time with us to…get a…perspective on…what it could be like."

"So that's a yes," I say flatly. "Is that what you've been doing with me?"

"Jesus Christ. No. Of course not." He looks so annoyed, I believe him.

"Do you want to give me a ride home?" I reach for his hand. "I have a death wish tonight. If we make it in one piece, I might have a bottle of cinnamon whiskey that I'd be willing to share over a late-night crime show."

"You're still watching those shows?" Zack never shared my interest in crime shows, but I loved them because they made me feel closer to my father.

"Crime never sleeps, and neither do I when I'm all wound up."

Zack throws a casual arm around my shoulder. "It will be like old times. The only thing missing will be your mom pounding on your bedroom door to tell you to turn off the television and go to sleep or Matt yelling that he knew I was there."

It turns out not to be like old times, because we have sex on the couch, and he uses the door instead of the window when he leaves at the first light of dawn to get in a workout before we start our morning training session.

And I don't tell him one hundred times that I love him.

20

Shayla

"I KICKED ASS IN THE UNDERGROUND ON THURSDAY NIGHT." I have cornered Torment at the snack bar in Redemption, incredibly without any fear for my safety. I don't know where this courage has come from, but I am determined to make my case. "Evil Elsa is ranked higher than me on the amateur circuit. If I had beaten her in a sanctioned fight, I would be in the running again for the finals."

Torment lifts a warning I-don't-like-to-be-cornered eyebrow, but I'm not moving. His only option for escape would involve knocking over the potted palm beside him, and he has too much class to do something like that.

"I want you to put me back on the circuit," I say into the silence. "TVA Promotion is holding a fight in three weeks at the Kezar Pavilion. It's a small event, but Carla Gordon will be there. She's ranked number ten. If I beat her, I might still have a shot at the finals."

"You're in my way."

I stiffen my spine, swallow hard. I just won an underground fight against a much higher-ranked opponent. I broke into a boathouse and had crazy rough sex in a public place with a man I hated until a few weeks ago. I can handle Torment.

"A recruiter from Radical Power was there. He came out to the Protein Palace to talk to me. He says if I beat Gordon, they'll make me an offer."

"Who?"

"Reg Knight."

Torment snorts. "He's lying."

"Maybe he is. Maybe he's not. All I know is there's a chance out there, and I want to take it. Get me on the card for the fight." With crazy determination, I plant myself in Torment's path and try not to look at his thunderous scowl. "Please. I called, and it's too late to get on the card, but they'll do it for you if you call before noon."

His gaze drops to my feet, and I take an involuntary step back as if my feet are powerless to resist his force of will.

"It's not my call. Slayer is your head coach." More glaring at my feet. More steps back. When he is finally "uncornered," he strides past me and down the hall, forcing me to run to catch up and feed his alpha ego.

"Slayer and I had a difference of opinion about the fight last night, and I can't get in touch with him this morning. He was supposed to be here, but I can't find him and he's not answering my texts."

"Your inability to communicate with your coach isn't my problem," he barks without looking back. "But talk to Sandy.

They came in together about an hour ago. Maybe she knows where he went."

"Oh." My feet stop following Torment around and freeze on the floor.

He looks back, and he must see something in my face, because he says, "Ah." And not in a now-you-realize-you-should-have-been-in-touch-with-your-coach kind of way but in a didn't-you-know-about-Sandy? kind of way. At least I think that's why his face softens the tiniest bit.

"You asked him to be your coach, so you need to respect his opinion. If you don't want him as your coach, then you can ask me again." He frowns. "Nicely."

"Okay. Thanks," I say, although I'm not sure why I'm thanking him except for ruining my day by telling me about Sandy and Zack. Did he go straight to her place after mine?

After sending another text to Zack letting him know the promotion might be convinced to let me on the card if they hear from him or Torment by noon, I head into the gym to find Sandy.

"Well, look who's decided to join us." Stan's sarcastic snort is audible through Redemption's cardio section when I step onto the treadmill between Blade Saw and Sandy. "Thank you for gracing us with your presence thirty minutes late on a Monday morning," he continues. "Why don't you just jump right in without a warm-up? Always good for tearing muscles and ligaments."

"Did you see Slayer this morning?" I whisper to Sandy.

"He came over to my place first thing, and we lost track of

time. I missed the first few minutes of class because of him."
She gives me a self-satisfied smile, and my stomach heaves.

"I think I need that warm-up after all." I head over to the
stretching area and sit on the mat. What the hell was he doing
with Sandy? Was Reg right about Zack? Am I just meant to
be another notch in his recruitment belt, or is he genuinely
interested in rekindling our relationship?

"So, what did Sandy say to piss you off?" Doctor Death joins
me on the mat, and Sadist follows a few moments later.

"Why do you think she said something to annoy me?"

"You had the look."

"What look?"

"The Sandy-pissed-me-off look." He scrunches his face into
something between a glare and a scowl. "Like this."

"Funny." I glare at Doctor Death and also at Sadist behind
him, who is laughing a little too hard. "Very funny. Such a
comedian. I'm in stitches."

"Were you fighting over Slayer?" Doctor Death asks. "I saw
her draped over him this morning in the snack bar. Was she
poaching your man?"

"He's not my man."

"Shame." Doctor Death shakes his head. "He was the first
guy you've been with that we could actually respect. Not like
that sniveling Richard, the cord-wearing performance artist
who drove a gray Ford Taurus, the dullest car on the planet, and
couldn't have a beer with us because he couldn't handle fizz."

"He didn't snivel," I huff, regretting yet again my poor decision
to introduce a few of my hookups to the guys at Redemption.

"I don't snivel either," Doctor Death says. "Are you free tonight?"

"I have to work."

"How about tomorrow? We can play doctor. I have all the right equipment."

I hear a growl. And then he's gone.

Zack slams Doctor Death down on the mat. Then he fists Doctor Death's shirt and shakes him back and forth like a rag doll. Doctor Death scrambles to his feet and curses in medicalese, referencing certain parts of Zack's anatomy that are off-limits in sanctioned fights. He charges Zack, and the fight begins.

"Well, that's your name scratched off the singles list again." Sadist sighs. "I was gonna set you up with my friend Gino. Only guy I know, other than Zack, who is worthy of you."

"As far as I know, I'm still single." I watch Zack and Doctor Death grapple on the mat, but I make no move to intervene. They are both big boys. They know the consequences of fighting outside the ring. And I'm pretty damn sure Torment will be storming into the gym any minute to take them to task.

Sadist gives me a sympathetic pat. "Once Doctor Death puts the moves on a woman, it's a sign that she's taken. He can't help it. He's instinctively attracted to women he can't have—Makayla, Amanda, Sia, even my Penny—and the guy who shows up to beat the shit out of him is the one."

"The one?"

"Your one. Slayer is telling you he cares."

"I'd like it better if he said it with flowers."

A few short minutes later, Torment arrives and rips Zack

and Doctor Death apart. Zack makes a beeline straight for me amid the cheers of the Redemption crowd. Everyone loves an illegal fight.

He stops a foot away from me, chest puffed out, preening like he just won the title belt. He's wearing a bright-blue T-shirt that clings to his pecs and a pair of navy-blue gym pants that sit low on his narrow hips. On another man, the casual attire would have made him look soft, but with the hard muscles rippling beneath his clothing and the five-o'clock shadow darkening his jaw, he's all raw power. All man. And, if I want to take the chance, all mine.

"Was that really necessary?" I ask him when Sadist and the guys have finished with the hand slapping, fist bumping, and shoulder thumping and returned to training under Torment's watchful scowl.

"Yes."

"Why?"

Zack gives an irritated sigh. "I heard him. He was trying to get in your pants."

"No one takes him seriously. He's a man whore. That's what they do." I fix him with an admonishing glare, but Zack doesn't seem to notice.

"Not to my woman."

"Apparently, Sandy is your woman." I fold my arms across my chest. "I wondered why you were in such a rush to leave this morning. But I heard you went straight to her place from mine."

Zack's brow creases with a frown. "Sandy? I stopped at her place after leaving you to drop off some documents for her parents. They run a charity for underprivileged kids, and Sandy asked me to be a sponsor. It was on my way, and I didn't want our training session to be interrupted today. She had a few more things for me to sign, and then I gave her a lift to the gym."

My cheeks flame. Oh God. I thought he was screwing me over, when really he was doing a good deed. "That's all?"

"That's all." His lips quirk at the corners. "Did you think—"

"No." I cut him off quickly. "Of course not."

He tucks a rogue lock of hair behind my ear, and his voice drops to a sensual purr. "Tell me again how you thought I was with Sandy."

"Zachary Grayson. Do not tell me you get off on my jealousy."

A slow smile spreads across his face. "You admit you were jealous."

"Even if I was, I wouldn't tell you, because your ego is already so big, I have to step around it."

He leans forward and whispers in my ear. "That's not the only big thing I've got."

I tip my head back and groan, but I feel his words as a delicious throb in my core. "How about we get back to being professional?"

He lifts an eyebrow. "Professionals don't slack off, miss their cardio workout, and stand around jibber-jabbering with their friends."

"I had to talk to Torment about the TVA event," I say defensively. "If you call them before noon…"

"No."

"No?" I shake off his hand. "You saw the fight on Thursday

night. I kicked Evil Elsa's ass. If I win the TVA fight, I might
have a shot at the finals and a professional contract."

"You're not ready. You aren't willing to put yourself out
there."

"Are you crazy? There's nothing I want more."

Zack makes a dismissive gesture with his hand. "You forget I
know you. I watched you take risks most kids wouldn't take—
biking down Devil's Hill, swinging on a rope over Fisher's
Creek, climbing out on the roof, rolling under a train car to
meet me, dancing until your feet were bleeding and I had to
carry you home, and that time you jumped across the stage, not
knowing if the male dancer they hired had the skill and strength
to catch you…"

He shakes his head, and I can't help but feel nostalgic for the
days where fear was my friend and not my enemy.

"Those are the kind of risks you need to take if you want to
win," he continues. "You need to be willing to be vulnerable,
to get hurt. If you can open yourself up, your opponent will let
her guard down. Right now, you're so focused on defense, you
are missing the benefits of an offensive position. I watched the
videos of your fights. Most of your points came when you were
defending and your opponent slipped up. Yes, you were quick
to seize the opportunity, but at this level, you need to make the
opportunities. You need to be the one in control, but you're still
afraid to take that next step."

My breath leaves me in a rush, and I feel his words as a stab
of truth in my heart. I learned to fight so I could defend myself
if I was ever in a bad situation again. I didn't learn to fight to

become a fighter. What if I've been doing the right thing for the wrong reason? What if this is as far as I can go?

"Shay? Talk to me."

He reaches for me, and I back away, trying to process everything he has said. Why did no one ever see what he sees? Why didn't I?

"What are we practicing today? Do you want me in the training area or on the mats?" I take the maelstrom of emotion that is threatening to overwhelm me and lock it away. If I don't distract myself quickly, I'm going to crack.

A pained expression crosses his face. "Mats. We'll do submission flow drills from half guard. How long do you have?"

Submissions. I would laugh at the irony, but it's taking all my effort not to run out the door. "Cheryl is coming to pick me up for work at noon," I mumble.

We walk to the mats, and Zack explains the moves he wants to practice and where he thinks I can improve. I lie on my back on the floor, and he straddles my right leg, then leans over my body to grab my left arm to demonstrate the three moves that put pressure on an opponent's arm. He drops his weight, and I shudder as something snaps inside me. He is warm and solid and safe, and every breath I take is filled with the scent of him.

"Did you get that? Kimura, Americana, armbar. You need me to do it again?"

My throat constricts as emotion swells inside me. I can't stop thinking that I might never make it as a professional fighter. Maybe Damian didn't just break my body, he broke who I was inside. I will never be able to take the risks I used to take—not in the ring, and not with my heart.

I shake my head, and he moves into an arm triangle that involves him lying fully over my body, one arm wrapped around me in what should be a restricting move but feels like a hug instead.

I want to be hugged. I want to be held. I want to lie beneath his strong, muscular body and hide away from the world.

"You okay?" he says quietly, pushing up to the next move, which involves a switch of arms that puts us face-to-face, his body cradling mine.

"Yes." I can't look at him, so I turn my head as if preparing for the next move, a Swedish roll.

"I wasn't trying to hurt you." He pushes to his elbows. "Deep inside, you are still the girl I knew who wasn't afraid of anything. She showed me what it meant to be brave. She inspired me to be more than I was. If it wasn't for you, I would still be living in that trailer park, dreaming of the kind of life I have now."

"What life? Being a recruiter?" Pain turns to anger in a heartbeat. "You tell me I'm afraid, that I need to take risks, but what about you? I know you love MMA. I feel it. I see it every time you walk into the gym. MMA is not what you do. It's who you are, and you are slowly killing yourself by denying it."

His head jerks back as if I hit him, and his eyes harden. "It's not the same, and you know it. If you take a risk, you could win a fight. If I take a risk, another man might die."

"No one died in the ring at the underground fight." I'm taking out my anger on him, and I know I should stop, but I can't. He told me some difficult truths. I owe it to him to challenge him, too.

"That was different." Zack pushes up, still straddling my leg, and I hug myself against the loss of his warmth. "I was in control. That wasn't the case during the Okami fight. He pushed and he pushed and he pushed until instinct took over. If I'd been in control, I would have seen the signs. Instead, I was on autopilot, hitting until he was down."

Just like my dad. He doesn't have to say it, but I know. Following in his father's footsteps was always his biggest fear.

"There is nothing of your father in you, Zack. You are a good person, a kind, protective, and selfless person. I know you left me because you thought you were doing the right thing, and I'm still trying to come to terms with that. But I know one thing for certain. There is a line you would never cross. You think I'm afraid to take risks, but you are, too."

He folds his arms over his chest. "This isn't about me."

"It's about us," I say. "And each of us finding a way to overcome our fear."

———

"Look what the cat dragged in." Cheryl snorts a laugh when Joe limps into Symbian, his back stiff and his arm in a sling. "Yup. Those criminals are going be scared," she continues. "Maybe you could threaten to hit them over the head with your cast."

"Nice to see you, too. You're in my chair." An uncharacteristically irritable Joe waves her away. "I'm on the desk for the next few weeks, so you two are gonna be stuck with Sol on patrol. Think you can handle him?"

"Sol's not gonna mess with us now that he's seen what Shayla can do." Cheryl squeezes my bicep. "Our girl here can kick some real ass."

"My fists and your gun. We're a good team." I smack a fist into my palm, and finally, Joe laughs.

"We need to set Joe up with someone," Cheryl says quietly as we get ready for our patrol. "He hasn't gone out on a date since his wife died. My heart breaks thinking about him hobbling around his house alone, no one to talk to. All that passion and no one to share it with."

I never thought of Joe as a passionate man, but Cheryl is right. He loved Lizzie with everything he was. He gave her his heart, his soul, and last week, he almost gave his life to see her again. After losing both Zack and my ballet career, I locked up my passion. I lost touch with who I was and what I wanted out of life. I stopped letting the music take me away.

Sol arrives late for his evening shift. He takes one look at me, and his lips turn down at the corners. "Well, if it isn't the little girl who thinks she's hot shit 'cause she can throw a few punches and knock down guys who can barely stand."

"At least I made an effort."

He snorts in disgust. "In a real fight, you wouldn't have stood a chance. You woulda been begging me to save you. Women aren't made to—"

"Don't go there." I cut him off before he starts on yet another misogynistic rant. Usually, I just turn my back and walk away, but I'm still riled up after my conversation with Zack. Who is he to get in the way of my dream? Or to tell me I'm afraid of taking risks. I'm going to take one right now.

"Come on, Sol." I open my arms and walk up to him. "Take a shot. I'm sick and tired of listening to you go on about what women can and can't do. No one here is going to say anything. You have my word. This is your big chance to prove yourself. Show us what you've got. Show us what you would have done to those intruders if I hadn't been there."

He looks at me in disgust. "I'm not fighting a girl."

"Oh. So you're afraid."

"Afraid to hurt you and lose my job." He looks to Joe for some manly support, but all he gets is disdain.

"You couldn't take her even if she was blindfolded with one arm tied behind her back," Joe says.

"Fuck you." Sol walks right up to me and gets in my face. "You're a fucking woman. I could break you like that." He snaps his fingers.

I grab his wrist, twist his hand behind his back, and force him to his knees.

"You want to show me that again?" I release him, and he spins around, fist finally clenched with the punch that has been a long time in coming.

Ducking down, I sweep his leg, knocking him to the ground. With a roar, he stands, and I grab him and knock him down again. I straddle his leg like Zack showed me in the gym and twist his arm into a painful armbar.

"Here's what's going to happen from now on," I tell him as he grunts and strains beneath me. "You are never going to touch Cheryl's ass. Or my ass. Or the ass of any woman in this facility. You are not going to make derogatory comments about women or hide in people's offices watching porn when you are supposed to be on shift. You do all that, and I won't report you for sexual harassment, nor will I finish what I've started right now. Do we understand each other?"

"Get the fuck off me, bitch. You're breaking my fucking arm."

I sigh and shift my weight, tightening my lock on his arm. "*Bitch* is a derogatory word. You want to rephrase that, or should I make my threat a reality?"

"Jesus Christ. I was just fooling around. You can't even take a joke."

"I like funny jokes." I push up and release him. "Chickens crossing the road, priests in a bar…"

"That's my girl. Right there," Cheryl mutters under her breath as Sol stalks away to the back room to change into his uniform. "She's so damn awesome, I am not worthy to be breathing her air."

"Cheryl…"

"A bit much?" She grins. "Or should I be louder next time?"

"Not too loud," Joe warns, gesturing to the door. "We have company."

Officer Morrison and Detective Waterton join us at the front desk. Cheryl's cheeks turn pink when Officer Morrison smiles.

"Hi, Jim."

"Jim?" Detective Waterton smirks at Officer Morrison. "Is that why you didn't stay to play cards with us on Friday night?"

"Shut it, Waterton." Officer Morrison gives Cheryl a kiss on the cheek, and a smile spreads across her face.

Joe and I share an amused look. Cheryl usually makes bad choices when it comes to men, which is why she's been married and divorced four times and she hasn't hit thirty. Unless Officer Morrison has some hidden secrets, he is the first decent guy we've ever seen her with.

They ask a few questions, and we check over our statements. Detective Waterton asks me about MMA and tries to convince me to join the police force. He's a bit of a flirt, and he makes me laugh with his stories about crimes gone bad. While we're talking, Sol slips out the side entrance. His attempt to avoid talking to the police is foiled by the eagle-eyed Waterton, who follows after him with Morrison in tow.

Detective Waterton is waiting at the front entrance when Cheryl and I head out on patrol ten minutes later. At first, I think he's doing something police related, but when he says, "Shayla, I was waiting for you," I clue in pretty fast.

"More questions?"

"Just one. I was wondering if you wanted to go for a coffee when you're done with your shift."

Cheryl indiscreetly splutters and jabs me in the ribs. I'm about to admonish her for her childish behavior when she jerks her chin toward the parking lot, and I realize her outburst isn't because Officer Waterton is asking me out on a date but because there is something I need to see.

I follow the direction of her furiously jerking chin and spot Zack, leaning against his blue Acura in the parking lot, his arms folded over his chest. He's wearing ripped, low-rise jeans that are a feast of seams in all the right places and put all sorts of naughty ideas in my head.

His gaze flicks to Detective Waterton and then back to me. He breaks away from the Acura and stalks toward us. Even from here, I can see his eyes narrow like laser beams on the police officer, as if he knows the competition is sniffing around.

"Thanks." I give Officer Waterton a polite smile. "But I've got plans tonight."

"Another night then?" Watertown digs into his pocket and hands me his card. "My private number is on there. You can call—"

Whoosh. The card disappears from my fingers, and Zack hands it back to the startled detective.

"I'm her coach. She's training tonight."

I glare when he slides a possessive arm around my shoulders. "I'm not training with you tonight, because I'm going to…" I scramble for a plausible reason to turn both men down.

"Amber's ballet recital," Cheryl says. "It's tonight at seven. Shayla was coming with me, because none of my family could make it, and she didn't want me to be alone."

"I'm coming with you," Zack says. "I like ballet."

"Were you listening? It's a ballet with little girls." I look over at Cheryl for a little more help, but she's too busy trying not to laugh.

"Even better."

"That doesn't sound good, Zack. Especially when there's a police officer present."

Zack tips his chin at Detective Waterton. "He's a guy. He understands."

Waterton laughs and gives Zack a manly thump on the arm. "Sorry, bud. Didn't mean to step on your toes. My fault for not asking Shayla if she was with someone."

"I'm not with someone," I protest. "Especially not him after what he did today."

"Being a guy," Detective Waterton says, "and understanding things as guys do, I don't want to get in the way." He holds out a hand, proving just what a nice guy he is, and shakes hands with Zack. "Nice to meet you. Enjoy the recital."

"What are you doing here?" I mutter as Cheryl walks the detective to his car.

"You're here."

For a moment, I'm at a loss for words. He makes it sound so simple. Like where else would he be?

His gaze travels up and down my unflattering polyester uniform. "Did I ever mention how hot you look in your uniform?"

"Save your smoldering intensity and sexual innuendo for someone who cares."

Zack leans against the metal railing. He grabs my security belt and pulls me toward him, settling me between his legs. "We didn't get a chance to finish our talk."

"You were in an I-don't-want-to-talk-I-want-to-glare-and-say-mean-things-and-kill-your-dreams kind of mood."

He cups my jaw in his hand, strokes his thumb over my cheek. "I told you the truth."

"The truth hurts."

"It usually does."

"Is this your attempt at apologizing for going all fight coach on my ass this afternoon?" I lean into his heat, inhaling his scent. God, he smells good, like beer and whiskey, with a hint of leather.

"You know I don't grovel well."

I laugh despite myself. "Actually, I don't know, because we almost never fought. Looking back, that probably means we didn't have a healthy relationship."

"Or it means we were meant to be together." He captures me with his gaze, studies me like he's trying to look into my soul.

"So why are you here really?" I smooth my hands over his chest, take a step closer. I can't help myself. Whenever I'm with him, I need to touch him. He's like a drug, and I need my fix.

"I got you on the card for the TVA event. You wanted it so much, I couldn't stand in your way."

My breath catches, and I wrap my arms around him. "What happened to 'you're not ready'?"

His smile broadens, warms my heart. "We have three weeks. You will be ready."

"Thank you."

"Pleasure." He leans down, nuzzles my hair in a very uncoachlike way. "Used a little star power to make it happen."

"You are a total star." I let him go, just as the police officers drive by.

"You should thank me for that, too," he says, nodding at the departing car. "We're gonna need a new set of rules while I'm coaching you to greatness. No other men."

My mouth drops open, and for a moment, I am at a loss for words. How could he even think I would want to be with another man? Even if Zack hadn't shown up, I would have turned Detective Waterton down.

"And no sex with other men," he says, filling in the silence. "I can't focus if I'm thinking about you with someone else."

"Then don't think about them."

"You're sleeping with other guys?" His voice rises in alarm, and although I'm tempted to play the femme fatale, I don't want to set him off after he got me into the TVA event.

"Calm down." I give his arm a soothing pat. "I don't have time to sleep around."

"Ahem." Cheryl clears her throat, announcing her return. "Not that I'm trying to guilt you into it in any way, but Amber *would* be thrilled if you came to her recital tonight. She's in primary A now and she's dancing the Imperial Orchid."

Zack frowns. "You weren't really planning to go?"

"I haven't been to a ballet in four years. I don't think I could watch. Anytime I see ads for the ballet or hear classical music, I have to break out a box of tissues."

"Don't worry about it." Cheryl waves a dismissive hand. "It's no big deal. I just thought it would be nice for Amber to have a cheering section, and you needed an out, but I totally forgot about—"

"You're afraid," Zack says to me, cutting her off.

I drop my head back and sigh. "We're not having this conversation again."

"Afraid? Are you kidding me?" Cheryl laughs. "My girl isn't

afraid of anything. You should have seen her bounce Sol around this afternoon. He'll never touch a woman's ass again."

Zack goes utterly still. "He touched you?"

"No," I say quickly, because I can see his muscles tensing, his feet ready to move. "It was all talk. However, I might have goaded him into punching me—"

"Jesus Christ." Zack scrapes a hand through his hair. "Where is he?"

"It doesn't matter where he is. He won't touch me again."

"*Bam.*" Cheryl smacks a fist into her palm. "She had him down on the ground faster than you could say 'misogynist pig,' and then she threw herself over him and did some kind of twisty thing and almost broke his arm."

I shrug in response to Zack's questioning look, although I'm damn proud of what I did. "Kimura, Americana, armbar. It worked pretty well."

Zack's lips quiver with a smile. "I can't condone fighting outside the ring. But damn. I would have liked to see that."

I would have liked him to see it, too, because it was exactly what he said I needed to do. All offence. No defense. No fear.

No fear. Maybe I should go with Cheryl tonight. Ballet was such a huge part of my life, and I have shut it out for the last four years. I'm afraid, just like Zack said. I'm afraid of the pain of loss that has been such a constant in my life. What would it feel like to be as brave with my emotions as I was in the ring with Elsa or with Sol tonight?

"What time is the recital?"

"Seven." Cheryl's eyes light up. "You're coming? Amber will be so excited. You're her ballet idol."

"I'm coming, too." Zack presses a kiss to my forehead. "It will be like old times."

"Except I won't be dancing."

"You will be dancing." He taps my chest above my heart. "In here."

21

Shayla

ZACK TAKES ME HOME TO CHANGE AFTER MY SHIFT. WE HAVE HALF an hour to kill before we have to leave for the concert, and Zack has some ideas about how he wants to spend it.

"Take off your uniform."

"No need to get bossy. I was planning to change. I can't show up at a ballet recital with a belt full of weapons."

He sits on my bed and leans back on the pillows, arms folded behind his head. "Leave the belt on. Take the rest off."

"You want to fuck me in my security belt?"

Zack licks his lips. "Very much."

"It's not safe." I unbuckle my belt and place it carefully on the dresser. Sexing it up with a Colt 1911 handgun strapped to my side is just asking for trouble.

"I'm not safe if I don't get what I want." His mouth turns down in a pout, and I laugh.

"I don't want safe." I unbutton my shirt and drop it on the floor. "But we have to be fast. We only have half an hour."

"A lot can happen in half an hour."

"Like what?" I rip open the Velcro on my bulletproof vest and shrug it off.

"You're going to sit on your dresser across from me, feet on the edge, knees spread, and show me your pretty pussy." He unbuckles his belt and tears open his fly.

"Will I be touching myself?" I pull off my T-shirt and unhook my bra.

"You're going to show me how happy you are to see me. Then you're going to show me what you like." He shoves his clothing over his hips.

"What will you be doing?"

"This." He fists his thick cock and pumps it hard. A moan leaves my lips, and he growls. "Naked. Now."

"Bossy."

"You love it."

I do love it. Although I never imagined wanting to give up the control I fight so hard for in the ring, it is deliciously erotic to give it up in the bedroom and let Zack run the show.

It takes me only moments to slip off the rest of my clothes. I shove aside makeup, magazines, and fight gear and position myself on the cold, hard surface of my dresser, back braced against the wall.

"Open for me, beautiful girl. I want to see how you touch yourself when you're alone."

Swallowing hard, I part my legs. Everything he says makes me wet. I could probably come just listening to the sound of his voice.

"Wider. Show me how wet you are."

I tremble, slide my feet past my hips. Although there are at least ten feet separating us and my gun is within reach, I feel deeply vulnerable, utterly exposed, and my stomach knots in protest.

"Such a pretty pussy." Zack pumps himself in earnest, and the sight of his powerful body, rocking with every rough stroke of his cock, sends a shock wave of need through me that banishes my fears.

There isn't enough time for a slow, gentle build. And I don't need to imagine a dark, dominant man manipulating my body, because the object of my deepest fantasies is sitting right in front of me. Emboldened by his obvious arousal, I slide two fingers through my labia and dip inside my entrance to make them slick.

"Show me how much you want me."

My fingers glisten under the light when I hold them in the air. Zack groans, and the tip of his shaft gleams wet.

"Touch yourself."

I rub my fingers on either side of my clit, gently at first, and then with firmer strokes as pleasure builds inside me. A gentle squeeze of my breast with my free hand rips another groan from his throat, and he grips his shaft so hard, I can't imagine it doesn't hurt.

"Are you close?" His gaze flicks between my hand and my face, his eyes heavy with arousal, his body taut and straining.

"Yes."

"I want to watch you come."

His words send blood rushing downward to my swollen clit. Desire spirals through me, lifting me higher and higher, and my body heats. I push two fingers deep inside me, rubbing my palm against my needy clit. That small amount of pressure is all it takes to send me over the edge. My climax rolls through me in a thunderous wave. My back arches, and my head slams against the wall as I give up the last of my inhibitions to the exquisite sensation.

"Fuck. Yes." With a hard grunt, he pumps his swollen shaft and releases against his belly, his hips jerking with each shuddering pulse.

I lean languidly against the wall, memorizing the rare softness of his face in the few precious moments where he is not haunted by memories of the past. This is the Zack I remember. The Zack of my dreams.

"That was damn good," I murmur. "And we still have time left."

A slow, sensual smile spreads across his face. "Get your ass over here, woman. That was just the warm-up."

An hour and two orgasms later, we meet Cheryl and Amber backstage at the Kofman Auditorium in Alameda. I've met Amber a few times before, and she greets me with a hug. Zack gets a wary look that makes him laugh.

"I'm scared." Amber clings to Cheryl's hand so hard, her fingers turn white.

"You'll be fine," I say to Cheryl's mini-me. Luckily for Amber, there is no sign of her dad in her beautiful face. "The toddlers will be going on first and then the big girls like you, so you'll be able to watch them from behind the curtain at the side."

We look for Amber's class, and I fight back waves of nostalgia as I breathe in the familiar scents of sweat and flowers, dust and makeup. Girls race past in light, floaty dresses, the sound of their ballet shoes tapping on the wooden floor so painfully familiar, I ache inside. Amber isn't the only one who is scared to be here tonight.

"You're doing good, sweetheart." Zack puts a warm hand on my shoulder, and my anxiety eases. Nothing could dissuade him from coming backstage with us. He said he had good memories of being backstage, but I know he didn't want to leave me.

We find Amber's teacher, Madame Rambert, warming the girls up with some demi-pliés in first and second.

"Point and close, point lift, point and close, and arms, fairy wings, and fifth."

"Don't go," Amber begs when we lead her to the circle. "Stay with me."

So Cheryl and I sit on the floor beside her, and suddenly, I'm five years old and desperate to be the best ballerina on stage and make my mother proud.

"Toes next," I whisper. "Good toes and naughty toes." I kick off my shoes, and do the movements in my sock feet just like her, then bend forward. "And touch toes. Hello toes!"

A few girls giggle, and I look up. The teacher is watching, and she motions me over. "You look like you know what you're doing. Could you finish warming the girls up? The toddlers are running amok, and I need to get them ready."

"It's been a long time…"

"Just a few minutes," she begs.

"Okay." I look up at Zack, leaning casually against the wall along with a few parents. "You don't have to stay. We won't be long."

He lifts an eyebrow, and his silent admonishment makes me feel all warm and tingly inside. He's not going to leave me. I am not alone.

Cheryl and I get the girls up, and we practice ballerina walks around the room, walking on demi-pointe and skipping. Then we do jumps in first, spring points, and petit jetés. The moves come back easily, as do the memories. We finish with a curtsy, and the girls clap.

After Madame Rambert returns, we find our seats in the auditorium. Zack holds my hand when the three- and four-year-olds delightfully stumble their way through the theme song from "The Twelve Dancing Princesses," losing tutus and tiaras in the process. Zack chuckles through the entire performance, and I can't help but join him.

"I didn't think a hard-core MMA fighter would enjoy something like this," I whisper.

"It reminds me of the first recital you did when you volunteered to teach."

I remember that performance, too. It was an utter disaster. From tears to tantrums, it was a mortifying three minutes that made me think I wasn't cut out to do anything but dance. "You were there?"

"Of course I was there." He squeezes my hand. "I thought you might need some support. But when I met you afterward and the first thing you said was 'I'm glad you weren't there,' I decided not to tell you."

Emotion wells up in my chest. He was there for me even when I didn't know it.

Amber's group is up next, and the first few notes of the music take me away to the thrill of my first recital and the excitement I felt every time I was on stage. Bittersweet tears prickle my eyes. I love fighting, but if I hadn't had my accident, I don't think I would have ever stopped dancing.

"You okay?" Zack puts an arm around me and pulls me close.

"I miss it," I admit, taking strength from his warmth.

"I thought there was nothing more beautiful than watching you dance."

I swallow past the lump in my throat. "That's not the kind of thing you say when a person can't do what they love anymore."

"Why not? There is no point pretending you weren't good. You were amazing, and you should never forget it. But I was wrong. There is one thing more beautiful than watching you dance."

Thrown off-kilter by his brutally candid words, I am almost afraid to ask. "What?"

"Watching you fight."

I snort a laugh. "Fighting isn't beautiful."

"It is to me when you're in the ring."

Zack whispers his happy memories of my performances in my ear for the rest of the show. The time one of the dancers fell on her rear and split her costume, and when the male lead in a performance of *The Nutcracker* got stuck in his papier-mâché head. He tells me how he was thrown out of the auditorium when he shouted and fist-pumped after I landed my first grand jeté.

I can't be sad when I'm smiling. By the time the intermission rolls around and we have to pick Amber up backstage, I am lost in bittersweet memories of a past that gave me much joy.

"You were wonderful," I tell Amber as we wait for Zack to return from the snack bar. "Lovely demi-pointe and skipping and petit jetés."

"How was my hair?" She pats her bun, seemingly unconcerned about her performance. "Did any pieces come out?"

Zack joins us in the lobby. He has a rose in a beautiful cellophane wrapper behind his back, which he slips over to Cheryl when Amber stops to talk to a friend.

"Give her this," he whispers to her. "It's traditional to give flowers after a ballet performance."

"Thank you. That's so sweet." Cheryl looks from me to Zack and back to me. "If you don't want him, I'm gonna be first in line."

After we say goodbye to Amber and Cheryl, Zack speeds through the city. Lost in thought, I don't realize he is driving in the wrong direction until the city lights have faded away.

"Where are we going?"

"Bay Area Ridge Trail." He turns right on Girard. "I heard it was a good place to watch the stars."

"Thank you." I squeeze his hand. "I was dreading going home. It was one thing being there with you and Cheryl, but being alone after that…"

"I know."

"You always knew." My voice catches, and I look out the window to hide my tears. "I haven't been out to look at the stars since I left Glenwood."

He squeezes my hand. "Me either."

Ten minutes and one stop at a shopping mall later, we are hiking along one of the well-used trails. Zack bought blankets, flashlights, water, and protein bars. He guides us through the semidarkness to a clearing below the ridge line on the mostly unpopulated side of the coastal range as if he's been coming here for years.

"How did you know about this place?" I ask as we spread the blanket on the grass. Although there are no lights around us, the glowing sky makes it easy to see the trees and rocks and a large skunk that scuttles away through the underbrush.

"I asked around." He drops his bag on the ground. "There are better places for star gazing, but none are so close. We might only be able to see a few hundred stars because of the city lights. Not like the thousands we saw at home."

Zack stretches out on the blanket, and I lie beside him, shoulder to shoulder like we used to do. Although the night air is warm and fragrant with the smell of pine, I'm glad of my jacket and the extra blanket he bought on his way here.

"There they are." He points to our stars. "Vega and Altair. They are almost together again."

Zack once told me the story of the two brightest stars in the Milky Way, Vega and Altair. The goddess Vega fell in love with Altair, a mortal peasant. Their love was so powerful, the gods could not stop them from coming together, and they were punished by being placed in the sky where they were separated by the Milky Way. Once a year, a bridge appears, and they can be together again. But the path is treacherous. If Altair fails to make the crossing, Vega's tears fall as raindrops on the land. But if he makes the crossing, the sky gods will allow them to be together.

"Except for the Milky Way." I point to the white streak in the sky between them.

Zack threads his fingers through my hand. "It's not that far."

"You always were the optimist." I tip my head until I'm leaning on his shoulder. "No matter what I did, you always said it would be okay."

Zack laughs. "I said that for me more than for you. I knew I wouldn't be able to stop you from doing whatever you set your mind to, no matter how crazy, so I had to try and reassure myself."

"So you didn't always believe what you said?"

Zack turns and presses a kiss to my temple. "I knew that as long as I was there, you could take any risk, because I would never let you get hurt."

I don't know if I'm emotionally drained after weeks of fighting the connection between us or if I am still feeling fragile after the ballet, but his words resonate deep inside me. I took a risk going to New York alone and an even bigger risk ignoring the warning signs and marrying a man I didn't love. It was the worst of decisions, but it needed to happen. Zack had always protected me, but sometimes you need to get hurt so you learn to see the danger ahead of you. You need to fall so you learn how to get up again.

"Shh."

I don't even realize I am crying until Zack gently pulls me across his body. His arms wrap around me, and I sob into his chest—loud, ugly, broken cries that shake my body. And all

I can get out are four words—words that have been buried beneath the walls around my heart, words that I have never admitted, not even to myself.

"It wasn't your fault." It was my choice to move to New York. My choice to get involved with Damian. My choice to marry him even though I didn't love him. My choice to ignore the signs that his insecurities about his age and position were being manifested in his increasingly possessive and controlling behavior. My choice not to walk away before my marriage imploded. I took a risk and I fell, but I learned how to get back up.

"Shay…" His voice cracks, breaks.

"I missed you."

"I missed you, too, sweetheart." He holds me through an endless torrent of tears, stroking my hair, my back, whispering things in my ear that I am desperate to hear but are inaudible above the sound of my pain.

"I was never meant to go to Redemption," he says quietly when my sobs become hiccups and I have soaked his MEFC shirt with snot and tears. "I was on a red-eye to Brazil, and the plane stopped to refuel in San Francisco. But when they started the plane up again, there was an engine problem, and we were rescheduled on a flight the next day. After sitting for so long, I needed to work out. I called up MEFC and asked if there were any local training centers with potential fighters of interest. I thought I'd kill two birds with one stone. They mentioned someone at Redemption. I walked in the door, and I found you."

"And I slapped you." My face burns at the memory.

"That was the moment I knew I'd found you again," he says with a hint of humor in his voice.

"Zack?" I scrunch his shirt in my hand, squeeze my eyes closed.

"Yeah?"

"Why does it bother you so much that I was married?"

He is silent for so long, my pulse kicks up a notch, and I tighten my grip on his shirt.

"I'm not going to lie to you, Shay. I always thought you were mine. Even when I left you, it never occurred to me you would wind up with someone else. I was determined to make something of my life, just as you were going to make something of yours. I wanted to be worthy. For you. For me. For the family we talked about having. But I always planned to come after you. The future I dreamed about always had you in it. Now I've had a chance to think about it, and I realize it wasn't fair. I'm glad you found someone who loved you and made you happy, even though it didn't work out in the end."

Safe in the circle of Zack's arms, my walls down, relieved of the burdens of anger and blame, I give him the same gift of honesty he has given to me. "I wasn't always happy."

He tenses the tiniest bit, and I push myself up to meet his gaze. "I didn't love him, and I don't think he loved me, but at first it didn't matter. We both got something we needed out of the relationship He was kind and generous and caring. We shared a love of ballet. And we had fun together. But slowly things changed, and because we didn't have love, there was nothing to stop our marriage from crumbling." I brace myself and tell him the secret no one at Redemption knows. "I didn't fall down the stairs."

His body goes rock solid beneath me, his arms turning to steel bands around my back.

"He pushed me."

"Jesus Christ." He pushes himself to sit, carrying me with him until I'm in his lap.

"After he beat me," I continue. "He was drunk. He drank a lot when we first got together, but it got worse when my career took off and his started to decline. He was a lot older than me. A lot older than most of the dancers in the company. It made him very insecure, especially after they hired two young choreographers to work with him. He became obsessed with the idea that I was going to leave him for a younger man."

"Shay." His voice cracks, breaks. "Fuck. I can't even—"

"He never hit me until that day. But he had become possessive and controlling and verbally abusive. Matt came for a weekend and talked with him, and things seemed to calm down, but then he got fired." I draw in a ragged breath. "The night it happened, he got very drunk and checked my computer history. I had seen a video of your fight with Okami online, and read about what happened after. I was worried about you, so I would periodically run your name through the search engine to see what you were doing. He knew who you were because I told him about you when we first got together. He thought I was going to leave him for you. And he lost it."

"All the broken bones…" His hands clench into fists. "He did that?"

"My leg shattered in the fall. There were two steep flights of concrete stairs. But yes, he did everything else." I hesitate and then tell him the truth. It's time he knows everything. "He said if he couldn't have me, no one else would."

"Aaaagh," he roars. "I can't…" He stands abruptly, pushing me off his lap. "Fuck. I saw him with you. I came to New York, and I saw you together. I thought you were happy. If I'd just crossed the street, this would never have happened."

"I blamed you for everything." I sit up, hug myself against the chill. "I blamed you for leaving me, for forcing me to make the wrong choices, for being overprotective and not letting me learn how to tell the good guys from the bad. I blamed you for leaving me emotionally vulnerable. I blamed you for not being there to rescue me. I blamed you for destroying my dreams of love and marriage and destiny bringing us together."

A low groan erupts from his throat, and he drops his head to one hand. "If I'd known, I would have come. If you'd called me…"

"I couldn't call you. I hated you. I didn't understand why you left and especially why it had to be that night. Maybe I wasn't good enough in bed. Maybe that night wasn't what you'd expected. Maybe my brother was right and I was the ultimate challenge, and once you had what you wanted, you moved on. Maybe everything you'd said about love was a lie."

"Fuck. FUCK. FUCK." He slams his palm against a tree. "Did you not know me at all? Could you ever imagine me turning my back on my sisters if they needed me? Or that you meant any less? How could you think I wouldn't be there for you?" His voice rises in anger. "You were the world to me."

"I didn't believe that anymore."

"The way I felt about you never changed."

Aside from the odd scamper in the underbrush and the whisper of wind through the leaves, there is no sound but the rasp of our breaths and the words that still hang in the air between us. I want to say the same thing to him, but I can't, and he knows it.

"Did he go to jail for what he did?"

"No." I wrap my arms around my legs and stare at my feet. "He was arrested and charged, but he got out on bail, hired an expensive lawyer, and plea-bargained his way out of jail. He's got a criminal record now, and he paid a fine and had to do community service and attend anger management courses, and of course no ballet company would hire him after that. I suppose that's justice. I lost my career, and so did he."

"That's not justice." His face turns fierce and hard. "I swear to you, Shay, that bastard is going to pay for what he did."

"I didn't tell you the truth right now because I want you to go after him. I started MMA and trained in security so I could defend myself if he ever showed up at my door. I was scared he would try and find me, and I didn't want to be a victim ever again. I'm not afraid of him now, but I don't want him thinking of me. Ever."

"He won't be able to think, because he'll be fucking dead."

"You're scaring me." I push myself up and close the distance between us.

"I'm going to scare him more."

"No, you're not." I press up against him and run my tongue over the seam of his lips. "I don't want to lose you after I've only just found you again, and that's what will happen if you go looking for him and lose control."

He groans and opens for me. Lips press against lips. Tongues tangle. His hand slides down to cup my ass, and he grinds his erection against my hips. "I won't lose control. I know exactly what I want to do to that bastard."

I know what I want to do to Damian, too. Despite my insistence that I just want to move on, a part of me has always longed for justice. Real justice. I want Damian to suffer as I suffered. Because he didn't just want to hurt me that night.

He wanted me dead.

"You want to go. Then go." Damian shoves me through the open door.

I stagger back, my leg so badly bruised by the beating, I can barely stand. I can't tell anymore if he's drunk or high or just so angry, he's lost control, but the things he's saying make me fear for my life. Wary of the steep staircase behind me, I reach for the railing, but my hand won't move.

"I'm going. Please just go back inside."

"Yes, you're going. But you won't be going to anyone else. If I can't have you, no one can."

He shoves me again, and I am falling, falling, falling. Pain shoots through every part of my body.

And then everything goes black.

22
Zack

GUILT AND LONGING WARRED IN ZACK'S CHEST AS HE DEEPENED the kiss. Part of him wanted to leave right now and hunt down the man who had hurt her. But the other part understood she was giving him a gift by asking him to come back to her—trust. She trusted that he would respect her wishes and leave her abusive ex alive. And she trusted that he would have the self-control to make that happen.

Going after Damian wasn't a choice; it was a foregone conclusion. But before he went hunting, he needed to know if he truly had lost control in the ring with Okami. The only way to do that was to go up against a man who could drive him to the edge.

Torment.

Slayer would have to return to the cage for the ultimate fight.

But first, he would have to run the gauntlet of fighters who stood between him and his goal. It wasn't going to be easy. Although he'd kept up with his training over the years, he hadn't stepped foot in a ring or cage until Shayla's underground fight.

He had a lot to relearn and not much time to do it. Once Shayla went pro—and he had no doubt she would—her face would be splashed all over the internet. He didn't know if the bastard was looking for her, but Zack wanted to find him before that happened. Not just so Shayla had the justice he had promised her, but so she could sleep easy at night knowing Damian would never bother her again.

He would do anything for Shayla. She was his Vega, and he wanted to come home.

He didn't remember moving. He had no idea how he found himself pressed up against her, pinning her to a tree as he covered her mouth and kissed her like it was the first time all over again.

"I want to take all your pain away, all the bad memories, the past you want to forget." It wasn't what he'd had in mind when he brought her here. He had intended only to share a moment under the stars after the emotional evening. But after hearing the truth, he wanted to replace her pain with pleasure, connect with her on a deeper level than they had until now.

"I need you, sweetheart."

"You have me." She wrapped her arms around his neck and pushed her tongue into his mouth.

She tasted sweet and minty, like the candy Amber had given her before she left, but it wasn't sweet he wanted tonight. Unsettled by what she'd shared with him, he needed the certainty of control, but he was reluctant to let go with her after she'd shared the violence she'd suffered at Damian's hands.

"I need you a different way." He unbuckled his belt and

yanked it through the loops. They had played with bondage before, especially as she neared eighteen and Zack had found it almost impossible to hold back when she got her naughty hands on him.

"Why? Are you afraid I'm going to do this?" She slid her hand into his pants. Her fingers brushed the tip of his erection, and he bit back a groan.

"Yes." But he couldn't move when her cool hand closed around his cock and she began to stroke. Shayla still knew just how to touch him, how firm to grip, how fast to move, how to use one finger on his balls on the downstroke.

His hand smoothed over her ass and under her skirt. He'd insisted on the skirt when they'd finally rolled out of bed at her place. Mentally congratulating himself on his foresight, he slid her underwear down and off. When he had her back in position, he kicked her legs apart and slipped a finger into her entrance. She gasped and arched into him without breaking the rhythm of her stroke.

"You're already wet for me."

"And you're ready for me." She squeezed his shaft tight, and he rocked into her grip. "Maybe we should forget the belt."

He added a second finger, thrusting and stretching as her wetness slid down his fingers. Her head fell back against the tree, and he took advantage of her bared throat to feather kisses up the column of her neck. He felt the vibration of her groan against his lips, and her stroke faltered.

Walking the line between pleasure and pain, he added a third finger and pulsed inside her. She was panting now, riding his hand, her grip stuttering over his cock. When he felt her tissues swell around his fingers, he angled the tips to press against her G-spot and rubbed his thumb gently over her clit.

"Oh God. Zack!" She came with a cry, her pussy pulsing around him. The scent of her arousal made him painfully hard, but it wasn't her hand he wanted.

When she started to come down, he withdrew his fingers and swept her up in his arms. Placing her gently on the blanket, he straddled her hips. "Hands over your head."

Without hesitation, she raised her hands, her back arching as he bound them above her with his belt.

"Close your eyes. Don't open them until I say."

A shiver ran through her body, but she did as he asked, and he took a moment to drink her in, from the light, filmy blouse that teased a man's senses to the short, dark skirt that had ridden up her thighs, baring the swollen lips of her cunt.

He kissed lightly down her throat to the vee of her shirt. She thrust up her breasts, offering them for his nuzzling pleasure.

"Who's in charge here?" he murmured.

"I'm not sure. Not much is happening."

"A lot is happening." He unbuttoned her shirt and shoved her bra up over her breasts. "This is happening." He drew a rosy nipple between his teeth and licked and sucked until it peaked.

She drew in a sharp breath, and he turned his attention to her other nipple, one hand gently squeezing her soft breast. "And this."

Her cheeks flushed with pleasure, and he pushed her skirt up to her waist. Although the windy trail below would give them fair warning if anyone came this way, he didn't want to take the risk of leaving her exposed.

Moonlight glinted off the scars on her legs, and he fought back a wave of nausea at the thought of how she'd suffered, how hard she must have worked to get to where she was now.

"You are so fucking strong." Without thinking, he leaned down and kissed one of the scars.

"Zack. No."

He could hear the pain in her voice, but he couldn't stop. He hadn't been there for her when she needed him, but he would spend the rest of his life trying to take her pain away. Gently, he kissed his way along the length of the worst scar and then down along the next. Her legs trembled, and when he looked up, he saw tears glistening at the corners of her eyes.

"They're hideous," she said. "For the longest time, I wore leggings under my fight shorts. But then one day, I decided I wasn't going to let him affect me that way. I'd passed all my security guard training. I was licensed to use a gun. I was feeling confident about my fight skills. Why should I be embarrassed about my scars? Most of the Redemption fighters knew my story about falling down the stairs. So one day, I took off the leggings and let them see."

"That took courage." But then his Shayla had always been brave.

"I was worried for nothing. The fighters at Redemption are like family. They knew it was the one thing I wasn't ready to laugh about."

His fist clenched involuntarily on the blanket, and his mouth watered in anticipation of the moment when he had her tormentor at his feet.

When he'd kissed every inch of every scar, he worked his way up the sensitive skin of her inner thigh, breathing in the scent of her arousal.

"Spread your legs for me, sweetheart. Show me your pretty pussy."

"You're dirty talking makes me hot," she said, her voice thick with desire.

"Because you're a dirty girl." He pushed her legs apart and positioned himself between her thighs. "A very dirty, very naughty girl. I think we need to get you clean." He settled himself between her thighs and licked up through her folds and right over her clit. She sucked in a sharp breath, and her legs tightened against his shoulders. Still sensitive from before. Just how he liked her.

Gently, he spread her labia, exposing her clit, and sucked it into his mouth. She cried out, her body jerking so hard, he had to put a firm hand over her stomach to hold her in place. He licked up one side of her clit and down the other, over and over until she was trembling all over, ready to come again. All it would take was just one lick.

He pushed back and studied her as he fought to get himself under control. She was all lean, hard muscle, and yet the softness was still there in her breasts, the curve of her hip, and the dip of her stomach. He wanted to lick his way along each of the muscles that had brought her back from the brink, trace every dip and swell with his tongue, taste the salt on her skin from a day of training and the nectar between her thighs after a night of loving.

Shayla gave a grunt of disapproval. "If you want to move along to the fucking part of the evening, I would be on board for that."

"The *fucking* part of the evening, as you so delicately put it, is a long way off." He leaned over and pinched a rosy nipple, rolling it between his thumb and forefinger until it peaked. "You forget I hold the world record in restraint. You can't imagine what it was like to be with you and not touch you when I had all those teenage hormones raging through my veins."

"Um…yes, I can, and I'm not waiting anymore." She wrapped her legs around him in a closed guard position, trapping him between her thighs as she ground her wet pussy against his erection. If he hadn't been so close to the edge, he would have laughed. He hadn't considered the down side to becoming intimate with an MMA fighter. Closed guard was used to control larger, more powerful opponents, and if he hadn't restrained her hands, he might have been in trouble.

"Do you really think that was a good idea?" he warned, sitting up. If they'd been in the ring, she would have been vulnerable to a strike. But there was only one thing she wanted, and when she arched her back and thrust both her knees into his chest, opening her guard, he was powerless not to give it to her.

Ripping open his fly, he freed his cock and positioned himself at her slick entrance.

She licked her lips and grinned, her gaze locked on his shaft. "It appears that was."

With a groan, Zack grabbed her hips and plunged into her, straight to the hilt. She cried out, and her arms came up as if to touch him, but he was too close. One touch and she would set him off. He lowered his voice to a warning growl. "Hands over your head."

Her pussy clenched around him, and her reaction made him harden even more. She was so wet. So hot. So fucking tight. Holding her gaze, he started to thrust, burying himself deep inside her. He wanted to stay here forever, connected to her, balanced on the edge of pleasure and pain.

He had planned to love her face to face, with his body covering hers, but holding her like this felt right. She was a fighter and a lover, at once vulnerable and strong. She had opened herself to him, yielded her control, and yet the legs she had wrapped tight around his hips were more than capable of pushing him away.

He widened his knees, braced himself, and slammed into her until her thighs quivered and her pussy tightened around him. But he wanted to draw this out, drive her so high, she could think of nothing but the need to come.

Releasing her hips, he slowed his rhythm, breathing deep between strokes to control his own arousal. With one hand around her hips, holding her in place, he teased her swollen clit, slicking her wetness up and around but never where she wanted him to go.

"Zack. Please." She groaned, her body shaking with need.

"Everything I ever felt for you is still there," he said. "No matter how long it takes for you to come back to me, I'll be here. I want to ease your pain, Shay." His voice cracked, broke on her name. He leaned down and kissed her softly as he stroked inside her as if his cock wasn't painfully hard and he could last all night. "I'll try to make good everything that bastard did to you. Starting with justice and ending only when you feel safe and whole again."

"It's not your responsibility. I forgive you, Zack. The choices I made after you left were my own."

"It's what I want." He couldn't stand it any longer. He pulled out and then thrust into her again. "You are what I want."

"Don't stop. Please." Her legs dropped from his hips, and she opened for him completely.

Whether it was the permission or the plea, he finally broke. With one hand on each of her knees, he spread her wide and surged forward, pounding into her so hard, the blanket slid across the grass.

"Take me deep, sweetheart." He had his rhythm now, a fierce hammering accompanied by the percussion of panting breaths that shattered the silence of the night. His brain fuzzed with the pleasure of her slick, wet sheath. He slid his fingers over her clit and rubbed a firm circle, then over the top.

"Come with me."

Shayla groaned and her pussy clamped around him as she came. Zack followed her over the edge, pleasure shooting down his spine as his cock throbbed and pulsed inside her.

When he had ridden out the last wave of his orgasm, he dropped forward, holding his weight with his elbows, and brushed a kiss over her lips. She sighed, and when she seemed content, he withdrew to yank his jeans back on.

After she had straightened her clothes, he lay down beside her and pulled her over his chest. "We missed out on this last time."

"I thought you were happy with hot, quick, and dirty sex," she said softly.

"I like anything that involves you naked." He stroked her hair, ran his hand lightly over her curves. She fit perfectly against him, felt right in his arms.

"I guess that means our relationship isn't going to be purely professional."

Zack didn't know what it meant. But he knew he wasn't leaving her. Never again.

―⁓―

Zack showed up at Redemption the next morning ready to fight for the first time in four years.

"Okay. Let's go." He held out a pair of fight gloves to Torment and gestured to the practice ring. "I'm going back in the ring again."

Shayla, who had warned him against approaching Torment at this early stage in his training, hissed in a breath and took two steps back, pivoting like she was ready to run.

"Good for you." Fresh off the treadmill, Torment wiped himself down with a towel.

When Torment made no move to take the gloves, Zack frowned. "Let's do a few rounds in the ring."

Torment laughed. "In this gym, you don't get to fight me until you've beaten everyone else."

"You're kidding." Zack looked to Shayla for confirmation

that Torment was pulling his leg, but she wasn't laughing. "Even just to spar? I thought that rule was only about real fights."

"I don't waste my time with amateurs…or retirees," Torment said. "I only fight the best, and I only spar with people I think are worthy."

"I'm no amateur."

Torment tossed the towel in the laundry basket with the flare of an NBA star. "Four years out of the ring says you are."

Zack bristled at the challenge. He may not have fought for four years, but he still trained, still kept up with new advances and techniques. No doubt, he had a long road ahead of him to regain his skill, but he could damned well hold his own against the fighters at Redemption.

"So I pay for a piece of you by defeating all your fighters?"

Torment laughed. "You can earn the right to spar with me. If you're good, you may even get the privilege of fighting me. I don't fight everyone who asks."

Arrogant bastard. He reminded Zack of himself when he was at the top of his game. Well, if that's what it took to prove to himself that he could keep control, he would do it. Every day that Shayla's ex walked the earth, thinking he had gotten away with his crimes, was one day too many. Zack wanted him to suffer. But he didn't want him to die. Jail held little appeal when he'd just found the woman who made his heart beat again.

"Fine. Who's first?"

"Newbies corner is over there." Torment pointed to a practice ring in the far corner of the gym. "I don't expect they'll put up much of a fight. The real challenge will start with the

midlevel fighters: Homicide Hank, Doctor Death, and Blade
Saw. If you beat them, then you'll have to face Renegade,
Sadist, and the Predator. And if you beat them, maybe I'll let
you fight me. But I promise, you won't win."

———

The next few weeks passed quickly. Zack trained in the early
morning and late at night and coached Shayla during the day.
Although it was a struggle to maintain the boundary between
personal and professional, especially when they were rolling
on the mats, her training progressed at a rapid pace, and they
worked off their passion every night while sharing a bed.

Respecting Shayla's obvious reluctance to have another discussion about their relationship or what the future might hold,
Zack didn't raise the subject again, but as the days passed, he
couldn't help but worry that forgiveness wasn't enough to completely bridge the gap between them. Had there been more to
her decision to marry Damian than loneliness and vulnerability?
Had he broken something that could never be repaired? His
concerns translated into an increasing reluctance to second-guess
her decisions, even when he began to suspect that she had still
not overcome her aversion to risk. He had taken her choice
away from her once; he wasn't prepared to do it again.

When she wasn't training or teaching her class, Shayla helped
him prepare for his fights after he'd decimated the ranks of the
junior team and graduated to Torment's midlevel fighters. He
started with Harry "Homicide Hank" Carter, a middleweight
with long, stringy red hair, a lean, lanky body, and a gaggle of
red-haired kids who swarmed around him wherever he went.

"He spent his early childhood watching staged TV wrestling," Shayla warned Zack. "His signature move is to climb the ropes, scream, and drop on you from above. It's the scream that really gets you. Triggers that first fight-or-flight response that freezes you in place, and that's when he drops."

Zack wore earplugs for the fight. He caught Homicide Hank midflight and took him to the canvas, easily submitting him with a triangle choke that made it impossible for him to breathe much less scream again.

He was much easier on good-natured, by-the-book Blade Saw, allowing the fight to run a full thirty seconds before taking him down. Zack almost felt bad at the win. Blade Saw's sorrowful eyes and hunched shoulders made him want to throw the fight just to see the dude smile again.

Zack wasted no time with Doctor Death, who had been a thorn in his side since the first time he caught him staring at Shayla's breasts. Although he wanted to make the dude suffer, he reminded himself he was going through these fights as a means to practice cultivating emotional control. And he did just that. Even when he floored the agile fighter fifteen seconds into the fight with a submission that made him scream. That last parting shot to the nose? Totally controlled.

"You hit him after he tapped out," Torment remarked as Zack exited the ring. It hadn't been lost on Zack that Torment had watched every one of his fights, including his bouts with the juniors, just as Zack had been watching him train.

"Must have slipped."

Zack wiped down with a towel, glad that Shayla was at work

and hadn't been around to see him toy with Doctor Death. "Renegade is free tomorrow evening," he said to Torment. "Can we set up a fight?"

"Isn't Shayla fighting in the TVA event tomorrow?"

Zack shrugged. "It's early in the afternoon."

"Is she ready?"

He felt a warning niggle at the back of his mind and pushed it away. She had upped her game over the last few weeks, although not as much as he had hoped. If a fear of risk had been holding her back, it hadn't affected her in the underground fight or during their training sessions, and he wasn't about to make the mistake of assuming he knew what was best for her again.

"She's trained hard, and she's confident about the fight."

Torment gave him a sideways glance. "What do you think?"

"I've seen a huge improvement in her striking over the last few weeks. She's putting herself out there, taking risks and reaping the rewards." He tossed the towel and picked up his gym bag as he waited for a response, his skin prickling at the uncomfortable silence between them. "I've suggested she still lean on her defensive game," he added.

"Part of being a coach is giving your fighters messages they don't want to hear," Torment said quietly. "Gordon is a very strong striker. She can do a lot of damage to a fighter who isn't on the ball."

"And sometimes you have to let your fighters make their own choices and learn from their mistakes."

"Don't confuse the personal with the professional." Torment folded his arms and leaned against the ring. "What she needs to hear from her coach is not the same as what she needs to hear from her man."

Zack could feel the vein on his neck pulsing, and he clenched his hands into fists. "Don't tell me how to do my job."

"I'm just making sure you know what your job is."

"She knows the risks."

Torment raised an eyebrow. "You of all people should know a fighter can be blinded to the risks by the size of the reward."

And there it was. Out in the open. He would never be able to leave Okami behind. Everyone knew Okami's coach had tried to stop him from fighting, but Okami was determined to go on.

Shayla was not Okami. She had been cleared for the fight by the CSAC doctors and had no lasting effects from her concussion. She felt good about the fight and was excited about the prospect of a professional contract if she won. Although Zack had reservations, he wasn't going to interfere with her decision. He hadn't given her the respect she deserved back in Glenwood, but he was giving it to her now.

Shayla

23

I ARRIVE EARLY AT THE KEZAR PAVILION ON SATURDAY afternoon for my fight with Carla Gordon. Torment, Sadist, and the rest of the Redemption team are in the arena to cheer me on. Zack is outside the changing room, fussing over me like a mother hen, making me wonder if I made a mistake crossing the personal/professional boundary with him. Over the last few weeks, we've caught each other up on our missing years, watched crime shows together, trained together, and had raunchy sex on every surface in my apartment. We've shared everything from fight diet meals to nutrition and training tips and from saliva to strawberry protein shakes. I feel like I've found my friend again, although friendship isn't all he wants from me.

"Have you got your tape?"

"Yes, Zack."

"Mouth guard?"

"Yes."

"Gloves?"

"Yes."

"Don't forget to warm up before you come out. Wear your track suit to the ring."

"Yes, Zack. Did you pack my lunch for me and remember my library books?" I grin as I take my gym bag from him. Such a gentleman. He carries my gym bag when I'm about to go into an MMA ring and hopefully knock Carla Gordon unconscious.

Zack's lips tighten. "I think you should reconsider wearing a chest guard."

"Too late. I've practiced without one. I'm not about to put one on now. If I get hit in the boobs, I promise you can kiss them better."

Not even the little sexual innuendo can make him smile, and I realize he is probably just as stressed as I am.

"Keep your face away from her fists." Zack kisses my cheek outside the door, finishing the litany of advice I have heard three times already. "We don't need a repeat of what happened in the ring with Sandy."

"I highly doubt a man from my past is going to walk into the event and distract me at the exact moment my opponent decides to throw a punch."

His brow creases in a scowl that has become all too familiar after weeks of brutal workouts and an intense training regime.

"I know." I sigh before he can make another comment. "She's a striker, and I'm a submission specialist. I need to take her to the mat where I have the advantage." Carla Gordon is a nine-year amateur veteran who is still looking for that "break-through" fight. She had a five-fight skid over the last two years as a featherweight and has revitalized her career by dropping to my bantamweight class. She is 6–1 since making the change and ranked number ten on the amateur circuit. She has a reputation for unnecessary brutality, and I am scared as hell of facing her. Not that I would ever tell Zack.

"I'll be in your corner." Zack is my corner man for the fight, which means he is there to give support and advice and help me with water or minor injuries during break times, if there are any. As with professional fights, no one is allowed in the ring except the referee and the ring doctor, and the referee is the only person authorized to stop a fight.

After Zack leaves, I head into the changing room. Mats have been spread out on the floor for prefight stretching, and the promotion has provided water, sports drinks, and snacks. My opponent is already changed and stretching on the mats. Although we're equally matched in weight, Carla is taller, with ropier muscles and a face slightly twisted by a number of breaks.

We share a few tense words, and then Carla is called out to the ring. I follow a few moments later. The modest crowd cheers as I climb the steps to the raised platform that holds the fight ring, but not as loudly as the Redemption team, who fill the mostly empty pavilion with a loud roar of my name.

Zack checks my gloves when I reach my corner and pulls me forward for a quick kiss to the forehead. "Go kick some ass, sweetheart."

"That's a contradiction in terms," I tell him as I warm up with a few jumps. "Ass kickers are not sweethearts."

"Mine is."

Carla and I shake gloves in front of the referee. He turns to answer a question from one of the judges, and Carla tightens her grip and pulls me toward her. "I'm gonna break you, fucking bitch," she mutters.

Is that the best she can do? I hear worse from the Redemption fighters in yoga class. I growl in return. "It's going to be hard to break me when you're unconscious on the mat."

The buzzer sounds. Professional matches are three rounds of five minutes each, but for amateurs, we only have three minutes to get the points we need to win.

Carla cracks me low off the counter, and I respond with a stiff jab and then another. She goes over the top with a right, but I keep right on jabbing, using the new offensive techniques I practiced with Zack. But something feels off. She moves so quickly, I can't land a blow, and her punches just keep coming. Zack wasn't kidding when he said she was a striker. She hasn't used her legs, and we're already a good thirty seconds into the fight.

Taking a deep breath, I reassess. My best chance is to get her down to the canvas, but with her speed and rapid-fire punches, I'm afraid to take the risk of leaving myself open.

Damn. Wasn't this the exact thought pattern I've been working with Zack to avoid? I need to take risks. I need to give her an opening so she leaves herself vulnerable. I try to imagine her as Damian and this is my one chance for revenge. I get in a good uppercut and then another. She retaliates with a one-two punch followed by a spinning back fist, leaving me the opening I need, but by the time I work up the nerve to take advantage of her moment of vulnerability, the opening is gone.

This isn't working. Nothing is working. I'm using the moves and routines I practiced with Zack, but I can't get past her guard. Carla shoots in for a takedown and drives me to the canvas. This is good. I have an advantage here. But my advantage doesn't last. She rolls and gets me in a triangle choke. I manage to slip free and get to my feet, but now my confidence is shaken. She is vastly more skilled than me, easily outmaneuvering me on both the canvas and on our feet.

I try to find my passion for the fight. I imagine how I used to feel on stage, how I would become part of the music. But there is no music here. There is only the relentless thud of Carla's feet on the mat, the harsh rasp of her breath, the look of death in her eyes.

Another fist comes my way. I duck and clinch, drive her to the ropes. She hits hard with her back. Just as I'm moving in with another fist, she delivers a devastating knee to the head. I stagger back, blinded by a fierce rush of pain. Carla pushes me to the mat and delivers three right hands to my head. Barely conscious, I see the referee as a blur before he pulls her away.

For the longest time, there is no sound. No Redemption team cheering. No Carla shrieking with victory. No words coming from the referee's mouth, although I can see his lips moving. My arms and legs aren't interested in obeying my brain, so I turn my head to the side and look around. There is Zack, struggling to get into the ring. But Torment and Sadist are holding him back.

Another man kneels beside the referee, blocking my view of Zack. He has dark hair and dark eyes, and he is wearing a shirt with a red cross on it. Doctor Death has a shirt just like that, so I guess he is the ring doctor. I move my mouth and discover I have regained control over that part of my body, so I say "Hi, Doc," to be friendly, but that just makes him frown.

"Did she lose consciousness?" he asks the referee.

"I don't think so."

"No." I find my voice, speak for myself. "No. I didn't lose consciousness." I push up on my elbows, fighting a wave of dizziness. "I'm fine. I'll get out of the ring so you can get the next fight started."

"I called time," the referee says. "Gordon fouled you with the knee to the head. You have five minutes to recuperate. I don't think it was intentional. She was bouncing off the ropes, and she says she lost her balance. If you don't get up, it's no contest."

My only chance at making it to the state finals and getting a professional contract comes with a win. A no contest isn't good enough. Gritting my teeth, I push to my feet. "I'm up."

The ring doctor helps me to the corner of the ring where someone has placed a nice comfy stool. I sag down, and Zack holds an ice pack to my head as the ring doctor kneels down in front of me and rummages in his bag.

"Why didn't you stop the bout?" Zack shouts. Both the ring doctor and the referee have the power to stop the fight.

"She didn't lose consciousness, and she was able to get up. I see no reason—"

Zack cuts him off with a furious glare. "She's had two damn head injuries in the last two months where she's lost consciousness, and one of them was only three weeks ago."

"No." I shake my head and then wish I hadn't, because the pain is so much worse. "I didn't lose consciousness the last time."

"You did," Zack barks. "It was only for a few seconds, but you did."

"I was there. I would know."

"I was fucking there, too. I watched you go limp in the ring."

"I was stunned, not unconscious. I got up and won the damn fight." My head throbs and pounds, and I wish he would shut up, because all this shouting is making the pain worse. I thought Torment was overprotective when he told me I wasn't ready for tonight, but Zack is taking it to a whole new level. "Don't interfere."

"So this fight you're talking about was three weeks ago?" The ring doctor waves his shiny flashlight in my eyes.

"Just over three weeks. And don't listen to him. He's making a big deal out of nothing."

"You can't let her fight," Zack says to the ring doctor as if I'm not there. "She might have a serious head injury. Sometimes they don't present themselves right away. Or sometimes it takes a few hits to the head—"

"Zack!" I push to my feet, shout his name. "Your issues about Okami are not my issues. I say I'm fine. I was medically certified as healthy before the fight. The ring doctor says I'm fine—"

"Okami?" The ring doctor frowns. "Zack? Zack Grayson! Slayer! You're Slayer!"

Zack shrugs. "Yeah."

"Big fan." The ring doctor pumps Zack's hand. "I watched that Okami fight. Sorry you had to go through it. I don't know how everyone missed the signs when he stepped into the cage. I would have had him DQ'd before the fight even started. It was only thirty days after his last knockout."

Zack freezes, and his face shutters, but not before I see a flicker of pain. I open my mouth to assure him that the signs a professional ring doctor would have noticed are not the kind of signs a fighter would notice when the doctor shakes his head.

"You know, that does raise a concern here." The doctor gives me a gentle pat on the arm. "I'm sorry, but I'm going to end the bout. Slayer is right. We can't be too careful with head injuries, and talking about the Okami fight just reminded me of the rules."

"What?" I stare at him, aghast. "It was nothing. I didn't even need to see a doctor the second time. He's just being over-protective. I'm good to go. A no-contest result means I can't get into the finals. I have a professional contract riding on this fight."

"I'm sorry." The doctor shakes his head. "I'm not ending it because of what happened in this fight. I'm ending it because of the thirty-day rule. You aren't allowed to compete within thirty days of a knockout. You'll be disqualified for breaking that rule. Gordon will advance despite the final. I hate doing this, but part of my job is to protect fighters, even from themselves. And I'm sure Slayer can attest to the devastating effects of a head injury, not just for the friends and family of the injured fighter, but for the opponent as well."

My heart drops into my stomach, and not just because of the doctor's decision. This wouldn't have happened if Zack hadn't opened his mouth.

"No. You can't." I try to stand, and my knees wobble. Grabbing the rope for balance, I take a step toward the doctor as he picks up his bag. "He's not right about that last fight. I didn't lose consciousness. And not in the fight before that either. Tell him, Zack. Tell him you made a mistake."

But Zack doesn't tell the doctor anything. He just glares at me as if I'm the one doing something wrong.

"Wait. Please." I grab the doctor's arm. "Ask Torment. He's really my head coach. He runs Redemption. Or Sadist. He's a pro fighter, too. He was at the last fight. If you just give me a minute to find them—"

"My decision stands." The doctor shakes Zack's hand. "Good to meet you. Hope to see you some day in the cage. Everyone's rooting for you to come back. You were my son's idol. Your fights were really something to watch."

He crosses the ring to speak to the ref, who then goes to speak to the judges. Within minutes, I have been disqualified for fighting while on a "CAMO ill" designation, meaning I have been accused of doing exactly what Okami did—fighting after a concussion when I should have been on the unavailable list. Carla Gordon shrieks with joy when she hears the news, and bounces around the ring.

"We should go." Zack moves to help me stand, and I slap his hand away.

"Don't touch me."

"You can't walk alone, Shay. You were unsteady even when you stood up." He puts an arm around me, and I push him away.

"I said don't touch me. Don't look at me. Don't speak to

me. You know I didn't lose consciousness, and he didn't need to know what happened at that fight. It was an underground fight that *you* set up. I shouldn't have a CAMO ill designation from an underground fight, but I couldn't tell him I was in an underground fight or I'd lose my amateur license. Is that what you planned? Did you set it up so I couldn't fight again?"

He shakes his head. "No. Of course not."

"Then why?" My head is hurting so much, I can barely see. Every time I shout, the world turns red, and I don't know if it's because of the blow or my anger or the tears that are leaking from my eyes. "Why did you do that? Why did you think you knew what I needed better than me? Why did you betray me all over again?"

I'm losing it so badly, both physically and emotionally, I know I'll never make it out of the ring on my own, but damned if I'm going to lean on him ever again. "Sadist!" I shout for my Redemption buddy. "Sadist!"

"Shay. Let me take you home. We can talk." Zack holds out his hand, and I step away.

"You thought this was Okami all over again, didn't you?" I am reaching, but when he flinches, I know I've hit the mark. "Is this your idea of redemption? You save me from an imaginary danger to make up for what happened with Okami?"

"No." He runs his hand through his hair. "Of course not."

"I've got you." Sadist's deep voice rumbles through me. Warm broad hands reach through the ropes, and he helps me through. He doesn't ask if I need help. He just puts his strong arm around me and half walks, half carries me away from the ring.

I don't even look back at Zack, and Sadist doesn't ask why we're leaving my coach behind. When we reach the changing room, I rest my head against the cool door and let out a sob.

"What happened?" he asks quietly.

"He told the ring doctor I was knocked out in my last fight, which wasn't true. I was DQ'd under the thirty-day rule, and I couldn't tell them it was in the underground, because that would be a breach of the rules. I could have won that fight, or at the very least had her disqualified. It was an intentional foul."

"They ruled it accidental."

"Then I could have had a no contest and fought next week. Now I'm facing a penalty, and I'm on CAMO ill for at least another week, which means no training. I'll need a doctor's note and permission to compete again. There's no chance I'll make it to the state finals now. And I will lose my shot at a professional contract. Zack is still carrying that damn chip on his shoulder about the Okami fight, and today, he gave it to me."

Sadist gives me a friendly hug. "You want me to talk to Torment? See if he can appeal the foul? Or maybe he can smooth things over? He knows everybody. There's gotta be something he can do."

Defeated, I give a shrug. "I can't imagine he'll be pulling strings to get me another fight when he thought I wasn't ready for this one, and on its face, it looks like I proved him right."

"I'm sorry, Shill," he says, inadvertently reminding me that I will be stuck with that damned ring name for at least another year, maybe forever. "I wish there was something I can do. Maybe Zack—"

"No. I'm done with him." I push open the door, look back over my shoulder. "I'm going back to how things were. I want Torment and Fuzzy coaching me again and Stan beating me up on the treadmill when I show up late in the morning. I want to train like I was training before. Things were simple before Zack showed up. I want them to be simple again."

"You improved a lot when you were training with him," he calls out.

"Maybe I did, but the price was just too high."

24

Shayla

"So, no more Mr. Hotness." Cheryl follows me into Symbian the week after my devastating fight. I was off work for a few days on doctor's orders, and our shifts haven't coordinated until today. We've spent the last hour catching up while we patrolled the grounds, and she now sums up a few hours' worth of considered reflection in five succinct words.

"No, he's gone. He came to the hospital where I was being checked over after the fight, and I asked him to leave. I'd had it with him interfering in my life, and I told him I didn't want to see him again."

"You didn't pull any punches."

I roll my eyes at her pun. Cheryl can always find the bright side to any bad situation. "I could have said a lot of things to him, but I bit my tongue. For a while, I thought things were different between us, but in the end, he was still his same overprotective self. He thought he knew what was best for me, and this time, it cost me a fight and possibly a professional contract."

We head over to the security desk, and I sit in Joe's chair while

she checks the monitors. "I think it's for the best. Things were getting too intense. He was pretty much living at my apartment, and I
was starting to feel about him the way I did in Glenwood. I felt like I
wanted to drown in him back then. I couldn't breathe unless he was
around. He made me feel safe and protected, and I don't want that
anymore. I can't rely on anyone else. I need to look after myself."

"You loved him."

"I don't know. Maybe it was infatuation. I was very young,
and he was my whole world."

"I thought I had that with Amber's father," Cheryl says. "I
lived and breathed him. He was everything to me. I thought he
was perfect in every way. I gave up everything to be with him—
my job, my family, even my dog, because he was a cat person.
And then six months after we got married, I found him in bed
with the next-door neighbor and her sister. Instead of apologizing, the bastard asked me to join them. It took me another try
before I realized the difference between love and infatuation.
Love does not explode onto the scene and utterly consume you.
It grows, wraps around you, holds you tight, and no matter what
you do, it won't let go. Sometimes you don't see it or feel it, but
love is always there. I had that with my first husband, and I've
been looking for it ever since."

"I once thought Zack and I had love. I even started thinking
we were finding it again, but now, I'm not so sure."

We study the monitors for the next few minutes. Everything is quiet outside. Joe is due to arrive shortly to take over
desk duty, and Cheryl and I will head out to relieve Sol on patrol.

"Is he still in town?" Cheryl asks.

"I don't know. I haven't seen or heard from him since I told him to leave the hospital, and my friends at the gym haven't seen him either."

"Holy crap. Lookit your face." Joe walks in the door, and I manage a smile now that the swelling has gone down and my bruises are fading.

"Better or worse than the raccoon look I had going last time?"

"Any bruises are bad bruises." Joe grimaces. "At least tell me you won."

"No. My opponent fouled but it was ruled accidental." My voice tightens, because the ruling still irritates me. "How is it an accident when someone grabs your hair, smashes your face down into their knee, and says 'take that, bitch'? I asked Torment if there was anything we could do, and he said he'd look into it, but he didn't seem very hopeful. Not that it would matter. I was disqualified because they thought I'd had a concussion in the last thirty days and tried to hide it. It ruined my chance of getting into the finals and maybe going pro."

I give up my seat to Joe, and he signs in on the computer. "Don't you dare give up," he says as he pulls up the security log. "You're a damn good fighter. Look what you did the other week here at Symbian. Maybe it won't be this year, but your time is coming, and Cheryl and I will be there when it does, and we'll be expecting front-row seats."

"I'm not giving up, but I am stepping back to reassess my training strategy." I lean against the console and fold my arms across my chest. "I'm training with Torment and Fuzzy again, and Stan is back to doing his old fitness torture sessions. But I'm off the competitive circuit, so I'm pretty much back to where I was two months ago, right down to the bruised face and black eyes."

His face softens. "She really did a number on you."

And Zack did a number on my heart.

"What the hell?" Joe stares at the monitor. "Sol logged out half an hour early. Did you see him go?"

Cheryl shakes her head. "We both got here five minutes before our shift was due to start."

"Christ. This is the last straw." He picks up the phone. "I don't know what's been going on with him. Ever since he came back from suspension, he's been acting strange. He's been patrolling buildings he doesn't need to patrol, not answering his pager, showing up late, and leaving early. At first I thought it was because he lost all that money and Babs left, but I've seen him go through that kind of rough time before and make it out the other end. It's like he wants to be fired this time. And now it's going to happen. I can't cover for him anymore."

I tighten my utility belt and check my weapons. "Do you want us to get out there? If he did leave early, it means no one has been on patrol for about forty minutes. That's a long time if the higher-ups have something secret in the works."

"Yeah." He covers the mouthpiece of the phone. "You guys go. I'm reporting him now."

Cheryl and I make our way across the grounds, checking the buildings one by one. It's a cool evening, the stars barely visible through the clouds. Cheryl fills me in on her most recent date with Officer Morrison and their plans for a weekend outing with Amber. We reach building three, and I give each door a perfunctory tug. Usually, everything is locked up tight, but the last door I check opens when I pull.

"Unlocked door in building three," Cheryl reports over her radio. "We're going to check it out."

"Sol should have reported this," I say as we walk down the main hallway, checking the office doors. "I don't think he'll get away with a slap on the wrist this time."

We check the upper levels, and Cheryl radios Joe to let him know we're heading downstairs to check out the plant room and the building manager's office.

I follow Cheryl down the concrete stairs. The main electricity meters, electricity distribution board, and water and gas meters are located in the plant room, along with the building management system computer, a server computer, and the data backup storage tapes, which are accessible only by the building manager and authorized staff.

We push open the door and step into suffocating darkness. Cheryl flicks the switch a few times, and then her hand drops to her utility belt.

"What's wrong?"

"The lights aren't working." She pulls out her flashlight and takes a few steps forward, shining the beam in an arc around the room. I hear a gasp, a thud, and the crack of the flashlight hitting the concrete floor. Through the stairway light behind me, I see Cheryl lying motionless on the ground.

"Cheryl?" Heart pounding, I pull out my gun and take a step back. "Whoever is in there, I'm armed, and this is the only way out. Come out with your hands up."

"Put down the fucking gun, or I'll put a bullet in her brain." Sol emerges from the darkness, his gun pointed at Cheryl's head.

Bang. Bang. Bang. Rational thought is trampled by the fierce thudding of my pulse. My mind screams a warning, but my body won't obey.

"Now. On your knees. Left hand on your head, the other putting the gun down."

I do as he says, tightening my left fist in my hair in frustration. My radio has an emergency button, but it is holstered on my left side. I can't press it without obviously reaching across my body. I can only hope Cheryl's radio triggers the alarm when it senses she is no longer moving. One of the benefits of working at a high-tech company is the high-tech equipment they gave us. Our radio alarms are automatically triggered if there is no response to a call or if the radio isn't moving, is moving too much, or is out of range. But if I know that, Sol knows it, too.

"One hand on the buckle. Take off the belt nice and slow."

"What's this about?" I undo my belt with my right hand. "Is it because you were suspended?"

He gives a snort of derision. "Throw the belt over here, and put both hands on your head."

I follow his instructions, throwing the belt as hard and fast as I can, hoping the excess movement will trigger the alarm.

Sol catches it with his free hand and places it on the ground beside Cheryl. He points the gun at me and motions to the ground. "Facedown on the ground. Hands behind your head."

When I'm in position, he comes up behind me and drops a knee into my back. "Not so tough now, are you, bitch?"

"What the fuck are you doing?" I don't recognize the second voice in the darkness or the shadow of the man sitting in front of the computer monitor that has just flickered to life.

"She thinks she's so tough playing at a man's game." Sol grabs my hair and yanks my head back. "Look at her now. How damn easy was it to bring her down and disarm her? Where's your fight now, cunt?"

"Fucking idiot." Sol's partner in crime taps on the keyboard in front of him. "We don't have time for your stupid games. We're already running behind. Give me the passwords and the flash drive. You need the money worse than I do."

"On the table beside you." Sol releases my hair and jabs his knee harder into my back, hitting one of the bruises Gordon left behind.

"You weren't watching sports games in the computer labs, were you?" I say, putting the pieces together. "You were stealing passwords."

"So smart and yet so fucking dumb." Sol shoves my head down until my cheek is pressed against the cold floor. "You know what this technology is worth? Billions. I'm gonna be a rich man. I'll pay off all my bookies, buy myself an island, and spend the rest of my life in the fanciest casinos in the world, fucking girls like you who think they're hot shit. But in the end, you are all just another piece of pussy."

"Do you really think they won't track you down? They're an IT company. One of the top ones in Silicon Valley. How are you—"

"Shut the fuck up." Sol's partner pulls some fancy equipment from a bag at his feet and hooks it up to the computer. Now illuminated by the dual screens in front of him, he is clearly the more imposing of the two. Tall and dark with a suit jacket hanging loosely off his shoulders and a T-shirt stretched tight over his chest, he's got a mafia look and the attitude to match. "Tie up the fucking girl, and give me a hand while I decide what to do with them. They've seen too much."

Even as fear wraps an icy hand around my heart, his slight accent over the word *girl* niggles something at the back of my brain.

It's a fucking girl, the thief said a few weeks ago before he escaped over the fence.

And what did I say then? *Not a girl like you've ever seen before.*

No, I'm not a girl anymore. I'm a woman who has been through hell and back. I became a wife for the wrong reasons and a success for the right ones, lost everything, and got back on my feet to chase a new dream.

Chasing. But never catching. And now I know why.

I've been afraid of losing my MMA dream, just like I lost my dreams of love and marriage and becoming a professional dancer. I've been afraid to go on the offensive, to take that final step, throw that final punch, open myself up to the success that is waiting on the other side of fear.

It is time to stop being afraid. In the underground, when the outcome of the fight didn't matter, I took those steps and threw those punches. That is the fighter I need to be.

The fighter and the woman I truly am.

I breath in deep, pushing away my fear, just as I did in the underground. "Were you behind the last break-in, Sol? Is that why you didn't fight? Or are you just the loser I always thought you were? Did you pretend to throw a few punches because you couldn't stand the thought that you were bested by a girl? Now you're hiding behind that gun, so you'll never know if you could really beat me."

Sol drops the gun and grabs the collar of my jacket, hauling me to my feet. He slams me against the wall so hard, I lose my breath, but the pain clears my mind, helps me focus on what I need to do. My body comes to life, and I find my fight. I spin and throw a kick and then a punch, forcing Sol back to the doorway. With a combo that would make even Torment proud, I drive him into the dark room and move in for a takedown.

"Enough." Sol's partner holds up the gun, and I raise my hands in surrender. "Sol, get the fucking flash drive and the bag, and get the hell out so I can clean up your damn mess."

"I can deal with her myself," Sol snaps, breathing hard. "She just caught me off guard. Just gimme a minute, Clive, and I'll wipe the floor with her ass."

"Get. The. Damn. Bag." Clive's gaze stays locked on me, and adrenaline surges through my body. I might only get once chance, and I need to be ready. I won't let Cheryl die and miss out on the chance for real love with a good man. I won't let Amber be raised by deadbeat husband number four. I won't give up my dreams of becoming a professional fighter, or of loving the man of my heart and seeing him again.

Even if it means putting myself out there in front of a bullet.

"What are you going to do? You can't kill them." Worry laces Sol's tone as he brushes past me, and it hits me that he would never have pulled the trigger. All the big talk and self-aggrandizement hid a coward through and through.

"I'll do what needs to be done."

I meet Clive's cold, steely gaze, and I have no doubt he's telling the truth.

Sol sighs. "I can't find the flash drive."

Clive shifts his gaze, just the slightest bit, and I take advantage of his distraction just as I've been trained to do, just as Sandy did when she knocked me down in the ring. I lunge, throwing myself forward with everything I have, aiming low for a take-down, beneath his outstretched arm. We crash to the ground, rolling on the cold cement, fighting for control of the gun that could turn the tide of this fight in the very worst way. I use every move I know, including the tricks I learned from Zack when we rolled together on the mats. I manage to take a dominant position on top of him, straddling his body. Using all my strength, I smash his gun hand on the concrete over and over again until I hear something crack. Clive screams and drops his weapon. I smash my fist into his face, and he shudders beneath me.

Bang. A door slams in the distance. I hear footsteps on the stairs, and then Joe appears in the doorway.

"Shayla! What's going on? Cheryl's alarm went off."

"They're stealing software. Watch out for Sol."

Too late. Sol bursts from the shadows, slamming Joe into the doorframe as he barrels down the hallway.

"Go after him," I shout. "I've got this situation under control."

And I do. I have found my fight on the other side of fear in the basement of Symbian Cloud Computing.

Zack

ZACK KNEW SOMETHING WAS UP AS SOON AS HE SAW SADIST standing in front of the red line painted on the ground at Redemption's entrance, his arms folded over his massive chest. When Sadist stopped him with a firm hand on his shoulder, he had a strong suspicion whatever it was had to do with him.

"Sorry, Slayer. Only members are allowed to cross the red line."

"I've got a three-month pass."

Sadist held out a meaty paw. "Let me see."

Zack handed over the pass Shayla had given him. He hadn't been to Redemption for a week, but he was damn sure the pass hadn't expired, because he'd only had it for a month and a half.

Sadist inspected the plastic card. Then he crushed it in his massive fist and scattered the pieces on the ground. "Looks like it was a three-week pass and not a three-month pass. You must have made a mistake."

Zack was disappointed but not surprised. In all his years in the business, he had never met a team as close-knit as the team at

Redemption. They truly were a family, and as any family would do when a member had been hurt, they were closing ranks and shutting him out.

No Redemption meant no training. No training meant no Torment. No Torment meant he wouldn't have the opportunity to put himself to the test. When he went after Shayla's ex—and nothing had changed his resolve to give her justice—he would have to do it not knowing whether he had the self-control to pull back before things got out of hand.

"I'm just here to work out."

Sadist shrugged. "You need a new membership to get in, and the membership desk is closed."

"I'll buy a day pass."

"We've run out."

Damn. He needed to work off some of his anger and frustration in a proper MMA facility and not the cold, poorly outfitted hotel gym that he'd been forced to use after picking up his stuff from Shayla's apartment.

"Okay, man. I get the message. I'm out of here." He lifted his hands in mock defeat. "Tell everyone I said goodbye. I'm back on the recruitment circuit and flying out to New York tomorrow."

"So that's it?" Sadist scowled. "You're going to San Francisco?"

"I was here to coach Shilla. She doesn't need me anymore, and she doesn't want to see me. I need to get back to work."

"Are you kidding me?" Sadist's voice rose in pitch. "She's your girl. You don't walk away. You don't give up because you lost your card."

"I do if she says that's what she wants." His hands curled into fists. "You think it's easy for me? I've called. I've texted. She's made her feelings clear, so I'm going to do a few trips and hope she cools down before I come back." He wasn't giving up. Not yet. But he was going to give her some space.

Sadist gave an indignant snort. "You betray her and then you abandon her. Nice."

Zack bristled at Sadist's sarcastic tone. "I watched her go down when Sandy hit her, and I watched her go down in the underground fight. To me, her reaction looked exactly the same. I even suggested she see a doctor after the underground fight, but she said she was fine, and I respected her decision. I made the mistake of not letting her make her own choices before, and I wasn't going to do it again. But a third time? When she could barely stand? She wasn't going to quit so I did what I had to do to protect her."

"Is that what you're telling yourself so you can sleep at night? That she hit her head hard enough to have another concussion?"

Zack folded his arms and glared. "It's what I saw."

"Through your Okami-colored glasses?"

"You don't know anything," Zack bit out. "What happened with Gordon was the nightmare of my fucking life. Yeah, maybe I've still got a hang-up about brain injuries because of Okami, but she could barely walk a straight line after Gordon's foul. I could have just let her go back in the ring like she wanted, and if I had, I wouldn't be here alone. But the risk was too damn high. So I told the doc about the fight the way I saw it, and he made his call. Even if I do lose her, I would make the same decision. I'd rather a world with her alive and hating me than one in which she's gone."

Sadist stroked a hand over his jaw and studied him, considering. "Wait there." He didn't wait for Zack's response but crossed the red line and disappeared into Redemption.

What the hell? Zack was tempted to walk away, but curiosity and a deep reluctance to return alone to his hotel held him in place.

A few minutes later, Sadist returned. "The Predator is waiting for you out back."

Puzzled, Zack frowned. "Why?"

"He has an extra membership card."

If Zack hadn't wanted that card so badly, he would have laughed. But he did want it. Although it had only been a week, he missed working out at Redemption. He missed the training, the camaraderie, the scents of vinyl and sweat, the sounds of speed bags drumming, weights clanking, and treadmills whirring. He missed being part of the sport that had been his life for so many years, the endorphin rush he got when he pushed his body to the max, and the hope that maybe one day he would be able to fight in the ring again.

"I'm a recruiter. Not a fighter."

"So check the Predator out," Sadist suggested. "Everyone thinks he's good enough to go pro. Maybe you'll want to sign him to MEFC before you head out of town. You don't want to lose him to Radical Power. I heard they've been sniffing around."

Zack sighed. "The Predator's a street fighter. He's got too much unlearning to do."

"Last I heard, you started out as a street fighter, too." Sadist closed the door behind him. "Maybe you can unlearn a few things with him. Or maybe you're too scared. I get it. The whole Okami thing. And then Shayla taking a few knocks to the head, making it all come back…"

"Fuck you." He knew exactly what Sadist was doing, and yet he was finding it hard to resist.

"Yeah, that's about what the Predator would do to you if you fought him. He is undefeated in the underground and a damn dirty fighter. If a man were wanting to push himself to his limit, a street fight in an alley with the Predator would be the best way to go about it. But I get that you're too afraid to face him. Hell, even if I weighed fifty pounds less, had spent time in Black Ops, and had been trained in covert operations by the CIA like him, I'd be afraid, too."

Zack didn't rise to the bait. "Anyone ever tell you that you're a bastard?"

Sadist laughed. "They tell me I'm a sadist. But today, I'm being a nice guy and giving you a choice to walk into the parking lot behind Redemption like a man instead of being picked up and thrown to the wolves for betraying our teammate. It's the kind of choice you didn't give to her."

Sadist was right. When he'd seen Gordon's knee slam into Shayla's head, all he could think about was getting Shayla the hell out of the fight so she didn't wind up dead like Okami. He'd been just as ruthless about making it happen as he'd been the night he walked away and left her in Glenwood.

"That leaves me with a choice that's no choice at all."

A grin split Sadist's face. "You could probably outrun me, but I have a feeling you're not the kind of man to turn down a challenge. And the Predator is one hell of a challenge."

"He's not Torment."

"You aren't ready for Torment."

Zack studied the heavyweight fighter, considering. He was flying to New York tomorrow to sign an upcoming new fighter from the Bronx, and he had planned to hunt down Damian while he was there. This was the perfect chance to really test himself against a worthy competitor. The Predator wasn't Torment, but he was damn close. "I'll walk."

"Good man." Sadist clapped him on the shoulder. "Most of the team should be out there already. I wish Shilla could have been here, too. She loves watching the Predator fight."

"You said he was in the CIA?" He lengthened his stride to keep up with Sadist as they walked along the building.

"Second-worst kept secret at Redemption, but he'll deny it, so don't ask. If you ever get his wife, Sia, drunk at the annual Redemption Christmas party, she has a good story to tell about what happened when she was kidnapped, and that will pretty much tell you all you need to know."

"What's the first-worst kept secret?" He didn't want to know, but he did. Everything about Redemption interested him, from its history to its fighters and from their stories to their bond.

"Shilla's accident that wasn't an accident." Sadist heaved in a ragged breath. "You probably know more about it than we do. When she first walked in the door, she was a wreck. Casts, slings, bruises, bandages…you name it. She told us she'd fallen down some stairs. Torment tried to send her to a rehab center, but she insisted she wanted to learn MMA. That's when we knew for sure there was more to her story. You don't look the way she looked from a fall down the stairs."

Zack stopped midstride. "I know what happened. Why are you telling me this?"

"There are benefits to having a history with the CIA. Friends you can call up for a favor. The Predator is a protective sort, especially when it comes to the team. He might be persuaded to do a little investigating for you if there was someone you were trying to find."

"And the price for the information?"

Sadist shrugged. "You have to be part of the team."

The Predator was waiting for him in the alley wearing a T-shirt, fight shorts, and a pair of running shoes. Two Redemption fighters were stationed on either end as lookouts. Torment leaned casually against the back door, like he had known Zack would show up. Zack was glad he'd worn his track pants to the gym. Although he'd always fought in street clothes as a kid, he was used to the range of movement afforded by sportswear.

No words were exchanged. None were necessary. It was an underground fight. No rules. No limits. No mercy.

The fight began with a nod from Torment. The Predator wasted no time and moved in quickly to smash his fist into Zack's cheek. Zack welcomed the pain as the payback he deserved and dropped into his fight stance, fending off the attack with an overhand left, followed by a right. The Predator landed a left kick, and Zack countered with a spinning back kick that the Predator easily blocked. The Predator retaliated with a dirty right hook, slicing Zack's forehead. Blood trickled over his brow, dripped down his eye, and he wiped it away, a familiar heat curling in his belly as the beast that he'd locked away inside himself raised its head.

Fighting the junior and midlevel fighters had been easy. But the Predator was in a different league. For the first time, Zack felt off his game, unprepared, and acutely aware that he was nowhere near the level he had been at four years ago. Although he hated to admit it, he wouldn't have lasted three minutes in the ring with Torment.

The Predator moved in with a right and then unloaded a flurry of punches to Zack's head. Zack moved to counter, but the Predator was gone, moving like a ghost through the shadows of the alley. He was everywhere and nowhere. The blows came hard and fast, with no discernible pattern except that he never hit the same place twice and nothing was out of bounds. He used moves that would have had him disqualified from sanctioned fights, and for all Zack's skill, he couldn't get close enough to take the Predator down to the ground where he would have the advantage.

He wiped the sweat from his forehead, took a breather while the Predator jeered from across the alley.

"That all you got, Slayer? Let me know when we're done warming up and I can really get started."

Zack was used to posturing and trash talk. When he had fought professionally, it was part of the show. The fans loved to hear the fighters threaten each other, and their scripted comments were the highlight of weigh-ins and interviews. But here, where there were no fans or cameras, he took the Predator's comments for what they were—a message that Zack wasn't worthy of what the Predator was holding back.

Not worthy.

It was the story of his life.

Without warning, the Predator rushed him, forcing him back against the building. He landed a leg kick that made Zack's teeth rattle and connected with huge shots to the head. Stunned, Zack threw a pair of counter rights, but the Predator's right hand flattened him against the wall, and he poured on the hurt, wrenching Zack out of the present and thrusting him into the brutal past.

"Don't tell me how to live my life, boy. You know why your mother killed herself? Because she had a fucking worthless piece of shit for a son. If I want to drink, I'll fucking drink. If I want to slap any one of you kids around to shut you the hell up, then I'll slap you. You think you can stop me? Think again. You don't have what it takes. You are good for fucking nothing."

Jab. Jab. Jab. The Predator wouldn't stop, wouldn't let Zack off the wall. Zack tried to advance, landed some right hands, but couldn't get enough room to go in for a takedown. He ate some savage knees and fell back, scrambling.

"You're nothing, Grayson. A high school dropout. Living in a fucking trailer with your sisters. Your parents were trailer trash. Your grandparents were trailer trash. You've got trailer trash in your blood. You aren't worthy of my sister. If I see you near her again, this fucking beat down will be nothing compared to what I'll do to you."

"C'mon, Slayer. This is pathetic. I'm getting bored punching your ugly face. Do something, or I'm gonna fall asleep. How did you win a fucking title belt if you don't know how to fight?"

"Four." The word dropped from his lips before he could catch it. "I won four belts. Not one." Adrenaline surged through his body, clearing the haze from his mind and unleashing the anger he held tightly in check. He was the best middleweight fighter in the country. An MEFC all-star. He had come from nothing and made something of himself through hard work and dedication.

He was worthy.

Worthy of respect.

Worthy of the ballerina who had stolen his heart.

He threw a big left hand, holding nothing back, and moved on the advance, taking the Predator by surprise. He connected with a vicious combo of fists and kicks, followed by a movie fight rear back punch that got the Predator weak in the knees. Zack grabbed the Predator's shirt, lifted his hand for the knock-out strike.

And then the Predator cursed.

Zack sucked in a breath as the word unlocked a memory of his very last fight.

Okami had cursed.

He had fallen to his knees, fully lucid and engaged in the fight even as Zack threw his last punch. There had been no sign. No warning. Until the end, it had been a fight like any other. And Zack had been fully present. Aware. In control. Even after he'd released the beast, he could remember every detail of the fight—the roar of the crowd, the scents of sweat and vinyl, the taste of blood in his mouth, the fury in Okami's eyes. And Okami's last words…

Fuck you.

He hadn't hit a man when he was down. He'd hit a fighter who had gone down fighting—a fighter who had chosen to take the risk of stepping into the ring against medical advice. Zack wasn't responsible for Okami's choices. He could forgive himself, because he was worthy. Not just as a fighter, but as a man. He had been in control then, just as he was in control now.

He dropped his fist, and the Predator surged up and landed a vicious uppercut to his chin, and then one to his nose. Blood splattered across the pavement. Reeling, Zack fell forward, and the Predator met him with big shots and knees. Zack dropped and ate some more shots before he fell to the ground, tapping out as the world went topsy-turvy and Okami finally had his revenge.

"Someone call a medic."

"Hey, buddy." Sadist crouched down beside him, gently pushing him down when he tried to rise. "Probably better if you just lie back and chill. Lucky for you, Makayla's on duty tonight. She's got a light touch with stitches and broken bones."

"I'm good." Zack wheezed out his words as blood trickled into his mouth. "Just need some ice."

"Yeah." Sadist patted his shoulder. "Sure. How about we wait for her anyway, just in case. Your ribs made a cracking sound when he threw that spinning back kick your way, and your nose might need a little reset."

Zack gritted his teeth against the pain of each breath. "Got a flight to catch in the morning."

"I think you might have to delay your trip a couple of days." Sadist cocked his head to the side. "You had the advantage until you pulled your last punch. Why did you do it?"

Zack lay back and stared up at the stars. "Because I could."

26

Shayla

"I'M LOOKING FOR ZACK GRAYSON." I GIVE MY BEST "I BELONG in your ritzy hotel smile" to the clerk at the front desk of the Devonian Palace Hotel. She checks out my *Cute but Psycho* tank top, flannel check shirt, and cargo skirt and responds with a tight-lipped smirk.

"Do you have a room number?"

"Um…no."

"Is he expecting you?" She tilts her head, and her perfectly coiffed, sleek black bob swings along her jawline.

"No." But I know he's staying here. Sadist gave me the details, and when it comes to information, no one knows more than him.

"Then I'm afraid I can't help you."

"Could you just call and let him know I'm here? He was hurt in a fight last night, and I'm worried about him. He hasn't answered any of my texts or phone messages." With each passing minute, I regret even more my decision to visit Zack, but after Sadist told me what happened with the Predator last night, I had to come.

"If he were staying with us, and I'm not saying he is, because we are very careful about the privacy of our celebrity guests—"

Celebrity guest. Sometimes I forget just how famous Zack still is.

"I wouldn't wish to disturb him unnecessarily." Her gaze flicks to my purse and back to me.

Hope flickers in my chest, and I pull a few bills out of my purse that I can ill afford to part with. "I'm sure he'll be happy to see me."

"The lounge is very comfortable," she says, slipping the money in her jacket. "You never know who you'll meet."

I follow the low hum of voices into a chic, dark wood-paneled lounge, all yellow leather chairs and eclectic designs. Men in suits or chinos, and button-down shirts wine and dine with women in slinky evening wear, their faces abnormally tanned and their bodies so thin that they almost look anorexic. I look around for Zack, and then I hear her.

Sandy's distinctive high, shrill laugh filters through the low hum of chatter and the clink of glassware.

I search the crowd and find her only a few tables away. She is wearing a beautiful sleeveless cream cocktail dress, and her long, blond hair falls in artful curls over her shoulders. With her back to me, she doesn't know I'm here, but Zack, sitting across the table from her, does.

His gaze locks on me, and his eyes widen. He's wearing a long-sleeved black shirt, mouth-wateringly tight around his broad chest, tucked into a pair of dress pants. Except for the fact that his face is battered and bruised and he sports a white bandage over his nose, he fits right in. Zack the celebrity fighter and Sandy the socialite. And the two people at the table, the blond woman dripping in diamonds and the man in Armani, must be her parents.

And then there's me. Grunge in every sense of the word but now comfortable in my skin.

"Shay." Zack stands so abruptly, his chair almost falls over.

Sandy turns, her perfectly tweezed brow lifts, and she gives me a slightly puzzled frown. "What are you doing here?"

My fingers tighten around my gym bag containing a first aid kit and a few boxes of bandages. What am I doing here? Maybe I'm a glutton for punishment. Or maybe I learned nothing about establishing boundaries when I was with Damian. Most likely I'm here because I have not suffered enough pain in my life, and I am obviously needing some more. Or maybe, after bringing down an armed intruder with the skills I learned at Redemption, I'm finally ready to overcome my fear, take a risk, and embrace the things I want in life.

"I heard about the fight," I say to Zack. "I just came to make sure you were okay." I give Sandy a tight smile. "Looks like you're just fine."

Poised to leave, I imagine myself turning and walking away, leaving Zack in Sandy's clutches, just as I did a few weeks ago when I told her we weren't together. And then I imagine a new Shayla. A now Shayla. A woman who survived a broken heart and a broken body. A woman who destroyed Evil Elsa and faced a much more seasoned competitor in a sanctioned amateur fight. A woman who stared down the barrel of a gun and didn't for one moment accept that she might die.

I wrap the strength and passion of that woman around me. And then I close the distance between Zack and me. I slide one arm around his neck, and I kiss him the way he kissed me when he found me outside the Protein Palace with Reg.

I kiss him with passion. I kiss him because I want him. I kiss him because he's mine and I want the world to know.

"I'm Shayla Tanner. It's nice to meet you," I say to Sandy's parents as I turn away. "Sorry to interrupt."

"Shay." Zack calls after me, and I can hear him offer his excuses to Sandy and her family.

"Shayla. Wait."

I walk faster, weave in and out of the crowds. I want him to chase me. I want him to want me. I want him to beg for forgiveness. This time, nothing less will do.

He catches up with me just outside the hotel. Raindrops fall lightly from the sky, washing away the dust and grime. Strong arms wrap around me from behind, and he hugs me tight.

"You came."

"I thought you were hurt." He feels so good against me, it's hard not to sink into his warmth.

Not yet, I tell myself. *You are worth an apology. You are owed an explanation.*

"Let's get out of the rain and where people aren't watching us." He walks me down the alley beside the building where an overhang from the side entrance shelters us.

"So," he says, looking down at me, his eyes warm and soft.

"So. Sandy…"

"Her parents are here to finalize the paperwork for the sponsorship deal I told you about. I'm back at work as a recruiter and leaving for New York tomorrow so it had to be today. We were supposed to take some pictures for the promo materials, too, but I guess this isn't the image they want to project." He gently touches his nose.

I would laugh, but I'm still trying to process what he said. *He's leaving.* I try not to let him see my shock, because I should be happy. This is what I wanted. I told him to get out of my room and out of my life. I told him I never wanted to see him again.

And yet, here I am.

"You don't look as bad as me," I say, running a finger over my puffy face.

He studies me and his eyes narrow. "You have fresh bruises."

"Cheryl and I might have come across Sol and his friend engaged in a little corporate espionage the other night. And I may have had a gun pointed at me by a not-very-nice guy."

Zack tenses, and his eyes go wide. "What the hell?"

"Calm down," I say in a soothing tone. "I wrestled the gun away from him, took him down to the ground, and had him pinned by the time Joe arrived. Cheryl's in the hospital with a concussion, but she'll be okay."

Even in the semidarkness, I can tell he's about to lose it from the way the pulse throbs in his neck, the stark look in his eyes, and the fact that his chest isn't moving.

"Breathe." I lean up and nuzzle his neck. "I'm okay. More

than okay. I was offered a promotion, although it would mean moving to another facility."

Zack lets out his breath with a rush of curses and exclamations and ties it all up in a bow of, "Where is he? I'm going to kill him."

"He's in jail. Sol, too. He got away but I'd beat him up so badly, he had to go to a hospital and the police found him." I lift an eyebrow. "You should be reassured by the fact that I can clearly take care of myself both in and out of the ring. I don't need anyone to protect me or to take my choices away."

We stare at each other as the rain patters around us, muffling the sounds of the city streets. We are alone in our bubble of darkness. Me and Zack against the world.

"What do you want?" he asks. "I'll do anything, give anything, to have you back."

"I want you. The real you, and not the idealized image I had when we were together in Glenwood. I want you with the pain you carry in your heart and the anger you carry inside. I want your strength and your courage. I want your overprotectiveness and willingness to cross any line for the people you care about. I want your beauty and your flaws. And I want an apology."

He lets out a relieved breath and his shoulders slump. "I'm sorry, sweetheart. I saw you fall, and all I could think about was Okami. I would have done anything to stop you getting back into that ring. I can't lose you. Not again." He leans down and kisses me, his lips warm despite the cool, moist air.

"But you're leaving."

"I'll be back." He pulls out his wallet and shows me a purple plastic card. "I have a permanent membership to Redemption."

"I heard you lost your fight with the Predator," I say as he tucks his wallet away.

"I lost that fight but won another. Apparently, it was enough to earn the card." He slips his hand under my clothes, cups my breast in his hand, his cool, wet skin making me shiver.

With a sigh of longing, I run my tongue over the seam of his lips. Touching. Tasting. Committing his mouth to memory as if I might never get the chance to kiss him again.

Zack groans and tightens one arm around me, molding me to him as if we were one person, not two. I feel his strength in the easy way he holds me, lose myself in his familiar scent, taste him on my tongue. He deepens our kiss, and I feel like this is how we should have always been. Together. Safe. Hidden from the world in a veil of tears.

"How badly are you hurt?" I want him inside me. Here. Now. When we are bruised and broken, wet and exposed. I want to bandage all our hurts with love, and make them go away.

"Not enough to stop." Without breaking our kiss, he slips his hand beneath my skirt. His warm fingers trace lazy circles along my inner thighs to the edge of my panties. He tugs on the elastic and then shoves my panties aside to slick one thick finger through my folds.

"You're so wet for me, sweetheart."

"I missed you."

"I'll make it up to you. In every way I can." He pushes his finger deep inside me, and I gasp, relishing the pleasure of a deeper connection while at the same time feeling greedy for more.

"Zack. We're outside. You're still a celebrity and if someone sees us together…" I lever myself up and push down on his thick finger, seeking more friction than he's willing to give.

"I don't give a damn. I want everyone to know you're my girl and I'm showing her how I feel in the best way I can." He adds a second finger and gently rubs his thumb around my clit, using my wetness for more lubrication before circling the aching bundle of nerves again. I am shaking, gripping his shoulders so hard, I'm sure my fingers will leave marks, but still he teases, alternating thrusts with slow, steady circles of my clit. Each stroke takes me closer and closer to the edge.

I have never been as turned on as I am now. Never felt so free that I don't give a damn if a horde of Zack's fans find us and take pictures to send to the press. Never felt so connected to anyone in my life.

"So fucking beautiful," he murmurs as he adds a third finger.

"Ahh." I bite off my cry when I feel the wet slide of his thumb over my clit, the firm pulse of his fingers deep inside me.

My orgasm starts as a low rolling heat in my belly that crashes over me and floods my veins with molten pleasure. I clamp my thighs around his hand and buck against him. But he holds me tight and keeps me safe, his mouth finding mine to swallow my scream.

I collapse against his broad chest, bracing myself on his shoulders as he undoes his fly, freeing his cock from its restraint.

"Are you ready for me?" His hands slide under my ass, and he lifts me, bracing me against the cold, brick wall. I wrap my legs around him and grind against his shaft.

"Always ready. More than ready. Even when you're away ready." I mean to tease, but Zack shakes his head.

"I'm not going anywhere," he says. "You are my life, Shay. I'm leaving tomorrow on a job, but I'm coming back when it's done, and I'll keep coming back until we've fixed everything that is broken between us."

Slowly, he pushes inside me, stretching me, filling me, driving in so deep, I can feel him everywhere. He gives me a moment to adjust, and then he starts to move.

Oh God. I wrap my arms around his neck and brace myself as I catch his rhythm, driving myself down to meet every thrust. Zack groans and slams into me harder, and I feel another climax begin to build.

"Promise you'll wait for me." He pants his breaths as he moves. "Promise you'll give us a chance."

"I promise."

Overwhelmed, my body tight and aching, I climax again, this time in a rush of white-hot heat. My inner muscles clamp around his cock as he hammers into me. He comes with a guttural groan, one arm wrapped around my body, holding me tight, his cock pulsing deep inside me.

I take Zack back to my apartment when we're done.

He holds me all night long.

When the sun rises, he slips out of bed to get ready to catch his flight, but I am so attuned to him, I am fully awake by the time he comes in to say goodbye.

"Don't get into any fights." I lean up and press a soft kiss to his bandaged nose.

Zack laughs. "I'm a fighter."

"I thought you were a recruiter."

"And I thought I'd lost you forever."

I lift my head and kiss him. He groans softly and pulls me closer, his tongue diving deep to possess every inch of my mouth.

"Come back to me," I say when he finally pulls away.

I am unsettled by his dark, thoughtful expression. But then he smiles, and his face lightens again. "Always."

27 Zack

NEW YORK HADN'T CHANGED IN THE SIX YEARS SINCE ZACK had visited for his Newark fight. It was still as noisy, dirty, and busy as he remembered. As a kid, he'd always dreamed about leaving Glenwood and living in the big city, but now he longed for the peace of the mountain trails, the whisper of the wind in the trees, and a future with the woman he loved.

After he reached his hotel, he went straight to the gym to check out the fighter Kip wanted him to see. He never told anyone who had caught MEFC's interest. Over the years, he'd discovered he could learn more about the prospective fighters by watching them train and socializing with the team than he could by watching them fight. At the end of a boozy evening, he called Kip and gave his report. The fighter had a serious drinking problem, and Zack pegged him as a wasted investment.

With the day's work done, he called Shayla.

"How's New York?" she asked.

"So far so good. I have one more thing I need to do tomorrow, and then Kip wants me to fly to Cape Town."

Silence.

He liked it. A lot. It meant she cared, and although she had showed him in a variety of different ways how she felt before he left, she hadn't said the words he longed to hear.

"I'm not going," he said. "I told Kip I wanted to stick around the West Coast for a while."

He heard a soft sigh and then a laugh. "West is best."

"How was training today?" They hadn't talked about what was happening with her fight career, and Zack didn't want to push. She was on CAMO ill for another two weeks, and she had voluntarily pulled out of the competitive circuit. They had decided last night that it would be best for her to find a new full-time coach. She needed someone who could keep an emotional distance, and that clearly wasn't him.

"Torment was an ass. Fuzzy was his backup bitch. And Stan just added to the pain. So nothing unusual. But I do have some exciting news."

His heart squeezed in his chest at her upbeat tone. When she was happy, he was happy. "Tell me."

"I've been helping Cheryl out with Amber. She's still not feeling great after that hit she took to her head, and she asked me to take Amber to her ballet class. Madame Rambert recognized me from the recital, and we had a long chat. She's been looking for a new teacher for the little ones, and I agreed to teach part-time. The pay isn't great, but it means I don't have to take the promotion at Symbian, which I was considering to cover the costs of hiring a new coach. I really don't want to leave Joe and Cheryl, and this way I get to do two things I love."

"I can't think of anything better than reconnecting with something that was such a big part of your life," he said. "It must not have been an easy decision, but you've always been brave."

"I'm scared," she admitted. "But I'm going to do it anyway. Just being in the studio watching the class brought back all sorts of memories, and I want to focus on the good ones and push away the bad."

Her courage put him to shame. What the hell was he doing traveling across the world looking for fighters when he should be in the ring?

The next morning, he headed out to the first of the two addresses the Predator had taped to the back of his new Redemption membership card. He hadn't asked how the Predator had found Damian, and he didn't want to know. Apparently, the bastard had opened his own ballet studio in the Hudson Valley after he'd been blacklisted by the ballet community for his attack on Shayla, and when he wasn't there, he was at his condo only a few blocks away.

Although Zack desperately wanted to grab Damian the moment he saw him and give him the beat down he deserved, he had made a promise to return to Shayla, and that wouldn't happen if he wound up in jail. He had to approach this the way he approached every fight. First, he would do a little recon, then he would form a plan, and finally, he would attack.

In theory, it made sense, and the recon part went well. The ballet studio was housed in a small, run-down brick building at a crossroads with windows facing both streets. Posters of dancers in various poses lined the tops of the windows, and a neon sign above the front door flashed "Peters' School of Dance."

After walking around the block a few times looking for alleys and back exits, Zack sat across the street with a protein shake and watched the young dancers go in and out over the course of the afternoon. Although there was no receptionist, a young woman in loose dance wear came out each time the door opened to greet all the dancers and parents. When the flow of dancers into the studio trickled to a lonely few, he called the number stenciled on the window and arranged an appointment for the end of the day, ostensibly to discuss his fictitious daughter's interest in starting ballet.

"I'm June Peters. We spoke on the phone." The young woman he had watched all afternoon held out her hand to Zack as he walked in the door at his appointed time. She had the lean, toned body and narrow hips of a young dancer, and with her smooth, rounded face and her long, blond hair tied up with a pink flowered hair tie, Zack figured her to be no older than twenty-five. But her eyes told a different story, and when Zack drew close to take her hand, he could see the bruises on her face that she had clearly tried to hide with makeup.

"I understand you have a daughter interested in ballet." Her gaze fixed on Zack's nose, now without the bandage but still badly swollen and bruised after his fight with the Predator.

"Car accident," he said quickly, making her blush at her indiscretion. "And yes. As I said on the phone, her name is Amber, and she's five." He sent a mental apology to Cheryl for using her daughter as an excuse to get close to the man who had hurt his Shayla.

"A little old to start, but I'm sure with a little extra effort, she can catch up."

"Who teaches the younger girls?" Zack moved forward, forcing her to step back down the narrow hallway as he searched for Damian. He could hear music coming from one of the studios and the sound of a man's voice.

"I do." She forced a smile, but her consternation was clear in her face.

"And when they're older?" He kept walking, and she kept stepping backward. Zack knew he should stop, but he couldn't help himself. Now that he was inside, he needed to see Damian with his own eyes, and he needed to see him now.

"Damian Peters. He was a dancer with Joffrey and the artistic director of the New York Ballet, along with many other accomplishments. He is an excellent teacher, very demanding, and he works the girls hard, but he gets incredible results."

"I'm sure he does." Zack stopped a few feet from the door and stared at the girl in front of him. From the way she held herself, he suspected she was hiding more bruises beneath her clothes. The thought of Shayla suffering during her marriage made him sick inside, and he took a deep breath to calm himself down. He hadn't been there for her, but there was another woman he could save.

Unable to wait another moment, Zack pushed past her and opened the studio door. There was only one person in the room, a tall, blond man standing beside the barre. Zack had only seen Damian at a distance when he had come to New York to find Shayla, but he recognized the harsh, square jaw and heavy features of Shayla's ex. He was shorter than Zack by about three inches, and his stocky body was thickly muscled without an ounce of fat.

A growl rose in Zack's throat. This was the man who had hurt his Shayla, broken her bones, crushed her fingers, and destroyed her dreams. This was the man she feared, who made her scared to open herself fully to love and life. He could redeem himself by defeating this monster. He could avenge Shayla, eliminate the threat, and make the horror of her past go away.

"Are you okay, sir?" June's forehead creased in a puzzled frown.

"Pain." He touched his nose. "From the accident. It comes and goes." His gaze flicked to the barely concealed bruises around her eye. "It looks like you were in an accident, too."

June's face heated, and she dropped her gaze. "I could get you some ice."

Although it was tempting to send her away, he didn't want to be left alone with Damian just yet. He needed to get himself under control, and right now, he was too close to the edge.

"Thank you, but I'm fine." He studied Damian as he warmed up. He wore knit warm-up tights and a tight white shirt as he did his barre. He would have stamina and strength but no skills as a fighter. Still, Zack could see he wouldn't go down easy, which meant he'd have to find somewhere to avenge Shayla where they wouldn't be disturbed.

"June." Damian barked without turning around. "You know better than to disturb me during practice."

"I'm sorry. This is a…new client. He has a daughter who is interested in joining the studio. He just wanted to look around." She turned to Zack. "I didn't get your name."

"Slayer, isn't it?" Damian met his gaze through the mirror that ran the entire length of the wall. "Or do you go by Zack now that you've retired?"

Only years of learning how to hide his emotions in the ring saved Zack from showing his shock. The bastard knew him.

"You can go, darling." Damian said, not unkindly. "This doesn't concern you. I'll lock up after I'm done and meet you at home."

Zack closed the door after June had gone. There were no windows in the dance studio. And the door he was now leaning against was the only way out. "You don't seem surprised to see me."

"I'm surprised it took you this long." Damian did a slow *tendu*, extending his left leg to the front, side, and back. For the first time, Zack hated that he knew the standard ballet barre warm-up routine.

"I thought she ran right back to you after she left me."

A growl escaped Zack's lips. "It's not that easy to run after you've been beaten and pushed down the stairs."

Damian sighed and changed position. "Is she still telling people that story? The doctors thought her memories might come back after a year or two. The hospital psychiatrist said the mind will create plausible fictions after a traumatic event to deal with overwhelming emotion. She was very distraught after I told her I was leaving her that night, and she couldn't cope with the fact that she had ruined her dance career when she tripped and fell down the stairs when she ran after me begging me to stay. I stayed beside her for three days at the hospital. When she woke up, she told everyone I had assaulted her. It was soul destroying. I hadn't stopped loving her, and to be accused of hurting her…"

"You ended the marriage?" He didn't want to ask, but he did.

"It was time." Damian moved to a fast *tendu*. "We'd grown apart. Our age gap was becoming a problem. We wanted different things out of life. And, to be honest, she was becoming obsessed with you. I told her it was over. She begged me not to go, clung to my legs when I tried to leave. She was hysterical. Screaming and crying as I walked down the stairs. We lived two flights up from the street at the top of a concrete stairwell. She ran to catch me, tripped on the top stair, and then she fell." He drew in a ragged breath. "I was already in the foyer. I turned when I heard the noise, but I couldn't catch her."

Zack didn't buy it. The Shayla he knew was reserved and not at all demonstrative. He hadn't known her feelings toward him had changed until one day, when she was fourteen, he'd told her she looked pretty, and her cheeks had flamed. He'd waited until she was fifteen to hold her hand, and even then, he hadn't known whether she'd accepted it out of friendship or something more. When he'd left her in Glenwood, her voice had shaken, and tears had filled her eyes, but she hadn't begged him not to go. There was no screaming or crying or hysteria. No declarations of love. Looking back, he wondered if such an extreme show of emotion would have changed his mind. Her poise and self-possession had made it easy to walk away.

"That doesn't sound like her."

"You clearly didn't know her well." Damian changed position into a slow *dégagé,* the foot of his left leg sharply brushing through the floor. "But then you weren't married to her, and I was."

Zack's skin prickled in response to the challenge, and he made a quick, mental reassessment of the man in tights. He clearly still felt he had a claim to Shayla, and his total lack of fear at Zack's presence in the gym suggested he shouldn't be underestimated.

"The police and the district attorney clearly didn't believe your story. Nor the ballet community, or you wouldn't be working here. If she made it up, why were you charged and convicted of a crime?" Along with the name and address, the Predator had dug up the details of Damian's conviction plea bargain and sentence.

A shadow crossed Damian's face so quickly, Zack wondered if he'd seen it. "A total miscarriage of justice. People are inclined to believe young pretty ballerinas even if they're telling lies. Even I had trouble believing she had been so badly injured from a fall down the stairs. But the idea that I had hurt my wife…" He increased the speed of his *dégagé,* his foot pointed at forty-five degrees to the floor.

Zack's gut clenched. Wife. She had been this man's wife. Not his. "Shayla wouldn't lie."

"I misspoke." He extended his leg to the back in a way that made Zack wince. "She believes her fabricated story. Her mind

just couldn't cope with losing me. That's why she ran away."
He did a *rond de jambe*, tracing out the letter *D* in the air. The
cool detachment with which he discussed the end of his marriage, his wife's horrific accident, and her supposed brain injury
was disconcerting and no small bit alarming. Did he feel nothing
for the woman he professed to love?

"I wanted to go after her and tell her I was prepared to work
on our marriage," he continued. "I hadn't realized the depth of
her feelings until then, or mine for that matter. But the hospital
psychiatrist told me it was better to leave her alone. He said until
she accepted what really happened, we could never be whole.
I hoped someday she would come back me. But as I suspected,
she went running back to you."

"Damn right." He wasn't about to tell Damian that Shayla
hadn't come running back to him at all. Instead, she'd forged
a new life out of the ashes of her childhood dream. She had
been beaten, but she had gotten back up. Why couldn't Zack
do the same?

"I don't know what she sees in you." Damian placed his left
leg on the barre and grabbed his toes, his chest flat on his thigh,
demonstrating the kind of flexibility that was every fighter's
dream. "She was a shell of a girl when she came to New York,
and all because of you. It was only after she was mugged and I
helped her pick up the pieces that she began to shine. She was
my creation, my muse, so young and beautiful, I was the envy
of other men." He lowered his leg and raised the other for a
stretch. "As I suppose you are now."

Zack grunted as he studied Damian. He had come with a plan

to beat on Damian until he felt the bastard had suffered enough that Shayla would have true justice. And yet, as he watched the dancer bend one leg and lower himself into a *fondu*, he wondered what that would truly accomplish.

He had learned to read people as part of his training—thought processes could be telegraphed by the subtlest signals, and the ability to predict a fighter's next move could make the difference between a win or a loss in the cage—and what he read from Damian was a total lack of feeling. Whatever had broken Damian, and turned him from the caring man Shayla had married, to the vain, self-aggrandizing, delusional, and fundamentally insecure man he was now, had never been repaired.

Zack could beat him. He could break his legs so he could never dance again, but looking around the small, run-down studio filled with children's costumes and drawings, a battered piano, and a barre worn smooth by hundreds of tiny hands, he doubted he could punish Damian more than he had been punished already. He would never have the power and prestige he'd had as the husband of a young, beautiful prima ballerina and artistic director of a world-famous ballet company. Instead of being treated as a star, traveling the world, and attending lavish balls and parties and hobnobbing with the artistic elite, he had become ordinary. Given what Zack knew of the man, this was the equivalent of Hell.

"How is she?" Damian turned and bent to do the *fondu* with his right leg.

"Good. No great. Fantastic. She's a fighter now."

Damian laughed. "So you turned her to the dark side. It's

for the best. Her career was already on a downslide when the accident happened. She was a classically trained dancer, but she wanted to do modern dance, and she just didn't have what it took to succeed. It was just a matter of time." He straightened and studied Zack. "Much like you coming to visit."

Zack's hands curled into fists. "What did you think would happen when we met?"

"Given you're the kind of man who could destroy a young girl who loved you for the betterment of your career and then kill a man with your bare hands to win a fight, I suspect you came here with violence on your mind." He brushed a flexed foot from *cou-de-pied*, resting against the side of his ankle, through the floor, the ball of his foot tapping lightly on the wood in a double *frappé*.

In Zack's state of heightened anger, the move had the hallmark of a bull pawing at the ground in challenge, and he fought the urge to respond with the violence Damian was clearly expecting despite his seeming lack of concern.

"Or maybe, now that you're retired, you've forgotten how to fight."

C'mon, Slayer. This is pathetic. I'm getting bored punching your ugly face. The Predator's words rang in his mind, and then Okami's, *Fuck you*, goading him into throwing that last punch.

Damian was goading him, he suddenly realized. The nonchalance. The casual conversation. The seemingly unaffected air. Only when Zack hadn't risen to the bait had he finally showed his hand with the comment about forgetting how to fight.

Why?

Jealousy? Revenge? Did he really think he could beat Zack in a fight? Or did he have some advantage? A weapon? There was no way he could be hiding anything under those skintight clothes. What about video surveillance? Did he think a leaked video of Zack beating on him would destroy Zack's career as a recruiter? Or did he think such a video would tear Zack and Shayla apart?

Zack looked around the room. He could have hidden a camera anywhere, or even a weapon. But it didn't matter. He was totally and utterly in control. He wouldn't be goaded into doing something he didn't want to do, and this wasn't a fight he needed to win. He had no interest in hitting this pathetic excuse for a man if it meant losing Shayla all over again. She didn't need to be saved. But he knew someone who did. There was more than one way to hurt a man. In Zack's experience, losing a partner was worse than physical pain.

"Grand battement." Zack turned and reached for the door.

"What did you say?"

"Grand battement." Zack looked back over his shoulder. "It's your last move."

"Aren't you going to hit me?"

Zack looked around the studio and shook his head. "No. It's time to move on."

Shayla

"SHAYLA TANNER TO SEE ZACK GRAYSON IN ROOM 869." I smile at the desk clerk at the Devonian Palace Hotel. "He's expecting me."

If she recognizes me from the other night, she gives no sign when she dials his number. But then, I don't blame her. I've just come from the ballet studio after a fun three hours teaching little girls the basics of ballet. My hair is up in a tidy bun, and I'm wearing a pink sweater over my dance leotard and a light gray skirt with a pair of pink flats. No grunge in sight. I also have a huge smile plastered on my face because Zack is back.

"Please go on up," she says, putting down the phone.

My heart pounds with excitement as I ride the elevator to the top floor, my happiness diminishing only slightly when I have to knock on Zack's door. If he was coming to see me after being away, I'd be in the hallway to meet him.

I know something is wrong as soon as he opens the door. Instead of softness and smiles, his face is taut and hard. Still, I wrap my arms around him and give him a hug. "I'm so glad you're back."

My excitement deflates like a burst balloon when he stiffens in my arms. I let him go and make my way into his suite, decorated in rich cream and brown, with shiny brass accents and a sitting area beside a wall of windows, with a separate bedroom off to the side.

"What's wrong?"

Zack closes the door and walks over to the window, stares out at the city in the fading light.

"Zack?"

"Was there something you forgot to tell me?" he says mildly, but I can hear the undercurrent of tension in his voice.

Bang, bang, bang goes my heart as I mentally run through any secrets that I might have kept. "About what?"

"About Damian."

Puzzled, I frown. "What about Damian?"

"He says you made the story up about him pushing you down the stairs. He said you had a concussion that caused memory loss, and you suffered a reality break because of the trauma of him deciding to leave you."

I don't know whether I should laugh at the absurdity of that statement or scowl because Zack has clearly done what I asked him not to do and hunted down my ex. I choose the scowl.

"You went after him."

Zack shrugs. "Of course I did. What kind of man would I be if I didn't?"

"A man with a girlfriend, which is not going to be you, because that was my fight."

"Your fight?" He turns, scrubs his hand through his hair. "I thought you didn't want me to go after him because you were scared he would find you."

"Do I look scared?" My hands find my hips, and I narrow my eyes and glare.

Zack's lips twitch at the corners. "You look angry and not very interested in taking off your clothes and welcoming me home."

"Damn right," I mutter. "I can't believe you went after him. And I can't believe he's still peddling those lies. Do you think the police didn't consider that possibility before they charged him with attempted murder and assault? He's delusional."

"I agree. He's also beating his new wife, who doesn't look older than twenty-five. Did he hurt you before the night he pushed you down the stairs?" His body tenses like he's waiting for a blow.

"No." I close the distance between us, drawn by his obvious agitation. This is what's bothering him. He thinks Damian beat me even before that awful night. "Can you imagine what the company would have done if I showed up at the studio covered in bruises, especially when we were on tour? You know pretty much everything is on display."

"What did he do?" Still, he doesn't touch me.

"Nothing at first. And then when he started to get worried about his career and I started making friends my age and spending time away from him, he started drinking. He shouted a lot when he was drunk and said a lot of unkind things, especially when I told him I was interested in modern dance. When he started pushing me around, I decided to leave. His behavior was escalating, and I could see where that would lead. I just never expected it to happen so fast."

He lets out a long, low, ragged breath and strokes my cheek. "He says I broke you."

"You did. But it just made me a stronger, more resilient version of myself. I never opened myself up to him the way I did with you, because I wasn't going to let anyone hurt me again. Emotionally or physically."

He draws me close, presses a tender kiss to my head. "What about now?"

"Now, I think I could let my guard down, but only for you."

He wraps his arms around me and holds me tight. "You should thank me for leaving you in Glenwood. If I hadn't made you strong—"

"Don't push it," I mumble against his chest. "You're already in the doghouse for going after him in the first place. Is he still alive?"

Zack laughs. "I didn't touch him, but I may have caught up with his wife on her way home and told her what happened to you. She didn't know the full story. I don't think she's going to stick around for long."

"You didn't hit him?" I almost don't believe him. The Zack I know has a jealous streak a mile wide. Only a few weeks ago, he was bouncing Doctor Death around the ring and going all possessive alpha with Reg. What's changed?

"There wasn't much I could do to him that he hadn't already done to himself. He's fallen so far, he'll never get up. He feels no shame about what he did and accepts no responsibility. He recognized me, and I think he wanted to set me up, but I didn't take the bait. I was in control, Shay. There was nothing I have ever wanted more than to see that bastard suffer, but I couldn't take the risk of losing you again."

I get a warm, tingly feeling all over, and I look up and smile. "I suddenly feel like taking off my clothes."

Zack gives a contented rumble and slides his warm hands under my shirt. "I want you naked every time I come home."

My heart sinks the tiniest bit. "You have to go away again?"

"One more trip. Three countries. Three weeks. Then I'm done." He unhooks my bra and pushes my shirt and bra over my breasts. "I have a lot of training to do if I want to defend my title next year." He leans down and draws my nipple into his warm mouth.

"Wait." I tug his head away. "What did you say?"

Zack gives my nipple a long, languid lick. "I'm going to fight again. I told Kip this morning."

Slayer back in the cage. The MMA world will go crazy.

My heart pounds a frantic beat, and I hold his face between my hands. "Where are you going to train?"

A slow smile spreads across his face. "Redemption."

29
Shayla

MY NEW COACH TURNS UP A FEW DAYS LATER. HIS NAME IS DICK. He is a good-looking, ex-military general with a crew cut and a rock-hard physique. He wears fatigues to the gym and likes to shout out my name in two loud syllables—SHILL-LAAAA—whenever I do anything wrong, which is pretty much every five minutes. He becomes best friends with the Predator his first day in the gym, and the two of them do a full workout and a five-mile run every morning together before the sun comes up while discussing how military training can translate into making my life a living hell.

Dick treats Redemption like his own personal boot camp and refers to his coaching as "advanced individual training." If someone gets in our way or dares to be on equipment he has booked for us to use, he grabs them and body-slams them to the ground. When someone complains that he has broken the rules about fighting outside the ring, he tells Torment it is discipline, not fighting, and if he actually fought them, they would be dead.

Torment loves Dick. He agrees to let Dick start a new course called Discipline with Dick.

Of course, the team can't let the name go. They snicker behind Dick's back and constantly crack immature jokes, culminating in Sadist showing up one morning with a black leather flogger. Unsurprisingly, with Zack out of the picture, Sandy is the first to sign up for the new class.

Three weeks into my new training program, I receive a surprise visit from Reg.

Dick is rolling with me on the mat and is not at all inclined to cut our submission session short so I can "waste time" talking to a Radical Power recruiter. Between submissions, I shoot apologetic glances at Reg, but he just smiles.

When Dick finally lets me go, I take Reg to the Redemption snack bar for a chat. Curiously, most of the senior Redemption fighters happen to be getting protein shakes at the exact same time.

"Is this meant to be a private conversation?" I ask Reg after we get our protein shakes. I gesture to the cluster of Redemption fighters pretending to be having a casual chat while leaning indiscreetly in our direction.

"It will be public soon." He looks over at the fighters and laughs. "You have lots of friends."

"Nosy friends."

"Sometimes, they are the best kind." He gestures to a table near a potted palm, and we take a seat.

"I came to see you because the CSAC reviewed the tapes of your last fight with Carla Gordon after Torment filed an appeal. They've ruled that the foul was intentional, and Gordon should not have been awarded the fight. They also couldn't find any record of you being injured in a sanctioned fight, so you shouldn't have been disqualified and given that CAMO ill designation."

It takes me a minute before I work out what's he's trying to tell me. "I won?"

"They've called for a rematch for this weekend," Reg says. "Because the situation was so unusual, they've decided to let you and Gordon fight again. You get another chance. And I'm still here if you win."

———

"She's Gordon," Dick shouts the next day as I spar with Sandy in the practice ring. "Pretend she's Gordon. What are you going to do when Gordon gets in your face?"

"I know what I want to do if he gets in my face," I mutter, throwing a punch that Sandy easily evades. "He's worse than Torment and Fuzzy combined. Worse than Zack. He doesn't seem to understand that muscles need time to recover. It's go, go, go all the time."

"Have you heard from Zack?" Sandy tips her head to the side, and her ponytail swishes across her back. I remember how she was always after Zack, so I send a left uppercut her way and clip her in the chin.

"That's good if you're a damned six-year-old," Dick shouts. "Put some power behind it."

"Every day." By now, everyone at Redemption knows Zack and I are together. My attempt to keep the secret lasted one whole week, and then Sadist caught me blowing kisses to Zack during an online chat.

"We need him for a photo shoot for the summer camp sponsorship." Sandy hesitates. "If that's okay with you."

"Of course." I can afford to be magnanimous. Everyone knows he's mine.

"We want to do a few shots of him in just his fight shorts…"

Suddenly, I'm not feeling the magnanimity anymore. *Bam*. I smash my fist into her perfect nose, and she staggers back. "Sorry. I slipped."

"This isn't a fucking street fight. Get it together," Dick calls out.

There are things I want to call out to Dick, too, most of which make fun of his name, but I am much too classy for that.

"Are you fighting over me?" The low, rough rumble of Zack's voice steals my breath away, freezes me in place. Swallowing hard, I look back over my shoulder…

Bam. Sandy hits me with a right uppercut. I stagger back, hit the ropes, but this time, Zack catches me when I fall.

"You're back early," I say, looking up into the face I have imagined night after night since he left.

"I'm back, sweetheart. And I'm here to stay."

"SHILL-LAAAA! What the hell? You've got a fight in four days. Get back in the ring."

"He's the new coach I texted you about." I turn and wind my arms around Zack's neck. "He makes you look like a pussycat."

"I like him." He cups my face in his hands and kisses me so deeply that I can feel our souls join in the breath we share. The world goes out from under me, and when he pulls away, I feel our connection like it was never gone.

"But if he touches you…"

"I thought you'd changed."

He kisses me again. His lips are hot and soft against mine, gentle. He owns me with that kiss, takes me home, and makes me whole again. "Not that much."

—⁂—

My last meal before final fasting for weigh-ins for the big event consists of four boiled eggs. Blade Saw, Homicide Hank, and I sit in a booth at the Protein Palace and contemplate the feast in front of us. They are fighting in the men's amateur division in the upcoming event, and the last few days have been hell as we try to shed as much weight as we can. Sadist has joined us to give us support, although we all resent him for the protein shake he is noisily slurping beside us.

"I fucking hate fasting." Homicide Hank peels open his egg, rips out the yolk, and then stuffs the white into his mouth all at once. "If I was living on my own, it would be easier, but when you've got kids, life is about food. Every second of the day, one of them needs food. You give them breakfast, and they want a snack. Then they're thirsty. Then they need another snack. Then it's nine a.m., and the sprogs are gnawing on my legs, although the damn food is everywhere. Every damned corner of the house. Every surface. Dry, fresh, hardened, and growing shit. Food, food, fucking food."

"Slayer once dropped so much weight for a fight," Sadist says, "he could barely stand on the scale, and when they took pictures at the weigh-in, he looked like a skeleton."

Homicide Hank pops another egg in his mouth. "I heard

MEFC offered to pay him three million to fight a title fight to defend his belt, but he turned it down. He said he wants to start from the beginning and work his way up. You gotta respect a man like that."

"I never heard about that." Sadist slams his cup on the table. "How the hell did you know about that and I didn't?"

"Dick knows the owner of the gym in Seattle where Slayer used to train. Slayer was in Seattle visiting his sisters and went to see the dude to share the news, and the dude told Dick. Dick told the Predator. The Predator told his wife, Sia. She was covering a tattoo for Doctor Death, 'cause he needed to get rid of the last girlfriend's name he'd had inked onto his back. Sia told him. Death told Makayla when he saw her at the hospital getting a baby scan—that secret got out fast. Makayla told Amanda when they were shopping for Amanda's wedding dress for the wedding in June. Amanda told Renegade. He told Blade Saw in jiu-jitsu class. Blade Saw told his girl, Cora. She told your girl, Penny. Penny told Fuzzy when she was taking one of his classes. He told his girl, Jess. She told Sandy during a Redemption girls' night out. Sandy told me."

"So everyone knows except me?" Sadist stares at Homicide Hank, incredulous. Not once has he ever missed out on a juicy piece of gossip—or ten.

"You could have just asked me," I say. "I can tell you anything about Slayer you want to know."

Sadist shakes his head. "I'm losing my touch."

After devouring our eggs at the Protein Palace, we head together to a casino, hefting our water jugs with our day's allocation of water. Although we make a few token attempts to win at the tables, we spend most of our time sitting outside the restaurant section, smelling the food and talking about our post fight feast the next day. My head throbs, and I use a few precious sips of water to take some painkillers, but really, all I want to do is go home, lie in front of the couch, and watch the Food Network.

"You're not looking so good," Sadist says when I rest my head on the table. "Maybe we should call up Doctor Death and get him to check you over."

"I'm fine. But I will skip the sauna tonight and take a nap before my run."

Apparently, my idea to skip the sauna triggers alarm bells in the minds of my overprotective friends. Sadist bundles me into his car, and an hour later, I'm at home, and Doctor Death is knocking at the door.

"You're extremely dehydrated," he says after he checks me out.

"That's the point." I fall back on the couch. "I have a bag of Pedialyte ready for after the weigh-in."

"Normally, I would agree," he says. "But what about the recent trauma to your head? I heard you were knocked out for a second time at that underground fight—"

"I wasn't. Zack was being overly cautious."

"—and then again in your fight against Gordon," he continues as if I hadn't spoken. "The brain is cushioned by water, and if you did have a subdural—"

"I don't, and I feel much better since I came home to lie down. I still have a few pounds to go. How about if I promise to skip the run?"

Doctor Death scrubs a hand over his face. "There's still a five percent risk."

"I like risk."

Unfortunately, he doesn't go away. Instead, he gives a dramatic sigh and joins me on the couch. After he tidies up his stuff and sends a couple of texts, we watch Delia Smith bake her triple-layer chocolate fudge cake, then learn two ways to prepare roast chicken and how to make a six-pound taco with only two pounds of beef. A screech outside cuts off the chef's secret ingredient for taco sauce, and I frown at the interruption.

"Did you hear that?"

"I didn't hear anything." He looks at me with a decidedly guilty expression. "Gee. Look at the time. I'd better go. I have lives to save, including my own."

He frees himself from my grasp and grabs his bag just as Zack bursts in the door.

"You're going to die, Death," I shout as Doctor Death makes a run for it. "As soon as I can get off this damn couch, they're going to call you Doctor Dead."

Zack follows him into the hallway. Through the open door, I see some manly handshaking, shoulder patting, and money being exchanged. When Zack returns, I fold my arms over my chest and glare. "We've been through this overprotective nonsense too many times. I know how to fast, and I know how it feels. I heard about how you starved yourself for a fight. You know what this is all about."

He presses his lips together and scowls. "This isn't easy for me."

"I know." I look up at him and smile. "But I'm proud of you for trying."

After two hours of watching TV, I feel good enough to get up for my run. I make a move to leave the couch, but Zack pulls me in a straddle across his lap.

"I know something that can burn calories better than a run."

"What's that?" I ask as if I don't already know from the rock-hard erection pressed tight against my pussy.

"Sex." He pulls his shirt over his head.

"Hmm." I press a kiss to his warm chest. "I like to have a lot of sex before a fight to get my testosterone level up."

"I'd prefer to be the only one in the relationship with testosterone." He helps me off with my shirt and unhooks my bra.

"You do have a lot of it."

He gives a satisfied grunt. "In spades."

"I hope you're planning to put it to good use tonight. Otherwise, I might have to put up a Craigslist ad for the multiple partners I'll need to get ready for my fight tomorrow."

He slips my bra off my shoulders. "You're not gonna pass out on me?"

"Depends how hard you make me come."

"I've always wanted to make a woman come so hard, she passed out." He leans down and draws my nipple into his mouth.

"You mean, you haven't already?" I sink my hands into his soft, thick hair. "Zack Grayson? Fantasy of women everywhere? Never seen with the same woman twice?"

He switches to my other nipple, and I arch into his hot, wet mouth. "I've been saving it all for you."

Zack slides his hand down my hips and drags me close. I grind my hips against the bulge in his jeans. "Don't save it too long. Once isn't enough when there's a fight the next day."

He swings me down to the couch and cups the curve of my sex. "As you command, beautiful ballerina." His fingers slide into my yoga pants, and he yanks them down, leaving me in only a skimpy pair of panties.

"Um…" I point down. "You forgot something."

"I forget nothing." He slips his fingers beneath the elastic and strokes my folds. "If I take those off, I'm going in, and I want you ready for me first."

"Did you not notice I'm ready for you now? Or did you think that wetness was something else?"

"More ready." He strips off his jeans and stretches on top of me.

His cock, thick and hard, presses against my clit, and I plant my heels on the couch and rub up against him like a contented cat.

"Naughty girl," he growls. "You think you're gonna push me over the edge, but you don't appreciate my self-restraint."

"Your woman is wet, almost naked, and her vibrator is out of batteries after having to make up for your absence. This isn't the time for self-restraint."

Zack runs his hand over my body, and his face softens. "You're gonna get hurt in the ring." He slides his arms around me. "You're gonna come back to me covered in blood and bruises, maybe even broken bones."

"I had bruises after that night you spanked me. You didn't seem to mind then."

"My bruises." His hand drifts down my back to my ass. "Sexy bruises."

I sit back and cup his face between my hands. "Please don't ask me not to fight."

"I won't. I'll be there with you. In your corner. But I won't pretend it will be easy." He leans in to kiss me, his lips soft against mine. And then he eases me down on the couch, his lips skimming down my neck to my collarbone. "I'm going to kiss every part of your body, so when you get hit tomorrow, you'll remember I was there first."

He kisses me everywhere. Soft kisses. Hard kisses. A brush of his lips, and then deep passionate kisses that arouse me more than his games. We make up for the weeks of missed kisses, our tongues tangling together as if we have all the time in the world. We share our bodies and our souls. We share our breaths, our hopes, and our dreams.

He kisses my face, my eyes, my nose, my chin, his whiskers rough on my skin. Then he moves down, flicking his tongue over the pulse at the base of my neck, tasting my collarbones, my arms, the insides of my elbows, even my wrists, and my fingers one by one.

I have never felt worshipped before. So utterly adored.

His mouth brushes over my ribs, now visible after days of fasting, and my concave belly. His breath is hot on my skin, tongue warm and wet where he licks and nibbles—the curve of my hip, my belly button, the top of my mound…

"Lower," I whisper, sliding my fingers through the thickness of his hair.

He slides my panties off and then lavishes attention on my clit, sending tiny bolts of pleasure shivering up my spine. His tongue is gentle, slick, lapping me up as if I were a delectable dessert.

He teases out my orgasm with the soft steady brush of his tongue. It rushes over me like the tide, pebbling my skin, filling every nook and cranny of my body. An irresistible, unstoppable force that flutters, flows, and ebbs, sending me drifting as it pulls me with it.

"Beautiful." Zack slides up my body. "I love watching you come."

With one firm thrust, he fills me, his cock deliciously thick and hard. We groan together. Move together. Breathe as one person, not two.

"Deeper, Zack," I whisper. "I want to feel all of you."

He takes his weight on his hands and pushes until he is seated as far as he can go. Our hips rock together, and then he pounds into me, filling me utterly and completely.

Finally, his body stiffens, and he comes with a hoarse cry, the pulse of his climax against my swollen tissue sending me over the edge again.

Zack collapses on top of me, buries his neck in my shoulder, and for a moment, we hold each other, chests heaving, bodies sated.

"I want to do this for you when you fight." I stroke my hand through his thick, soft hair.

"Once won't be enough."

"Twice?" I wiggle, rubbing my breasts against his chest, and he groans softly.

"More."

"How much more?"

"I'll need you every day of the year before the fight and every day after. Sometimes two or three times." He pushes himself up and runs his tongue over the seam of my lips.

"Hmm. How are we going to have all that sex unless we're together all the time?"

"We'll have to live together." He nuzzles my neck. "Then I can sex you up whenever I want."

"That sounds serious."

He studies me, his face intense. "It is serious. We've wasted enough time. I don't want to waste a second more. I love you, Shay. I want to be with you forever."

I hold him tight and whisper in his ear. "I love you, too."

And for the first time, I am not afraid to open myself up, because I have found my passion again, and he has found me.

30 Shayla

"SHAYLA."

A shadow detaches from the wall outside Redemption, and I recognize Damian in the fading evening light before he comes into view. Everything about him, from the angle of his neck to the set of his shoulders, from the slight wave of his hair to the timbre of his voice, is so painfully familiar, watching him walk toward me is almost like coming home.

Except I am home. At Redemption. And all my friends are inside, waiting to throw a celebration party just for me after my big win against Carla Gordon last night. Zack will be joining us later, after he finishes his charity photoshoot.

Damian stops under one of the parking lot lights, only a few feet away. In some ways, I have been waiting for this moment since the day I left New York, knowing in my heart he would eventually come. But of all the emotions I expected to experience when I saw him again, I feel only one—relief.

"How did you find me?"

"Zack Grayson paid me a visit. It wasn't hard to track him down now that he's in the news because of his big comeback. I called the MEFC office and said I was a reporter looking for a story. They told me he was training here. I knew you'd be with him." His gaze drifts down my body, lingering on my Symbian uniform and the utility belt around my waist. Sadist told me to come straight from work for the party, and I didn't stop to change.

"I watched your fight last night…" He trails off when my face tightens.

"I'm glad I didn't see you there."

"After seeing you in the ring, I'm glad, too." He looks me up and down, and then he smiles—that cool, slightly detached smile that should have warned me from the start that there was a monster lurking beneath the man. "You look good. Different. Stronger."

"You look older."

His smile fades the tiniest bit. "You've changed, too. You're more confident, self-assured."

"I don't let people beat me up is what I think you're trying to say." I take a step toward him. "I don't let them hit me or kick me or punch me or beat me with bats. I don't let them tell me they love me and then push me down the stairs. I am not a toy or a treasure or a piece of arm candy or a stepping stone to success. And I don't run away from the things that scare me."

He runs his hand through his mop of blond hair. Once, I thought his hair was beautiful, artistic, cut long in the front and glistening gold in the sun, but now it looks dirty, unkempt, and badly in need of a brush. "I missed you, darling."

The affectionate term makes me cringe, not just because I don't want to be his darling, but because he only ever used it when he was drunk, as I suspect he is now from the way he slurs his words and tilts his head.

"Then maybe you shouldn't have tried to kill me."

Anger flickers across his face, and then it's gone. "I see your memory still hasn't returned. You lost your balance when you were trying to stop me leaving you."

"Seriously?" My voice rises in pitch. "You are totally delusional. You think I cared about you so much that I would risk killing myself over you? That I suffered these injuries because I was that desperate for you to stay? Do you think a fall can crush every bone in a hand? Or that stairs leave boot prints in your side?"

He holds up a warding hand. "You've always been so emotional. It was one of the things I had hoped you might grow out of as you matured so you could see the world in a more logical way. We were good together. We could be good together again. I've researched MMA. My choreography skills can help you in the ring. And you need someone experienced to guide you."

It's like he doesn't even hear me. But then, maybe he never did. "Don't be ridiculous. Even if you were the only trainer on earth, I wouldn't work with you. And I'm with Zack, now. As you well know."

Damian sighs. "I can see you're upset. We can discuss it another time."

"I'm not upset." I close the distance between us, stopping

only a foot away. "I'm angry. Angry and disgusted that I wasted years of my life with you. I thought I loved you, and you took that love and broke it."

"I loved you." His voice softens. "Never doubt that."

"You don't know what love is." My hand clenches into a fist by my side. "Love is sacrifice. Love is giving. Love is taking the long, hard road back when it's easier to walk away. Love fills all the cracks in your heart and gives you strength in the darkest of times. Love never leaves. It is there when the lights go out and in the depths of despair. I know love now, and what we had wasn't it."

I thought I fought my best fight yesterday, but as I lift my hand, I realize I am fighting my best fight now.

Everything I have learned—every fight, every class, every loss, every win, every ounce of blood, sweat, and tears I have shed, Sol and Clive and the other burglar I caught at Symbian— has prepared me for this.

My fight.

With all my power, I smash my fist into Damian's face. He staggers back into the car behind him, making no move to defend himself.

"That is for everything you did to me, for twisting my love, for breaking me, for destroying my dreams." I hit him again and again until he slides down the side of the car.

Damian wipes the blood off his face and pushes to his feet. He puts one hand under his jacket and pulls out a gun.

"This is for everything you did to me," he spits out. "I lost my career because of you, my respect in the community, my friends, my life, and now because of your boyfriend's meddling, I've lost my wife. All you had to do was keep your mouth shut instead of blabbing to the police. Loyalty. That's what love is. And gratitude. Forgiveness. You protect the people who looked after you and made you a star. You honor the vows you said in church to love, cherish, and obey."

Given this was my biggest fear, the cause of the nightmares that drove me to train as a security guard and join Redemption, I am curiously unafraid of the gun. Maybe it's because I have been threatened with a gun before. Maybe it's because I've faced death and won. Maybe it's because I am a damned good fighter who has been offered not one, but two professional contracts. Or maybe it's because, after what happened to Joe, I never go to work without my bulletproof vest.

"Don't be a hypocrite." I mentally calculate my distance and angle, weighing the option of another Clive-like takedown. "In what world did you honor your vows by beating me and trying to kill me?"

"A world where your wife doesn't walk out on you when you need her the most for the man she professed to hate most in the world."

"I didn't leave you for him," I say. "I left for me."

"Now you can leave forever." He raises the gun. "And when I'm done with you, he's next."

A door crashes open. Feet pound on the pavement.

Torment takes the safety of his fighters very seriously. He has cameras all over the parking lot. He will have seen Damian approach me and he will have watched the scene play out. And if he knows, Redemption knows. I just wonder how he was able to hold them back for so long.

Taking advantage of the distraction, I go low and shoot in for a takedown. A bullet cracks the silence. Glass shatters. I grab Damian and carry him down, knocking the gun from his hand before I straddle him and pin him to the ground.

Redemption fighters swarm around us. I am plucked off my prize and unnecessarily deposited a safe distance away. Then the frenzy begins.

I hear the screech of tires in the distance, and I press my lips together and glare at the fighters gathered around Damian, arguing over who gets to hit him next. "Who called Zack?"

No one looks at me directly. Instead, they become interested in the vehicles, in the parking lot, the streetlights, and the faint stars in the night sky.

"Yeah. I thought so," I mutter, fighting back a smile. "All of you." I gesture to Damian as I walk toward Redemption. "Make sure you leave a piece for Zack. He deserves at least one punch."

31 Zack

"WINNER BY A KNOCKOUT, THE NEW MEFC MIDDLEWEIGHT world champion and holder of five MEFC title belts...Slayer!"

Zack raised his arms in triumph as Blade Saw announced his arrival at Redemption, playing to the packed gym going wild for his return from his championship fight in Vegas. Even after a two-day media junket, he could still feel the sheer and utter thrill of holding the title belt in his hand. He had done it. He had come back from oblivion, defeated the Terminator, and achieved his dream. And he couldn't have done it without the Redemption team.

He hadn't come to Redemption to return to fighting. He had come to recruit another body for the MEFC stable. Who knew his entire life would change the moment he walked in the door? Not only had he found the ballerina who had stolen his heart, he had found redemption, and he had found a home.

"Welcome back," Sadist said, clearing a path through the eager fans. "How did it go?"

Zack shook his head. "It was easier before everyone and his dog started streaming their broadcasts. I lost count of the number of interviews I did. MEFC had a team of publicists, and even they couldn't keep up with the requests."

"I saw the one of you with Shayla after the fight. You were great together. Very entertaining."

A new MMA streaming service had asked for a joint interview with Zack and Shayla, who had become a hot celebrity couple after they had announced their engagement. Media interest had intensified after Shayla won the amateur featherweight title belt and was signed by MEFC, prompting them to elope to Glenwood. They'd had a small outdoor wedding with only their family and close friends in attendance, including, of course, the entire Redemption team.

"I'm looking forward to picking her up and just having a quiet night at home."

"Yeah. About that…" Sadist grimaced. "Something's come up."

"What are you talking about?" Zack followed Sadist's gaze as he looked around Redemption, but everything appeared to be business as usual. Cheryl and Shayla had finally convinced their colleague, Joe, to join the gym, and Cheryl and he were sweating their way through Fuzzy's Punch or Perish class. Blade Saw and Homicide Hank were sparring in one of the cages. Doctor Death was rolling on the mats with Renegade. The Predator was drum rolling a speed bag, and Makayla, Sia, Amanda, and

Penny were clustered together on the bleachers, whispering like they were up to no good.

"You'd better ask your Daredevil." He gestured to the practice ring at the far end of the gym where Shayla was sparring with Sandy.

A smile spread across Zack's lips. After Shayla had won her amateur title and signed her professional contract with MEFC, the team had put her "Shilla the Killa" name to bed and asked him for a ring name worthy of Redemption's top female fighter and California's newest women's featherweight amateur champion.

What was she like when you first met? they'd asked.

Fearless. Unstoppable. A risk taker. Just like she is now.

Zack crossed the mats toward the practice ring, taking in the enormity of what was now considered to be one of the top MMA training gyms in the state. With three title belt holders and a shelf full of amateur cups, Redemption was fast becoming the place to be.

His place to be.

Torment had put Zack's picture on the wall the first day he had come out of retirement and started to train. Zack had been deeply moved by the gesture. He hadn't earned his title belts at Redemption, but Torment had recognized his achievements alongside those of his fighters. It had made Zack even more determined to reclaim his title so he could credit the team. Shayla's picture now hung beside his own, the fulfillment of a promise he had made to her the night he had traded his ring for a path to Redemption.

Torment was standing outside the ring with his daughter,

Brianna, on his shoulders, watching Shayla and Sandy fight. Zack felt a curious sense of longing as he gave his favorite toddler a high five. He had never wanted kids, never thought he could be a good father because he had no good role model in his life, but Shayla had made him see that he'd been his own role model. Taking care of his sisters had been all the training he needed to be a good dad. And now that Viv was in remission again and living with an intern she'd met in the hospital and Lily was married, he only had one person to look after and room in his heart to welcome another.

Sandy's gaze flicked to him as he climbed through the ropes, hoping to surprise Shayla by coming up behind her. He'd pulled the same trick the first day he'd come to Redemption when he'd had the shock of his life, seeing her in the ring.

"Oh my Lord." Sandy's eyes widened. "Look who it is."

Taking advantage of her lack of focus, Shayla lunged forward and wrapped her arm around Sandy's neck in a choke hold.

"It's…Slayer," Sandy wheezed.

Shayla's head jerked up, and her gaze locked on his. A lifetime of memories filled the space between them. The day he'd found her at the bottom of Devil's Hill. The touch that had woken his soul and stirred a fierce protectiveness in him that even now he could not contain. The friendship that had sustained him during his darkest times. Stolen kisses and furtive cuddles. Desperate longing. Sexual awakening. The night they had come together and broken apart. And the day he had found her again.

She had wanted to make something of herself, and she did. Twice over. Prima ballerina with the New York Ballet, winner of the amateur featherweight title belt, and now professional MEFC fighter. She was her ring name personified. A "Daredevil" in every sense of the word. But he knew what kind of woman she really was. The woman of his heart.

Frozen in shock, Shayla loosened her grip. Sandy spun out of the hold and clipped Shayla a good one in the chin.

She stumbled back and lost her balance, but before her head could hit the pole, Zack was there. He caught her and spun her around, pulling her into his chest.

"Still determined to protect me, I see." Shayla smiled at him as he bent to kiss away the hurt on her chin. "Welcome home."

"You two can have matching bruises." Sandy gestured to Zack, who was still sporting the evidence of his championship fight. "Did the Terminator spend all his time pounding on your face?"

"You mean in the seven seconds before I knocked him out?"

Sandy laughed. "I hope we can get a play-by-play over drinks tonight."

"Another time."

Shayla mocked a frown. "Someone isn't very sociable this evening."

Zack pressed his lips to her ear and whispered, "Someone just spent the day giving interviews, flew in from Vegas, and came straight to Redemption to pick up his wife whom he hasn't seen for two days. Drinks are the last thing on my mind."

She looked up at him through her dark lashes. "What is on your mind?"

"Fucking you wearing your title belt and nothing else."

"We've done that six times already."

"Then we'll do it six times with you wearing my title belt."
He nuzzled her neck. "Once in every room of our apartment."

"Think how much better it would be if we had a house."
She smoothed her hands over his chest. "We would have a yard
to lie out and look up at Vega and Altair and extra rooms for
christening title belts or even for visitors."

"What visitors?" His skin prickled when Shayla pulled
away. Turning, he realized they had an audience. The entire
Redemption team—kids and significant others, too—were
crowded around the ring.

"This visitor." Shayla handed him a small white box with the
Redemption logo emblazoned on top.

"What's going on?"

"Open it."

Zack glanced up at the smiling faces of his teammates and
lifted the lid off the box. "What is this?" He held up a tiny
pair of red Redemption fight gloves. "Slayer" had been printed
across one glove and "Daredevil" across the other.

"I figured we should get our baby started early."

"Our baby?" His gaze flicked from the gloves to Shayla and
back to the gloves. "You're pregnant?"

"Two months. I found out last week, but I didn't want to
distract you from your training."

Emotion overwhelmed him, and he pulled Shayla into his
arms, burying his head in her hair as the team cheered around
them.

"I love you," he whispered. "I can't believe we are going to
be a family."

"I'm sorry it had to be so public. I was so excited, I had to tell someone."

Zack sighed. "You told Sadist?"

"No. I told Cheryl, and she told Joe. He went for drinks after class with Fuzzy and let it slip. Of course, Fuzz told his sister, Sia, and she told the Predator and...well, you know how it goes here at Redemption. Sadist is still annoyed he was the last to know." She moved to pull away, and he tightened his grip.

"Hold on a minute longer. I've got something in my eyes."

"I hope those are happy tears," she whispered.

"I thought I couldn't be happier than the day I found you again," he said. "But then you agreed to marry me, and I thought my heart would burst. But now I've got it all. You, our baby, my career, and Redemption."

EPILOGUE

"TORMENT WANTS TO SEE YOU." SADIST STEPPED IN FRONT OF Zack as he emerged from the Redemption locker room, blocking his path to the exit.

"I promised Shayla I'd be home by eleven tonight. I'll talk with him tomorrow."

"Now." Sadist folded his thick arms over his chest.

Zack bristled. What the hell was going on? "Excuse me?"

"You heard me." Sadist pointed toward Torment's office. "Let's get going."

"You've got to be fucking kidding me." No way was he going to let anyone order him around. He'd earned his respect at Redemption. Over the last seven months, he'd fought every member of the team, including Sadist, and he'd won every fight. The Predator was next on his list and the only man standing between him and his dream of fighting Torment.

"Do I look like I'm kidding?" Sadist scowled. "If you want

to keep your membership at the gym, you'll come with me. Otherwise, hand in your card."

"Jesus Christ." Zack brushed past Sadist. "What's this all about?"

"You'll find out soon enough." He trailed Zack until they reached Torment's office, and then he knocked on the door.

"Come in," Torment called out.

"I'll be waiting out here," Sadist said. "In case you need me."

The hair on the back of Zack's neck stood on end. Had he done something wrong? Broken a rule? Had something happened in the week he'd been away at a training camp in Florida? It had been hard enough being away from Shayla and their new baby, but if he'd missed something important at Redemption...

"Slayer." Torment motioned him in, and Sadist closed the door behind him.

"What's this all about?"

"How's the baby?"

"Good." He shifted his weight, disconcerted by Torment's friendly tone. "We named him Dylan after Shayla's dad."

"Strong name. How's Shayla doing?" Torment leaned back in his chair, his black Redemption T-shirt stretching taut over his broad chest.

"Great. She'll be in next week to start training again. The doctor said light exercise. We're having a difference of opinion over what that means."

Torment laughed. "Are you all trained up now? Ready for your fight next week?"

Zack shifted his weight again, glanced back over his shoulder to where Sadist was standing guard. What was this? Why was Torment trying to put him at ease when he'd sent Sadist to threaten him to get him to come to the office? "Yeah. Kinda wishing it was this week 'cause I'm at my peak."

"Excellent." Torment threw something across the desk, and Zack caught it midair.

"My title ring." He'd forgotten about the ring he'd given up to save Shayla from Torment's wrath. "Why are you giving it to me now?"

"Challenge accepted." Torment gestured to the door. "Renegade is clearing the gym now. We'll have it all to ourselves. No one will be around. It will just be you and me."

Zack swallowed hard. It was the ultimate challenge.

"What about the Predator? I didn't beat him."

"You did on points. And I know you pulled that last punch." He nodded at the ring. "This has been a long time coming."

Zack flexed his shoulders, tipped his head from side to side, making it crack. "You want to take a minute and call Makayla and Brianna to say goodbye?"

Torment stood, pushing away his chair. "The only call I'll be making is to tell them how I kicked your ass."

"You won't be able to see my ass when you're lying unconscious on the mat."

They walked out into the hallway, and Sadist followed them to the gym.

"No one comes in," Torment said to Sadist when they reached the entrance. "If the doors aren't open in thirty minutes, call two ambulances."

Zack handed Sadist the ring after Torment walked into the now-empty gym. "Make sure this gets to Dylan."

Sadist tucked the ring in his pocket. "You think you're gonna lose?"

"No." Zack grinned. "I'm going to win. I just don't want it to get lost when I'm celebrating."

"How can you be so sure?"

"Every one of my dreams has come true since I came to Redemption," Zack said. "I dreamed about fighting Torment, not beating him. Even if I lose, I win."

AGAINST THE ROPES

"You come in. You fight. It's simple."

Me fight? He can't be serious. Do I look like I pound on people for fun?

"Sorry. I think there's been a misunderstanding." Forcing a tight laugh, I shuffle back to the red line marking the fighters' entrance to Redemption, a full-service gym and training center that is home to one of Oakland's few remaining unsanctioned, underground fight clubs. Maybe I should have read the rules posted at the door.

"No, you don't." The hefty blond grabs my shoulders and pulls me toward him. My nose sinks into the yellow happy face tank top stretched tight over his keg-size belly. The pungent odor of unwashed gorilla invades my nostrils, bringing back memories of school trips to the San Diego Zoo. Lovely.

Gasping for air, I glance up and flash my best fake smile. "I'm just here to sell tickets. One of your fighters, Jake, asked my friend Amanda to work the door and she asked me to help her.

Why don't we just pretend you didn't see me cross the red line and I'll get back to work?"

If I were a different type of girl, wearing a different—and lower cut—shirt, I might try another kind of technique to get out of this predicament, but right now, a smile is all I've got.

It backfires.

"Mmm. Pretty." He releases my shoulders and paws at my hair, mussing it from my crown to the middle of my back. What a waste of two hours with the flat iron.

"I'm not too sure about pretty." My voice goes from a low quiver to a thin whine as he strokes my jaw with a thick finger. "But I am small, fragile, delicate, easily frightened, and given to high-pitched screams in situations involving violence." In an attempt to make my lies a reality, I suck in my stomach and tuck in my tush.

He frowns, and for the first time I notice the missing teeth, jagged scar across his throat, and the skull and crossbones tattoos covering his arms like sleeves. Not quite the cuddly teddy bear I had thought he was. More like a Viking berserker.

My heart kicks up a notch, and I hold up my hands in a defensive gesture. "Listen. I was chasing after some deadbeat who didn't buy a ticket. He came in just before me. Tall, broad shoulders, black leather jacket, bandana—I only saw him from the back. He was in line talking to people, and then suddenly he breezed past the ticket counter and went through this entrance. Did you see him?"

A smile ghosts his lips. "You'll have to talk to Torment. He deals with all line crossers and ticket dodgers. Usually takes them into the ring for a lesson in following the rules. He likes to hear people scream." His chuckle is as menacing as his breath. Maybe he ate a small child for lunch.

"Let's go. I'll introduce you." His hand clamps around my arm and he tugs me forward.

A shiver of fear races down my spine. "You're kidding, right? I mean, look at me. Do I look like I could take on someone named Torment?" My smile wavers, so I add a few eyelash flutters and a desperate breast jiggle to the mix. Unfortunately, my ass decides to join the party, and my thighs aren't far behind.

Wrong message. His heated gaze rakes over my body, and a lascivious grin splits his wide face from ear to ear. "Torment likes the curvy ones."

Now there's a slap in the face. But maybe I can use the curves to my advantage. If I can't talk my way out of this mess, I'll just wiggle.

"Come on. He'll decide what to do with you."

Heart pounding, I scramble behind the self-styled Cerberus deep into the belly of Hell. I wish I had written a will.

Upon first glance, Hell disappoints.

The giant sheet-metal warehouse, probably around 20,000 square feet, boasts corrugated metal walls, concrete floors, and the stale sweat stench of one hundred high-school gym lockers. The ceiling is easily twenty-five feet above me. At the far end, a few freight containers are stacked in the corner, and a circular, metal staircase leads up to a second level.

Our end of the warehouse has a dedicated training area and a fully equipped gym. Half-naked, sweaty, pumped up alpha males grapple on scarred red mats and spar in the two practice rings. Fight posters and pennants are plastered on the walls. In one corner a man dressed as a drill sergeant is barking orders at a motley group of huffing, puffing fighter wannabes.

My stomach clenches as the drumroll of speed bags, the slap of jump ropes, the whir of the treadmill, and the thud of gloves on flesh create a gut-churning symphony of violent sound.

"Hey, Rampage, you get us a new ring girl?" A small, wiry, bald fighter with red-rimmed pupil-less psycho eyes points to the "FCUK Me" lettering on my T-shirt and makes an obscene gesture with his hips. "Answer is yes, honey. Find me after the show."

I berate myself for my poor choice of attire. But really, it is my sister Susie's fault. She sends me the strangest gifts from London.

Rampage leads me toward an enormous raised boxing ring in the center of the warehouse. Spiky-haired punkers, clean-cut jocks, hip-hop headers, businessmen in suits, and leather-vested bikers fill the metal bleachers and folding chairs surrounding the main attraction. I've never seen a more eclectic group. There must be at least two hundred people here with seating for probably two hundred more. But there's no sign of Amanda. Some best friend.

We stop in front of a small, roped-off area about ten feet square. Rampage opens a steel-framed gate and shoves me inside. "You can wait in the pen. It's for your own safety. We can't have people wandering too close to the ring."

"I am not an animal," I mumble as the gate slams shut. He doesn't even crack a smile. Maybe he doesn't go to the movies.

I walk to the back of the pen for a good view of the ring and instantly recognize the man with the black bandana, despite the fact he has changed into a pleasantly tight pair of white board shorts with black winged skulls emblazoned on the sides. "That's him," I shriek. "That's the guy who didn't buy a ticket."

Amusement flashes in Rampage's beady black eyes. He stalks over to the pen and throws open the gate. "You get that guy to buy a ticket, and we'll call everything off. I won't make you face the ring."

My brow crinkles. "Isn't he a fighter? Does he even need a ticket?"

"I made you an offer. You gonna stand around talking or are you gonna take it?"

I lean up against the gate. "This has got to be a joke. And guess what? I'm not playing anymore. Just let me find Amanda and I'll get out of here."

Rampage glowers at me and his voice drops to a menacing growl. "You get up those stairs or I'll take you up myself and I can guarantee it ain't gonna be pretty."

I sigh an exasperated sigh.

"I'm going. I'm going." What the hell. Even if this is some kind of joke, the guy in the ring has mouth-watering shoulders and a great ass. I can also make out some tattoos on his back. It can't hurt to get a closer look. Maybe make a new friend.

Stiffening my spine, I climb the stairs and slide between the ropes and onto the spongy canvas mat. Hesitating, I take one last look over my shoulder. Rampage smirks and waves me forward.

My target is leaning over the ropes on the other side of the ring talking to an excessively curvy blonde wearing a one-piece, pink Lycra bodysuit. Her mountain of platinum hair is cinched on top of her head in a tight ponytail. Her huge, brown doe eyes are enhanced by her orange, spray-on tan and a slash of hot pink lipstick. She is pink and she is luscious. She is Pinkaluscious.

She rests a dainty, pink-tipped hand on Torment's foot and gazes up at him until he slides his foot back and away. Ah. Unrequited love. My heart goes out to Pinkaluscious, but really, she could do better than some two-bit, cheapskate fighter.

"Hey, Torment. I brought you a treat." Rampage's voice booms over the excited murmur of the crowd.

In one smooth, quick movement, Torment spins around to face me. My eyes are slow to react. No doubt he caught me staring at his ass, and now I am staring at something even more enticing. Something big. My cheeks burn, and I study the worn vinyl under my feet. Someone needs to make a few repairs.

Footsteps thud across the mat. The platform vibrates under my bare feet sending tremors through my body.

Swallowing hard, I look up. My eyes widen as well over six feet of lean, hard muscle stalks toward me.

Run. I should run. But all I can do is stare.

His fight shorts are slung deliciously low on his narrow hips, hugging his powerful thighs. Hard, thick muscles ripple across the broad expanse of his chest, tapering down to a taut, corrugated abdomen. But most striking are the tattoos covering over half of his upper body—a hypnotizing cocktail of curving, flowing, tribal designs that just beg to be touched.

He stops only a foot away and I crane my neck up to look at his face.

God is he gorgeous.

His high cheekbones are sharply cut, his jaw square, and his eyes dark brown and flecked with gold. His aquiline nose is slightly off-center, as if it had been broken and not properly reset, but instead of detracting from his breathtaking good looks, it gives him a dangerous appeal. His hair is hidden beneath a black bandana, but a few tawny, brown tufts have escaped from the edges and curl down past the base of his neck.

His full lips quirk into a faint smile as he studies me. A lithe and powerful animal assessing its prey.

My finely tuned instinct of self-preservation forces me back against the ropes and away from his intoxicating scent of soap and leather and the faintest kiss of the ocean.

"Excuse me…Torment. I…thought you forgot to buy a ticket, but…um…I don't think you really need one. Do you?"

"A ticket?" His low-pitched, husky, sensual voice could seduce a saint. Or a young college grad trying to supplement her meager salary by selling tickets at a fight club.

My heart thunders in my chest and I lick my lips. His eyes lock on my mouth, and my tongue freezes mid-stroke before beating a hasty retreat behind my Pink Innocence glossed lips.

He steps forward and I press myself harder against the springy ropes, wincing as they bite into my skin through my thin T-shirt.

"Are you Amanda?"

With herculean effort, I manage to pry my tongue off the roof of my mouth. "I'm the best friend."

He lifts an eyebrow. "Does the best friend have a name?"

"Mac."

"Doesn't suit you. Do you have a different name?"

"What do you mean a different name? That's my name. Well, it's my nickname. But that's what people call me. I'm not going to choose another name just because you don't like it." My hands find my hips, and I give him my second-best scowl—my best scowl being reserved for less handsome irritating men.

His gaze drifts down to the bright white "FCUK Me" lettering now stretched tight across my overly generous breasts. With my every breath, the letters expand and retract like a flashing neon sign. I hate my sister.

He leans so close I can see every contour of bone and sinew in his chest and the more intricate patterns in his tribal tattoos. The flexible ropes accommodate my last retreat, and I brace myself, trembling, against them.

"What's your real name?" he rumbles.

"Makayla." Oh, betraying lips.

He smiles and his eyes crinkle at the corners. "Makayla is a beautiful name. I'll call you Makayla."

Heat roars through me like a tidal wave. He likes my name. "So…about that ticket—"

He snorts a laugh. "I don't need to buy a ticket."

About the Author

New York Times and *USA Today* bestselling author Sarah Castille writes contemporary erotic romance and romantic suspense featuring blazingly hot alpha males and the women who tame them. A recovering lawyer and caffeine addict, she worked and traveled abroad before trading in her briefcase and stilettos for a handful of magic beans and a home on Vancouver Island. Readers can find her at sarahcastille.com.